BLINDLY INDICTED

OUT OF SIGHT BOOK 1

KATIE MAY

EXPRESSO PUBLISHER, LLC

PARANORMAL
PRISON

Edited by Expresso Publishing, LLC

Proofread by Autumn Reed

Cover Design by Covers by Christian

This book is dedicated to student loans—the only thing that consistently fucks me in the ass.

CONTENTS

Foreword   ix

Chapter 1   1
Chapter 2   11
Chapter 3   20
Chapter 4   27
Chapter 5   33
Chapter 6   41
Chapter 7   50
Chapter 8   57
Chapter 9   68
Chapter 10   75
Chapter 11   84
Chapter 12   93
Chapter 13   101
Chapter 14   108
Chapter 15   116
Chapter 16   124
Chapter 17   131
Chapter 18   138
Chapter 19   146
Chapter 20   152
Chapter 21   162
Chapter 22   170
Chapter 23   177
Chapter 24   184
Chapter 25   192
Chapter 26   198
Chapter 27   205
Chapter 28   215
Chapter 29   222
Chapter 30   230
Chapter 31   234

Chapter 32	241
Chapter 33	248
Chapter 34	255
Chapter 35	265
Chapter 36	273
Chapter 37	280
Chapter 38	289
Chapter 39	297
Chapter 40	312
Chapter 41	324
Chapter 42	332
Chapter 43	340
Chapter 44	344
Chapter 45	352
Chapter 46	359
Chapter 47	366
Chapter 48	377
Chapter 49	385
Chapter 50	393
Chapter 51	402
Chapter 52	409
Chapter 53	414
Chapter 54	423
Chapter 55	429
Chapter 56	438
Afterword	453
Supernatural Prison Series	455
Acknowledgments	457
About the Author	459
Also by Katie May	461

FOREWORD

Thank you so much for reading my book! There are a couple of triggers I would like to warn you about before you dive in. Skip this if you don't want spoilers!!!

The main character lived as a prisoner and was tortured and raped repeatedly. Some of her men were sexually assaulted as well in the past. Nothing is explicitly detailed. I want you to read my book, but I also want you to take care of yourself. There's also a lot of violence, main characters with questionable morals, and sexual content. However, none of the harem members treat the main character as anything less than a queen.

This is a reverse harem romance meaning that the female lead will end up with at least three men! If that bothers you, then this book is not for you.

CHAPTER 1

NINA

I push aside another swaying branch, my bare feet pounding against the forest floor. Grit, pebbles, and other unsavory substances have embedded themselves into my skin, but I barely notice the pain.

Faster.

Faster.

Faster.

I need to move faster.

My dress catches on a branch, the fabric ripping, and I let out a startled cry as something sharp cuts my skin. I feel a sticky liquid slide down my stomach—blood.

Run straight until you reach the tree cut in two. Then turn left. Run until you see the road. At the road, make sure you go right. Do not stop. Do not look behind you. Do not allow yourself to be seen.

The instructions reverberate in my head as I pick up my pace. My lungs struggle to replenish their oxygen supply, and my heart is hammering in my chest.

Faster.

Faster.

Faster.

I extend my senses towards the nearest animal and immediately implant myself in the mind of a squirrel. It's running through the underbrush, its eyes fixated on the human beside him.

Me.

Through its eyes, I'm able to see my tangled black hair, blood-stained white dress, and dirty face. The moonlight illuminates my haggard appearance.

The squirrel, startled by my approach, attempts to scurry off in the opposite direction. It's at that moment, before it climbs up a nearby tree, that I see it.

In the distance, silhouetted in the inky gray darkness, I spot a strange tree cleaved in two. Without a moment of hesitation, I pull myself out of the squirrel's mind and veer to the left.

Faster.

Faster.

Faster.

In some distant cavity of my mind, I become aware of dogs howling and motors revving. However, it's all background noise, overshadowed by the breath rushing in and out of my lungs. My legs ache from the physical exertion, and I find myself stopping, one hand bracing against a tree trunk to hold myself up.

No stopping.

With a cry, I force myself to run even faster. Everything hurts. Branches whip at my face, drawing blood, and more than once, I trip over a tree stub.

Usually, I'm more apt at using my other senses, but not today. Not when my life and freedom are quite literally on the line.

I can't go back there again.

I don't know how long I run. Minutes? Hours? Time sludges by slowly. In a demented way, I'm used to it. My life as a prisoner and punching bag has assured me that time doesn't exist. It's just an abstract concept.

I run until my bare feet touch something hard and grainy. Asphalt.

Make sure you go right.

I run.

My chest tightens to unbearable levels, and the pain in my stomach intensifies. I'm weak—starved, really—and haven't done more than walk from my cell to the torture room in months.

Why did I think I could do this?

Still, I can taste freedom on my tongue. I can hear the crickets in the distance. I can feel the wind against my face.

It's within my grasp...

My legs give out from underneath me, and I collapse on the ground. I only have a second to pray, a second to plead, before unconsciousness overtakes me.

∼

His grip on my hair is punishingly tight as he drags me down the long, barren hallway. I'm in his mind yet again—a power I discovered many years ago. Gray stone walls surround me on every side, and the distinct smell of copper and urine permeates the air.

"I'm sorry," I cry, attempting to dig my feet into the floor. That small act of disobedience proves to be futile, as his grip only tightens. Pain erupts on my scalp as I'm dragged, kicking and screaming, into a familiar bright room.

This room has been the star of numerous nightmares.

Floor-to-ceiling windows create the walls, allowing copious light through. It's the only room in the facility that allows natural sunlight to penetrate the monotony of darkness. The rest of the rooms are bathed in artificial fluorescent lights, or, in the case of my cell, a single hanging bulb.

I remember the first time I'd been dragged into this particular room. I'd been three, maybe four, and more confused than scared. Where was I, and where was my momma? But those thoughts quickly dissipated as the pain consumed me.

Now, the pain is something I am used to.

He pushes me down onto a cold slab of cement raised in the center of the room. It resembles a macabre altar used for sacrificial rituals. At least, that's what Kai always told me.

Kai...

His absence in my life is a physical pain, a gaping hole that is growing to a chasm. He has been the one constant in my life for years, and every day he's not here is the slash of a whip against my back.

Kai, I need you.

I wrench myself out of the bad man's head as iron chains clamp down on both of my wrists and ankles. The last thing I want to see is my own torture.

"What should we use today, Little Monster?" *he teases, and I don't need vision to know his lips are curled into a sinister sneer.*

I don't whimper, don't cry. My eyes stare sightlessly at the ceiling as he glides across the room, to the wall hosting a variety of weapons. Everything from machetes, to knives, to grenades.

There's only one rule the psychopaths have to follow: don't kill me.

I hear the sound of a blade being unsheathed, but I remain oblivious to what weapon he selected. Sometimes, ignorance is bliss.

I brace myself for the pain—the never-ending agony.

It's just another day in the dissonant chaos of my life.

∽

I WAKE UP TO BEEPING.

My head is foggy, as if I've been drugged, and my body aches something fierce. I attempt to bring my hand to the back of my head...

Only to realize it's restrained.

I tug, the cold metal biting into my wrist.

They found me.

Terror thrums through me—a physical bolt of lightning to my senses. The incessant beeping becomes louder until it drowns out everything but the pounding of my heart.

"You need to calm down. You're safe," a calm voice tells me, and I flinch at the hands touching my shoulders. It's entirely instinctive. Flinching has been ingrained in my very anatomy since I could first walk. Every touch has a second agenda.

Taking a deep breath, meant to calm my racing heart and mind, I push myself into the woman's head.

She's staring down at me.

I look like a *mess*. I must've been washed off, for the dirt and blood are nowhere to be seen. The white, gauzy dress has been replaced by something much less comfortable. Paper, maybe? A paper dress?

A black screen is adjacent to the bed, a line steadily creating waves. I try to recall the name of the strange contraption. I know Kai told me...

A heart monitor!

I mentally grin at my own epiphany.

I appear to be lying on a small cot, a scratchy white blanket pulled over my lower half. Both my wrists are secured to the bed by silver handcuffs.

Any comfort I previously felt diminishes at the sight of those things. How many times have I been strapped to a table just like this?

The woman seems kind, compassionate, but what darkness is lurking just beneath the surface?

Everyone has a darkness. Some wear it like a badge of honor, while others hide it away. Which one is she?

"Where am I?" I whimper. It's the strangest sensation to

see my lips move but not be consciously in my body. It's a gift I've always had, and one I can't explain.

I don't know how or when I lost my vision. It could've been from birth, or it could've been a product of the constant torture. Either way, darkness is all I have ever known. When I was younger, and I found myself randomly popping into people's minds, I thought I was insane. Normal people can't do what I can. From what little I gathered, the person can't sense my presence in their mind. I can last as long as my concentration holds—the longest has been a few hours, and the shortest was a couple seconds.

Kai was the one who told me to be quiet, to keep my power a secret.

But when Kai left...

I had nothing to live for, nothing I cared about. Like a volcano erupting, I confessed everything during one particularly painful session. I told them that, while my eyes couldn't see, my mind was more than capable.

I thought it would help me, would save me, would provide me a relief from the persistent pain.

I was wrong.

Heart hammering, I pull out of the nurse's head and inventory my body. My eyelids feel heavy and crusty, as if I had partaken in a long cry. Both of my wrists feel as if they had gone through a meat grinder. I know, without having to look, that the skin will be red and blistered from the cuffs.

My lungs struggle to refill with air as my thoughts race in tandem to my heart. I may be in a hospital, but the cuffs demote me as a prisoner. I thought I was free. I thought I had escaped...

The heart monitor reaches a crescendo as my thoughts run unattended.

"You need to calm down," the nurse instructs, not unkindly. "You're safe."

"I'm a prisoner," I retort, my voice a breathy whisper. It hurts to speak any louder, as if sandpaper is rubbing at my vocal cords. My words make her pause; I no longer hear her hustling above me.

After a pronounced moment of silence, she resumes connecting a tube to my arm. An IV? I think I recall Kai telling me about one, but all his lessons blur together. "I wouldn't recommend talking until you have a lawyer present."

What?

Try as I might, I can't understand her words. They just don't make sense in any context. Why would I need a lawyer? I'm not a complete imbecile. I know what a lawyer is and what they are used for. What I don't understand, however, is why I would need one.

The nurse finishes her thorough checkup before hurrying away, muttering under her breath.

Alone with only my thoughts, I allow my mind to wander.

I'm...free. Free. That word feels foreign, unnatural, as if I'm describing the situation of someone else entirely. For as long as I can remember, that word has never applied to me.

Maybe when I was a child...

A vivid memory of my three-year-old self being tied down to a table assaults me.

No, not even then.

I release a semi-hysterical giggle as tears burn my eyes. I want to shout from the rooftops, scream it to the world, brand it on my skin.

I'm free!

And yet...

I helplessly wiggle in the restraints containing me to the bed. The metal is cool against my skin, almost uncomfortably so.

If I'm truly free, then why do I still feel like a prisoner?

I try to ignore the nagging voice in the back of my head—

a voice that sounds eerily similar to my main torturer—telling me that I'll never be free. That I'll never escape.

For the longest time, I had relied on someone else to save me. A knight in shining armor or a handsome prince. Kai frequently told me stories about the beautiful princess trapped in a tower and how a handsome prince killed the monster and saved her. When no princes arrived and my knight was taken from me, I decided I needed to save myself.

My stomach is a tumultuous mixture of dread and anxiety as I wait for the nurse to arrive again. When the door is pushed open and footsteps pound against the stark white tiles, I know innately that it isn't the nurse visiting me.

With great trepidation, I push myself into the newcomer's head. Fortunately for me, the direction he's staring at gives me an unrestricted view of his reflection in the hospital window.

The man appears to be older—mid-forties, if I had to guess—and he has a thinning hairline freckled with gray. His eyes are chips of obsidian in a decidedly cold face. He's immaculately dressed in a black suit with gray cufflinks and a periwinkle-colored tie. Everything about this man screams wealth and power. Lots and lots of power.

When he moves to stand at the foot of my bed, staring down at me, I retreat from his mind and embrace the darkness. It consumes my vision like a dark curtain being drawn closed.

"What is your name, child?" he asks briskly. His voice is as cold as his features. Unease skates down my spine, unfurling in my stomach like a heavy ball of lead. My breathing is painfully shallow, sawing in and out. I have heard that tone of voice. Once, when Kai had beaten one of our guards because of a leering look directed at me.

That tone? It's accusing.

"My name?" I repeat meekly. I wish desperately I could

fiddle with my long black hair. It's a nervous habit I developed when I was younger, and it drove Kai crazy.

"Don't make me ask again," he snaps, and that previously mentioned ball of lead tangles with the nerves already present.

"Nina," I reply, voice a hushed murmur. And then, louder, I repeat, "Nina."

"Nina." He speaks my name as if it's something disgusting, a curse word spoken in church. The bed dips as his heavy weight settles at the end. "Do you know a Raphael Turner?"

His question takes me off guard, mainly because I have never heard that name before in my life. Granted, the guards at the Compound never gave me their true names (Kai referred to them as Asshole One, Asshole Two, Asshole Three... and, well, you get the picture), but even then, that name had never even been mentioned.

"This will be much more difficult if you play dumb," the man points out scathingly.

I flinch instinctively at his tone of voice. God, when will I never not cower when someone yells at me? I don't know how I'm expected to survive this new world if the slightest noise sends insidious fear snaking down my spine.

"I don't know what you're talking about," I reply honestly. He releases a disgruntled sigh, and I resist the urge to peek into his head one more time. All I'll see is myself...pathetic and trapped, like a feral dog taken off the streets but immediately locked in a cage.

"Councilman Raphael Turner." His words are spoken succinctly, a no-nonsense manner used commonly at the Compound.

I stare at him blankly, attempting to calm down my rabbiting heart.

"I've never heard of him," I say slowly, carefully. It feels as if I'm tiptoeing along a thin rope, miles above shark-infested waters. One wrong move and I'll tumble over, never to be seen again.

"You had blood on you," the man announces curtly. At my raised brow, he elaborates. "When we found you. You had blood on you."

My own blood, I think somewhat amusedly. Definitely macabre amusement. I picture a knife descending on the sensitive skin of my stomach...

"I was tortured," I admit quietly. The very words hurt to say, as if confessing them out loud somehow makes them more real. "I've been there since I was two or three—"

"The blood we found on you belonged to Raphael Turner," he cuts me off, and I can practically hear the banked anger and frustration lurking just beneath the surface. His next words take the remaining air from my lungs. I exhale heavily, my muscles losing strength, as tears prick at my eyes. "You're under arrest for the murder of Councilman Raphael Turner."

CHAPTER 2

NINA

They don't tell you that, when you're arrested for murder, you learn that the world isn't black and white.

They don't tell you that you discover humans aren't the only people roaming this earth.

The supernatural exists.

When I first entered my holding cell—after a stern-faced doctor ushered me into a separate room to test me for powers —I was left reeling. From her, I learned that vampires, demons, sirens, witches, and so much more live side by side with us humans.

It's...not at all shocking.

To some, it might be a life-changing epiphany, but I have always suspected I wasn't human. Humans can't do what I can. Seeing through others' eyes, for one, but also my accelerated healing.

When the doctor had asked me what I was, I merely quirked a single brow at her. I was confused, hungry, and terrified—that's what. After numerous tests and prodding, my results came back inconclusive.

Even in the supernatural world, I am a freak.

The first few days, I was absolutely terrified. I sobbed, yelled, and pounded my fists against the stone walls of my dank cell until blood formed on my knuckles. When I requested a lawyer, the guard scoffed—literally scoffed—before promising I'll get the "best help available."

Even I could hear the sarcasm in those words.

My "lawyer" was a ditzy man who'd never held a law book in his hand. I believe he worked at a grocery store before being pulled in as my attorney.

And that's how the court works: I'm guilty until proven innocent. The problem? They don't allow me a fair and fighting chance to prove my innocence.

My trial itself lasted only a month before the ancient judge declared me guilty of all charges. William—the man who had questioned me at the hospital—sat in the audience with a smug smile on his face. I could see him through the judge's eyes.

Nightmare Penitentiary.

I haven't heard of the elusive prison designed to host the most dangerous and fearsome supernatural creatures. How could I? I lived in one cage my entire life, then immediately traded it in for a second. My view of the world is extremely limited. Until my arrest, I didn't even know the supernatural world existed.

I allow darkness to overtake my vision like a cauldron of spilt ink as I'm loaded into a van. The guilty verdict reverberates in my head, accompanied by a gut-clenching fear. Terror thrums through me, an electric wire, and I shift uncomfortably in the leather seat. Iron handcuffs are clasped tightly around my wrists, the skin beneath them red and bleeding.

From what little I garnered eavesdropping, Nightmare Penitentiary is home to murderers, rapists, serial killers, and

thieves of all ages and genders. It's the Land of Misfit Toys...
only for monsters.

A category I'm now grouped into.

Beneath the terror, something akin to resolve settles over
me. I know I'm going to die. How could I not? I'm a blind
female entering a prison so dangerous, the staff themselves
have to be the best of the best. I'm a gazelle entering a den of
lions.

I don't like to think of myself as weak, but I know I am.
My body is frail and starved, and the slightest sound sends me
into a tailspin.

And what do I have to fight for?

Freedom is an illusion, one that evaporates with the
slightest pressure. I can fight for myself, sure, but where did
that lead me last time? My "freedom" consists of nothing but
pain and numbness—the juxtaposition not lost on me.

I'm trembling like a leaf in the wind when the van finally
pulls to an abrupt stop.

A door is opened, and then a hand grabs my arm, roughly
pulling me onto the pebbled street. I take the opportunity to
survey our location through my captor's eyes—my new
prison.

The guard—at least, I'm assuming he's a guard—is staring
at an immense stone building splashed with gray. Numerous
gables and turrets are erected on the roof, and I spot a
gargoyle standing sentry. Gray clouds clot the sky overhead,
somehow making the entire scene appear even more
ominous. Everything is banked in monochromatic colors. Silver
fences sprout from the ground and swoop steeply inward,
creating a makeshift roof over a courtyard. The prongs at the
top resemble jagged teeth. Almost irrationally, I picture them
as teeth...devouring me whole.

"Come on," the guard says gruffly, giving my arm a shake.
"The warden wants to speak with you."

The warden...

I contemplate mounting a case to prove my innocence, but I know the effort will be futile. From the moment the judge laid eyes on me, he construed I was guilty. I still don't know the full story of how Raphael Turner died, and my lawyer didn't deem it necessary to divulge the facts.

But what defense could I give? The judge didn't believe me when I claimed I'd been held captive my entire life, tortured by a secret organization seeking to understand my powers. It sounds ridiculous even to me.

The facts remain consistent: I was found passed out on a highway, covered in the blood of a dead man. A homeless, nameless female.

The verdict had been swift and brutal.

"She's nothing but skin and bones," a new voice scoffs from nearby. A moment later, a second hand wraps around my upper arm, tight enough to bruise. I whimper at the initial sting of pain before stubbornly clamping my mouth closed.

You can't cry. You can't show weakness.

But... a dry voice begins in my head. *Aren't you already dead?*

It's a funny thing to question your mortality. How much can a person actually endure? How many times can you be twisted and bent until you snap? I'm still standing, even after being broken one too many times. But how much longer can I last? I'm running in a never-ending race, and I'm only just now realizing that the track is a circle with no definitive beginning or end. Freedom is an abstract illusion, a mirage in a desert.

Shaking myself out of my demented reverie, I allow the guards to lead me up a steep staircase.

The air changes the second I enter the inside of the prison. It seems staler, somehow, and smells vaguely of copper and urine. Two smells I'm familiar with.

Heart galloping like a herd of wild horses, I focus on my other senses.

What do you hear?

It sounds like...men crying. The melancholic sound sends pinpricks of unease down my spine. It's both haunting and heartbreaking. Woven intermittently with the cries are men laughing—loud, humorous guffaws at odds with the other noise.

What do you feel?

Nothing but the hands wrapped around my arms and the handcuffs secured to my wrists in front of my stomach. I am still wearing the pure white dress from a month ago—when I first escaped the Compound. Every night, I would dress in court-issued pajamas. When I woke up the next morning, the dress would be miraculously clean. The fabric is soft and breathable, airy around my chest and lower regions.

What do you smell?

Copper. Blood. Urine. Vomit. Those distinct scents contaminate the air until I'm practically choking on it.

What do you see?

I push my consciousness into the nearest guard...only to quickly retreat when I discover he's focused intently on my heaving breasts. Shuddering, I settle on the second man instead, who is, thankfully, watching where he is going.

The hallway is long, the walls made up of roughly hewn cement blocks. From what I can see, there are very few doors down this expanse.

"I don't feel right about this," the guard whose head I'm in mutters to his comrade. "She's just a kid. She'll be killed in seconds."

The second man releases a harsh bark of laughter. "She's a fucking murderer. She deserves whatever is coming for her." His hand slips from my arm to land on my ass and cop a feel. I tremble, fear coursing through me.

Men are...evil.

Correction: not all men. There are facets of every aspect of nature. Not one person—or gender—is inherently evil. There are light and dark aspects in everyone.

This man, though? He's evil.

I feel violated and disgusted, but I know I don't have a voice. They stole it from me the second they secured handcuffs to my wrists and accused me of a crime I didn't commit. We live in an unfortunate world where the accused is glorified and the victim is blamed. It can't be a dog-eat-dog world when I'm nothing more than a pathetic mouse.

"Come on, bitch. The warden wants to speak with you," the creepy man announces.

Together, the men drag me into a large room, directly at odds with the rest of the prison.

The room is beautiful. Ethereal. A five-tiered chandelier hangs in the center of the room, flames casting odd shadows on the furniture. Plush blue chairs, lined with gold trim, sit directly in front of a mahogany desk. There appears to be more than one level, and everywhere I look, bookshelves sprout from the ground. It reminds me of the story Kai used to tell me—Belle visiting the Beast's library.

Only, in this situation, I'm the Beast.

The guards lead me through the throng of dark-painted bookshelves.

What secrets lurk in these yellowing pages? What is so important to be kept reserved in a glass case?

A man leans against a desk, his arms crossed over his chest and a cigarette dangling from his plush lips. He wears a long, flowing trench coat with more pockets than I thought possible. A black tie is haphazardly undone, as well as the first few buttons of his shirt. A shock of disheveled dark hair grazes his eyes as he stands to his full, impressive height.

"Is this her?" he asks, voice raspy.

The evil guard gives my arm a shake for good measure. "It's her," he agrees before nodding his head respectfully. "Warden."

"Terry." He nods first to the creepy guard and then to the guard whose head I'm occupying. "Brad."

The warden steps even closer to me, out of Brad's line of sight, and I feel his hot breath waft across my cheeks. For what feels like a century, he merely surveys me. Silent. Deadly.

A lion that isn't just out for the hunt, but for the kill. After a moment, he steps back, removes his cigarette, and blows out a puff of smoke.

"You don't look like much," he murmurs, almost dismissively. To the others, he asks, "Did she really kill Raphael Turner?"

There's a long moment of silence as the guards shuffle from foot to foot, unable to answer. Or maybe unwilling to answer.

The warden's deranged laughter implodes the silence. "Good job, girly!" He claps a hand against my back, the force of it making me stagger forward a few steps.

The guards make a strangled sound but don't comment.

"Now, do you want my advice, girly?" the warden continues, either oblivious or choosing to ignore the reactions to his dogmatic comment. When I remain silent, shaking, he places a calloused hand on my shoulder. "To survive the Labyrinth, you have to make friends. Get it, girl? You can't do this by yourself."

God...I. Can't. Stop. Shaking.

Labyrinth?

I know what one is, of course. Kai used to tell me stories about the maze guarded by the minotaur. What does this have to do with prison? Is it code for something? I don't dare to ask the numerous questions clamoring for attention in my mind.

"I'm going to be generous with you, Nina. I don't know why. Maybe I like you." The warden scoffs at his own words before chuckling darkly. "The labyrinth is constantly changing. The second you think you're familiar with the layout... just know that you're not. Fortunately for you, only political prisoners are placed in the maze. Everything from hacking into top-secret information to assassinating council members." Through the guard's eyes, I can see the warden leveling me with a pointed look. It feels as if my heart is shrinking in a rapidly growing vise. I can barely hear him over the pounding in my ears. "When you wake up, you'll be confused and disoriented. You, more than anyone else." He presses the pad of his thumb to first one eyelid, then the other to indicate my blindness. I stagger back a step...directly into the evil guard's arms.

"Hello, princess," he purrs, and I immediately step forward, closer to the warden. You learn very, very quickly how necessary it is to choose your monsters. It becomes ingrained within you—that ability to sense evil in others.

Wait...

"When I wake up?" I stutter out.

"I'm rooting for you, Nina Doe," the warden says, using the last name the court gave me. I didn't have an "identity," and the courts could find nothing in their databases.

"Wait!" Before I can mount a protest, something sharp penetrates my skin. I sway on my feet, the familiar sensation of dread and terror increasing tenfold. Anything can happen when you're unconscious.

Anything.

"Night, night," the warden says just before unconsciousness claims me.

At least I understand the darkness. The rest of the world? Not so much.

CHAPTER 3

BLADE

The pathetic excuse for a man falls at my feet.

A spineless, disgusting werewolf.

Bronson has a large hand around the man's neck, keeping him in place. I narrow my eyes into thin slits, enjoying the way the man—Jean—quivers. There's something very, very satisfying about instilling fear in a dangerous prisoner such as Jean. Does it make me fucked up? Probably. Do I care? Absolutely fucking not.

"Jean, Jean, Jean." I tsk, shaking my head slowly. The man's eyes widen almost imperceptibly, his terror evident. I know I can be intimidating as fuck. I'm large, larger than the rest of the freak shows around here, with muscle upon muscle. Tattoos and scars line the length of my body. There isn't a spot of me that isn't covered, including my dick— though no one in this shit show has seen those particular tattoos.

As one of the last remaining dragons, evoking fear is ingrained in my very genetic makeup. One piercing glare, and I have men falling to their knees. One strident word, and I can take over this godforsaken world.

Unfortunately, this "world" only exists in the basement of a maximum-security supernatural prison.

"Blade, do you have to toy with your food?" Damien drawls from beside me, using the nickname given to me by the other inmates.

Damien, as always, is impeccably dressed in a form-fitting suit and shiny loafers. It's the outfit he wore when he first arrived at the prison, nearly two years ago, and one he has stubbornly refused to get rid of. As a powerful mage, he is more than capable of washing the suit every night before bed. I imagine wearing it gives him some semblance of control—a reminder of the life he once had before it was brutally ripped from his hands.

Currently, his pants are undone, cock on display, as he fucks one of the prison whores. Their words, not mine. He barely seems aware of the panting girl beneath him, her eyes closed in bliss. As always, Damien's hands are firmly by his sides, not even touching the girl's waist. It's one of his rules: get your cock wet, but nothing else.

The girl, Teegan or whatever, begins shouting inarticulate praises as Damien increases his speed. I just barely resist the urge to roll my eyes. She—like so many other females who offer themselves to my gang—probably thinks she'll be the one to tame his beast. The mere concept is laughable. Damien is a psychopath, through and through. If I wasn't a continual benefit to him, I had no doubt he would kill me.

"I'm not playing," I huff, crossing my muscular arms over my chest. I cast a side-eyed glance at the simpering wolf. Pathetic. I'm not usually one to judge an entire species based on one man—Bronson is ten times the werewolf this man could ever be—but come on. This is the third shifter I've dragged into my "office" in the past week. They've been getting restless, volatile, and I know it's only a matter of time until they snap.

Abruptly, Damien pulls out of Terry—Tasha?—and stalks forward, ignoring her cries of protest. His dick is still hard and bobbing as he steps in front of the werewolf. Bronson, after a quick look at me, steps away with barely veiled disgust.

"I'm a lot of things, Jean, but a rapist is not one of them. Do you know what I do to rapists?" Damien, almost methodically, tucks his cock back into his pants. I swear the sick bastard is harder now than he was a minute ago, balls deep in his whore.

Jean trembles pathetically, ducking his head in what I would almost describe as a submissive gesture.

I want to scoff.

If he thinks kissing my ass now will save his life, he's sorely mistaken. I didn't become the unofficial leader of the Labyrinth through my good looks alone. For the most part, the warden and his slimy guards leave us alone. We're the forgotten monsters. As long as there's no obvious dissent, we don't have to worry about a visit from the big man above.

Thank fuck. I'm not one to believe urban legends, but if the rumors are true, the warden stalks through the shadows at night and devours parts of your soul. Creepy shit, if you ask me. I prefer my soul intact, thank you very much.

"I don't like you, Jean. I never did. And not just because you're a disgusting rapist," Damien says coldly. The man is always cold, though, his eyes sky blue and frosty in an arresting face. I swear he scares me more than anyone else in this prison.

"You going to let Dam take the reins?" Abel asks dryly. His back is against the wall as a girl kneels before him, sucking him off. While his eyes are fixed firmly on the scene before him, his hands are in her hair, guiding her movements.

"He's going to kill him," Cain, Abel's twin (yes, I see the irony), points out. Unlike his brother, there are no girls fawning over him. They learned their lesson the hard way when he practically ripped off their heads. There are two people in my gang the girls know not to touch: me and Cain.

"I don't care," I reply, turning back to the scene at hand. Damien has unsheathed a long, keen blade and is holding it millimeters from Jean's throat. Don't ask me how the psychopath got the blade. I'm pretty sure the man has connections outside of the prison...and inside. "You know I have a zero-tolerance policy for rapists."

Jean had been discovered by a lower gang member of mine —not a part of my inner circle—with his cock inside a struggling, terrified female. There are very few things I don't tolerate in my prison, and rape is one. Even thinking about it makes me see red.

I'm a murderous asshole, and even I know consent is necessary.

So, no. I don't feel bad about whatever Damien plans to do to him. I hope he burns.

As if privy to my thoughts, Damien abruptly lowers the knife to the man's groin. With one swooping strike, the man's dick falls to the ground, and blood stains his pants.

Jean's cry of agony? Music to my fucking ears.

"According to my source," Damien begins in a slow, dangerous voice. The man practically exudes power. If I was into guys—or anyone, for that matter—I would totally be sporting a boner. "You had your dick inside an unwilling female. Is that true?"

Jean releases a pained gasp, pressing his face into the blood-soaked floor.

"Is that true?" Damien repeats, gripping the other man's hair and holding his head up. Bronson, now hovering near the wall, covers his junk with a wince.

Same, man. Same.

"Yes!" Jean explodes at last, his voice a sob. It always strikes me as funny how some men can act like big, macho badasses when confronting unwilling women, but the second the tides are turned, they're simpering fools. If you have to assert your dominance over people weaker than you to feel like a man, then I feel sorry for you.

"And did your hands touch this female as well?" Damien queries dangerously. The only answer is a snot-filled sob.

One hand and then the other drop to the ground beside the severed dick.

I have to give Damien credit: he's a classy motherfucker.

Cut the hand that did the deed and all that crap.

I turn away from the gruesome sight and survey the room. Our base of operation always changes, depending on the Labyrinth's needs. I swear the building is a living entity. Still, we've been here long enough to understand how it works.

This room in particular has drainpipes on the wall and puddles on the ground. Probably piss, if I am being honest. Not that I would test it. Hmmm. Maybe I should ask Jean to take a lick...?

The only people present are my inner circle (Bronson, the twins, and Damien), the prison girls, and Jean. The rest of my gang is probably traipsing through the ever-changing halls in search of the cafeteria. It's a pain in my ass to never know where the food will be on a day-to-day basis. We dragons need to eat.

A shrilling cry has me glancing back at Damien and Jean. The werewolf has lost both of his hands, his dick, and now his legs. He's trying futilely, desperately, to crawl toward the door, blood trailing behind him in his wake.

Damien just laughs, the sound sending—admittedly—shivers of terror down my spine. If Damien ever chooses to betray me...

The next swing of the knife proves to be fatal. Jean collapses on the ground, his head dismembered from his body. I stare impassively at the head as it rolls to my feet.

Disgusting prick.

Damien, with a smile capable of making angels cry, turns towards me, blood coating his entire body. With a whoop, he runs towards his discarded female, whips out his dick, and begins to pound into her earnestly.

Fucking psycho.

Turning towards Bronson, I gesture at Jean's body...errr... body parts. "Take care of that." It's not a question.

Bronson grunts, not even hesitating before he picks up one body part at a time.

Abel chuckles—actually fucking chuckles—as Bronson wraps one of the severed hands in Jean's discarded shirt. "Do you need a *hand* with that?" the twin asks, laughing even harder at his own joke. Cain gives a disgruntled snort, rolling his eyes to the heavens. Unfortunately for him, he should be looking the other way for help with his brother. As Bronson grabs a strand of Jean's black hair, hefting his head up, Abel adds, "Next time you're going to get all murdery, give me a *heads* up."

"Good lord," Cain mumbles, pinching the bridge of his nose. "You're a regular old comedian, aren't you?"

"I wouldn't say old..." Abel retorts, elbowing him in the stomach. "I'm technically a few minutes younger than your ugly ass. And thanks, sweetheart, I'm done now." Abel extracts himself from the swollen-lipped female and moves to stand beside me, tucking his now flaccid dick back in his pants and zipping it up. Whatever he's about to say is interrupted by a red-faced, sweaty warlock (different from a mage) running into the room. He pants, placing one hand against the wall to steady himself.

"Gary, what's the meaning of this?" The men know not to interrupt us when we're having a "meeting." Read as: murder spree. I'm not pretending to do anything I'm not.

"New prisoner," he huffs. "Female. Young. Beautiful."

My lips purse into a frown.

When a new inmate arrives in the Labyrinth, they're usually unconscious in order to not see the entrance and exit. When they wake up, they're confused and terrified, especially the females. I have taken it upon myself to ensure no harm comes to these women—unless they deserve it. I'll never hurt a female, but the other men here? They kill indiscriminately. I can't save every asshole.

Turning toward Terry...Tallia ...Terrance—shit, I need to remember her name—I nod towards the door.

"Find the female and make sure no harm comes to her." Smiling darkly, I crack my knuckles. "When she wakes up, bring her to me."

CHAPTER 4

NINA

There is one thing the prison guards failed to take into consideration when administering the sedative: I had been drugged before. Numerous times, actually. I lost track of how many times after one hundred and thirty-five.

Needless to say, I have developed a sort of immunity to it.

When awareness first grips me in an iron hold, I keep my eyelids closed. If there's one thing I'm used to, it's darkness. Pure, unending darkness. I know my appearance juxtaposes what my eyes actually see: my skin is as pale as moonlight, only a shade or two darker than my glaringly bright gown. My hair is long and luscious, dark tendrils that cascade to mid-back. At first glance, I appear to be a beam of light—at least, that's how Kai always described me. It's ironic that all I have ever known is darkness.

Focusing on the guard to my right, I submerge myself in his subconscious, allowing his eyes to work as my own.

We appear to be in a tunnel. Bright fluorescent lights overhead illuminate the dark stone walls and wet floors. It smells vaguely of mildew and bodily fluids, the combined scents making me want to gag.

My body, held between the two guards, is weak, the drugs still in effect at least that much. I could no sooner move my head than I could fight them off.

"Here?" guard one asks.

"Here," the second one agrees. A moment later, I'm dropped unceremoniously onto the floor, my back aching at the impact. I clamp my mouth closed against the impending whimper that wants to escape. Heaven only knows what these men will do to me if they discover I'm awake.

"It was nice knowing you, Nina Doe," one of the men says, not unkindly.

The second one snorts, and a moment later, his boot collides with my rib cage. "Fucking murderer." A blob of spit lands on my face. "Bitch."

He hurls more insults at me, but his words bounce off my rock-hard skin. I have dealt with worse during my days as a prisoner.

The other guard finally gets control of his comrade and practically drags him back the way they came from. The entire exchange lasts less than a few minutes, but it feels like a century.

And then, I'm alone.

For the first time in my entire existence, there is no mind near enough for me to delve into. Darkness obscures my vision like bloated storm clouds clotting the sky. It's all I can see, this darkness, all I'm aware of.

I can't stay here. The thought comes to me with an almost blistering speed, my heart thumping in tandem with my racing thoughts. Icy fear trails its finger down my spine. I know how dangerous it can be for a woman like me—alone and vulnerable—in a prison that breeds predators. If the rumors whispered by the prison guards are true, monsters lurk these halls at night.

And I'll be damned if I'm the helpless prey.

It takes considerable effort to stagger to my feet. Everything hurts—my legs, my arms, my head. Each step forward is how I imagined wading through tar would feel like.

Keep walking.

I repeat those two words in my head like a mantra. A prayer. A reminder that, if I fight, I won't go down as a helpless victim. It's a lesson Kai drilled into my head back at the Compound: always fight, for there's a chance you might emerge victorious.

A small, demented part of me wants to give up and give in. That same part craves the comfort only my darkness can offer me—an escape. An escape from this world, my fear, and the monsters that lurk under my bed at night.

I reach out and touch the nearest wall, palming it desperately. It's wet to the touch, almost as if the stone is weeping. It leaves my hand disgustingly sticky.

After a few more painfully slow steps forward, I branch out my awareness once more, searching for anyone in the general vicinity. My search proves to be futile; there are no eyes for me to see through.

How many people are in this prison?

How large is it?

My panic continues to grow and grow until it resembles a bowling ball in my stomach. Not that I know what a bowling ball looks like. I only have vague descriptions from a story Kai told me.

Speaking of stories...

I recollect the story of the maze and the minotaur. How did it go again? Did the hero survive?

I venture forward another step, my body practically plastered against the wall. My head is foggy, and I struggle to formulate coherent sentences. Still, I forge on. Vomit churns in my stomach, and I instinctively wrap my arms around my midsection.

My searching hand comes across something abnormally sharp, almost like a piece of rock protruding from the wall. I caress the object for an extended period of time, memorizing the shape, before continuing on.

Where am I going?

I don't have an answer to that. I'm unsure of which option is safer: finding others or remaining free of them. Still, a tinny voice in my head tells me I need to *move*. Where? I'll cross that path when I find it.

Quite literally.

My hand abruptly touches air, and I pause, canting my head to the side. Focusing on my senses, I note open air in both directions. A fork in the road, I suppose.

Nibbling on my bottom lip, I decide to travel down the right one. Once more, I place my hand back on the wall and walk slowly.

One step. Two steps. Three steps.

I pause when my hand stumbles across something sharp. Something familiar. Frowning, I trace the object with careful reverence.

It's...the same rock I had stumbled upon only a few minutes earlier.

Did I just walk in a circle?

Heart thundering, I choose the left pathway this time. Each movement is slow, unhurried, painstakingly patient. My hand memorizes each and every crook and crevice of the hallway as my feet propel me forward.

A left, then a right, then straight, then right again.

For the third time, a sharp piece of rock pokes at my palm.

No. No. No. No.

This can't be happening.

Tears spring to life in my eyes as I stumble down hall after hall, turn after turn, fork after fork, all of which lead me back to the same rock protruding from the wall. My fear turns into frustration, which turns into an almost elemental fury.

After a few more futile efforts, I collapse against the wet wall, the stench of dried blood and urine wafting to me. I bang my head against the hard stone once, twice, three times.

My body is still reeling from the effects of the drugs, and I feel unbelievably tired. My eyelids droop threateningly as my head falls to the side, my ear touching my shoulder.

Stay awake, Nina! Stay awake!

The monsters come out to play when I'm asleep.

Still, the pull is enticing, and I'm just so darn frustrated. Maybe my prison is a new form of psychological torture —loneliness.

Who would've thought I'd miss my cell at the Compound?

A quiet, barely audible mewl reverberates from farther down the tunnel. My head snaps up as I glance in one direction and then the other. Breath sawing in and out, I push my attention out, towards the creature rapidly approaching.

It's lower to the ground, but through its eyes, I can see a clear view of myself leaning against the dirty wall. My hair is snarled, a disheveled mess of black silk, and my dress is stained with blood and dirt. Dark circles mar the skin underneath both of my eyes, painfully noticeable on my too-pale skin.

The creature steps forward, and I brace myself...

Until it pounces onto my lap and curls into a ball. A contented purr echoes through its chest.

I pull myself out of the cat's eyes, my hand smoothing down the mangled fur.

"Hello, little guy. What are you doing here?" The cat

continues to purr in earnest as I stroke its back. "Are you a girl cat or a guy cat?"

This time, I'm almost positive the little creature releases an *oomph*. I wonder if my time down here is already making me crazy.

"Guy cat?" I ask, and a sharp tongue licks my hand. Giggling, I resume my careful strokes. "I always wanted a cat. Kai said..." I trial off, the mere mention of Kai bringing tears to my eyes. The cat makes a pathetic whining noise, curling itself farther against me. "Kai said he'll get me a cat. When we escaped. But you know? That's a story for a different day, isn't that right, Mr. Scruffles?"

The cat's blissful purrs cut off abruptly, and I can practically see his head cocking to the side.

"Do you not like the name?" I tease, stroking him behind the ears. "I always told myself that I'll name my future cat Mr. Scruffles. Of course, that was when I was, like, three..." I giggle as Mr. Scruffles begins to knead my leg. "So, what are you doing here, sweet boy?"

Of course, the cat can't actually respond, but it makes me feel better imagining he can. The loneliness and fear doesn't completely dissipate, but Mr. Scruffles's presence definitely helps.

"Let me guess," I continue, tapping my chin. My tears dried up the second this little fur ball climbed into my lap and offered me sweet kitty kisses. "You're a familiar to a warlock. Yup. I just learned this month that the supernatural exists. Before that? It was nothing but a story Kai used to tell me." I freeze suddenly, my hand pausing in Mr. Scruffle's fur. "I don't belong here. And I don't want to be here. I think..." My eyelids droop as I once more rest my head against the wall. "I think I'm going to die here."

CHAPTER 5

NINA

I wake up feeling oddly refreshed. Not one hundred percent, but better than I was the night before. My eyelids are heavy and crusty, and I blink rapidly to dispel some of the gunk that formed overnight. There's a pain in my neck that doesn't alleviate, no matter how many times I twist and turn my head from side to side.

In my lap, purring melodically, is my new furry friend.

I don't quite understand how a cat found himself in a dangerous prison, but I don't dare articulate the questions on the tip of my tongue. For all I know, he is a pet of a fellow prisoner. Hell, maybe he *is* the familiar to a witch or warlock (if that's not an urban legend). I still remember the stories Kai told me about a black cat...

Absentmindedly, I stroke his gnarled fur. It's matted in numerous places, the texture coarse beneath my fingers. I wonder what color he is. For some reason, I imagine him to be orange with white stripes. Don't ask me why that particular image comes to the forefront of my mind. The only cat I have ever seen was Fluffy, a white kitten one of my kinder captors brought to the Compound.

I suddenly become aware of a gripping sensation in my lower stomach—my bladder.

I really, really need to pee.

Staggering to my feet—and ignoring Mr. Scruffles's disgruntled huff—I place my hand against the wall.

"I need to go to the bathroom," I whisper to the cat, pushing myself into his head. It's the strangest sensation to see through an animal's eyes. For one, he's lower to the ground than a normal human, and for two, he sees everything in shades of black and white. The monochromatic colors used to give me a headache, but over time, I got used to them. It's either that or darkness.

Mr. Scruffles places his paw on my calf, kneading me, and I scratch behind his furry ears. In the next moment, he's hurrying down the hall, pausing once to glance over his shoulder. Through his eyes, I can see my vacant gaze staring at a spot over his head, my jaw slackened in shock as I try to process the cat's unusual behavior.

Is the…?

Is the cat trying to lead me somewhere?

There's not a lot I know—and less I understand—about the supernatural world. I know it exists, for one, and I'm suspected to be a part of it. I know that this region of the United States is led by the elusive, dangerous council. I know that William is an enforcer for said council.

And I know that monsters exist.

Is it completely out of the realm of possibilities that a cat can have coherent thoughts? Not particularly. For all I know, he's as intelligent as me.

Can I trust him?

I remain standing, understandably wary. And then I immediately feel ridiculous for being afraid of a cat. A freaking cat.

Mr. Scruffles releases a pathetic meow, and I sigh, relenting. Using the cat's eyes, we maneuver the maze-like basement. The first half of the journey consists of nothing but grimy stone walls, leaking pipes, and flickering lights.

It is only when we turn at a fork in the hall—left—that the scenery changes. There are various holes in the wall, each one the size of a modest closet or small room. All that remains of the doors are broken, rotting wood and charred bits of undefinable material. What appears to be a table is now nothing more than a pile of assorted debris, ravaged by vandalism and time. We stop at one of the largest rooms, and my heart ratchets up a notch.

"Is this...?" I begin, venturing a tentative step forward at Mr. Scruffles's pressing. "Is this where your owner lives?"

It doesn't resemble a prison cell—though, I'm not an expert, by any means, on what one is supposed to look like. Chairs are scattered around the room facing a small, static-filled television. A simple cot is pressed against the far wall, and on the opposite side, a toilet and sink sit.

"I don't know if I can be in here," I whisper, fear gripping me in an iron claw and refusing to release. What if the owner comes back and sees me in his or her space?

The cat rolls his eyes upwards, a decidedly human gesture.

I should go. I really should go...

But my bladder protests otherwise.

Before I can reconsider, I push down my panties and relieve myself in the toilet. I notice, somewhat amusedly, that Mr. Scruffles turns around the second I pull down my underwear. After I'm done washing my hands in the rustic sink, I perch myself daintily on one of the wooden chairs.

"Thank you," I tell my new friend as he climbs up onto the table and presses his face into my hand. His whiskers tickle my skin, and I can't stop the instinctive smile that pulls at my lips.

Now that I'm no longer in agonizing discomfort, I can focus on other stuff. Namely, my gnawing hunger.

As if on cue, my stomach growls, the noise drum-shattering loud. My cheeks instantly go up in flames as I remove my hand from Mr. Scruffles and touch my stomach.

Gracefully, the cat jumps off the table and races towards the open door. Once more, he releases a loud meow to indicate I follow him.

What the heck am I doing?

Trusting a cat?

I heard stories about how prison can make you lose your mind. Is that what's happening to me?

I don't know what possesses me, but I obediently amble to my feet and follow the cat down the twisting passageways.

As I walk farther, I note that the tunnels extend into large rooms. Some appear to be recreational halls, while others still look to be dining rooms. Desks and tables are knocked over more often than not, and papers are practically plastered to the damp floor. Mold covers the walls, the stench nearly as pervasive as the smell of urine and blood.

Mr. Scruffles leads me to the largest room I have seen so far in the Labyrinth. Table after table are placed in perfect lines in the middle of the room. Against the far wall, a separate table seems to glimmer with bright light. As I watch through his eyes, transfixed, a collection of entrées appears.

Magic.

The food doesn't look appetizing—stale-looking bread, a glob of brown and red meat, and decaying bananas—but it's a feast to my growling, gnawing stomach.

"Thank you," I whisper, bending down to press a kiss on Mr. Scruffles's tiny head. I swear the cat leans into me like a flower straining towards the sun.

Scrunching my nose at the not-so-pleasant scent of the food, I scoop first the meat and then the bread onto my plate. I opt not to eat the banana. I survived this long—the last thing I need is to be killed by food poisoning.

Mr. Scruffles jumps onto one of the far tables, and I move to sit beside him. At some point, I must've pulled myself out of his head, for darkness once more monopolizes my vision. Using only my hands for guidance, I spear some of the meat onto my plastic fork.

The taste is...tolerable. It isn't the worst food I have ever eaten, but it's definitely not the best. The spicy tang of the meat is countered by the dryness of the bread. To drink, they only provide water in small paper cups.

"It's not bad," I tell Mr. Scruffles seriously. He makes a somewhat incredulous scoff. Maybe I have a future career in reading cats—I swear I understand him better than most humans. "Seriously, it's not awful." I giggle, pulling apart chunks of bread and feeding one to me and then one to Mr. Scruffles. "Once, at the Compound, I had to go a whole week only eating celery and water. *That* was awful. I think I prefer this junk to that."

The cat nudges my hand, demanding pets, and I comply easily.

"I've never had a pet before," I continue, my voice sounding far away and distant even to me. "Tay—that's what everyone called her, at least—had a cat she would bring in. Fluffy. He was a pretty white cat. Actually, it might've been a she. Anyway, Tay would bring the cat in to visit me. I liked Tay. She never participated in the... torture sessions. Of course, she didn't do anything to stop them, either." I trail off, my hand stilling on the cat's head. I could be mistaken—I usually am—but it almost feels as if the cat bristles at my words. His back hunches, and an ear-piercing hiss escapes. I bop his head playfully. "Shush."

I resume my strokes, and Mr. Scruffles settles down

enough to lay on the table indolently. His furry tail swishes back and forth, whacking against my hand with each thrust.

I have just finished my meal when I become aware of footsteps behind me. If I was anyone else, anyone with perfect vision, the sound might not have been noticeable. As it is now, the footsteps sound thunderous in the quietness of the room. The tiny hairs on the back of my neck stand on end, saluting the world.

Mr. Scruffles goes tense beside me, his coarse fur prickling.

"New girl!" a strident voice says from behind me. A second later, large hands squeeze my shoulders.

A ball of terror forms in my gut, churning the contents of my stomach. I attempt to calm my uneven breathing.

While the voice isn't necessarily unfriendly...

You can't trust anyone.

Ducking my head, I ignore the newcomer and stab at my meat.

Go away.

Don't hurt me.

Please don't hurt me.

I don't think I can survive it.

"I heard that you just arrived," he continues easily.

I wonder, briefly, what he looks like. While his voice is low and charming, his appearance could be the exact opposite. You can learn so much about a person through their eyes. Philosophers aren't kidding when they say that eyes are the windows to your soul. In one glance, you can see a person's hopes and fears, their anger and desire.

Like Kai. He was the only person who didn't stare at me like I was a tasty morsel he wanted to devour. He stared at me like I was a person, as necessary to his life as the air he breathed. Kai can only be comparable to the ocean. A deep and dark abyss you are forced to sink into in order to understand. You may drown, but death would be worth it.

"Are you dumb, bitch?" the newcomer asks snidely. His words are a slap to the face, and I blanch. "Answer me!" He grabs hold of my hair, yanking my head back. The momentum pulls me off the bench and onto the floor, slick with something wet. Hopefully, it's not blood.

Fear explodes through me, kicking my body into action. I jerk my leg out and strike him in the knee. There are a few places Kai taught me to hit when in a pinch—the nuts, the knees, and the throat.

But without diving into his head, I'm relying solely on instinct. Fortunately, my foot aims true, a resounding crack and pained growl following the kick.

With a gurgling laugh, the man grabs my hair once more, tilting my head to the side. "You filthy—"

A ferocious roar has the man releasing me with a sharp, pained gasp. I remain submerged in my pit of darkness, shaking, as screams reverberate in the once-silent room. It almost sounds as if...

As if...

As if a monster is attacking the man.

I scramble onto my knees, hands tightening on the table edge, and push into the nearest mind available.

All I can see is blood. Lots and lots of blood. The man's face—he's uglier than I imagined—is horribly disfigured, grotesque, with bloody slashes down both his cheeks and neck.

I push myself out of the monster's eyes quickly, seconds from hyperventilating.

Am I next?

All I have ever known is pain. Inevitable pain. There's not a second that goes by when I don't experience some form of it.

It's only fitting I would die experiencing the worst pain imaginable.

I feel hot breath on my cheek from the monster, and I squeeze my eyes shut, tears cascading down both my cheeks.

I'm not ready to die.

When no pain arrives, I push my consciousness once more into the nearest mind.

Mr. Scruffles—the mind I find myself in—glances at the disgusting, disfigured body lying in a pool of his own blood on the floor. The man's face is nearly unrecognizable, nothing but blood, guts, and skin. My stomach heaves and tightens, and I cover my mouth, gagging. The cat turns away to focus on me, slithering between my legs and resuming its contented purr.

My hand freezes inches from the cat's fur.

Had he just...?

What the heck just happened?

CHAPTER 6

NINA

I somewhat reluctantly follow Mr. Scruffles back to the cell I had gone to the bathroom in. My pulse skitters in trepidation as I use my hands to familiarize myself with my surroundings.

What just happened?

It sounds surreal to say that the cat had transformed into a beast and killed that man...but what other option is there? Someone—or some*thing*—had hurt him, and the cat was the only other occupant in the room.

Terror thrums through me as my heart ricochets around my ribcage. There's a very real threat sitting only a few inches away from me, his tail swinging languidly.

Am I going to be next?

I want to run as far as I can, but I know my attempted escape will be futile. It's apparent that the cat—monster—has taken a liking to me, practically herding me towards the bedroom. How long will that "liking" last? The last thing I want to do is provoke the creature and shorten my time left on earth.

I sift through my memories for any monster, creature, or

paranormal entity that fits the cat's description. Nothing springs to mind.

Still, despite my fear, I can't ignore how tempting an actual bed sounds. While I slept peacefully only a few hours ago, there's something about an actual mattress, pillow, and blanket that appeals to me immensely. Even staring at it through Mr. Scuffles's eyes reminds my body how weak and leaden it has become. I pull out of the cat's head, and darkness presses in thickly all around me.

Using my hands for guidance, I stumble around the numerous chairs until I touch the mattress. It smells clean, the scent almost floral, and it's softer than my mattress at the Compound.

I sink onto the fluffy surface and rest my head on the pillow. I hear Mr. Scuffles climb onto the foot of my bed and rest between my feet. In only seconds, his breathing is even and steady as sleep claims him.

Despite my earlier qualms, I find myself drifting off as well. It doesn't matter that I just slept for hours in the dank hallway. It doesn't matter that a monster is purring away at my feet.

I want to sleep, want to forget everything that has transpired in the last month. It feels as if I've aged years in a matter of hours. As the first pull of unconsciousness grips me, I think about death. My death, in particular.

How many times did I wish for such a relief in the Compound?

Now, death is quite literally breathing down my neck, but the allure is no longer present. I don't know if I'm capable of fighting it, but I'll sure as hell try.

I WAKE UP TO WATER BEING SQUIRTED IN MY FACE WITH THE force of a tsunami. It enters my nostrils and gaping mouth, evoking unimaginable pain. Twisting, I press my forehead against the now-soaked pillow.

As abruptly as it began, the water shuts off.

"Get up, Little Monster," a cold voice demands. When I remain immobile, I hear the telltale sound of my cage being thrown open.

I mean cage literally.

My cell consists of nothing but gray slabs of stone and bars in front of the only doorway. There are no windows—no sunlight penetrating the suffocatingly small room. Only a cot and pot reside inside my prison. The cot itself smells distinctly of mildew and piss, and the pot reeks something fierce. They're supposed to clean it out every day, but it has been sitting here for weeks now, overflowing and staining the cement floor.

A moment later, a rough hand fists around my hair, yanking my head back. I just barely manage to contain my yelp of pain, my teeth destroying my lower lip.

"Don't be a bitch," he snaps.

Instead of fighting, I go limp in his arms. Call me a coward. Call me weak.

I learned long ago that fighting only leads to more pain.

He shifts me so I'm sitting somewhat comfortably in his arms, one of his hands under my butt and the other around my shoulders. I wince as he begins to grope me, but I know better than to open my mouth.

There's no reason to fight. Not anymore.

Not after Kai left me.

Tears spring to my eyes instinctively, his mere name evoking such a reaction. I stubbornly hold them in, refusing to shed another tear in front of this man. Maybe later, in the solitude of my cell, I will fall apart. For now, I will pretend that my puzzle pieces aren't jagged and broken, chewed up and discarded. I will pretend that I'm whole.

Maybe I'll begin to believe it myself.

I slide into his head as he leads me through the Compound. Instead of the torture chamber, he leads me to a familiar room consisting of a wooden desk and two plastic chairs. I'm deposited on one, and he moves to sit opposite me, his legs kicked up and his hands behind his head.

"You're being watched and recorded," he says almost conversationally, nodding first to the camera in the corner of the room and then to the wall-length mirror. He leans forward suddenly, resting his forearms on the table. "So, tell me, Little Monster, what you know about immortality."

～

I AWAKE WITH A GASP, BREATHS FEATHERING IN AND OUT. My heart feels like it is clamped in a spiky vise, bleeding with each consecutive harried pump. The dream replays on repeat in my mind. No, not a dream.

A memory.

Why did he ask me that question? What did he mean? Does it have something to do with my enhanced healing capabilities?

Each question clamors for attention in my head, but I'm unable to settle on just one. A splitting headache forms behind my eyes, and I rub at the sensitive skin with my thumbs.

Was it possible that the facility knew about the supernatural world?

The more I consider it, the more probable it seems. It's no secret that the men and women present suspected I was something other than human. The tests administered and questions asked confirm as much.

But why me?

Why Kai?

Almost lazily, I push my mind into the nearest set of eyes...only to discover that I'm alone.

Where is Mr. Scruffles? I pat down the blankets, but my searching hands come up empty. Panic surges through me, completely unexpected. I'm struck by the intensity of it.

I don't trust the cat, yet I'm grieving his absence. Maybe it's because he was my first friend in years, not just my first friend in this prison. Maybe because his absence causes loneliness to press in on me on all sides, like a steadily shrinking room. As the walls push in, I begin to suffocate.

Breathing unsteady, I stumble around the room, searching futilely for the missing cat.

Did he go back to his owner?

Irrational tears trail down my cheeks, and I scrub them away.

No crying, Nina. You have to be strong. You're not going to survive another day if you show weakness.

I don't know how much time has passed, but I'm not hungry. I imagine it's only been a few hours since I last ate. Since the monster killed...

Don't think about that.

I debate my options. I could stay in this room, where I've been relatively safe so far, or I could take my chances somewhere else in the Labyrinth. The main problem with the former idea is the owner of this room. I have no idea who or what he is and what he will do to me if he discovers me in his space. But if I travel by myself in the Labyrinth...

I'm under no misconception that I'm a strong fighter. Not every heroine has to be one. I know the basics of throwing a punch, but if you were to put me in a fight against a hardened criminal, I would be dead in seconds. That is, if they kill me. I'm not completely oblivious of what can be done to females in today's society.

Before I can make my decision, there's a rustling noise to

the left of me, and I whip my head in that direction. Deciding quickly, I slide into the newcomer's mind just as she staggers to a stop in front of the open door, panting.

"I've been..." Pant. "Looking for you..." Pant. "Everywhere."

Her voice is decidedly feminine, and when she glances down, I see ample breasts and a ruby red gown. It's far nicer than anything I would've expected to see in a prison.

She fixes her gaze on me, trembling in the corner of the room.

"Looking for me?" I ask softly, watching my mouth move through her eyes. It will never not be weird.

"Blade told me to look after you," she explains, but I have no idea who this "Blade" is. If he's anything like his namesake, I don't want to find out. "I went to where the guards usually drop off the new inmates, but you weren't there. Then I started asking around, but no one saw you. "Usually, Blade likes new females seeing other females when they wake up. It makes them feel more comfortable. I'm Tessa, by the way. And you are...?" She steps forward, hand extended, only to pause when she's directly in front of me.

I know she can see my white, sightless eyes.

"Holy shit!" she curses. "You're blind?" Before I can reply, she releases a melodic laugh that instantly puts me at ease. "How have you survived this long?" She tsks her tongue before kneeling down to stare at me.

"I'm Nina," I stutter out at last. She seems friendly, charismatic, but is it an act? There were only a few females in the Compound with me, and all of them were captors instead of captives. Evil doesn't discriminate against gender.

"Nina," she says softly. "That's a pretty name." With a sigh, she rises to her full height and lifts a hand to help me up. "Come on. Blade wants to meet you."

Those words freeze every organ in my body. My heart

struggles to pump blood. My mouth parts in shock and terror.

"What?" I ask meekly.

"He's not that bad," Tessa says, and I can imagine she's rolling her eyes. She seems like the type. "None of his inner circle is that bad...well, except for Damien. He's an asshole. A sexy asshole, but an asshole all the same. And I swear Cain looks as if he's seconds away from snapping my neck..." She trails off thoughtfully, but her words do the opposite of what she intended.

Fear like no other claims me in an impenetrable chain. I scramble on my hands and knees until my back is against the wall.

Tessa releases a heavy sigh. "Look, I can either force you, or you can come willingly. Either way, you're coming with me. Got it? Good."

Without waiting for me to respond, she lifts her hand and my entire body freezes. Abruptly, I'm yanked out of her mind and back into my solitary darkness. A pathetic squeak escapes me as my feet hover just above the ground, never touching.

What does she plan to do with me?

I've never missed Mr. Scruffles more than I do in this moment.

Air brushes my cheeks, whipping my hair around my face, as I move down the hall. Only, I'm not actually moving. *Tessa* is moving me. My feet never once touch the ground.

I don't know how long we walk until Tessa releases me, my slippered feet landing gently on the cold cement. I stagger, head pounding, as a delicate hand rests on my shoulder.

"It's better me than the others," she tells me sincerely. "But I promise, Nina, that I'll protect you. You don't have to be scared of them."

I don't know why, but a part of me believes her. I have

dealt with liars and crooks my entire life, but there's nothing but truth emanating from her. Maybe it'll be beneficial to have someone like her as an ally.

"Now, when the door opens, you're going to have to step inside. I'll be right behind you, okay? They're going to be straight ahead. Take maybe about seven steps, okay? Stop and then bow. Don't say anything until you're spoken to. I know this is scary for you, but you'll be safe. Promise. Blade doesn't harm women. The worst that could happen is one of the others propositioning you, but if you say no, they'll back off. Okay?" She squeezes my shoulder, and I take the moment to once again slip into her head.

I wonder, briefly, if the spell she performed on me prohibited me from entering her head before. It would be interesting to experiment with. Does her magic cancel out my magic? Is that even what this is? Magic?

Tessa's facing me currently, but through her eyes, I can see an immense doorway directly over my shoulder. What appears to be snakes and dragons are etched into the silver lining. It's by far fancier than the rest of the prison, but it does nothing to quell the full body shivers overtaking me.

"You'll be okay," Tessa assures me before pushing open the door. It slides open silently, revealing a room with stark white walls, gray flooring, and a high-backed chair against the far wall of the room.

A man is sitting on the chair currently, talking to a man wearing a pressed suit and tie. Out of Tessa's peripheral, I spot other men, but she doesn't focus long enough for me to get a good look at them.

Even if she did, I wouldn't.

My entire attention—my entire *being*—is fixated on the man in the chair.

His dark hair cascades to his shoulders in disheveled waves. A wicked scar runs down his left cheek, somehow accentuating his handsome features. Tattoos climb up his throat, and his white shirt sleeves are pushed up to reveal more on his forearms. He's a vision of chiseled muscle and rugged sexiness.

And he's also painfully familiar.

"Kai," I whisper softly. Before I realize what I'm doing, I'm running forward. It appears as if there are miles between us, miles I wish desperately to breach...

He stiffens, but he doesn't look away from the man he's deep in conversation with.

My vision shifts suddenly, and I release a startled *oomph* as I'm tackled to the ground.

CHAPTER 7

BRONSON

I want to kill the twins.

No surprise. I'm pretty sure I want to kill the twins at least once a day.

Abel smirks at me, the little asshole, and waves the pendant in the air like the fucking American flag.

My pendant.

I'm not one to be vindictive—preferring to remain in the shadows and listen attentively—but the twins have pushed it too far this time.

With a roar, I shed my human skin and pounce forward, three hundred pounds of pure beast. I know my wolf can be intimidating as fuck. My fur is a contrast to my hair—while my tresses are blond, my fur is the shade of molten onyx stones. It's a distinct characteristic of my lineage: a shadow wolf.

In three easy strides, I'm across the room with my paws on Abel's chest. Despite my towering, hulking frame looming over him, the asshole still has the nerve to smile.

Crazy fucker.

With a huff of annoyance, I take the pendant between my

sharp canines and saunter away. Abel's deranged laugh follows me, even as Cain grunts at his twin's antics. Unfortunately for the quieter demon, they're both on my shit list.

I spit the pendant onto the ground, allowing the change to wash over me. It feels like thousands of needles pricking my arms and legs, not keen enough to break skin and draw blood but enough to hurt. My furry body shudders, contorts, as the magic wafts over me in a silver sheen. In only seconds, I'm standing on two very human feet, as naked as the day I was born. My clothes were ripped to shreds during my initial shift.

"Asshole," I growl at Abel, and his laughter only increases. I notice a few appreciative stares from the females lingering, but I ignore them all. They know not to approach me—I'll approach them.

I bend down to open my backpack and grab a change of clothes: a flannel shirt, dark jeans, and a white undershirt. After quickly dressing, sans boxers, I turn back around with my customary scowl firmly in place.

A few of our lower gang members are gathered in the far corner of the room, attempting to be invisible. The prison females are flirting with them shamelessly. Probably hoping to secure a man who will protect them.

They know they won't find it in us.

The guys and I...we're assholes. Too hard and cruel to truly care for anyone. The women know this. We use them when we have an itch and then discard them the next day. Usually, we don't bang the same female in the same month. Don't want them to get too attached.

The twins are talking amongst themselves, and I mentally plan their demise. I may be quiet, but that doesn't mean I'm stupid. It just means I see more than the average person.

Like how Abel is oddly attached to his dick.

It would be a shame if something happened to it...

Smirking at my macabre thoughts, I grab the pendant from the ground and place it around my neck. It was a gift from my father many years ago, before he passed away. It's my most prized possession, and it's a miracle I was able to sneak it into the prison in the first place.

Not that anyone cared. The guards threw us in here without a second thought.

Forgotten. Discarded. Used. We're nothing but a child's old toy that was spit on and then thrown away.

The pendant glints in the artificial lighting like freshly spun gold. Engraved in the heart is my momma's initials. How Abel stumbled upon it remains a mystery—I always keep it around my neck or hidden in my room—but I'll make him pay for stealing it. I already have to deal with Blade's longing, wistful looks.

Not that I blame him. The superstition about dragons hoarding gold and other shiny objects is true. I'm pretty sure Blade has an entire room dedicated just to his collection.

Across the room, Abel catches my eye, and I pantomime slitting his throat. His grin grows even wider while Cain frowns. I always knew Cain was the smarter twin. You can never be too careful with a volatile werewolf.

In the front of the room, on a dais, Blade talks in soft tones to Damien. I know exactly what he's talking about: the increase in fights and dissent within the prison community. For years, Blade has ruled the Labyrinth uncontested. What has changed in the last few months? Why are the shifters protesting a system that keeps us all safe? It makes me immensely worried.

The second Blade is kicked off his throne...

Hell will reign.

The Labyrinth isn't perfect, but it works. It's relatively calm and peaceful—for a prison, that is.

The air suddenly leaves my lungs, and I gasp, my large

palm sliding down the wall. Pain explodes in my chest, and I keel over. Something is happening, something indecipherable, but something irrevocably *right*. My heart drops to my stomach as all my senses focus on one being. One bright, pure light that breaks apart the darkness. A ray of sunshine in the gray, overcast skies that have defined my life.

Her.

She steps into the room, body shaking with what I suspect to be terror. Her hair is as dark as obsidian and cascades down to her waist in thick, luscious waves. Her body is frail and slim, a product more from starvation than exercise and diet if my senses are correct. She's so entirely delicate and breakable that I want nothing more than to cross the distance between us, take her in my arms, and protect her from this entire world.

One word reverberates in my ears, over and over again, like the sweetest song imaginable.

Mate.

This slight, unassuming, gorgeous female is my mate. I know that as innately as I know my name is Bronson and I'm left-handed. My wolf howls in my mind, demanding to be free. Beneath the ecstatic joy is bone-crushing terror.

How did my mate end up here?

I want to lunge forward and take her in my arms, but she already looks so frightened. Tessa stands directly behind her, and I'm grateful that, out of all the women who had to find my mate, it was Tessa. She's the nicest.

What's her name?

What's her story?

Where did she come from?

Question after question fill my mind until I want to shout them from the rooftop.

My mate.

My fucking mate.

I've heard the stories of a werewolf's fated mate—the one person who completes your heart and soul. I've even seen it happen firsthand. First with my mother and then with my sister. I have never, not in a million years, believed that I would stumble across my fated mate, the person irrecoverably meant for me.

Especially not in this hellhole.

What did she do to arrive here? She looks as if she could barely hurt a fly, let alone a person. Is she a government spy? Everything about her is delicate and fragile, like a real-life angel statue. I yearn to take her in my arms and shield her from the horrors of this world.

There are a lot of fucking horrors.

Her mouth parts suddenly as she stares in Blade's direction. Stares with...sightless, white eyes.

Is she blind?

Terror squeezes my heart in iron chains and tightens painfully. I need to go to her. I need to protect her. I need—

As the female begins to rush forward, towards Blade (what the fuck?), Tessa tackles her from behind, pushing her into the ground. My mate whimpers and covers her head with her hands, almost as if she's expecting another blow.

A growl escapes my lips before I can contain it, and I find myself marching forward.

"You can't touch him," Tessa whispers urgently to my mate, the *him* meaning Blade. "I told you. Walk seven steps and then bow."

My mate will bow to no one. If anything, we will bow to her.

I will bow to her.

With a ferocious roar, the noise nearly unrecognizable, I grab Tessa and wrench her off my mate. It's entirely irrational. Logically, I know Tessa isn't hurting my female, but my wolf bristles at the sight of someone tackling her small frame.

My beautiful, gorgeous mate turns her face in my direction, terror evident in her glossy white eyes.

All I can do is stare.

This close, she's even more beautiful than I imagined. Her dewy, heart-shaped face is perfectly symmetrical, her skin like porcelain. Those large, white eyes, framed by thick lashes, somehow make her arresting features even more stunning. More beautiful.

Her sightless eyes stare up at me in horror and fear, and I immediately feel as if I've been struck by lightning. My mate should never, not ever, look at me like that.

But what did I expect? I'm a large, towering beast of a man hovering over her. Even if she can't see my features, she can sense my presence.

I should move away, give her space.

But fuck, she smells so damn good.

Blade cuts off his conversation mid-word, spinning to see what the commotion is all about. It's very, very rare for me to growl, let alone in the presence of a lady. His eyes drop to the female cowering on the ground, and something flickers in his hardened gaze. Something I have never seen before.

Disbelief. Horror. Hope.

And love. A love so deep and intense, I want to growl *again*.

Why is he looking at my mate like that?

"Nina," he whispers, staggering down a step, as if he is drunk. Damien turns to stare at us, his expression almost bored, but pauses when he catches sight of the petite female. His eyes widen almost imperceptibly in his stupidly handsome face, and he, too, takes a step forward.

"Kai?" my mate whimpers, turning her head to stare in his general direction.

Blade pauses a few steps away, his lips curling into a snarl.

"Everyone out!" he shouts, and I wonder if I'm the only

one who notices my mate wince. What has happened in her life to cause such an instinctive reaction to loud noises? I suddenly want to tear the world apart, watch it bleed. Whoever hurt her...

A growl resounds low in my throat.

In a matter of seconds, the females and lower members scatter as if their asses are on fire. Tessa hesitates, only a second, before hurrying out with the rest of them. She might be the nicest female, but she's still a coward, still driven by fear. Only the twins, Damien, and I remain.

Blade collapses to his knees before the female—Nina—with tears glimmering in his dark eyes. Blade, the man who once murdered twenty-two people without breaking a sweat, is crying. Who is this woman who brought a man like Blade to his knees?

She reaches for him at the same moment he reaches for her, pulling her onto his lap and wrapping her in his arms. She rubs her face against the skin of his neck as he rocks her.

I just barely bite down on the hiss threatening to escape.

What the fuck is going on?

CHAPTER 8

NINA

I used to have dreams of this exact moment.

Seeing Kai. Touching him. Reveling in his warmth. His distinct scent of cinnamon and peppermint is now tampered by the stench of cigarettes, but his arms around me are as familiar as the air I breathe.

He holds me reverently, like I'm fine glass he's afraid will break. Nuzzling my neck, he inhales me as desperately as I inhale him, as if he's committing my scent to memory.

"Nina," he whispers into my skin.

I gently tap his chin, urging his head up, and run my fingers over the sharp planes of his sinfully handsome face. I don't need sight to know he has looks that make angels weep. With sure strokes, I trace his high, chiseled cheekbones down to his strong jawline. And then up, towards his plush lower lip and thin upper one. His tongue instinctively snakes out to lick my thumb, and shivers take over my body. I could use my powers to see him, but somehow, this feels a hundred times more intimate. At this moment, it's just him and me in an embrace capable of melting the walls. I take my time mapping out every tight muscle of his body and the grooves of his numerous scars, more scars than he left the Compound with.

"Your hair's longer," I muse softly, brushing a hand down his shoulder-length black hair.

I can hear the smile in his voice as he cups the back of my head before lowering his hand down, following the cascade of my tresses. "So is yours."

"This is all sweet and shit, but who the fuck is this girl?" a sly voice demands, and I whip my head in the unfamiliar male's direction, ignoring Kai's threatening growl. Using his shoulders for purchase, I jump to my feet and smile in the new man's general direction.

"I'm Nina," I say softly, extending a hand. Any person who is a friend of Kai's is a friend of mine.

"No!" Kai bellows at the same time another male screams, "Don't!"

A cold hand grasps my own, and I can practically sense the tension in the room ratcheting up a notch. Everybody seems to be holding their breaths.

But why?

Who is this man?

"Nina," he says, my name leaving his lips like a decadent treat. For some undefinable reason, a flush enters my cheeks, and I duck my head. I don't quite understand my reaction. "I'm Damien."

"Damien," I repeat, offering him another tentative smile. "It's a pleasure to meet you."

Almost involuntarily, I slip into Kai's head—as familiar to me as my own—and survey the man from his eyes.

He's...gorgeous. That's the only word capable of encapsulating the six-foot man standing before me. He's skinnier than Kai, wearing a double-breasted suit coat with overlapping front flaps and two sets of buttons, a covered placket, and a red tie. His face is all sharp angles and smooth curves, accentuating his high cheekbones and brilliant sea-blue eyes. While his skin is as pale as my own, his hair is so dark it almost appears blue, carefully brushed away from his face.

It's a type of beauty I have only seen reserved in predators. An unmerciful, savage type of beauty that makes my heart thump in my chest. But beauty is beauty, and his ensnares me like a sword disguised in ribbons and bows.

This man, Damien, is watching me as intently as I watch him. There's curiosity in his gaze as his eyes skillfully travel over my body.

"That's enough, Damien," Kai growls, grabbing my waist. Damien's eyes flash briefly, and it's only then that I realize he's still holding my hand. That makes my cheeks flame even brighter as I quickly remove it and shove it into my dress pocket.

"Kai," I reprimand sternly. "Behave."

But I can't stop the giddy smile from cleaving my face in two.

Kai is here. With me.

It doesn't even matter that "here" is a virtual hellhole quite literally underground.

He had promised he'd come for me...and, apparently, I was the one who came for him.

I pull myself out of his head and turn toward him, a brilliant smile playing on my lips, only to be struck cold by his beseeching tone.

"What the fuck are you doing here?" he demands curtly.

"Don't talk to her like that!" a gruff voice snarls, and Kai's hands tighten imperceptibly on my shoulders. I don't know if he's going to pull me closer, push me away, or place me over his shoulder and run away. Any of the above are immensely appealing.

He's here.

He's with me.

I'm practically giddy—not even his sour mood can ruin my day.

"Take a walk, Bronson," Kai sneers. "You forget who's in charge."

The third man, Bronson, releases a low, threatening growl, but he doesn't move from where he's hovering nearby. I can't see him, but I can sense him. His presence, that is. The heat he emanates is almost palpable.

"I'll ask you one more time, Babygirl," Kai tells me, and his voice is considerably more gentle. "How did you get here?"

My lower lip begins to tremble as I think of the events that led me to this precise moment.

"I did what you said," I whisper, ducking my head. "During feeding time, I overpowered Miles and escaped. You were right. He is the weakest guard."

The silence in the room is suddenly stifling. How many people are listening to me recount the last month of horrors? Kai, for sure, and that Damien guy. Bronson too. And maybe a set of twins? I thought I saw them through Tessa's eyes, but they could've left with the others.

Kai's breathing is suddenly ragged and uneven, smoke perfuming the air around my face. At the Compound, I had suspected he was different like me. That he had some unexplainable powers.

Is he a part of this supernatural world too? He must be. How else would he end up in this prison?

That's something I need to ask him, but first, I need to focus on the topic at hand.

Taking a deep, steadying breath, I lift my hands to cover his on my shoulders, interlocking our fingers and bringing them down to my stomach. His touch burns me, but it's the sweetest heat imaginable. The fire enlivens something in my veins, pooling low in my stomach.

"I escaped." Tears form in my eyes as a small smile plays on my lips. "But then..."

"But then?" the gruff male, Bronson, asks darkly. I don't know the man, but his tone of voice makes me cringe. Something about the darkness he exudes...

Kai growls, and Bronson's breath hitches. Without having to see, I know he takes a few steps away from me, his larger-than-life presence no longer suffocating.

"I'm sorry," he mumbles forlornly.

I offer a weak smile in his general direction. "It's fine. Truly."

He's obviously someone Kai trusts, I tell myself sternly. *There's nothing to be afraid of. With any of these men.*

"What happened, Angel?" Damien asks, and the nickname makes me blush stupidly.

"I passed out," I admit. "When I woke up, I was in the hospital, and this man, William, accused me of hurting someone."

Murdering someone is a more adequate description, but I can't quite bring myself to say that dreaded m-word. I know I'm not a killer, and hearing that title makes my stomach twist and tighten.

"What's his name?" Kai asks gently. When I don't answer, shaking like a leaf, he elaborates. "The man they claimed you...hurt."

"Raphael Turner." My voice is barely above a whisper.

A flurry of curses precedes my declaration.

"He's a butt-munching dickwad," someone proclaims. The unfamiliar voice sounds from the corner of the room, and I turn my head in that direction. It must be one of the twins.

"What's a butt-munching dickwad?" I ask him, and his laughter abruptly cuts off.

"Is this chick serious?" he asks no one in particular. When

Kai and Bronson merely growl and Damien remains silent, the twin sighs heavily. "She is serious, isn't she?"

"I am...um ...very serious." Removing Kai's hands from my shoulders, I step closer. "I'm Nina."

"I heard the introduction the first time," he replies, a smirk in his voice. My cheeks turn red, but this time, it's from embarrassment.

"Well, yes," I stutter, fiddling with my fingers. "But it's polite for you to give me your names as well. Any friend of Kai's is a friend of mine." I trust Kai implicitly. The people he keeps around him must be amazing men. Maybe they're like me, falsely arrested for crimes they didn't commit. It would make sense for Kai to take them under his wing, as he did for me.

"Friend, huh?" And then, in a jovial voice, "And Kai? I always thought your name would be Bertrand or something."

My brows furrow. The twin almost acts as if he doesn't know Kai's name. But, if they are friends, Kai would've told him, right?

"His full name is Malakai," I confess, and Kai growls low beneath his breath.

"And how, beautiful Nina, do you know *Malakai*?" The twin moves to stand directly in front of me. At least, I'm assuming it's the same twin I've been talking to this entire time.

"We were at the Compound together," I answer easily, holding up my hands. I pause inches from his face, raising an eyebrow. "May I?"

"Um...you may?" His voice rises, turning the agreement into a question. Still, I don't hesitate to place both hands on his face and familiarize myself with his features. Lower cheekbones than Damien's, but with a face thinner than Kai's. His skin is smooth beneath my traveling fingers, not a scar or pimple to be felt.

I slide easily into Kai's head to stare at the mysterious twin.

His hair is golden, longer on the top than the sides, and his features are decidedly boyish. He's leaner than a lot of the other males—sans Damien—but still breathtakingly muscular. A sultry, mischievous smirk pulls up his thin lips.

Over his shoulder, I see a man similar in appearance to the guy I'm touching. Same blond hair, grassy green eyes, and thin build. Unlike his twin, this man's lips are curved into a scowl, and his eyes are narrowed on me in his brother's arms.

"What's your name?" I ask the smiling twin, pulling out of Kai's head and embracing my customary darkness.

"Why? Do you want to scream it?"

Ignoring Kai's enraged snarl, I frown. "Why would I scream it?" I drop my hands to my sides and stagger back a step. "Are you going to hurt me?"

Another step has me pressing my back against a man's front. Damien's, if the smell is any indication. Clover leaves and something sweet, something I can't pinpoint.

"Yes, Abel, are you going to hurt the beautiful lady?" Damien asks dryly.

"Of course not!" the twin, Abel, protests. "I was just... I was just trying to..." He groans, his voice muffled, as if he holds his head in his hands. "Fuck, that's not what I meant."

"What did you mean, brother?" the other twin asks with a hint of amusement in his voice.

"Fuck off," Abel mutters.

"Language," I reprimand immediately. "He's your brother. That isn't nice."

A loud guffaw sounds behind me, and without even having to look, I know it will belong to Bronson.

"Not nice at all," the unnamed twin agrees, a smirk evident in his voice.

"Listen," Abel begins, and he almost sounds hesitant and

unsure. For some reason, that makes Kai break into laughter behind me. "I didn't mean anything about the scream comment. I just..."

"You just?" I prompt when he trails off.

He blows a raspberry, stirring the hair by my ear. "Nothing," he settles on at last. "Never mind."

Turning away from Abel, I level my sightless eyes onto Kai. I know it can be unnerving to have the full extent of my white gaze on someone, but Kai never seemed to mind. He's the one who taught me that my blindness is a gift, not a hindrance. He made me feel special and beautiful despite my glaringly obvious flaw.

"Kai, you have a lot of explaining to do," I begin, attempting to adopt my best no-nonsense tone. Internally, I'm screaming. Dancing. Shaking my hips. I half wonder if I've died and gone to heaven. Being back with Kai...it's all I have ever wanted. Freedom means nothing without him to enjoy it with. "You said you were going to come back for me," I finish, and even I can't hide the sudden surge of vulnerability and pain in my voice.

Bronson releases another threatening growl, almost as if he's indignant on my behalf. Damien settles his chin on my shoulder, but I flick his nose to get him away. I'm not about to let an unfamiliar male get so close to me, thank you very much. They may be Kai's friends, but they aren't mine.

Though I'm not opposed to the idea. I've never had friends before. Maybe...

"Babygirl, I tried. I promise you. I thought about you every day and—"

Whatever he's about to say is interrupted by a door being pushed open. Heavy breathing follows next as someone enters the room, panting.

"Lord Blade," the newcomer huffs.

Lord Blade? Whose name is that? The second twin?

"Yes," Kai answers curtly, confusing me even more. "I thought I told you imbeciles not to interrupt."

I open my mouth to admonish Kai for calling this man an imbecile when Damien's hand tightens on my shoulder.

"You can give him hell later, Angel," he whispers in my ear, and his warm breath causes goose bumps to pebble on my skin.

"It's an emergency, sir," the man replies. "It's Rion. He and the other shifters are refusing to allow us to enter the cafeteria. A fight started. Three of our men are already dead, and two of theirs are wounded."

Kai growls, the sound so inhuman and downright terrifying that I jump, spinning around in Damien's arms and burying my face in his shirt. The man stiffens underneath me before placing his hands tentatively on my waist, holding me still. Terror pulsates through me—entirely irrational because I know Kai would never hurt me—and taints my body with the pungent, sour smell of it.

"Holy shit!" the man exclaims, and I automatically slip into Kai's mind to see what has captured the newcomer's attention. He's a small man, not as small as me, though, with thinning brown hair and wire-rimmed glasses. His eyes are fixed pointedly on me in Damien's arms.

Is it weird? Me being comforted by a stranger? I didn't think anything of it. For some reason, I feel safe with these men. Maybe because Kai trusts them, and I trust Kai.

Over my head, I watch Damien's eyes narrow into thin slits, and a threatening smile contorts his beautiful features. "You have something to say, worm?" he asks, his tone unrecognizable. Dark and terrifying, inducing full-body shivers.

"Of course not," the man stutters as Kai swivels his head back to him.

Releasing a low curse, Kai turns to Bronson first. It's the

first time I have gotten a good look at the man, and my heart
kick-starts, reverberating around in my ribcage.

He's enormous. A real giant of a man. He makes Kai look
thin and scrawny in comparison. Muscle upon muscle cover
his chest, stomach, legs, and arms. His thighs are the size of
tree trunks, and when he moves, his muscles ripple and flex.

"Bronson, Damien, you're with me. Cain and Abel, stay
with Nina."

Bronson's eyes flare hotly. "No."

"No?" Kai asks darkly. "You don't get to say no to me,
Bronson. You forget who I am." Whipping his head towards
Damien, Kai snarls, "Release Nina at once, Damien. She's not
one of your toys."

Of course I'm not a toy. I'm a human being. What the
heck has gotten into him? He knows better than anyone what
those degrading terms do to me. I will no longer be a weak,
defenseless doll for people to use, step on, and then throw
away. Not anymore. Not after I freed myself.

Finally, Kai turns to face the twins—one cheery and one
somber, their dispositions as different as night and day.

"And, you two, do not let any harm come to her, got it?
Do not, I repeat, *do not* do anything to her. Do you understand me?"

The smiling twin, who I assume is Abel, salutes while the
other one nods.

"Wait," I begin, detangling myself from Damien's arms. I
wrench myself out of Kai's head as I step forward. "You're
leaving me again? After we just found each other?"

The mere prospect sends my heart and head racing. Pain
thrums through me like a lightning bolt.

No. No. No. No.

I just got him back.

"I will be back," Kai reassures me, but his tone is no
longer that gentle one I love and adore. It's cold. Cruel. It's a

literal slap to the face. "Don't get all desperate and needy on me. It's not a good look for you."

Never, not ever, has Kai spoken to me that way. Tears burn my eyes, and I stagger back one step and then another. He's been my best friend for years, even when he left me all alone.

I had thought I was his as well. His reaction when he first saw me sure indicated as much.

But this? This is someone I hardly recognize.

"Okay," I whimper. The Compound's torture hurt less.

Maybe, just maybe, Kai could have come back for me.

And maybe, just maybe, he didn't want to.

CHAPTER 9

ABEL

Who the fuck is this woman with eyes as silver as the moon and hair like liquid night? With a body both supple and thin? With soft lips juxtaposed by the sharp planes of her face? With skin like alabaster?

And when the fuck did I start using words like "alabaster" and "liquid night" when describing a woman?

Normally, I'll look at their assets. Namely, their breasts and ass (there's a reason they're called *ass*ets). I'm a tits man, in case you were wondering.

Currently, her gorgeous doe eyes stare blindly up at me and my brother with pain emanating in their depths. I feel irrationally furious at the way Blade treated her. Logically, I know he did it for the scumbag's benefit—no one can know about Blade's (excuse me, *Malakai's*) attachment to her. I can't even begin to compute what Rion will do with that information.

Adopting my trademark, sultry smirk, one lost on the petite female, I say, "So, Nina, it seems that we find ourselves alone."

Blade must really trust me and my brother if he left her alone with us. Though, out of all the members of his inner circle, we're the least volatile and dangerous. We still have our powers in the Labyrinth, but as demons, my brother and I are unable to access the full extent of our skills. Can't really create portals to hell to rejuvenate our powers, now, can we? Besides, I have no doubt we will be a tasty dragon kabob if we so much as look at her inappropriately.

I've never seen Blade care about anyone but himself, let alone someone he obviously cares about *more* than himself. The fact that this diminutive slip of a female holds so much power over our esteemed leader terrifies me.

"So it seems." Nina sighs, turning a longing glance in the general direction Blade disappeared to. For some reason, that irritates the shit out of me.

And it irritates the shit out of me that it irritated the shit out of me in the first place. See my conundrum?

"Don't be so sad, Bambi," I jest, placing my arm around her shoulders. She tenses, the action almost instinctive, and I notice Cain's eyes narrowing in on that minuscule movement. Slowly, as to not startle her further, I remove my arm and rest it back by my side.

"Bambi," she parrots, narrowing her ethereal eyes in my direction. "That's not my name." She almost seems...put off, as if I'd purposely mistaken her name with that of another woman. Granted, it wouldn't be the first time, but that's not the case here.

"Bambi." I nod my head once, my smile growing in tandem with her confusion. "Like the movie."

One black brow quirks as she cocks her head to the side.

"Don't tell me you've never seen *Bambi*," I say in horror, placing a hand to my chest. "Have you been living under a rock?"

"More like in a compound," she murmurs, her cryptic statement leaving me with more questions than answers.

I exchange a bemused look with my brother, and he shrugs, feigning nonchalance. I can tell he's trying to act like he's not utterly captivated by the female who smells like blossoms and sunshine, but his eyes follow her as keenly as mine do.

"We'll have to rectify that straight away!" I say, and the melancholy in her eyes abates with my dogmatic words. "Wait. That's insensitive. I'm sorry. I forgot about..." I gesture vaguely towards her eyes, and Cain whacks me on the back of my head. Scowling, I flip him off.

An adorable giggle—seriously, when did I start saying words like "adorable?"—interrupts my retort. It's a sound I yearn to hear every second of every day.

What is it about her? Am I just that desperate to get in her pants?

Maybe I just need to get laid.

"I may be blind, but I would love to watch Bamble with you," she says softly, though her tone holds a hint of something in it, something I can't name. Amusement, maybe, like she is in the know of a secret we can't even begin to comprehend.

"*Bambi*," Cain corrects, speaking to her for the first time. She spins towards him with a wide smile, and I watch as my twin automatically takes a step back. A muscle in his jaw twitches as he crosses his arms over his chest and scowls at her.

"And you must be Cain. I don't think we've been formally introduced." She extends a hand—the nails chewed down to stubs—and I watch my brother narrow his gaze at the offending limb.

Taking control of the situation before it can escalate and implode, I gently wrap my hand around Nina's wrist and pull her towards me. "Enough of this," I say easily, bopping her nose. Apparently, I do cute shit around this female. The horror. "Let me give you an official tour of your new home."

Though the term "home" makes me want to vomit. A blow job it may giveth, but a home it does not maketh.

Pretty sure Shakespeare said that somewhere.

If Nina is confused by the abrupt change in topic, she doesn't show it. Her brows furrow at my initiation of contact, but she takes a deep, calming breath, and her body begins to relax incrementally until she is calm and flaccid—unlike my dick. Her hand is warm in mine, and that warmth seems to migrate straight to my groin. God, even her hand feels amazing.

Her small, dainty hand that I can just picture wrapped around my—

"How long have you known Kai?" she asks conversationally.

Cain wanders a few steps behind us. One glance over my shoulder shows his hands in his pockets and a wry grin playing on his lips.

"Oh, a few years, give or take," I say dismissively.

Her face practically glows, as if someone lit a candle beneath the surface. "He's a good man."

I just barely hold in my snort. Good man, my fucking ass. He's a good leader, for sure, and he's just and fair, but never would I consider Blade a good man. He keeps men like Damien around him, for fuck's sake.

"Shouldn't you be asking us the most important question?" Cain cuts in scathingly. Both Nina and I give him befuddled looks. I recognize the expression on Cain's face: cruel and cold. Icy terror skates down my spine, stealing the warmth from my body.

"Cain, what are you doing?" I warn darkly.

His smile grows, revealing sharp teeth. A flash of red

appears in his irises, the color nearly blocking out both pupils. The distinct stench of smoke and sulfur permeates the air.

Ignoring me, Cain keeps his attention on the trembling Nina. No doubt, she can feel the shift in the air as his demon form makes an appearance. Fucking asshole.

Blade will kill us.

"Don't you want to know what we're in for?" he asks, and I growl.

"Shut the fuck up," I hiss, my own teeth instinctively elongating.

"You see, my brother here is a trickster demon," Cain continues. "Me? I'm a sex demon." His voice takes on a seductive purr that brings most women to their knees. The power he exudes is almost staggering, a physical force thickening the air like syrup.

Most women, that is, except Nina, apparently.

To my shock and horror, her shoulders lift and her spine straightens. The only indication that Cain's power is affecting her is the tightening of her fists, dull nails digging into her palms.

"What are you in for?" she asks with more bravado than I'm sure she feels. Her chin lifts almost imperceptibly as she rests her blind, silver gaze on Cain.

"Well, well, well. I can't give you all our secrets, can I?" he taunts, smirking.

I take a threatening step closer until I'm nose to nose with my idiotic twin. "Seriously, Cain, shut the fuck up."

"Kai obviously trusts you enough to leave me alone with you," Nina insists, and Cain swivels his head to glare at her once more.

"Your precious Kai is the worst of us all," he hisses, and then Nina does the stupidest thing I have ever seen: she takes a step closer and places a hand on his arm.

An enraged roar escapes my brother as he staggers back a step, clutching at his stomach. I step in front of Nina, fully prepared to fight my brother until she's capable of escaping. It isn't just because I'm attracted to the dark-haired beauty. I would save anybody from my brother's unwarranted wrath.

The color drains from Nina's face, as if she is only now understanding the severity of the situation. The danger she unwittingly placed herself in.

Her next words, however, are a proverbial kick to the nuts. "I'm sorry."

What. The. Fuck?

"Why the hell are you sorry?" I ask, spinning towards her. Bambi's eyes aren't on me, but on my brother. Guilt swirls in that milky gaze, and she lowers her head submissively.

"I shouldn't have touched him," she whispers in a choked voice. To Cain, she adds, "I hate people touching me too."

Dozens of emotions flicker in my brother's garnet gaze before he settles on anger.

"Stay the fuck away from me!" he snarls before stomping away.

I watch my twin's retreating back before turning towards the trembling female. Miles upon miles of pain are buried in her expressive eyes. It would take a necromancer for me to uncover it all.

"I'm sorry," she repeats to me, and I manage a wobbly smile, suddenly grateful as fuck she's unable to see it.

"It's fine, Bambi. My brother has his issues."

"Don't we all..." The last is said in a hushed murmur, her expression contemplative.

But I have to wonder why my brother ran away. It's not his usual MO. He much prefers facing the problem head-on and snarling at it until it scampers away.

If I know my brother as well as I think I do—better than

I sometimes know myself—it's because he was just seen more clearly than ever before in his life, and that terrifies him.

"Let's take the tour, shall we?" I ask, clearing my sluggish head. And then, with more of my signature humor, I quip, "I'll let you touch whatever you want, as long as you're good."

When she laughs, not understanding my sexual innuendo, my smile grows.

Yeah, I'm an asshole. Sue me.

But fuck if something about this female isn't twisting me up inside.

CHAPTER 10

NINA

I can't stop thinking about Cain's explosive reaction.

There was a pain in his eyes, an agony that emanated in those gorgeous depths. As I stared at him through his brother's vision, I saw a man laden with pain and suffering. A man on the verge of breaking.

Clearing my head, I allow Abel to lead me down a twisting hallway. I have long since given up on trying to see through his eyes—his gaze is always on me.

"I'm sorry about my brother," Abel says easily, guiding me around a corner. I try not to flinch when his hand tightens imperceptibly around my upper arm to lead me.

He's Kai's friend. He's not going to hurt you.

But even I can sense the danger lurking just beneath the surface. The untamed beast. Everything about Abel is a contradiction. His golden hair and bright eyes give him an angelic appearance, but there's a darkness exuding from every pore in his body. What did Cain call him? A trickster demon? Of that, I have no doubt.

"Your brother," I begin slowly, choosing my words carefully. We stop abruptly, and I hear the telltale sound of a lock being undone. A moment later, Abel ushers me through a door. "Your brother hides a deep pain," I continue at last. "As do you."

"Me?" Abel scoffs. "The only pain I like is in the bedroom, Bambi."

My internal temperature rises a thousand degrees at his words. I may have lived my life in a bubble, but I'm not completely stupid. I have heard the guards talking enough to understand what, exactly, the trickster twin means.

Beneath the embarrassment is something else, something akin to...jealousy. My gut is buzzing like angry bees at the prospect of Abel with another woman.

What is wrong with me?

Maybe it's because I'm so desperate for love I'm willing to relish in any attention thrown my way.

"I still don't get why you call me that," I point out as Abel helps me step over something in the middle of the walkway.

"What? Bambi? We've been over this."

"What's it about?"

The air in this part of the prison is staler. I half wonder if we've ventured deeper into the abyss, though we never touched any stairs. My hand, stroking the wall, comes away wet and sticky. Grimacing, I move to rub it on my dress— before deciding against it and rubbing it on Abel's shirt.

"Hey!" he protests, and I giggle. There's a smile in his voice when he speaks next. A genuine smile, not the one he dons like a mask. "I don't really remember what the movie is about, but I remember there's a deer. And someone dies. The mom, maybe?"

"What?" I gasp, spinning to face him. "That's awful. Why would you call me that?"

"Because of your wide, gorgeous eyes," he replies easily, lifting his hands to caress the skin around them both. Just as quickly, he drops his hands to his sides and steps back. "Just like the deer's eyes. If you don't like the nickname, I can come up with a better one."

My heart is thundering a mile a minute. Did he just...? Did he just call my eyes *gorgeous*? They've been called a lot of things—creepy and ugly, yes, but never gorgeous.

"Is that a thing here?" I ask, quirking a brow. "Nicknames?"

Some of his familiar snark returns. "Only if they're given by you."

I smile, remembering snippets of conversation from my time in the Compound. One in particular sticks out more than the others. During a trip from my cell to the torture chamber, we stumbled across a couple in the throes of passion. Her nickname for him comes to the forefront of my mind.

"Okay, you want a nickname? I'll give you one. Anything for you...Daddy."

Abel stumbles over his own two feet, curses, and then places his hands on my shoulders.

"No...just ...no."

"What's the matter, Daddy?" I ask. Does he not like the nickname? At the Compound, the man had been overjoyed to be called such a thing, his moans of ecstasy increasing.

"Goddammit, woman," he curses, stepping away from me. "We are not going to be doing this shit."

"Doing what...shit?" I parrot, furrowing my brows. He exhales sharply.

"You know what? Let's just never talk about this again. Okay, Bambi?"

"Yes, Daddy."

"Motherfucker." With another muffled curse, he intertwines our fingers and pulls me after him down the hall. "Call me something else. Anything else."

"All right," I concede with a sigh. "How about...sunshine?"

He snorts, but this time, he doesn't stop moving. "Sunshine? Why that?"

"Because you're always sunny and cheerful while your brother is dark and broody," I surmise. There's a moment of silence as I'm pulled down another passageway. If I was with anyone else, anyone Kai didn't obviously trust, I would've been terrified. Right now, I'm more excited than anything. It feels as if we're going on an adventure, like in those books Kai used to read me at night.

"Don't mistake my smile for what it's not," Abel warns me, his tone unexpectedly serious. "There's more darkness in me than you know."

It almost sounds as if he's warning me of something. Warning me away from him.

But I have seen monsters—well, metaphorically, of course —and I don't believe Abel is one. There's a darkness in him, sure, but that darkness is nothing compared to the light I sense.

"And there's more light in you and Cain than you know," I retort back.

When he speaks next, something dark is in his tone, something that hints at his underlying darkness. And it scares me, but not in a way I can articulate. I fear that, if he submits himself fully to the darkness, he'll never again experience nature's ethereal light. I can't fathom a fate like that, bound eternally by pain and suffering.

"You don't know anything about us."

"I know that you're stuck in the shadows, pressed so far back that you're incapable of seeing the light. I know that you experience self-hatred, anger, and pain, but I can't begin to comprehend why. I know you and your brother don't see each other—or anyone else, for that matter—clearly. Sometimes we have to walk in the darkness. Sometimes we're left with no other alternative. But we must strive to find our way back into the light." The words come from deep within me, a part of me I didn't know existed.

I don't need vision to know I struck Abel speechless.

"Shit, Bambi, that's deep," he jests, but I can hear a slight quiver in his voice that wasn't there earlier. He places a hand on my lower back, guiding me forward. "Down this hall, we have some of the cells. Rooms. Whatever you want to call them."

I take the moment to slip into his eyes and survey our surroundings. We appear to be in a worn-down cellblock, rows of concrete gray cells lined up on either side. The one we stop in front of consists of a set of bunk beds, a bookshelf, and a scattering of clothes. The twins' room.

"Our...friend group resides in these cells," he continues, voice stumbling over "friend group," as though he actually wanted to call it something else. "Blade's—I mean, Kai's—cell is to the left of mine, near the door. Bronson's is across."

"What about Damien's?" I ask. I count at least four dozen cells expanding the length of the room. As we walk farther, I spot what appear to be female cells, stray bras and underwear thrown about. For some reason, that makes me furious. I don't want females so close to...

So close to whom, Nina? I ask myself. *Kai? The twins?*

Other male cells are spread intermittently throughout, some devoid of any memorabilia and others decorated with pictures and novels.

"Damien sleeps at the end of the hall." Abel points to a heavy metal door located opposite the rest of the room. "He doesn't like when people disturb him."

"What about the one cell I found?" I ask as Abel pauses to peer at a picture pinned to the wall. It shows an older man with graying black hair, his arm wrapped around a petite female. Two children stand in front of the smiling couple.

"What cell are you referring to, Bambi?" He glances away from the picture to stare at me intently.

"I..." For some reason, I feel stupid admitting that a cat led me there. No doubt, Abel will think I'm even more dense than he already believes. "I stumbled upon it when I first arrived here," I admit at last. A half-truth. I found that I'm better at telling half-truths than full-on lies.

I pull out of Abel's head when I begin to fidget, turning away from the intimidating man to run my hand over the metal cell bars.

"There are some shifters who are not a part of our... friend group," Abel admits at last. "They have a friend group of their own, scattered throughout the Labyrinth. With the maze always changing and twisting, we gave up on trying to find them all." Suddenly, Abel is in front of me, his hands once more on my shoulders. I stifle my scream at his sudden movement, closing my eyes to fight off the impending panic.

"Nina," Abel says slowly, seriously. I can feel the caress of his gaze on my forehead and cheeks. "How long did you stay in the cell?"

"What?" I manage to gasp.

He won't hurt you. He won't hurt you.

"Did you touch anything? Get your scent on anything?" There's an urgency in his voice, an urgency that belies his laid-back exterior.

"I... I slept on the bed," I admit at last, finally gaining my wits. The panic abates to be replaced by something far colder.

Fear.

"Shit," Abel murmurs, his nails digging into the skin of my shoulders. "Shit. Shit. Shit. Shit on a fucking duck."

"Why would you want to shit on a duck?" I ask half-heartedly, waiting with bated breath for Abel to explain what has him so worked up.

He takes a deep breath and then another one, his muscles relaxing slowly.

But even then, he can't quite dispel the tension tightening his body like the string on a bow.

"We should find you a place to sleep." Abel changes the subject, pulling me with him once more. "But Kai's going to probably want you to sleep with him."

I want to prod him for answers, demand that he tell me what has gotten his panties in a twist, but I keep my mouth shut. I'm not the greatest at speaking out of turn, especially around men.

"How long have you been friends with Kai and the others?" I inquire again, remembering he didn't quite answer me earlier, as we stop at the largest cell, sporting a queen-size bed, two dressers, and an assortment of novels and magazines. Kai's smoky scent surrounds me, comforts me, and I inhale deeply.

"We're not exactly friends, Bambi," Abel admits at last, nudging me forward. "Now, do what you need to do to familiarize yourself with the room. Touch everything or whatever." He pauses, staring at me intently. Through his eyes, I can see my head tilt to the side inquisitively. "You know, for a blind person, you're awfully good at walking and shit."

I snort at his ignorance. "And for a seeing person, you're awfully good at being a condescending prick." The words escape me before I can take them back, and I brace myself for the inevitable hit.

Abel surprises me by throwing back his head and laughing.

"You got me there. My momma said I came into this world calling the doctor an asshole." Once his laughter finally subsides, he adds, "But I meant, you seem to know your way around pretty good."

That's because I can see through your eyes, I think but don't say.

I'm determined to take my secret to my grave. If the Compound's reaction is any indication, the less people who know, the better.

"What do you mean that you're not friends with Kai?" I ask. If he can change the subject, so can I. "Why would he leave me with you if he doesn't trust you?"

My heart breaks at the thought that, maybe, I don't mean as much to Kai as he means to me. I had always thought our reunion would be joyous and exhilarating. Stumbling into a warm house after trekking through a frozen tundra for years. Instead, he had left me as quickly as he found me. I thought losing him had been the worst pain imaginable, but this might beat it. He scratched at a wound that hasn't quite scabbed over, drawing blood before it could heal properly.

"He left you because he knew we could protect you," Abel says at last. He perches on what sounds like the edge of the bed, and after a moment, I use my hands to find one of the chairs I spotted earlier before pulling out of his head.

"What do you mean?"

"He has stuff he needs to do to make this prison safe, safe for you. He left you because he loves you enough not to be selfish," he continues, almost reluctantly. "I don't like the guy, but we have an understanding. He knows we will protect you and take care of you until he can return."

"Abel," I whisper, my voice barely carrying across the small expanse of the room. "I'm very confused right now."

"I know you are, Bambi. But I promise you, no harm will come to you while you're here." He places a hand on my knee, and I jump, startled, before relaxing into his touch. A strange heat emits from his hand, and I have to wonder if it's a product of his demon blood.

"I don't belong here." The words are sluggish, as if being dragged through tar, and cause tears to prick at my eyes.

"I know." He squeezes once before releasing me. "And we'll find a way to get you out."

CHAPTER 11

NINA

The little boy engraved himself into my soul the second I set eyes on him.

Dirty black hair caked with grime cascades down a face sunken in from hunger. A simple brown shirt hangs loose on his slender frame. He's nothing but skin and bones, seconds away from toppling over.

He's dropped unceremoniously into the cell beside mine by a guard, his tiny body thudding against the concrete.

In all my years at the Compound, I have never seen another prisoner. And I have never, not ever, seen another child, least of all a boy.

I remain huddled in the corner of my cell as the boy begins to wail. My skin crawls at the haunting, oddly melodic, sound. It goes on for what feels like hours—but is probably more like a few minutes—until I finally whisper, "Don't cry."

He whips his head in my direction, startled, and scrubs a hand down his cheeks, tears smearing the dirt on his face. "What are you doing?"

"What are you doing?" I counter, ambling to my knees and crawling towards him. Thick metal bars separate us, but I know if I reach through, I'll be able to touch him.

I don't, of course, but my hand twitches with the sudden irrational need to.

"I just want my mom." Great, heaping sobs wrack his body, and any preconceived notions of ignoring him diminish. I timidly reach my scrawny arm through the bars and rub his back. His shirt, weighed down with sweat, dirt, and other unsavory substances, sticks to my fingers.

"Did they take you from her?" I whisper, and he sniffles, wiping at both his cheeks once more.

"I just want to go home," he says, and my heart breaks at the despondency in his voice. The heartbreak. I have just met this boy, and already, I want to soothe him. Nurse him back to health. Sing to the twisted and depraved pieces within him until he's whole.

"I'm Nina," I introduce, and he gives me a small, hesitant smile. It doesn't quite reach his eyes, but it's better than the agony previously radiating from his gaze.

"Kai."

～

RAUCOUS LAUGHTER DRIFTS TO MY EARS WHERE I'M CURLED up on Kai's bed. At some point, people began filtering in, males and females alike.

Abel, after depositing me in Kai's cell with the assurance he was only a wall away, retired for the night. I can hear his heavy breathing through the bars.

Sleep eludes me as I toss and turn.

Where is Kai?

Abel had assured me he would be here soon, but that was ages ago. Already, I feel itchy and uncomfortable, like a bump on my skin I know I shouldn't touch but do, anyway.

I hear footsteps pause right outside my cell. A heavy sigh. A muffled curse.

Cain.

Without a word to me, he moves into the cell he shares with his brother. Is it wrong that my heart palpitates in his presence? He hates me, I know that, and yet I can't stop myself from wanting to comfort him. As I told Abel, there's something dark inside Cain, something undeniable, and I don't know if any amount of light can banish it.

I strain my ears, listening to the brothers discuss something in low voices. A part of me wants to dive into their heads and see what they see. Are they alone? Is there another female with them?

Why does that thought gut me? It feels as if dozens of ants are crawling over my skin, eating me alive.

Shutting my eyes, I can feel myself drifting off.

Before sleep can completely consume me, strong hands lift me up and reposition me against a chiseled body.

"Kai," I murmur drowsily, "you're back."

"I'll always come back for you," he replies, placing my head on his chest, just under his chin. "Don't you believe me?"

I choose to remain silent. What I believe is he left me alone with virtual strangers. I can't forget the crude words he said to me—for the first time in my miserable life, he made me feel unwanted and used. A disgusting mold you can't quite eliminate.

"Hey," he whispers, placing a finger against my chin and tilting my head up. "Talk to me."

"There's nothing to talk about," I say easily, my heart plummeting and then bottoming out in my stomach.

"You're angry." It's not a question, but a statement.

"I'm not angry." Sighing, I twist my head so he's no longer capable of seeing my oddly expressive eyes. He once told me he could read a thousand stories by staring into their milky depths. I believe him. "I'm sad."

Kai is oddly silent, tracing patterns on the skin of my arm with his thumb.

"I made you sad." He brushes a kiss against my temple. "That was never my intention. I know I hurt you. I know I left you after I just promised I wouldn't. But...there's a lot you don't understand, Babygirl. If people know exactly how much you mean to me..." He trails off, his hand stilling its gentle strokes. "The people surrounding my cell right now are loyal to me and only me. They know the punishment for harming you or even talking about you to other inmates. But some of the shifters? They don't have the same restraint as my men do. They'll hurt you to hurt me. Do you understand?"

I roll over, resting my chin on his chest. His hands, rough and calloused, numerous scars zigzagging throughout, immediately cup both of my cheeks.

"You're talking about your...errr...gang?" I ask, point blank. When he's stunned into silence, I turn my head to kiss one palm and then the other. "I'm not completely stupid, Kai. You're Blade, aren't you? The man who runs this prison?"

I'm not completely oblivious to the duality of Kai's nature. Light and dark. He's two sides of the same coin. He's the moon and the sun, constantly chasing one another but never capturing. But unfortunately, the moon and the sun aren't normally visible at the same time.

Other times, however, the sun can be a brilliant swatch of color in the cerulean blue sky, and hanging below it, a dim shade of white, is the moon. Existing side by side in relative harmony.

"There's a lot of evil in this world," I begin when he doesn't immediately respond. "Especially here. I knew when I arrived that I might not survive this." His arms tighten around me, and a growl reverberates through his chest. His heart rate increases with each passing second, the *thump*

thump thump almost comforting. "There's some, like you and your friends, who embrace their darkness. They wield it like a weapon. They don't pretend to be one thing and then act another way. And then there's some who are immensely more dangerous—those who are willfully ignorant. They may not actively seek to hurt others or inflict pain, but they're aware of everything that is going on and do nothing to stop it. The judge. The warden. My lawyer. They knew what would happen to me, a young, blind female, and yet they saw it as their only option. Their self-preservation and self-interest overruled their sense of righteousness and justice. It's a subtler evil. Maybe that's what makes it insidious...because it's unintentional, not because the people have malevolent aspirations."

I trail off at Kai's sharp intake of breath. The cells in the immediate vicinity have quieted down as well, almost as if they were entranced by my passionate speech. Heat rushes to my cheeks at all that I said—words I hadn't intended to speak out loud.

"When did you get so wise?" Kai asks breathlessly. His lips seem to be hovering an inch from my own. Each word sends a gust of wind against my parted lips, and tingles erupt on my skin.

"I was in that Compound for a long time," I say solemnly. "Kai..." Hand trembling, I trace a pattern on his chest where his shirt dips down. "Do you consider yourself evil?"

He blows out a breath, the air stirring the loose tendrils of hair cascading down my cheeks. "That's a loaded question, Babygirl."

"Do you hurt people?" I continue sketching patterns into his skin, awaiting his answer with shaky breath.

When he speaks, his voice is a hushed murmur, nearly inaudible over the pounding of our combined hearts. "Only bad ones."

"So, if you hurt someone evil, someone who hurts others,

does that make you evil? Are there guidelines for what defines evil and what doesn't? If you kill one person who killed twenty others, does that make your act justifiable? Is it an act of evil or an act of goodwill?" I settle my head down once more in the crook of his neck.

"I don't have the answer to that," he whispers. Silence descends between us, but it's not uncomfortable. If anything, the quiet, combined with his gentle hands on my arm, is almost soothing. "Do you hate me?"

"Never," I reply adamantly. "I don't think you're evil, Kai. I think you do things that some may perceive as bad, but I don't think you're evil. You're my best friend. My savior."

He shudders underneath me, burying his face in my hair. "Sometimes, I think my choices and transgressions are piling up on me, like dirt engulfing a coffin."

His confession shakes me. I didn't realize he felt so strongly about the things he's done. But I wasn't lying when I said he is still inherently good. The man who sang me to sleep at night, read me stories, and held me so tenderly in his arms cannot possibly be bad. It just isn't comprehensible. I know our time apart might have changed him, but being in his arms once again only fortifies my resolve. Kai is *good*.

"Kai?" I ask, before I can lose my nerve. "There are a lot of females here. Have you ever…?"

God, I don't even know what I'm asking. My skin is suddenly crawling. The tension in the room is so thick, I'm gagging on it.

"No," Kai says immediately. "Never. There's only one girl for me." His voice is suddenly right next to my face.

What would it feel like to kiss him? To capture that full bottom lip with my own? Will he taste as he sweet as he smells? Would he even want me to kiss him?

I haven't kissed a boy. Ever. I have imagined it tons of times, all my fantasies featuring Kai, but we haven't ever taken that step. Does he feel the same way about me as I do him? His words make me think he does.

Just one kiss...

Banging on the metal cell bars startle us apart. Well, it startles me. Kai doesn't even flinch.

"What?" he snaps scathingly. A low growl is the only response. "Bronson, what the hell is the matter with you?"

Before I can ask what he's going on about, the bed dips with someone's heavy weight, and a snout pushes against my hand. Immediately, I slide into Kai's head and survey the creature resting on the bed with us.

It's...an animal.

But not any animal I have ever seen before. Unnaturally large with red piercing eyes, black fur, and sharp teeth, the creature seems to be plucked straight out of a horror novel.

"What is it?" I whisper to Kai as the animal whines, demanding to be pet.

Kai grumbles beneath his breath before saying, "It's a wolf."

"A wolf? Like Little Red Riding Hood?" I ask, recalling one of the stories Kai used to tell me. A little girl who wore a red cloak traveled into the woods to see her grandmother. While she was there, she discovered a big bad wolf was impersonating the old woman (though how anyone would be stupid enough to fall for that ruse is beyond me). And then, a handsome huntsman named Kai stormed in, killed the wolf, and saved the girl. Her name, of course, was Nina. They fell in love and lived happily ever after.

"As long as I get to kill it," Kai mutters, no doubt remembering the same story as me.

"He's adorable." I scratch him behind his ears as he licks my face. Giggling, I fall back onto the bed, and the wolf plops between my legs, his head resting on my stomach.

"*He's* Bronson," Kai hisses through clenched teeth.

"Bronson?" My mind recalls images of the strange man I had semi-met. Large and muscular, with a shock of blond, tousled hair. This wolf is...Bronson?

How can that be possible?

Seeing my dumbfounded expression, Kai elaborates. "He's a werewolf. Well, a shadow wolf, to be precise."

Despite knowing that this monster—wolf—is actually a human male, I don't stop petting him. Something inside of him calls to me, something I can't name or understand. His large, unbelievably sharp teeth may be inches from my face, but I know innately that he will never harm me.

Don't ask me how or why.

"What's a shadow wolf?"

"It's like a werewolf," Kai begins reluctantly. He seems furious that Bronson interrupted our private moment, but he also won't do anything to make me unhappy. "Only, he was born as a hideous beast, instead of being bitten or scratched to turn into one."

"I wouldn't say hideous..." I murmur, feeling indignant on Bronson's behalf. The wolf yips happily and playfully bites my finger.

"Most werewolves can only shift during the full moon, but shadow wolves are different. They're stronger, faster, and smarter than the average wolf. They still retain their human brain when they shift forms, unlike the average werewolf. But instead of relying on the full moon, a shadow wolf is able to shift at will—sort of like shifters—but only in the shadows."

"Shifters are real?" I query, attempting to wrap my head around all of this.

"Shifters are born into their powers, unlike werewolves. They, too, can shift at will, but unlike shadow wolves, they have no restrictions. Most of them have a large form and a small form, as well as their human one." He pauses, shifting in the bed to make himself more comfortable. "But we don't talk about them. They're not...our friends." His ominous words cause goose bumps to pebble on my skin. "Now, sleep. You're exhausted."

"Can Bronson stay?" I whisper. I feel protected with the giant wolf watching over me. Comforted. Safe.

Kai growls. "You know I can't say no to you. But..." His next statement is directed at the panting wolf. "If you pee on my leg, I'm cutting you up and eating you."

I giggle at his threat, swatting at his arm. "No, you wouldn't."

"Don't test me."

Still laughing, I cuddle into Kai's side, and he slides an arm under my neck. In the heated cocoon of muscular bodies, sleep comes easily.

CHAPTER 12

NINA

I sit in the chair adjacent to Kai's on a dais in the room where we had our bittersweet reunion. My heart is hammering a mile a minute as prisoners—all female— enter the room and present us with trays of food. Through Kai's eyes, I watch as he grabs a little bit of everything until his plate is mountain high, balancing precariously. The girl, a petite redhead, remains kneeling as Kai takes a small bite of each entrée.

Only after, does he hand it to me.

At my quirked brow, he explains, "Checking for poison."

His words make my blood turn cold. Why the heck would he eat it if he suspected it to be poisoned? I glare at him, but he merely laughs, filling up his own plate.

"Eat, my queen."

The food is nothing like the disgusting meat combination I had when I first arrived. Pancakes, laden with syrup, fluffy scrambled eggs, crispy bacon, and what appears to be oatmeal. I've had a meal similar to this only once before: when Kai snuck us both into the kitchen at the Compound for my tenth birthday.

My throat closes at the memory and Kai's thoughtful gift.

"Thank you," I whisper hoarsely, offering him a full smile.

"Anything for you," he replies. He takes my hand in his and gives it a squeeze.

"Is there anything else we can do to be of service?" one of the female prisoners inquires, and Kai turns to stare at her. She's beautiful, her toned body and ample breasts visible in the translucent dress she wears. Even from where we sit, I can see her nipples. Which means *Kai* can see her nipples.

Her blue-green gaze volleys between the twins to Damien and then to Bronson before finally settling on Kai. Realizing she has his attention, she languidly begins to stroke a finger up and down her cleavage.

"You are excused," Kai says sharply, and the woman pouts. Actually pouts.

"What about you, my love?" she asks in a low, raspy tone, sashaying to Abel. Her hand settles on his bicep, and I see red. The intensity of my jealousy takes me by surprise. It's almost crushing, this weight, like a wave burying me beneath the water's surface.

I tense, wondering what Abel will do and why I care so much.

His face goes still, hewn from stone, and his eyes seem to penetrate the offending limb caressing his skin.

"You heard Blade. You may leave." His tone is no longer the jovial, cheerful one I have grown accustomed to. It's cold, icy almost, and sends tingles vibrating up and down my spine. Tingles of...pleasure. Which is insane, right?

"Or I can make you leave," Damien suggests with a slight smile.

She gulps, stutters, before hurrying out of the room. The rest of the women follow her, sans one, who stands trembling in the center of the room.

Tessa.

"What's the meaning of this?" Bronson growls. "We told you to leave. Let us have our breakfast in peace."

We haven't talked yet about last night and how he slept with me as a wolf, and I'm too nervous to bring it up. No, I much prefer to stick my head in the sand, thank you very much.

Tessa gulps but refuses to cower beneath their combined piercing stares.

"Nina," she says stiffly, nodding towards me. "I want to make sure she's okay. You guys have shown...more interest in her than anyone else." She looks around nervously but continues with a determined set to her chin, directing her next question at me. "They're not hurting you or doing anything you don't want, are they?"

My heart swells. This girl is terrified, positively petrified, if her wide eyes and trembling hands are any indication, yet she holds up her chin imperiously and her gaze doesn't waver.

I've never had a female friend before, but maybe, just maybe, I found one in her.

The guys growl at what she implies, but I silence them with one raised hand. Tessa's eyes widen, barely perceptible, before she schools her features.

"I'm fine. More than fine," I assure her. "Thank you, Tessa."

She nods once, casts a worried look at the five males, then hurries out of the room with the rest of the ladies.

Only when we're alone do I pull out of Kai's head and focus on my food. After a few bites of eggs, I ask the question that has been burning a hole in my tongue.

"Are those your fuck buddies?"

Kai chokes on a piece of egg, Abel yelps, Bronson growls, Cain laughs, and Damien remains silent.

"What did you just say?" Kai manages to ask at last.

"That's what they said at the Compound," I say, slightly

offended at his incredulous tone. Did I use it in the wrong context? "For women they were...errr ...in relations with. Fuck buddies. Or is it buddy fucks?"

I push myself into Bronson's eyes, who is standing sentry near the door, and survey their reactions. Abel and Cain exchange a long, eloquent look that makes words almost unnecessary. Damien is staring at me intently, and Kai looks amused.

"You already know my answer, Babygirl," he purrs, wrapping an arm around my shoulders and continuing to eat with his free hand.

"Those wenches mean nothing to me," Damien insists vehemently. I'm shocked by his pragmatic tone.

"Dam," I say softly. "That's not a nice thing to say."

He grunts, grabbing a small dagger and picking at the skin underneath his nails. He's the only one who's not eating.

"A wise man once told me," Abel begins, breaking his staring contest with his brother, "that a past lay is a past lay, and nothing more."

"That doesn't make any sense," I point out.

He mutters something that sounds like, "Thank fuck," before digging into his pancakes with gusto.

Bronson, I notice, is the only one who doesn't answer my question. He's fixed his eyes firmly on me, and through his vision, I see myself blush and duck my head. It's unnerving to be the sole attention of his intense gaze.

I embrace my customary darkness once more, using my fork to cut up my pancake. Behind me, I hear the now familiar cling of metal against metal.

Before I can lose my nerve, I jump to my feet—taking my plate with me—and move expertly to where I know Damien leans against the wall.

He's different from the others. I've known that since the first moment I saw him. Hardened and savage in beauty. The power he exudes is dark and staggering, caressing my skin like a shadow. He's a part of them...and yet he's not. Every time they're all together, he's on the outskirts, looking in. Heck, he doesn't even sleep in the same area, preferring to have his quarters on the opposite side of the hall.

When I look at him, I see darkness. Pure and unrelenting darkness.

"You're not eating," I point out softly. The tension of the men behind me is almost palpable, growing by the second. Kai releases a low, threatening growl, and I sense a body moving closer.

For a long moment, Damien doesn't speak, but I know he's looking at me. I can feel his gaze like a burning brand on my skin.

"I'm not hungry," he settles on at last.

Abel snorts. Don't ask me how I know it's him, only that I do. Maybe it's because Cain would never be seen doing something as undignified as snorting. "He's paranoid that someone's going to kill him."

I gasp, my stomach a tumultuous mixture of dread and fear at the prospect. "Why would someone kill you?"

Damien doesn't answer, and once more, I hear the sound of metal against metal. I want to flinch at the familiar noise of sharpening knives but manage to rein in my innate reaction.

"Here," I say, scooping up some eggs and holding it up for him.

Someone gasps behind me, but I don't know who.

"Nina, be careful," Kai warns, but I wave him away as I focus on Damien, sliding into his mind.

Silence stretches between us like a taut rubber band seconds from snapping. Any moment now...

Damien grabs my hand and guides it to his open mouth. His lips close around the prongs once before he releases the fork. Everyone seems to be holding their breaths. Heck, even I'm holding my breath.

"That's delicious," Damien says at last, and I smile warmly, relieved.

"Can I join you?" I question. In response, he pulls us both onto the ground, my thigh flush against his. Giggling, I feed myself first and then offer a bite to Damien. Each time, he takes it eagerly, almost reveling in my attention.

"What the hell am I witnessing?" Cain exclaims, dumbfounded.

"A man losing his balls," Abel supplies.

"You, if you don't shut the fuck up," Damien deadpans, and I hear Abel's audible gulp.

Leaning to the side, I pinch Damien's muscular bicep through the thick fabric of his suit. "That's not nice," I scold.

Instead of responding, Damien takes the plate from my lap and begins to feed *me* tiny bites. A blush crawls up my neck and to my cheeks at the intimate exchange.

"The world has officially gone to hell," Cain murmurs.

The door to the "throne room" opens, and Damien jumps to his feet, the plate clattering to the ground. He moves to stand in front of me, blocking me from the intruder's gaze.

It's another unfamiliar man with hair caked with grime, a dirty face, and ripped clothing. He is held between two large and intimidating men.

"What's the meaning of this?" Kai demands, stalking forward. Gone is the sweet, passionate man who called me *Babygirl*. In his place is a predator. A monster.

The embodiment of darkness.

"Caught him sneaking around your stash," one of the muscular men says, shaking the trembling man's arm. I don't need to see Kai's face to know that his eyes have darkened.

Even at the Compound, Kai was obsessed with shiny things. It frequently got him into trouble. Gold, silver, ruby...

it didn't matter. If it sparkled, he had to have it. He told me once it was an instinctive need inside of him, something he couldn't control. The guards called him a kleptomaniac.

"Is that right?" Kai asks, stepping closer to the sniffling man. "What's your name?"

"Hunt...Hunter," he gasps, cowering under the full force of Kai's stare.

"Is it true, Hunter, what my friend said? Were you in my stash?" When Hunter doesn't immediately answer, Kai leans even closer until he casts a shadow over the other man. "Answer me."

"I was...I was just looking," he says at last, tear-filled eyes imploring. "Please."

"We found this on him." The second man procures a golden chain from his pocket and tosses it to Kai, who catches it easily.

"So, you stole from me," Kai deduces, volleying his gaze between the man and the chain.

"I'm so, so sorry." The man begins to cry in earnest, great, heaping sobs that wrack his body.

With a snarl, Kai turns from Hunter and faces me, still sitting behind Damien's imposing frame. "Get her out of here," he says, but his voice is unrecognizable. Guttural, almost, like he's speaking through elongated teeth.

Bronson, of all people, steps forward and gently grabs my hand. I wince instinctively at the contact before willing my body to relax.

He's not going to hurt me. He's not going to hurt me.

Bronson waits, painstakingly patient, before I allow him to pull me to my feet.

"What's going to happen to that man?" I whisper as Bronson drags me to the door, opens it, and pushes me out.

"They're just going to talk to him," the giant man assures me gruffly. But...

But I know he's lying.

On the other side of the door, I can no longer hear, but I can still see. I'm still in Damien's mind.

I watch as the mage indolently steps forward with his blade extended. The two thugs move aside as the twins take their places, each holding one of Hunter's arms. Kai's lips move, but this far away, I can't hear what he's saying. Maybe, in time, I can hone my gift. Maybe I can learn to use other people's senses instead of just their eyes.

For now, all I can do is watch.

Kai's hand shifts into a huge, scaly claw the color of rubies. His features change and contort, and in that moment, overlapping his human form, I see something I have never seen before.

The illusion lasts for only a second before it dissipates, leaving Kai visible once more, but it's enough.

Red scales. A body the size of a house. Horns protruding from the creature's head. A formidable tail covered in spikes.

A dragon.

Kai is a dragon.

Bronson's saying something to me, but I'm too lost in the vision to respond. To breathe. My legs feel like Jell-O, threatening to give out at any moment.

Kai lifts a clawed hand and slashes it across Hunter's neck. Blood sputters, like a red waterfall, and douses all four of the men.

No. No. No.

Bronson screams my name, his voice high with fear, but I can't hear him over the roaring in my ears.

The world around me fades to black.

CHAPTER 13

KAI

I'm a fucking dumbass.

Not just any dumbass, but the king of fucking dumbasses. I deserve to wear a crown of barbed wire and thorns.

"The door was closed," Bronson insists for the tenth time since he barreled back into the room, Nina unconscious in his arms. "I don't know what the hell happened."

What happened was my queen saw me kill that man, slicing his head clean off his body.

I don't say that to the other guys, though. The less they know about Nina—and her abilities—the better.

Fuck, what else did she see?

She's probably terrified and confused, her fragile mind unable to comprehend everything that just transpired.

Did she see my partial shift? Does she think I'm a monster?

Damien stalks forward, body lean and powerful, and points a dagger at Bronson's face. "What did you do to her?" he demands, eyes not wavering from the fierce shadow wolf.

Bronson's eyes flash with a ring of silver as a growl

rumbles his body. I immediately jump to my feet, prepared to rush between the two supernatural psychopaths before they can fight with my love in between them. Fortunately, Bronson calms down first, his body relaxing incrementally as his arms tighten around Nina.

Fuck, I'm going to have to ask him about his possessiveness towards her. The way he acts around my girl goes beyond a relationship between mere strangers.

Damien doesn't lower his dagger, but his eyes do flicker towards the sleeping girl. I could be mistaken, but I swear his eyes soften marginally before they harden once more.

"I will flay you alive, Wolfie. Cut your skin off and bathe in your blood. Eat your innards and then dance in them." The tip of the knife touches Bronson's throat. One sudden move, and the wolf will be very much dead.

Nina...

I need to get her away from them. *Now*.

"She was fine," Bronson growls, staring Damien in the eyes. "All of a sudden, she started rambling about monsters and dragons and Kai." He nods his head towards me, and Damien spins on his heel with a predatory grace that belies his nature. As a mage, you wouldn't consider the man high on the totem pole of life. Above a human, for sure, and maybe above dumbass shifters, but definitely not higher than a dragon.

Yet, if Damien ever felt the need, he could dominate not only the prison, but the world. He's a rabid dog tethered to a chewed-up leash that is seconds from snapping in half. He needs someone to control him, call the shots, warn him when he's going too far.

Frankly, the guy scares the shit out of me.

Being the sole focus of his piercing glare sends prickles of unease racing down my spine. Instead of showing my discomfort, I glower right back.

"Would you like to share with the class, Kai?" he asks coldly. He flexes his muscles once, the movement almost threatening. Brandishing his knife in the air, he takes another step closer. "How do you know the girl?"

"Why do you care?" I growl, crossing my arms over my chest. I know my eyes are vertical slits as my dragon comes out to play.

"Maybe..." Another step closer. That damn knife of his continuously twirls between his fingers. Is it wrong that I want it to cut one of them off? Or hell, maybe he'll drop it on his throat—one can only hope. "Maybe I just want to fuck her."

Smoke flares from my nostrils as my breath saws in and out. Damien's smile only grows, though his eyes remain cold.

"Maybe I just want to slide my cock into her sweet, virginal pussy. Is she a virgin, Blade? Or did you get to her first? Or did someone else—"

Before he can finish his sentence, I lunge forward, claws extended. Damien laughs jovially, as if this is the most fun he's had all year.

He sidesteps my blow stealthily, ducking beneath my clawed hand. A growl emanates from my chest as I spin around once more, preparing myself to strike. To maim. To kill.

Blistering pain erupts on my back, and I roar as Damien slashes at my skin with his knife.

"I won't hesitate to kill you," Damien says stoutly, backing away and crouching in a defensive maneuver. His eyes are cold, steely, devoid of any warmth. Those are the eyes of a killer. "But... I'm already tired of this."

My body quivers as my feet hover a foot above the ground. Glimmering, pearlescent manacles clasp both my wrists and ankles together, stilling my struggles. The bastard cast a spell on me.

"You going to kill a man who can't even fight back?" I hiss, my eyes flickering to an unconscious Nina. She's lying on the ground with her head in Bronson's lap as the twins hover over them both. "Fucking coward."

"What type of man do you take me for?" Damien queries, dusting imaginary lint off his suit jacket. "I'm many things, but a killer of an incapacitated man isn't one." He ventures a step closer, his eyes thin slits. "What is she, Blade?"

Scowling, I spit at his face.

The psychopath doesn't even bat an eye.

"What is she?" he asks again.

"I. Don't. Fucking. Know." And it's the truth. I don't think anyone in the Compound knows what she is. All I know for certain is that she's something other, something ethereal.

And she's mine.

From the first moment she comforted me—a sniveling little boy who had just been ripped away from his parents— my dragon claimed her as his to protect, fight for, and love. She's my star, moon, and sun. The entity I orbit around. My everything. She loves every piece of me, even the ones I haven't apologized for.

When I left her...

When I was taken from her...

I squeeze my eyelids shut, attempting to dispel the horrific images of those dark times. I hadn't intentionally broken my promise to come for her. I *had* tried.

And it's what brought me here. Still, the fact that I fought for her doesn't immediately assuage my guilt at leaving her behind.

"If you guys are done pissing on each other," Abel retorts, "you should come see this." His voice is high with wonderment and awe.

Damien—the asshole—moves forward silently, leaving me hovering above the ground in a vise of chains.

"Fucking asshole," I mutter, twisting and wiggling. I can easily shift into my dragon and burn the mythical chains, but I don't dare with Nina so close. The last thing I want to do is hurt her.

Stepping over Hunter's pool of blood, Damien leans over her, effectively obscuring her from view.

I don't like this.

At all.

My dragon hisses and howls, my struggles renewing with vigor. It takes time, but I'm eventually able to overpower Damien's magic and break free from the manacles, which lowers me back to the ground.

Eyes reptilian slits, I hurry to Nina's other side.

Her skin seems to...glow. That's the only word I can think to use, but even that doesn't fully encapsulate what I see. A golden sheen surrounds her still body, haloing her dark hair and pale skin. It flashes like errant fireworks with each breath she takes.

"What the hell is she?" Abel gasps, and I don't like the expression on his face. It's too wistful, too needy, as if he wants to lock her away and keep her to himself.

Come to think of it, I don't like any of their expressions. Cain's eyes are narrowed suspiciously, and Bronson's normally broody mask has been removed, revealing adoration and worship.

And Damien? He looks as if he's found a brand-new toy to play with. Something shiny to covet as his own.

Fuck, I need to get her out of here.

"Is there anything you want to share?" Damien asks me once again, voice curt and succinct.

I glare at him in return. He seems to have forgotten that *I'm* the leader. The king.

"Let's take her somewhere she can be more comfortable," Abel suggests, bending to take her from Bronson.

The shadow wolf growls, his arms grasping Nina's shoulders to hold her still. All four of us raise an eyebrow at that. His behavior is extremely territorial, possessive. Unlike anything I have ever seen before. Bronson doesn't have girlfriends. Hell, he barely even has lovers.

He's almost acting as if she's...his mate.

Oh.

Fuck.

Without a word, Bronson scoops her up in his arms and carries her to a small room dug into the wall of the one we're in. There's only one door leading in and out. Though I don't like having her out of my sight, I know she'll be safe and protected with us here.

"I've never seen anything like that before," Cain begins, brows furrowed. "And I've seen a lot of nasty shit."

"She's not nasty," Abel protests, hitting his brother on the back of the head. Cain scowls once at Abel before turning on his heel and stalking away.

Once he's gone, I turn towards the two that remain. Damien's expression is as impassive as always, but Abel is looking longingly in the direction Nina and Bronson disappeared in.

"She's *mine*," I stress, voice more dragon than human. Fire licks at my skin as I survey the threats to my mate, my beloved.

Damien smirks coldly, grabs a dagger out of his suit sleeve, and moves to sit in front of the bedroom door. Abel merely stares at me quizzically for a moment before placing a hand on my arm.

"Don't start a war that you can't win, brother," he advises.

And with that ominous statement—threat—he takes off after his twin.

What the fuck am I going to do now?

One thing is certain. Brother or not, friend or not, inner circle or not, if any of these men decide to hurt Nina, I will not hesitate to kill them.

It was my hesitation to kill that separated us in the first place.

CHAPTER 14

NINA

I'm dreaming...but I'm not.

At least, it doesn't feel like a dream. It almost feels as if I'm in someone's head again, but that's impossible. I haven't ever slipped into someone's head while sleeping before.

The man whose head I'm in is staring at Abel.

"You don't get to be an asshole and walk away," the trickster demon is saying assertively, arms moving in a flurry of motion.

That's strange. Usually, I can't hear through the head I'm in, only see. This must be a dream.

A very, very realistic one. From the scattering of freckles on Abel's nose to the slight wave of his blond hair, my memory has conjured up an exact replica.

"Don't talk to me like you understand." Cain's voice reverberates all around me. Deep. Husky.

Abel's eyes flash darkly. "I was in Beaunique too. Don't act like you're the only one who has shit to deal with." He takes a step closer until he's nose to nose with his brother. "But stop dragging her into your problems."

With that declaration, he turns on his heel and stomps away. Cain waits until he's out of sight before releasing a guttural roar, knocking a stack of books onto the ground. His breathing is ragged, erratic, as he sits on a bed and places his hands on his knees.

From this position, I can see that he is in the cell he shares with his twin. While the others consist of single beds, theirs has a bunk bed resting against the wall.

Cain abruptly jumps to his feet, grabs a sheet off the bottom bunk, and hooks it in front of his cell as a sort of makeshift veil.

He seems to be hesitating—his movements slow and uncertain—as he opens a drawer and grabs a bottle.

His gaze lowers to his pants as he unzips them, freeing his...

Oh my god.

If I was in my body, I'm sure I'd be bright red by now. It isn't the first time I have seen a...errr ...cock, but it's the first one I've seen that sent a lustful fire through me. It's longer and wider than any I have ever seen before, the tip slightly bent.

Cain lathers his hand with the liquid from the bottle before stroking the length of his throbbing cock.

I shouldn't be watching this.

I really, *really* shouldn't be watching this.

He begins to stroke himself faster and faster, his other hand cupping and fondling his balls.

What am I doing?!? I shouldn't watch this. Oh god, what is he going to think of me? The last thing I want to do is violate the privacy of someone who already hates me.

It's a dream, Nina. It's not real.

A white liquid squirts from the tip as he roars out what sounds like my name. For a moment, he sits there, breathing heavily, before grabbing a towel and wiping at his dick.

Did he just say...?

Oh yeah. I most definitely am imagining things.

But when did my dreams get so vivid?

I WAKE UP CONFUSED AND BEDRAGGLED. ALL I CAN RECALL are fragments of the strangest dream...

A warm body is on my breasts, purring contently.

"Mr. Scruffles?" I ask gruffly, blinking rapidly to orient myself to my surroundings. I feel something soft and fuzzy beneath my back. Dimly, I can hear muffled voices, as if coming from the next room over.

Where am I? How did I end up here?

My mind replays the moments leading up to this, and I gasp.

No. No. No.

Kai's feral smile...

Glowing eyes...

Scales clamoring up the side of his neck...

Claws...

Panic begins to rise, but I push it down, burying it in an iron sarcophagus. I can't allow myself to believe the worst of Kai. Not after everything we've been through.

Surely, he has a reason for doing what he did.

Surely.

Surely.

Surely.

Can I really defend a monster?

A tsunami of pain crashes over me, and a single tear slides down my cheek. I try to ignore the current of anger and betrayal swirling through my mind.

Taking a deep, calming breath, I focus on Mr. Scruffles on my chest. Absently, I begin to scratch behind his ears.

"You came back," I whisper, pressing a kiss to his furry head. "Where did you go?"

The cat, of course, doesn't answer, but his purring intensifies. A scratchy tongue presses against my cheek, and I giggle, swatting the cat away. "Ewww. Stop."

The cat suddenly jumps to his feet and bounds off the bed a second before a door opens and closes. I slip into his mind just as he hides beneath a table, staring intently at the approaching feet.

I pull back into my head as someone sits on the edge of the bed. Though I can't see him, his presence is unmistakable.

"Bronson," I whisper, hesitantly playing with the edge of the blanket.

He leans in closer, warm breath that smells distinctly of peppermint wafting across my face, before pulling away abruptly. He grunts something nonsensical.

"You probably have some questions," I venture. I did, after all, pass out in his arms.

Bronson grunts again, but this time, I take it as an affirmative.

"I can't..." he begins, trailing off and clearing his throat. His voice is deep and raspy, husky almost, and sends tremors of heat straight to my core. I can't quite understand my visceral reaction to the large man before me. "I can't protect you if I don't know what I'm protecting you from."

Protect me? Why would he want to protect me?

Is Kai forcing him to?

Questions continue to pile up in my head, but I swat them away impatiently.

I'll confront Kai...later. Once I wrap my head around everything I saw.

"I don't know how to explain it," I whisper, lowering my

eyes down to the blankets. I can't see him, but he can see me, and that is an unnerving sensation.

"Try," he growls, but I know his ire isn't directed at me, but the situation.

"I don't know you," I begin, and this time, his growling increases, and I *know* it's directed at me. Blanching, I attempt to curl in on myself, make myself as small as humanly possible. My instinctive reaction elicits a curse from the large man, and he rises from the bed, footsteps pacing the room. "Kai told me not to trust anyone."

"You can trust me," he protests vehemently. "I will never hurt you." There's no doubting the sincerity, the passion, in his words. A lump forms in my throat, making it impossible to swallow.

"Why? You don't know me, either."

He doesn't respond, and I wonder if I struck him speechless. I tend to have that effect.

The bed dips as he sits down once more.

"Ask me anything," he demands, his voice still that sultry growl.

"Excuse me?"

"Ask me anything."

"Umm..." I tap a finger against my chin. "What's your favorite color?"

"White," he replies gruffly. "It's the color of your eyes."

My heartbeat, which had returned to its normal rhythm, speeds up once again.

"What's yours?" he asks, then immediately curses. "Shit, I'm sorry."

"Pink," I admit shyly, lowering my eyes once more. "I like pink." It was my favorite color to see in the Compound. One of the workers, Anya or something, always wore that color. I thought it was pretty and happy, a vibrant hue that broke apart the drab grayness I had grown accustomed to.

"Pink," he repeats, and I can't quite read his tone. "When did you lose your sight?"

"I don't remember," I admit hesitantly, "but I must've been really young."

"So, how do you know what pink looks like?"

The tension in the room is so thick, I'm gagging on it. Trembling, I wrap my arms around my stomach.

"I'm sorry," Bronson says abruptly. Gruffly. "I didn't mean to sound confrontational."

"It's okay," I murmur. His face is suddenly inches from mine, his spicy, masculine scent surrounding me. Embracing me. It's the strangest thing—he's an absolute stranger, and yet, I feel the irresistible need to lean into him and revel in his warmth. My heart is palpitating in his presence. Overcome by emotions I can't quite put a name to, I place a hand on his shoulder and push him back.

"So...you're a shadow wolf," I begin, desperate to change the subject. I want to tell him everything, reveal to him my deepest, darkest secret, but a tinny voice in my head warns me against it. I can't trust anyone, even friends of Kai.

Even handsome wolves who make my heart do funny things in my chest.

I recall his beautiful wolf form. Glossy black fur. Sharp canines dripping with saliva. He was terrifying, but at the same time, heartbreakingly gorgeous and majestic.

"Yes," he grunts, and I wait, wondering if he's going to say more. Bronson doesn't seem like the type of man who talks more than he has to, though. After a moment, he places a hand on my knee and gives it a squeeze. "I can shift into a wolf."

"Well, that's kind of obvious," I reply with a smirk. His chuckle is dark and seductive, a surprisingly addictive sound.

"I can shift in the shadows at any time," he continues.

"Kai mentioned that you were born this way. How else

can you turn?" There's so much about this world I don't know. How can you turn? A bite? Scratch? Is it painful? And are both his parents wolves or only one?

Silence descends between us, suffocatingly pronounced. It feels as if his eyes are infernos burning my skin.

"Yes," he settles on at last, and he doesn't elaborate. I don't ask him to. The silence between us is precious, precarious almost, and I'm afraid that it will inevitably implode.

"What do you like to do?" I blurt, cheeks burning. Once more, he gifts me with his rare, salacious chuckle. He really should laugh more—he'll have the world eating out of his hand...paw.

I imagine his smile is wolfish when he speaks next. "Hunt."

Goose bumps blossom on my skin.

"I used to run with a pack," he admits, and his tone takes on a wistful, dreamy quality. "My momma and sisters, my cousins, my friends."

"How old are your sisters?" I imagine my voice is the same as his. I've never had sisters...or family. Heck, I never even had friends. I can't quite ignore the pang of jealousy that grips me.

"Marbella is sixteen now," he tells me. "And Lola will be thirteen. And Ali, if she was still with us, would be seventeen."

"What happened to Ali?" I ask on bated breath, though a part of me is dreading the answer.

"She was killed," he states at last, voice matter-of-fact.

"I'm sorry," I whisper, though I know my condolences aren't necessary. There's no amount of apologies I can give that will bring back his sister.

"She would've liked you, you know," he says.

I smile softly. "What was she like?"

"Wild. Crazy. Compassionate. She loved life and everything in it." There's an obvious smile in his voice as he talks about her. Love and warmth emanate from him in waves. This girl—this wild, crazy, compassionate girl—had stolen his heart and irrevocably broken it.

I have the strangest need to comfort him, to wrap him in my arms and assure him that he'll survive this. His scars are still raw, still bleeding, and I desperately want to provide that thread that stitches him back up. The need is almost a physical compulsion, my body arching towards his.

Before I can give in to these primal urges, the door to the room is pushed open, and I jump, shrieking. I immediately shy away, cowering beneath my arms.

"Bronson," Kai snaps.

The wolf growls low in his throat. "What?"

"There're guards here." I can hear the barely contained rage in his voice, a current of anger spiraling through him.

Bronson hisses slightly. "Why? They never fucking come down here."

I don't need vision to know Kai is looking directly at me. "They're here for Nina. Apparently, she has a visitor."

I don't get a chance to ask the thousands of questions mounting in my head before the pain begins.

CHAPTER 15

NINA

Have you ever stuck your finger into an electrical socket before? I did, back at the Compound. Not willingly, of course, but I still remember every excruciating detail.

A white light burst behind my eyes, and a humming sensation ran through my veins. My skin tingled, itched, as I experienced a momentary paralysis. During that agonizingly long second, on the grimy Compound floor, I thought I was going to die.

Actually, I was certain of it. As my body lit up like the Christmas trees Kai used to tell me about, I succumbed to my fate.

That's what it feels like now—an electrical current coursing through my body, setting my skin and nerves ablaze. I scream as white-hot pain pierces me in the gut. Somewhere in the distance, the noise muffled, I hear an enraged snarl and a startled cry.

"What's happening?" I sob, rolling off the bed and pressing my face against the floor. Both Bronson and Kai release identical pained growls before first one thump and then another resonates all around me. Their growls cut off abruptly.

Panting, I search for the nearest mind, only to come up empty. Either they left the room...

...or they're unconscious.

Or dead.

My head is spinning, reeling, turning constantly. I'm unable to grasp one thought through the blistering, agonizing pain.

Footsteps echo around me, and I eagerly slide into the nearest mind.

Dozens of guards in navy blue uniforms surround me, weapons strapped across their chests. One of the men steps forward, kneeling before me. He's only a few years older than I am, with light brown hair, twinkling blue eyes, and a malevolent smirk. He pushes at my shoulder, and I release a whimper at the contact. My body still feels as if it's been set on fire, stomped on, then skinned alive.

All of which I had endured more times than I can count.

"She's strong," the guard murmurs, poking me. "Most can't stay conscious for more than a second." I want to swat at him, demand he stop touching me and ask him about the others, but I'm afraid that, if I open my mouth, only a scream will emerge.

Pain. So. Much. Pain.

It's a tsunami crashing over me. Consuming me. Drowning me.

"How is she still conscious?" the guard whose head I'm in says to no one in particular. He turns, staring first at an unconscious Kai partially shifted into his dragon form and then at Bronson, fully shifted. My heart cries out as I note their limp bodies, closed eyes, and still chests.

No. No. No. No.

The guard kneeling in front of me glances up towards a man just in his peripheral.

"You can stop now," he directs. When the guard stares at him completely, I get my first look at someone who is obviously powerful. A mage or warlock, if I had to guess, given my limited supernatural knowledge. His white hair is blowing in an invisible wind, and his violet eyes emit a strange inner light. Power. The man exudes power.

Heck, it almost appears as if he *is* power.

The strange man stops chanting instantly, dropping his hands to his sides. Immediately, Kai and Bronson begin to murmur and shift.

"Now that I stopped the spell, they're not going to remain down for long," the white-haired man muses almost lazily.

"Good. We have what we need, anyway."

Two guards grip both my arms, pulling me up to my feet, and propel me out of the room and into the throne room. I'm too weak to walk on my own, so I'm forced to hang between them, my feet hovering just above the ground. The pain has ebbed, but my stomach somersaults repeatedly, threatening to expel the contents of my breakfast.

In the throne room, I can see Abel lying unconscious at the foot of the chair. Damien is leaning against the wall, head lolled, with at least a dozen guards surrounding him, weapons drawn. Even unconscious, the man is capable of evoking fear in guards and prisoners alike.

Is it strange that I feel a flurry of pride?

The guards move as one through the Labyrinth, only stopping when they reach the first fork in the hall.

"She needs to be unconscious," one of the guards insists snidely. The same asshole who poked and prodded me.

"She's blind," a different guy protests. "It's not like she'll see anything."

"You know the rules." The guard grabs a syringe dripping

with a strange, undefinable liquid. Leaning towards me, his smile grows exponentially, as if some sick, twisted part of him gets off on inflicting pain. "Nighty night."

I pull out of the mind I'm residing in just as the needle pierces the skin of my neck.

Kai.

Bronson.

Visitor.

Compound.

Nighty night.

Darkness pulls me under.

I REALLY NEED TO STOP PASSING OUT.

As awareness enters my body, I try to piece together where I am and how I got here. I remember talking with Bronson...

And Kai running inside, telling us that I had a visitor.

And then...pain. Agonizing pain, lighting up my bones like an incandescent flame. That man—that strange white-haired man with purple eyes—must've cast a pain spell on the others. For some reason, whether intentional or not, the spell hadn't rendered me unconscious, but the injection did.

Where am I?

I'm sitting with my hands handcuffed to something cold in front of me. A table? Yes, it feels to be a table made of metal, my hands latched to something protruding from it. There's a kink in my neck that I can't remove, no matter how many times I twist my head from side to side.

A door opens and closes, alerting me to the approaching figure. I tense, my back going ramrod straight, as he approaches the table.

"You must be Nina," a breathy voice exclaims as the chair across from me is pulled back with an audible screech.

Not a he.

I push into the female's head to get my bearings. The room is similar to the one I was interrogated in for weeks on end after I was arrested. Masculine white walls without a splash of color. Silver metal table in the center of the room. Two plastic chairs.

The woman turns her face away from mine, towards the one-way mirror, and I'm able to see her clearly for the first time.

She's beautiful. Gorgeous. Her chestnut curls cascade down to the middle of her back. Brilliant blue eyes, the exact shade of the core of a blistering hot flame, stand out on an already arresting face. She's slim and tall, and I know without having to see her move that she would be graceful and elegant. Her teal dress clings to her body like a second skin— tighter around the bodice and bedecked with jewels before sweeping outwards at her waist.

When she turns back towards me, I see my mouth parted slightly and white eyes wide. Gaping.

Regaining my senses, I clamp my mouth shut and try to remember her question.

"Yes, I'm Nina," I stutter.

Who is this woman, and why is she here to see me? My first thought is that she's from the Compound, but I'm positive I've never seen her before in my life.

"You don't know me," she begins softly, "but my name is Alyssa Timmer." She waits, as if expecting a reaction from me. Her name rings absolutely zero bells.

When I don't immediately reply, she shifts in her seat, staring down at her flowing skirt.

"Councilwoman Alyssa Timmer," she corrects, and I stiffen even more.

As in...? The same council that Raphael was on before he was killed and I was convicted of his death?

Oh god. I'm dead. So, so dead. She's here to kill me. Avenge her friend's death.

Goodbye, Kai.

Goodbye, Abel and Cain.

Goodbye, Bronson.

Goodbye, Damien.

Goodbye—

"I don't believe you killed him," Alyssa finishes at last, and all coherent thoughts flee. I blink at her like an imbecile. "Raphael had a lot of enemies," she continues, "and he was an extremely powerful vampire. I find it hard to believe that a little girl like you could be behind his death." Almost as an afterthought, she adds, "No offense."

"Um...none taken." Her words slam into me like a sledgehammer, stealing the breath from my lungs. "You believe me? That I'm innocent?"

What does this mean? Am I free? Can she get me out? But what about Kai and the others? I can't leave him, not after I just found him. And though I don't know the others well, a part of me feels like I *need* to. Know them, that is. It's almost an instinctual need, like crying when you're in pain or laughing when you're happy. I *need* to know them.

"I believe you, but there's nothing I can do." She sighs, the sound forlorn, and I wonder what kind of relationship she had with this Raphael guy. Come to think of it, I know next to nothing about the man I supposedly murdered. Was he young or old? Handsome or ugly? Compassionate or evil? His entire existence before his death is a mystery to me.

It's ironic, in a demented sort of way, that I know more about the man's death than anything else.

"Nothing you can do," I repeat numbly.

"The judge ruled you guilty," she explains, not unkindly.

She looks down at my locked hands, almost as if she wishes to reach across the table and put hers over mine. Instead, she balls them into fists and keeps them stubbornly on her lap. "In this world, you're guilty until proven innocent. Since you've already been convicted, the authorities don't feel the need to investigate further."

"But you don't believe that," I surmise.

"No, I don't. It just doesn't add up." She glances towards the window once more, a frown turning down her thin lips. "I've started my own investigation into things. Raphael was charismatic and kind, but he was also extremely ruthless and vicious. He had friends, but he also had enemies. I'm just trying to narrow down which ones wanted to see him dead." She turns towards me. "Most of them are already in this prison."

I keep my lips pressed into a thin line, unsure if she wants or is even expecting an answer.

"The council controls this area of the United States," she begins before snorting delicately. "I'm sure if we could, we would control the world." Shaking her head ruefully, she focuses back on me. I'm leaning over the table, entirely entranced by the snippets of information she's tossing at me. "The council is made up of supernaturals from each of the main species. There are seven of us in total. A mage, a shifter, a vampire, a demon, an angel, a werewolf, and a druid. There are other supernaturals out there, of course, but these are the ones who predominantly live in this area. We maintain the peace, create laws, and run a structured system. Raphael was one of the main proponents of peace between species— supporting things like interspecies marriages and breeding, among other things. Other supernaturals were not as progressive as him."

"And you think that's what got him killed," I guess, piecing together the puzzle with the minimal clues she gave me. She's offering them like breadcrumbs, and it's my job to follow the trail.

"I do." She nods once before gracefully moving to her feet, staring down at me. "I'm going to try to get you out of here, Nina, but I need your help."

"Anything," I answer immediately, and not just for my freedom. A man is dead. I want to help her find the true murderer before he or she can hurt someone else.

"There's a man in the prison that I think might have some information about Raphael Turner's murderer," she says candidly. "Ask him some questions, and I'll do what I can on my end. Together, we'll uncover the truth about what happened to my friend, and we'll get you out of here."

I clear my throat, shifting nervously in the uncomfortably cold chair. "What's his name?"

"Damien Gentry," she says. What little warmth I had leaves my body in a swooping whoosh. "He was one of the men sent to assassinate Raphael."

CHAPTER 16

DAMIEN

The girl intrigues me.

Knives intrigue me. Dead bodies intrigue me. Blood staining my hands intrigues me.

Girls—even pretty ones—should most definitely *not* intrigue me.

My tumultuous feelings for her are bordering on obsessive. When I close my eyes, I see her face. When they're open, I seek her out. My body is an epitome of contradictions: I want her close, yet I want her as far away as possible.

My magic flares brilliantly as my thoughts continue to circulate around little Miss Nina Doe. A flaming ball of fire heats up my palm, threatening to devour the entire godforsaken world.

Not that I would shed a tear. The world can burn, for all I care.

Blade's dragon roars, wings flapping as it remains dormant in the throne room. Fortunately for our *king*, the room is big enough for him to shift comfortably. His long, sharp claws dig into the cement floor, leaving behind jagged gashes.

Bronson is pacing, the wolf wild and untamed. Feral. It

almost gives me a giddy thrill. What will it be like when his monster is finally set loose on this world? I can close my eyes and visualize the destruction and pain left in his wake. The streets will be bathed in red...

Smile grim, I focus once more on the handle of my favorite dagger. Narian Teres had given it to me when I first arrived at the guild. *A present*, he said, *for his favorite assassin.*

God only knew what being his favorite entailed.

Narian was a lot of things—most of them sick and depraved—but he had a keen eye for weapons. This one has struck its target every time since I was ten, first sent out in the world to do a powerful man's bidding. A little monster unleashed.

Now, look at me...

My thoughts, as always, circle back to Nina. I can't help but wonder where she is, if she's hurt, if she's dead. The damn girl is a distraction—a mold that has spread to encompass an entire wall—and try as I might, I can't remove her.

A demented part of me wants to kill her. It would be so easy. A slash of blade against her fragile little neck. Then all my fears will be eliminated. I will no longer have to worry about this slip of a girl because she will no longer exist.

In that same wavelength, I try to envision a world without her in it. It's almost inconceivable.

As a mage, I'm capable of sensing powers in others. Most are a dull, monochromic gray. Some shine a little brighter than others, but not by much.

And then there's her.

She's a flame. An actual, brilliant flame that sets my skin on fire. I burn, but I welcome the pain. All I ever see is darkness—every corner, every crevice, every hallway. When she steps into a room, it's like she's bathed in her own personal light. Or maybe she collects the light of every person in the immediate vicinity because, at that moment, all I can see is her. She descended into my life like an angel, haloed in light, and that is what she is to me: my angel. My personal angel.

If those asshole guards harmed her in any way...

"You need to calm the fuck down and start talking," Cain snaps at Blade, and it shocks me to see the normally stoic demon lose his cool. Unlike the others, he doesn't have any... warm feelings towards the strange female. I can see heavy suspicion in his eyes and something resembling fear whenever he speaks of her.

"Seriously, man, you can't help her when you beast out," Abel adds. The twins' words finally seem to resonate inside the dragon's thick skull.

In a flash of blinding light, Blade returns to his human form. Wordlessly, Abel hands him a pair of pants and waits for him to get dressed.

Bronson, the undignified savage, remains in his wolf form, snarling in the shadows. I'm not sure he could even control his shift if he wanted to. It must feel like a knife in the gut to be separated from his mate so soon after meeting her.

The others may be oblivious, but not me. I pride myself on knowing the ins and outs of every mechanism in this facility, including the people. They're like machines with cogs and wheels that I'm able to skillfully turn and twist to do my bidding.

Leaning against the wall, I cut the dagger against the flesh of my wrist, watching with rapt interest as blood wells. The red color looks beautiful against my pale skin. Fuck, sometimes I wish I was born a vampire just to be able to lick it clean. Taste it. Taste the power and pain.

What would Nina taste like?

"You're right," Blade says, panting. He hasn't fully regained control of his beast. Reptilian eyes peer back at me in a face contorted from rage. "If Nina's in danger, you deserve to know the truth."

"We don't care about the blind slut," Cain snaps, and Blade bristles at the derogatory term. Even Abel glares at his brother. With anybody else, I'd have their tongue already on a fucking silver platter, but I know Cain's anger stems from something much, much deeper. Fear, for one. Pain, for two. Torturing him would be like kicking a downed puppy. As sadistic as I am, I'm not about to kill an already beaten man.

Though it's tempting. Very tempting.

Blade takes a deep breath, gathering his wits, before focusing on a water stain on the wall. "She was at the Compound with me."

"What the hell is that?" Abel queries. We've been acquaintances for years, but I don't know anything about these men. I know what they did to arrive here—I make it my business to know—but I don't know about their lives before they were placed inside these walls. Maybe I should rectify that.

"I was taken there when I was a young boy. Ten, maybe. Nine? I don't remember." Blade's eyes take on a hazy, distant quality, as if he's reaching for a memory only he can see. I can't help but think about how vulnerable he is currently. About how easy it would be to render him immobile with my powers and cut out his heart.

But alas, I'm too interested in his story. I hate how curious I am about Angel's life.

"It...wasn't a good place." He glances worriedly at Bronson, as if anxious for his reaction, and scrubs a hand down the back of his neck. Silly little boy. It's not the wolf he should be worried about.

"What do you mean?" Abel asks, his eyes already tinted with red.

"It was run by humans who tested on supernaturals," Blade admits at last, exhaling. My blood turns cold as I understand the implications behind his words.

What happened to my Angel?

I want to kill Blade for no reason at all, except the fact that he's the bearer of bad news.

"What do you mean *tested?*" Cain asks darkly. Abel puts a comforting hand on his brother's shoulder as the two exchange inscrutable looks. Interesting. What secrets are they hiding?

"She was tortured," Blade says bluntly, and Bronson lets out a wounded cry that quickly transforms into a growl. Abel, standing closest to the beast, takes an automatic step back, pulling his brother with him. "They sent her to the torture chamber every day. They would burn her, skin her alive, shoot her..."

Cain runs to the corner of the room and vomits out a black, smoky liquid. Abel's face is shockingly pale as he leans against the wall, sliding down until he lands on his ass. Bronson's whining increases.

Pathetic. All of them. Instead of cowering, they need to take action. Already, I'm planning the deaths of all the miserable cretins involved in Nina's torture. It will not be quick and painless. No, not at all.

I will make them scream for mercy.

If Nina is an angel, then I will have to be her devil. I will be her darkness, her fighting hand, her killer.

Hers.

"How long was she in this Compound?" Abel asks softly, dropping his head into his hands. At least he's doing better than Cain, who is close to losing it. Tiny horns sprout from his blond hair, and his skin crackles with waves of heat. Long lines zigzag down his cheeks, like a canyon forming.

"Her whole life," Blade answers miserably.

"And you left her there!" Bronson roars. At some point, he shifted back to his human form and is now towering over Blade, ass naked. The dragon drops his eyes almost guiltily.

If he left her there, I would have to kill him. It's in the rule book.

Death to all assholes.

I take a step closer with my knife drawn, and Blade's eyes snap to mine. He doesn't stop me, though, which makes it even more sad.

"I don't know what happened," he says softly. "We'd been planning our escape for months. I would have her look through the guards' eyes and describe exactly what she saw."

Look through the guards' eyes? What did he mean by that?

Blade continues to talk, unaware of what he gave away. "I planned out an escape route. When we had the chance, we would run. *Run straight until you reach the tree cut in two. Then turn left. Run until you see the road. At the road, make sure you go right. Do not stop. Do not look behind you. Do not allow yourself to be seen*," he recites, voice distant. "I remember, one night, we were talking—we had cells right next to each other—when I heard footsteps. No one was supposed to come down for at least a few hours. I was terrified they had discovered our plan."

He really needs to hurry the story along. I would like to kill him and then find Angel in a timely manner. Sometimes dragons can be so selfish.

"They opened my cell door and said 'you're going somewhere else. We don't need you anymore.' I promised Nina I would get her out. I fucking promised." His voice breaks, and I resist the urge to roll my eyes. Fucking dramatic. "When I woke up next, I was here. And she was there."

"Wow," I drawl at last, clapping my hands together slowly. The gesture is impeded by the dagger still tightly gripped between my fingers. "What a sad and touching story."

"You've never loved anyone," Blade bites out scathingly.

"You wouldn't even begin to comprehend what it's like to have her ripped away from you."

"You're right." I shrug cheerfully. "Love makes you weak. But it doesn't change the fact that you didn't answer one very important question: what is she?"

Blade's eyes shoot fire at me, even as his shoulders slump. "I don't know," he answers at last, and I vehemently curse. Dammit. This time, I'm positive he's telling the truth. There's no way he can lie that well.

"But I do know," Blade continues, recapturing everyone's attention, "that she's my fated mate."

Ohhh. Things just got interesting.

Bronson snarls, the sound more monster than human, and lunges forward, tackling Blade to the ground.

Smirking, I move back to lean against the wall and clean the inside of my nail out with my dagger. "Tsk, tsk, boys. Haven't you heard? Sharing is caring."

Inside, however, I'm fuming. Not at the mate thing—I don't give two fucks about that—but about what she endured. Our backgrounds aren't all that dissimilar, but while I came out sullied and tainted, she still shines with an inner light.

It's a light I need to live. A light that's vital to my very soul, my genetic makeup.

Now that I have her, no one is taking her from me.

I'll kill everyone here if I have to. And then, once I'm done with that, I'll kill everyone at that blasted Compound. I'll live in the darkness so my Angel is able to live in the light.

CHAPTER 17

NINA

I know something is going to happen before it does.

It's not a vivid image or even a voice inside my head. It's a feeling—spiders crawling up my spine and my heart a brick inside my chest, cracking my ribs.

The familiar tendrils of panic wrap around both my wrists. I may no longer be wearing handcuffs, but it feels as if I'm weighed down by iron manacles. My breathing is uneven as I'm forced down the ever-changing hallways of the Labyrinth, two guards on either side of me and one at my back.

I don't know why my emotions are so rampant and chaotic. I'm heading back to Kai and the others, right? I should be calm.

Instead, my heart is tap-dancing with fear and adrenaline. It's like I'm standing on broken glass, just waiting for one shard to break through skin and draw blood. The tiny hairs on my arms stand at attention while tremors rush through me.

Something is going to happen. Something big.

"Stop," the guard behind me announces suddenly, and like

obedient puppies, the two guards on either side of me slow their pace. I chance slipping inside one of their heads—the man on my right—to see what the commotion is about.

The guard behind me is leering, a decidedly predatory expression marring his ugly face. And no, he wouldn't normally be considered ugly. In any other circumstance, any other time, I might even call him handsome.

But there's a darkness in his eyes that surpasses even Damien's. I don't know how to explain it. Maybe it's different because the darkness is directed at me, not someone else. When evil acts are inflicted on evil people, you're able to look at it differently. It's an entirely different sensation, an unnerving one, to be the sole focus of it.

With tousled blond hair, gemstone green eyes, and a tapered waist, he rivals even the twins in the good looks department. A slow, beguiling smile turns up his lips as he takes a step closer, so close, I can feel his rancid breath against my face.

"I can take it from here," he says to the two guards on either side of me. They hesitate, no doubt recognizing the evil he exudes in tangible waves for what it is, but, like all cowards, they hurry away.

It's like I told Kai earlier: those who choose to remain ignorant to the horrors that plague this world are infinitely more dangerous than the ones who actively seek to inflict harm. They see the evil for what it is, yet still choose to look in the other direction. There are only so many times they can bury their heads in the sand, though, before the past catches up and suffocates them.

I'm trembling. God, I'm trembling so badly. I know I need to fight, scream, do *something*, but I can't bring my body to move. It's just not physically possible.

I pull out of the retreating guard's head and embrace the darkness. It cloaks my vision with the finality of a starless night. Only, in this case, I'm not sure there's going to be a morning. How can there be? How many times can I break and shatter until there's not enough left of me to piece back together?

I'm not oblivious to the guard's intentions. I have dealt with my fair share of evil men taking what they want without thinking of the consequences. They see me as a body—*their* body—to use and discard as they please. Even now, I'm nothing but a meat suit.

His hand clamps around my upper arm, and my trembling increases. Tears trail down my cheeks.

No. No. No. No.

It's all I can think—that one word muttered incoherently in my brain.

"Be a good bitch and spread your legs for me," he hisses.

I'm sobbing now. There are a thousand dangers I have to fight off, but the worst one is the demon inside my head. It conjures images of all the times I've fought before and how futile those efforts were.

What's the point?

Maybe, if I cooperate, I'll at least maintain some dignity.

I brace myself. Whatever this man does, I'll get past it. I have to.

A fierce, thunderous roar echoes from directly behind me. I freeze, muscles locking, as the hand on my arm drops abruptly.

"What the hell?" the guard asks, his voice high with shock and fear.

A body presses against my side before barreling past me. The guard begins to scream, high-pitched and keening, as sounds of flesh being torn apart echoes all around me. The growling increases in intensity as the screaming drifts off. I hear a deafening crack of bone before silence greets me.

My heart is hammering a mile a minute, playing

hopscotch, and I back up until I'm touching the cold stone wall.

Tears and snot drip down my face, but I don't raise a hand to wipe them away. Terror continues to thunder through me.

I'm terrified. Absolutely terrified.

But not of the monster who saved me, but of what might've happened if he *didn't*.

My legs give out, and I collapse onto the floor, still whimpering.

"I'll take care of you, *mi amor*," a soft voice says as arms lift me up. Everything about this man is unfamiliar, but I can't seem to stop myself from leaning farther against him, soaking up his warmth. He moves briskly through the twining passageways until I'm placed on a bed. One glance in the stranger's mind confirms that this is the same one Mr. Scruffles led me to that first night.

Is he the owner?

I curl into a ball and begin to cry harder. My body isn't the only thing that hurts now. What is it with men who believe they have the right to take liberties with females? Is this the prototype for the rest of my life?

A soft meow sounds from directly below me, and a moment later, Mr. Scruffles jumps onto the bed and curls himself beneath my chin. His purring comforts me, but even his presence isn't enough to stop the onslaught of tears.

What happened with the guard only solidified what I have always suspected: I'm weak. A liability.

No wonder Kai didn't come back for me. I wouldn't want to come back for myself.

~

SOMETIME LATER, I FIND MYSELF UNABLE TO CONJURE another tear. My face feels red and blotchy, and my hair sticks to the sides of my face. Throughout my entire meltdown, Mr. Scruffles remained on my chest, a calm and soothing presence. He hasn't quite eradicated all the holes, but he has helped fill them in.

"Thank you for staying with me," I whisper, kissing his furry head. His scratchy tongue licks my cheek once before he settles back down, his head beneath my chin.

I know I need to get up, find the guys, but my body feels disgusting. Maybe it's the phantom touch of the guard's hand on me, or maybe it's the dirt and grime growing a colony on my body. Either way, I don't think I can last much longer.

"Is there a shower here, little man?" I ask, and the cat jumps to his feet immediately.

Maybe I was right in my initial assessment. The cat seems too intelligent to be merely an animal.

I slip into his head as he leads me down one hallway, pauses, then retraces his steps. After a few tries, he stumbles in front of a coed bathroom, purring in satisfaction.

The shower beckons to me, but I hesitate. What if someone comes across me when I'm naked and bathing? Fear strikes me like a lightning bolt to the heart as I think about how vulnerable I will be.

Mr. Scruffles, as if sensing my internal dilemma, leads me into the bathroom and down the empty hall of stalls and open showers. He pauses at one in the far corner—the only one with a privacy curtain. At his nudging, I step inside and close the curtain.

I'm still seeing through his eyes, so I'm able to watch his view of the world shift suddenly. Before, he had been close to the ground, but to my horror and macabre fascination, he begins to grow and grow until it seems like he's the height of a tall man.

Did he just shift into his monster form?

Like a sentry at battle, Mr. Scruffles steps in front of the entrance to the bathing house and guards the door.

It shouldn't comfort me as much as it does.

Quickly, I strip out of my dirty white dress and fumble with the buttons to start the shower. Ice cold water greets me initially, and I yelp, stepping out from under the spray. After a few more tries, I'm able to warm the water somewhat. My searching hand stumbles across a bottle, and I inhale its floral scent deeply. With only a little trepidation, I squeeze some of the liquid onto my palm and lather it into my hair. Anything is better than the dirt coating my waves now.

I shower quickly, rubbing the undefinable substance into my skin.

Please, please be soap. Please be soap.

Mr. Scruffles would've warned me if it was anything else, right?

After I finish my shower, I search the ground for my dirty dress. The last thing I want to do is re-dress in that disgusting garment, but I have no other option.

Instead of the scratchy material, my hand finds something soft and fluffy.

A towel, neatly folded just under the curtain, as if someone had pushed it through. I relish in the towel's softness—softer than any blanket I've used before—and dry myself quickly.

Bending down once more, my searching fingers come across three objects that are most definitely not mine.

A clean bra, underpants, and a dress.

I pick up the underwear, and I can tell they're clean because they don't stink like mud and sweat, but I can also tell they're different from my old pair because of the silky fabric. I've never had something this comfortable.

Is this some other woman's undergarments?

My curious hand stumbles across what feels like a tag.

How did brand new clothing get here?

I know I shouldn't trust such a lavish gift, but it's either wear that or exit the stall naked. Deciding quickly, I dress in the bra, underwear, and dress. The dress itself feels like silk against my skin. Heck, for all I know, it *is* silk. It conforms to my breasts perfectly before swooping outwards around my waist. It's as if it was made for me. Even the bra and underwear are my exact size.

You know what? I'm not even going to worry about it.

Feeling more human than I have in the last few days, maybe the last month, I step out of the shower, using the towel to catch the remnants of water in my black hair.

Utilizing my powers, I slip into Mr. Scruffles's head to see him still standing guard at the door. It looks as if he hasn't budged an inch since my shower began.

Only, this time, he isn't alone.

Five familiar figures stand in front of my cat, weapons drawn and faces taut.

"Move out of the way," Kai hisses in an unrecognizable voice. "Before I kill you."

CHAPTER 18

NINA

I press myself flush against the wall, heart hammering against my ribcage.

"Where is she?" Kai's voice is more beast than human, more monster than man. Through Mr. Scruffles's eyes, I see just how intimidating and terrifying Kai can appear to a stranger. It's not just his bulk and height, though that certainly helps, but the power he exudes. He has a cold, dark presence that sends goose bumps racing up and down my spine.

And he's a *dragon*. A mother freaking dragon.

I still can't wrap my head around it. My best friend, the man who is an extension of me, is a mythical creature plucked straight out of a fairy-tale book. Suddenly, the stories he told me back at the Compound take on a whole new meaning.

The princess fell in love with the fire-breathing dragon shifter. She knew he would always protect and love her.

Shivering, I take another step backwards and wrap my arms around my stomach. It doesn't quite hold all my pieces together, but it's a start.

Mr. Scruffles cants his head to the side, my vision

distorting with the minimal movement, before he takes a step closer to the group of intimidating men gathered in front of him. Damien is suddenly in front of the beast, seeming to materialize out of the shadows, with a dagger in hand.

"I'm going to enjoy gutting you," he breathes with a malicious smirk on his face.

My eyes—well, Mr. Scruffles's eyes—track all the men intently, cataloging their movements.

Cain and Abel are standing just behind Kai, whispering to each other. Cain, as always, looks annoyed, and Abel is anxiously chewing on his lower lip. Bronson is in his wolf form, pacing in the shadows. His lips are pulled back from his teeth as deafening, ferocious snarls escape him.

Damien ventures a step closer, Kai shadowing him, and Mr. Scruffles instinctively takes one back. I can see how this will play out in my head. The cat is vastly outnumbered, but I know he is a formidable foe. I can't quite eradicate the memories assaulting me.

The ferocious snarls overshadow the desperate screams of the dying guard.

Innards splayed on the cafeteria floor.

Blood coating the walls.

This will be a bloodbath on both sides, but I have no doubt Mr. Scruffles will bear the worst of it.

"Don't hurt him!" I scream, running around Mr. Scruffles to plant myself in between them. Through the cat's—monster's—eyes, I can see Kai and Damien both gape at me. I wish to take back my plea, but there is no way I can scoop the words out of the air and put them back in my mouth. In a calmer voice, I repeat, "Please, don't hurt him."

"Nina," Kai says urgently, his features softening. Before, scales were covering both his cheeks and muscular arms, but to my amazement, they begin to recede. His reptilian eyes gradually return to their normal brown hue, and his sharp teeth retreat into his mouth. "Nina, take a careful step closer."

"What? Why?" My head is spinning rapidly as I attempt to understand the urgency of the situation. Walking backwards towards the cat, I add, "He won't hurt me. He's my cat. He's Mr. Scruffles."

"Nina, come here. Now."

Pulling myself out of Mr. Scruffles's mind, I implant myself immediately into Kai's.

I can see myself, pale and trembling with freshly washed hair. A sea-green dress shimmers in the artificial lighting like waves catching light.

Over my shoulder, I see Mr. Scruffles for the first time.

He's . . . a tiger.

An honest-to-God tiger.

He's nearly twice my size, with sleek orange fur, black stripes, and a white whiskered face. His lips are pulled back from his teeth, revealing razor-sharp canines.

Oh. My. God.

Kai takes a step closer, pushing Damien aside, until I consume his entire vision. This close, I can see the freckles dotting my cheeks and nose, the tendrils of blue in my midnight dark hair, and the scar curving down my neck from a torture session in the Compound.

"The lady is terrified," Abel points out, and Kai whips his head around to face him, thank god. I love Kai, I do, but there's only so much of his undivided attention I can take until it feels like my skin is itching. With Kai, I know he's not just seeing a pretty face.

He's seeing *me*.

Every scar. Every broken, twisted part of me. The darkness buried behind layers of light.

Darkness that he's partially responsible for.

Dismissing those melancholic thoughts, I focus once more on the twins.

The blond-haired trickster demon stands next to his brother, gaze on me. "Shall I serenade her? Calm her down?"

"Please don't," Cain deadpans.

Damien, from somewhere behind Kai, adds, "I'll cut out your tongue and shove it up your asshole."

Ignoring both of them, Abel clears his throat and takes a step closer—either oblivious or choosing to ignore the fact that each step takes him even closer to the enraged, pacing tiger. I know firsthand how powerful and deadly that cat can be.

Abel pretends to hold a microphone in front of his face and begins to sing about how I have a friend in him. And that I can lean on him when I'm not strong.

I wonder if he wrote that himself.

I can't help but crack a smile, my fear diminishing, as he skips around the room air-drumming on the others' heads. When he reaches Damien, the mage recites a single word in a weird, melodic language, and the demon collapses to the ground, unconscious.

At first, I think Abel's antics are merely that: stupid, childish antics.

But then I recognize them for what they actually are when a soft hand grabs my elbow and pulls me into a tight embrace.

Abel was the distraction.

In the span of seconds, Kai has me in his arms and is gradually backing away from the tiger. My body goes limp and pliable in his embrace, unwilling to fight him. Maybe, if I go willingly, I can stop any unnecessary bloodshed.

Through Kai's eyes, I can see Mr. Scruffles stare at me forlornly. His dark, penetrating eyes dig through layers of skin and bones and carve out a piece of my very soul.

"Kai," I whisper. "I promise you. He's a friend."

"He's no friend, Nina," he responds darkly.

Damien moves in front of us, blades extended, and I begin to struggle futilely.

"Don't hurt him!"

"He's a shifter, stupid girl," Cain drawls from where's he standing above his brother's body. When I turn towards him —in tandem to Kai turning—he flinches, as if my attention physically pains him. His eyes drift to his brother as his lips thin into a solemn line.

Fire lights inside my stomach and spews out in my next words. "Go fuck yourself, Cain."

Everybody pauses.

Everybody.

Even Damien and Mr. Scruffles, currently engaged in a standoff.

My cheeks blaze red, and I have the ridiculous urge to bury my face in Kai's neck. I can't remember the last time I allowed my anger to get the best of me. Maybe years ago, after a particularly brutal beating.

At the Compound, I learned that anger only led to more pain. If I gave the men and women a reaction, my own torment would only increase. That fear had been as effective as a gag.

"Did she just curse?" Abel murmurs groggily. I imagine he's still lying on the floor, but Kai has already looked away.

I'm instantly swamped with guilt, and I know I need to apologize to Cain as soon as possible.

"Babygirl," Kai says, changing the subject. "He...Mr. Scruffles...he's a shifter."

I remember Kai telling me about shifters. They have three forms. A small animal form, a large one, and a...

The tiger's body begins to fizzle and ripple like a mirage. I plaster myself against Kai's hewn-from-stone body and gasp as I watch the shift through his eyes.

As the intense glow fades, Mr. Scruffles is no longer a cat or a tiger.

He's a man.

Oh my god.

I'm such an idiot.

Even as I think that, I can't ignore the fact that he's the same animal who stayed with me when I broke apart. Comforted me. Was that his act? Did he merely want to lure me into a false sense of security?

He appears to be only a year or two older than me. His tanned skin is the color of burnt porcelain, and his muscular arms are sleeved in tattoos—everything from roses to wolves to lions. More tattoos are visible on his defined pecs, curving lower. His straight brown brows shadow even darker eyes, as dark as onyx stones. Puckered lips and a lip ring complete the bad boy look. His dark brown hair is buzzed on the sides with slightly longer waves on top.

And he's naked. Buck naked.

I immediately pull out of Kai's eyes before I catch a glimpse of his...thing.

"I can't control it any longer," a guttural voice rumbles from behind me, and a current of heat travels down my body at the primal sound. Bronson. He must've shifted into his human form at some point.

"Hold it in, wolfie!" Damien snaps.

"He can't control the mating call any more than I can," an unfamiliar voice says in a lilting accent. Is that... is that Mr. Scruffles?

Mating call?

My head swarms with confusion, like a nest of angry hornets. A knot the size of a walnut forms in my throat.

"Control your fucking wolf," Kai rages, but before he can

continue, I'm plucked out of his arms and thrown over someone's shoulder.

Bronson's, if the muscles are any indication.

"What are you doing?" I squeal, slapping at his rock-hard backside. My cheeks flame when I realize my hand drifted lower than I'd intended.

Behind me, I hear Abel whisper to someone, "He needs this. We'll find them in a moment."

Needs what?

What does he need?

We walk for only a few minutes before I'm gently placed on a warm bed. The smell reminds me of Bronson—no specific fragrance comes to mind, but it's both masculine and musky.

Bronson, with a huff, begins wrapping me in blankets until I can't even move my fingers. I remain rooted in place, more confused than anything.

One second, I think the men are going to kill my cat... errr...not my cat...

And the next, I'm being mummified by a shadow wolf.

Only when I'm safely cocooned does Bronson stop growling. He places his head in my lap with a happy hum.

"It's his wolf," Cain says scathingly from somewhere nearby. Bronson tenses, his growls returning, before he calms back down. Cain must've done something to placate him. "He needs to protect you. Nurture you. Be near you."

"Why?" I whisper, and I'm surprised when I realize my voice is soothing Bronson, which only exacerbates my confusion. His growls gradually decrease until they turn into contented purrs. He nuzzles his face against my neck, his beard prickling my skin.

I can hear the smirk in Cain's voice when he answers, though it now comes from farther away. "Long, long story, Trouble."

"Where's Mr. Scruffles?" I whisper, terrified of what Kai and the others will do to him. I know now that he's not actually a cat, that he lied to me, but I also know that he saved my life twice since I arrived here.

"They're just having a conversation," Cain replies amusedly.

Why don't I like the sound of that?

CHAPTER 19

MR. SCRUFFLES

Well...

This is fun.

Hanging from the rafters in the "king's" throne room is exactly how I thought my day would end. Add on to that the brutal beating his mage pet is inflicting...

Oh! Shiny!

My eyes latch onto the silver ring on Blade's finger as another punch connects with my face, ripping my precious lip ring out.

I have been betrayed by the shiny.

"Now, now, boys, that's not very nice," I gasp as blood forms in my mouth.

"Cut the shit, Rion," Blade growls. Honest-to-fuck growls. A little dramatic, if you ask me, but I'm not one to...

Oh. Is that a new ring? I always knew he had the one on his right hand, but the one on his left looks brand new. Rings are a bitch in a fight.

"What were you doing with Nina?" Mage Bitch asks coldly. I don't think that's his real name—pretty sure it starts with a B or D—but us shifters always refer to him as Mage Bitch or Blade's Bitch. Both work.

Mage Bitch is a scary fucker with cold eyes and an even colder smile. The man's colder than an icicle. I'm pretty sure his balls are cold too...you know, blue balls.

Speaking of icicles, I'm rather parched. Hanging from the rafters while being tortured does that to a man. Perhaps if I ask nicely, they'll humor me with a glass of water?

It's sort of ironic that they would hang me from the ceiling, considering that's how I've been stalking Nina. Technically, I wouldn't consider my actions "stalking." It sounds much darker than what it actually was. I much prefer "watching someone without their knowledge or permission." It's all about the words.

Damn. I'm a poet. I should really consider a career as an author—

Mage Bitch places his dagger against my throat.

"Start talking," he hisses darkly.

"Isn't it obvious?" I blow at a piece of hair that had gotten stuck to my blood-soaked mouth. "I'm her mate."

Blade roars and barrels forward like a bull. Both Man Whore and No Love hold him back. Yes, those are the names we have coined for the twins.

Man Whore...do I really need to explain? The trickster demon has more lovers than I have tattoos on my body, which is fucking saying something. We once joked that his dick is actually a fish that dies if it doesn't get wet at least twenty times a day. Of course, he hasn't used one of his playthings in days, not since Nina arrived. The women of the prison have begun to grumble.

Hell hath no fury like a woman without cock.

Okay, I apologize if that's sexist, but you haven't met the women in this prison. They scare me more than their esteemed "king" does. And, yes, *king* was said sarcastically.

I really want him to take a running dive off a cliff—

Damn. I can't wish for his death, not when he means so much to Nina. My heart refuses to allow me to continue that thought.

I want him to get a nasty, painful sunburn every day for the rest of his life. And he's not even allowed to put ointment on it. Ha!

There. That's better. My amended statement gets an internal smile from me. Apparently, Blade is allowed to endure minor torture at the hands of the dreaded sun.

"What the fuck are you talking about, shifter scum?" Blade demands, shaking off the twins and stalking closer. I give him an indolent look.

As a shifter, I have a lot of the same characteristics as my animals. That means I'm a lazy bitch who gets distracted by—

Blood.

I glance down at where Bitch Mage's—or is it Mage Bitch's?—dagger breaks skin.

Son of a biscuit.

"Are you supposed to be her mate too?" I direct at a glowering Blade. "Because you're a pretty shitty one." Smoke billows from his nostrils, and scales erupt on both his cheeks and arms. Little mister dragon is close to losing his self-proclaimed cool. "You didn't bother to ask her who her visitor was, did you? What if it was someone from her past? What if she was hurt? You are just so stuck in your ways—"

The scariest roar I've ever heard reverberates through the room. Even Damien, normally calm and collected, blinks rapidly. Blade looks seconds away from sinking his teeth into me, but I know I have him. Hook. Line. And sinker.

Without a word, he turns on his heel and stalks out of the room, no doubt to take Nina from her other mate and coddle her. I wonder how that will go.

Wolf Man seems like quite the intimidating asshole. It

goes against his primitive instincts to share his mate. If I had to take a gander, I would say he currently has her wrapped in a cocoon—symbolizing a wolf's nest—and is hand-feeding her berries. He's also probably growling and barking at anyone who gets too close.

Obsessive bastard.

Not that I can blame him.

I *am* the one who hid in the rafters and watched her as she slept. Again, not in a creepy way. More in a "you're my mate and I must protect you" sort of way. What can I say? Cats love climbing. And hunting.

Especially tasty treats like Nina.

Turning towards Mage Bitch, I flash him a cocky smirk. "What are you going to do now that your master is no longer here?" I query with genuine confusion. "Can you even piss without his permission?"

His eyes flash with unparalleled fury, and I know I hit a sore spot. Really, that should be the first indicator that I need to shut the fuck up, but my mouth doesn't know when to stop. I can't even blame the cat in me because, while cats are prissy, they're not stupid.

"How does it work? Does he bend over and have you wipe his ass? Do you use your tongue? That's pretty kinky, if you ask me. It's kind of sad, really, how little he values you. I mean, you're the most powerful person in the Labyrinth, maybe the entire prison, and yet, do you think he's going to allow you near his precious mate? Hell, no. I see the way your eyes follow her—like she's the only thing that matters. You want her...but you're never going to have her. He won't let you. Not someone as dark and twisted as you." I physically bite down on my lip to keep from going off on another rant.

Really, Rion?

For a moment, I think he's going to kill me. I can see the

intent in his eyes, the tautness of his muscles, the tension swarming through him like a thousand gnats.

Instead, he lowers his knife.

"You saved her?" he asks, brushing the blade on his suit sleeve. Crazy fucker. How he maintains his immaculate appearance while simultaneously being a psychopathic serial killer remains a mystery to me. I'm always drenched in blood and guts after I make a kill. And then I spin around in a circle, singing, *"Don't you rain on my parade."*

It's a cat thing.

"Nina?" I clarify, realizing I have yet to answer his question. At his impassive look, I nod like a fucking bobble head. "Oh, yeah. Twice. Like a badass motherfucker. Why do people say motherfucker, by the way? Because you can bet your mage ass that I never fucked my mother. That bitch is long dead. Anyway, yes. I killed two people. Disgusting men... I'm talking about their tastes, by the way, though their personalities were something else too. The first one put his hands on my girl. I couldn't let that stand. Bitch had to be taught a lesson." I cackle malevolently. Honestly, I sometimes terrify myself, but in a loving way. Can you lovingly terrify yourself? "The second man was a guard." Red flares over my vision as I think about what he tried to do. What he almost did.

"Did he suffer?" Mage Bitch, sick fuck, looks as if he's seconds from orgasming in his pants.

"Not enough."

"Hmmm..." He slides the dagger cleanly into his suit sleeve. "Next time, come get me."

"So, you're not going to kill me?" I inquire, quirking a brow at him.

Yes, Rion, remind the psychopath that he wants to kill you.

Fucking shit. How have I lived this long again? Oh, yeah.

I started my own fucking rebellion and murdered everyone who got in my way. Duh.

Whistling beneath his breath—I'm pretty sure it's some Beyoncé song—Bitch Mage meanders away, probably to go creep on Nina.

Now it's only me and the twins remaining.

Man Whore is staring at me with wide eyes, a mixture of bewilderment and awe in his gaze. No Love is scowling, though that's not a surprise. I don't think I've ever seen that man smile.

"You gentlemen going to let me go?" I question, pulling at the restraints. They're laced with magic designed to dull a shifter's natural strength. Only a very powerful mage—or in this case, Bitch Mage—is capable of performing such a spell.

"Mommy, I'm scared," Man Whore whispers to his brother, continuing to cast me side-eyed glares. No Love rolls his eyes to the heavens.

As the two of them depart as well, I call to their backs, "Don't mind me! I'll just be hanging around!"

Of course, I begin to cackle hysterically.

Sigh. The things I do for love.

CHAPTER 20

NINA

I wake up wrapped in blankets with a possessive wolf humming beneath his breath. I untangle myself quickly from the heated death trap and attempt to get my bearings.

Blinking sleep away, I cant my head to the side and follow the music. The second I'm in range, Bronson hooks an arm around my waist and deposits me onto his lap. An enticing smell permeates the air, and I slide into Bronson's mind to see already cut pancakes lathered with syrup on the table.

"How long was I asleep?" I question as he stabs a slice with his fork and feeds it to me. The last thing I remember was verbally sparring with Cain and then Kai arriving. My dragon had kissed my forehead, promising me we'll talk in the morning, before unconsciousness claimed me.

"Hours," Bronson huffs, offering me another bite of pancake. I open my mouth obediently, and he slides it in.

"Thank you," I say softly. "For taking care of me."

His chest rumbles, and he mutters something nonsensical before hugging me closer to him.

We eat for a moment in silence. Well, I eat. He feeds me. I'll never admit to anyone how much I like being taken care of. It's a drastic change from the vulnerable little girl I had been only a few months ago, forced to survive on stale bread and dirty water. The girl who couldn't trust anyone, because everyone had an agenda. The girl who trembled at her own shadow. The girl who embraced the darkness because the light was too much for her to bear.

"Where are the others?"

"I'm hurt, Angel, that you didn't notice my captivating, magnetic presence earlier," Damien answers dryly, and I startle. Bronson whips his head in the mage's direction.

He's standing in the shadows of the cell, like some sort of avenging angel of death and destruction. As always, he's immaculately dressed in another pressed black suit and stark white shirt. His black hair is styled away from his face, the perfect combination of unruly and gelled.

Staring up at him... It's the same as glancing at your feet, only to discover you're thousands of miles above ground on a tightrope. There's danger in his eyes, a savage type of beauty.

"The others are sleeping," Bronson whispers, focusing back on the plate of food.

"And Mr. Scruffles?" I tentatively inquire. A snake pit has formed in my stomach, and the slithering reptiles are hissing at me, their venom a physical pain.

"Mr. Scruffles." Damien snorts. "That's a good one. But alas, your pussy is still alive and well."

Bronson flicks his gaze upwards and growls. Though my vision of the mage is slightly askew, I'm able to see him twist his dagger between his fingers, the blade slicing at skin. Blood wells, a bright, startling red against his porcelain skin.

Alarmed, I jump to my feet and hurry over to him, easily slipping out of Bronson's head and into Damien's.

"Oh my gosh. Are you okay? Does it hurt?" The acid in my stomach churns like lava as I grab his hand and pull up his sleeve. Long gashes litter his skin—his wrist, his palm, his arm. I barely even hear Bronson's warning over the roaring in my ears.

Without thought, I rip off the sleeve of my dress and wrap it around the worst of the scars. It's the only thing I can think of to do. At the Compound, I often had to heal my own injuries, at least the ones that didn't heal by themselves. I still have a hideous scar marring my spine from when one of my torturer's cut deep enough to see bone. Though my skin knitted itself back together, the scar remains. A reminder.

"How did you know about my scars?" Damien questions softly. His eyes are no longer on his bleeding wrist, but on my face. I swear I feel stripped and vulnerable beneath his gaze. Though his eyes may be icy, they trail across my body like molten lava, setting me aflame.

"What?" I ask, using the pad of my finger to feel the raised, jagged lines. With his eyes intent on me instead of his arm, I'm forced to rely on touch alone. When my finger comes back sticky with blood, I use a portion of my dress to create a makeshift bandage.

"How did you see the scars?" His mouth is directly next to my ear, and goose bumps explode on my skin. My heart palpitates at his proximity, but I keep my face blank.

"I... I don't know what you mean."

Kai's warning plays on a continuous loop in my head. He told me that I can't trust the others, but surely, that's not true. They have been nothing but kind and welcoming since I arrived...except for Cain. He's been, for lack of better words, a butthole.

"You're a strange girl, Nina Doe," Damien whispers, a mixture of awe and reverence in his tone.

I drop my hand from his wrist and tilt my head back.

Though I can't see him, I know he can see me—see the sincerity in my cloudy eyes. "What do you mean?"

I also want to ask how he knows my court-appointed last name, but now doesn't seem like the time.

"No one has ever cared about my scars," Damien murmurs, and his words scratch at the hole in my chest.

Our moment is broken by the pounding of footsteps and then the presence of bodies surrounding me. One of the men —I'm assuming Kai—attempts to take me from Damien, but the mage actually growls. If I didn't know what he was, I would've assumed he was some type of shifter.

Damien moves us both until I'm resting on his lap in one of the spare chairs, Bronson on one side of me and Kai on the other. Both men hold one of my hands, seemingly oblivious or choosing not to care that I'm in someone else's lap.

I'll never understand men.

Is this normal?

I sift through the minds present until settling on Cain's. He's leaning against the wall, arms crossed, as he surveys the room. My cheeks take on a rosy quality as I realize how I look to the outside viewer.

Propped on Damien's lap, with his hands on my thighs...

Bronson tightly gripping one hand...

Kai holding the other...

I don't know enough about societal norms to be able to tell you if this is normal. I know some friends can be more touchy-feely than others. Maybe that's all this is.

"Awww. No fair. I want in on the cuddle orgy," Abel pouts. He's still in the entrance to Bronson's cell, eyes flickering over the four of us, like he's looking for a place to plant himself.

Orgy...orgy ...orgy.

I could've sworn I've heard that word before, yet it doesn't ring any bells.

Kai and Bronson both glare, but Damien offers the

demon a droll look. "Only people who contribute to the orgy are allowed to participate."

"I contribute!" Abel protests indignantly. His lower lip pushes out farther. "But only one of you is pretty enough for me." He emphasizes this with a waggle of his eyebrows in my direction.

"Sorry. Don't swing that way," Damien deadpans.

"Not cool, man. Not cool. You can't just reject the happy camper." Abel points towards his crotch, and if my cheeks weren't on fire before, they definitely are now. The only saving grace is that the guys—sans Kai—don't know I can see them. "If the happy camper chooses you, then you should consider yourself lucky."

"Wait, I'm confused," Cain butts in. "Did your happy camper choose Damien or Nina?"

"And why do you call your cock *happy camper*?" Damien adds, amusedly. His hands begin to absently knead my thighs, and I resist the urge to wiggle.

"It's more of an elephant's trunk, don't you think?" Abel jests. "Long and thick."

"Yeah, those aren't the first two words that come to mind when I think of an elephant's trunk," Cain grouses.

"Nina, say you agree with me, babe. Come on," Abel pleads. My face? Pretty sure it's one thousand degrees.

"How would she know?" Kai asks, still gripping my hand. "She hasn't seen it yet."

Seen what yet? Why don't I understand what the heck they're talking about? Does Kai want me to see his friend's... happy camper?!

"It has its ups and downs...and sometimes, it's a little hard...other times, it's a pain in the ass..." Abel trails off before throwing his head back in laughter. "Fuck, guys, that was good. I'm a regular comedian."

I turn towards Bronson—the only one not joining in on their antics—and whisper, "I'm confused."

He leans closer, his earthy, masculine scent surrounding me, and replies, "Ignore him. I do."

"That's not nice!" Abel tells Bronson once his laughter has receded. "It's bullying."

Through Cain's eyes, I watch Bronson roll his. I can't help but giggle at his annoyance.

"Now, are we going to be serious? Or are we going to continue behaving like children?" Kai asks, flashing a pointed look at first Abel and then Cain and then Damien. My giggling increases as Abel drops his head like a child being reprimanded by a parent. Still, I swear I see his lips twitch at my laugh.

"Sorry."

Ignoring his apology, Kai turns towards me and takes my cheeks between both of his hands. His palms are rough against my skin, but his touch causes fireworks to dance down my spine.

"I'm sorry I lost my control yesterday," Kai tells me earnestly. "I should've stayed with you, asked you questions. Instead, I allowed my anger to get the better of me, and for that, I apologize. You're the most important thing in the world to me, and I'll do better. I promise. And I should've told you the truth sooner about what I am, but I was afraid. Afraid you'll reject me or hate me or see me as a monster. Nina, I'm a dragon. An elemental dragon, to be exact. I'm different from shifters and werewolves, since I can transform at any time, and I only have one form. I'm so, so sorry. Please forgive me. Please know I will never, not ever, hurt you."

My eyes water at his heartfelt apology. I didn't even realize he had done something wrong. This is a learning curve for both of us, I realize. Before, we were nothing but kids attempting to understand this strange new world we'd been thrust into. Now, we are adults facing a similar problem. We have to understand the new game board, the new pawns, the new rules. All of us are going to make mistakes.

When his hands drop from my face, I interlock our fingers once more.

"I forgive you."

I'll always forgive you.

When Kai begins to smile, Cain quickly looks away, as if our shared happiness physically pains him. I'll have to talk to the sex demon, and soon. I'm beginning to consider all these men my friends...maybe something more, though what that more is remains a mystery. The last thing we need is discord within our group.

"Tell us what happened," Bronson demands gruffly. When I hesitate, Kai gives my hand a reassuring, encouraging squeeze.

"A councilman—woman—was here to see me," I begin. "Alyssa something...I can't remember her last name." I have the urge to do something with my hands. Fiddle with my ripped sleeve. Pluck at my nails. Twirl my hair around my finger. At the same time, I don't want to remove my hands from Bronson's and Kai's. Warmth migrates from where we touch and settles in my chest. "She believes me. She believes that I'm innocent."

"What does that mean? Are you leaving?" Abel asks, and I hear both hope and dread in his voice.

Shaking my head, I say, "No. She doesn't have any proof. Just a gut feeling. She told me a little about what Raphael hoped to implement in the supernatural world. Interspecies marriages and breeding, for one. She also mentioned that it's a controversial subject."

Bronson begins rubbing patterns against the back of my hand with his thumb, and full-body shivers take over me at the slight contact.

"It's true," he replies in his low, raspy voice. "Wolves are with wolves. Vampires are with vamps. Mages are with mages. And so on."

My heart drops into my stomach at his declaration. For some reason, a reason I can't name, that bothers me. A lot. Does he feel that way too? Does he only want to be with a wolf?

"So, she thinks someone opposed to those policies killed him," Kai clarifies.

Abel whistles between his teeth. "Damn. Whoever it is must have a lot of juice. Raphael Turner was extremely fucking powerful. Like, *he could turn water into wine* type of powerful. I'm grudgingly impressed."

Clearing my throat once, I wiggle in Damien's lap and remove my hand from Kai's. "She also mentioned you, Damien." I poke his arm—the only piece of his body I'm able to touch. "Is it true that you tried to kill Raphael?"

I hold my breath as I wait for his answer. Damien releases a heavy, prolonged sigh, his hands tightening on my thighs.

"Unfortunately. It was nothing personal—I don't give a shit about council politics. I was hired to do a job, and I failed. He had more security on him than the motherfucking president." As always, he delivers his speech without an ounce of inflection whatsoever. I might believe him to be numb if his hands hadn't tightened imperceptibly on my thighs once more.

"Do you know who sent you?" Kai asks eagerly, leaning forward.

Damien gives him a dry look. "Of course not. That's not the way things work."

"Could you find out?" Abel cuts in.

Damien taps a finger to his smooth-shaven chin, considering. After a moment, he gives a decisive bob of his head. "I can ask around."

"So, whoever killed Raphael was powerful enough to take out highly trained and powerful guards," Kai surmises. "As well as an extremely old and powerful vampire. Who has that type of power?"

I volley my head between all the men. I wish desperately I could contribute to the conversation, but my mind is swirling faster than a tornado.

"Lionel Green," Cain cuts in suddenly, snapping his head up. I note, out of Cain's peripheral, Abel ball his hands into fists as his face drains of color.

"The shifter representative?" Kai clarifies, and Cain nods once, the movement jerky.

"He hates Raphael and the policies. He believes every species should remain segregated from the others. He also voted the last ten times to reveal our existence to humans." Cain's voice is heady with loathing and something else, something almost akin to fear. It makes me want to wrap my arms around him and offer him my warmth. To fill up his cracks with what little light I can offer.

"He *would* be powerful enough to take out Raphael, especially if he had help," Abel adds almost reluctantly.

"And luckily for us, we have one of his ex-workers hanging around," Kai says with a manic grin. Ex-worker? Who is he talking about?

He doesn't mean Mr. Scruffles, does he?

"Bronson, Damien, and Abel...you're with me," Kai says, and all three men stiffen.

"Why me?" Abel whines.

"Because we need your crazy to deal with someone even more crazy," Kai answers immediately. When none of the guys move to do his bidding, he releases a low and threatening snarl that causes metaphorical bugs to skitter across my body. "Cain is more than capable of looking after her for a few minutes. Isn't that right, Cain?" His tone leaves no room for argument. Either he agrees or suffers the consequences.

I don't want to know what those consequences entail. Kai's wrath is as vengeful as a storm, shattering houses and leaving behind dead bodies.

Cain sounds as if his teeth are being pulled out one tooth at a time. "Right."

What have I gotten myself into?

CHAPTER 21

NINA

Cain is so mercurial. Sometimes, I want to punch him, and sometimes, I want to give him a long hug. Currently, it's the former option.

After he leads me to his cell, we sit in a long, potent silence. I know he's gazing at me as intently as I am him. While he may be focusing on the physical characteristics, I'm focusing on other things.

Like his heart that I can hear beating erratically. The uneven draws of his breath. The smoky scent emitting from his body, combined with something floral from his shampoo. The tap, tap, tap of his fingers against the armrest of his chair. He's tense. Anxious.

But he doesn't want anyone to know.

After a long, unnerving moment of silence, I jump to my feet and begin to trail my fingers over the table. Numerous boxes greet my searching hand.

"What's this?" I ask softly. I could always slip inside his head and see for myself, but I would rather hear the answer from him. Right now, he's barely holding himself together. I don't know if my curiosity will distract him or send him teetering over that steep edge.

"Game," he responds scathingly. "Have you played?"

"Well, I can't answer unless I know what game it is," I reply with an eye roll.

"Monopoly," he spits out.

Does he really hate me so much that we can't have a cordial conversation? For reasons I don't care to define, that hurts tremendously.

"Never played," I answer, caressing a second box.

"Chess," he names, almost reluctantly.

Smiling, I jiggle the box in front of his face enticingly. "Let's play!"

"You know how to play chess?" His voice is heady with disbelief and scorn. When I continue to smile, not answering, he relents with a disgruntled sigh. "Fine. Whatever."

"Perfect!" Clapping my hands together, I feel my way back to the chair and sit opposite him at the table. Kai's words from earlier volley around in my head like a loose basketball.

No one can know the truth.

"You'll have to tell me which square you place your pawn on," I decide quickly. "A6 or B2 or whatever. That's how Kai played with me."

And it was...until I mastered my gift and learned how to slip into his head with ease. For now, my powers are a closely guarded secret. I'll keep them under lock and key in an impenetrable coffin, buried miles below cement. No amount of digging can uncover it.

"Got it," Cain bites out. I'm beginning to believe the demon only has two moods: angry and very angry. It's such a contrast to sunny Abel that they're as different as night and day. Maybe that's not a bad analogy for them. Abel embodies an inner light, while Cain has an internal darkness. Yet, they need each other, each one intricately intertwined with the other.

Shaking my head to clear my thoughts, I watch through Cain's eyes as he sets up the board. He's black, unsurprisingly, leaving the white for me.

He moves his pawn first.

"Pawn to B5," he announces, sitting back in his chair and forking his fingers together just at the edge of his vision.

Absently, I feel for my pieces, memorizing the board, and move my own piece up two spaces. I remember from Kai's lessons that the first time you move a pawn, you're able to move it up two spaces instead of one. I know this game so well that I don't need someone to move my pieces for me—I can easily feel the ridges of the king's crown and the curve of the knight. I can play and win this game without eyesight.

Once more, Cain surveys the board before moving a different pawn forward. "Pawn to C5."

"So, Cain," I begin conversationally as I move my knight. "You don't like me very much."

"I never said that," he huffs. "Pawn to D5."

"You didn't have to," I point out. "You can't stand to be in the same room as me."

"Because you're an unknown," he sneers without preamble. "You just waltz into our prison, claiming you're innocent, and already, you have the most powerful males at your feet. What are you, Nina?"

It takes me two tries to swallow around the apple-sized knot in my throat. My hands tremble slightly. "It's your turn."

He doesn't even look at the board; his focus is fully, intently, on me.

"Bishop. C8 to F5."

I nod once before considering the pieces with an almost clinical detachment. It's all about moving the pawns to fit your needs. Destroying your enemies. It takes strategy and patience, both of which I have in abundance. Or you can seek to eliminate the opponent's most important piece—the king.

Win the game.

We play a few more rounds in silence. During that time, I'm able to capture two of his pawns and one of his bishops, and he's able to capture my knight.

"I don't know what I am," I admit at last, twirling his captured piece between my fingers. "I thought I was human with a strange and uncanny ability to heal. I only recently learned that the supernatural exists."

"Kai told us about the Compound," he says at last, once the silence contaminates the air like a sickly poison. My muscles lock together at his words as my breath leaves me. No. No. No. All I have ever wanted was to escape the Compound and the connotations that went with it. I don't want Cain's pity or his suspicion.

I thought, maybe, that coming here could be my chance to start over. A chance to reinvent myself without the threat of the Compound hanging ominously over my head like a sharpened blade.

If Kai told him about my past, what else did he tell him?

"So, you know that I'm not exactly the most socially apt person," I say, only half teasing.

"And it was only you and Kai there?" Cain presses, ignoring my attempt at a joke. A rather pathetic one, if I am being honest.

I move my second knight and sit back, waiting for him to take his turn. "That I know of. There may have been others, but I was kept apart from them. Kai was the only other prisoner that I met."

"And you don't think that's suspicious?" he questions, voice rising marginally. When I flinch, he works to keep his tone at a controlled volume. "It's just kind of odd, that's all."

My anger festers low in my stomach, like a swirling ball of

heat. His accusations sting—gut me—more than I care to admit.

"What are you saying, Cain? Just spit it out already." I ball my hand into a tight fist, and Cain's gaze drops to it immediately.

"I...I don't know what I'm saying," he admits at last. "Rook. H8 to H5."

"How about we make a deal?" I place my hands beneath my chin and tilt my head to the side. Cain's gaze lowers briefly to my lips before snapping back to attention. My heart flutters, but I keep my face blank.

"What kind of deal?"

"If I win, you have to at least try to be my friend." Acid forms low in my stomach, tangling with the ball of lead and nerves already present.

"And if I win?" he counters with a dismissive scoff.

"Then I'll leave you alone." I try to ignore the current of dread spiraling through my mind at the prospect, but I'll do it. If it's what he wants, I'll do it.

Cain considers me silently for a moment. A long, stifling moment that feels more like an eternity.

"All right," he agrees at last, nodding. "You have yourself a deal."

Hands sweating, I manage a frail, weary smile. "Be prepared to get your butt kicked."

"Butt kicked." He snorts once. "Do you really not swear? Not even 'ass'?"

I make a face, moving my pawn across the game board and capturing one of his. "Not really. I mean, not if I can help it. That's literally all I heard back at the Compound. I'm sure Kai told you, but it wasn't really a nice place." Understatement of the century. "I don't like things that remind me of there."

"Like loud noises and sudden touches," he deduces. My

face gets hot at how much he observed in such a short time. And this is coming from someone who hates me. I can't even imagine what a person like Kai has noticed.

"I could say the same about you," I muse as he announces and then moves his queen.

"I don't want to talk about me." His voice is curt, a crack of a whip, but I can sense an underlying pain beneath the surface. There's a part of his story that he doesn't want to talk about with me. A part of his story that made him the bitter man before me. Maybe, with time, he'll trust me enough to share that vulnerable piece of him, but I doubt it. At the moment, he's merely tolerating me, but that tolerance is as fragile as finely spun glass. One wrong move from either of us, and it will shatter into a thousand pieces.

"Then, we'll talk about me." I capture his rook with my bishop, barely managing to hide my squeal of excitement. "Ask me anything. I'm a book that is open."

There's almost a smile in his voice when he speaks next. Almost, but not quite. "I believe the saying is an open book."

"Book that is open. Open book. Is there really a difference?" I wave my hand in the air dismissively. "Either way, you can ask me anything."

He doesn't hesitate. "Did you kill Raphael Turner?"

"Of course not!" I protest immediately, adamantly. "I never even met the guy."

His vision dips once as he nods, almost as if he's confirming something to himself.

"How did you escape the Compound?"

It's the first time one of them has asked me that question. Not even Kai has bothered to ask. My throat is suddenly unbearably dry, while my hands become slick with sweat.

"They were moving me to what I called the torture room. It's a big room full of windows in the Compound, a few hallways away from my cell." My heart is doing somersaults in my chest as the memories bombard me—memories I have tried to keep dormant. But like with any ghost, they creep up and haunt you when you're least expecting them. "The usual guard and torturer was on duty that day. I don't know his name. Everyone just called him Man."

"Man?" Cain interrupts.

"I know. I thought it was a stupid nickname too."

I visualize Man the last time I saw him, through his own eyes as he stared at his reflection in the window. Body hunched over, with blood erupting from his stomach. Eyes flashing with pain and fury. Lips pulled back into a snarl.

"What happened?" Cain's voice is softer than I've ever heard it before. It travels over me like a lover's caress, as light as a butterfly's fragile wing.

"I fought back." My hands tighten around the edge of the table, knuckles turning white in Cain's vision. "I broke apart my wooden bed and used a prong to create a makeshift weapon. When a different guard—the weakest—tried to take me, I stabbed him and ran. Man came around the corner, no doubt hearing the commotion, and I attacked him too. Scratched his face, bit him, punched him. I wanted him to hurt the way he always made me hurt. I think I took him by surprise because, for some reason, I was able to overpower and escape him. I remembered my plan with Kai...our escape route. And I did it. I actually escaped. At least, I thought I did." I remember the fear of waking up in an unknown hospital room. William's visit and his accusatory voice. The month in a dirty prison cell, awaiting my inevitable fate.

That sense of security had been wrenched away from me only seconds after I'd found it.

"That doesn't seem fair," Cain points out as he stares down at the board. To my horror, I note that his queen now has easy access to my king. Checkmate.

"It's not," I whisper. *And neither is your own pain.*

My heart continues to pound a daunting rhythm inside my chest.

Cain is silent for a moment, fingers tapping against the table, before he moves his king one spot over.

In direct line of my queen.

"King to E8," he says softly.

My lips curl into a smile before I can stop them. "Checkmate."

CHAPTER 22

NINA

I don't hear from Mr. Scruffles in the following days.

The guys keep me contained to the cells and cafeteria, rotating shifts, so one is always with me while the others are away.

And while I don't see my shifter cat, I do run into Tessa.

Abel leaves me at a table in the cafeteria to go grab some food when I feel a hand on my arm. Startled, I whip my head in the direction of the intruder and inhale her unfamiliar lilac scent.

"Sorry." Tessa curses, pulling her hand back, as if I'm toxic. I try to calm my racing heart. It takes considerable effort, my breaths huffing in and out, before I'm finally able to plaster on a smile.

"It's okay. I just don't like being touched."

"Girl, with those sexy hunks of man meat around, how could you *not* like being touched?" she jests, jabbing her elbow into my side conspiratorially. I manage a weak chuckle, but jealousy grips my heart in a steel claw and clamps down. I don't like her referring to the guys as sexy hunks of man meat...and I don't know why. "I haven't seen you around."

"I've been...busy." To be honest, this is the first time I've been out of any of the guys' sight. They have different approaches for watching over me, but one thing remains the same: they track my every move.

Damien will often stand in the corner of the room, an extension of the shadows, as he listens to me babble about anything and everything. Sometimes, he'll add his own input, but mostly, he's content to let me rattle away.

Bronson will wrap me up like a delicate and precious package he wishes to treasure. Abel calls it "manhandling," but Bronson calls it "protecting." The giant shadow wolf will always find excuses to touch me, sniff me, or play with my hair. Oh, and feed me. I'm pretty sure that's his favorite pastime.

Kai will regale me with stories about his time before the Compound. We never address the elephant hovering over us, preparing to stomp down. We're merely biding our time, our heads in the gallows, waiting for that dreaded blade to drop. I know it isn't his fault that he never came back for me, but knowing it doesn't assuage the ache in my chest. We have years of tangled history we're only just beginning to unravel. Years of hurt and pain, but also love and joy. Though our conversations aren't stilted or awkward, by any means, they seem superficial compared to what we could have.

Cain, during the few times he took up "babysitting duty" (his words), humored me with various games. I finally learned how to play Monopoly, though I'll be the first to admit that I suck at it. I felt awful taking money from a grumpy Cain, so I gave him a free pass when he landed on my property. Every. Single. Time. He ended up with all the money, and I ended up with a bruised ego.

And then there's Abel...

Though I can't see him, I can sense him behind me, piling up meats, greens, and fruit onto my plate. Bronson gave all the men a "health diagram" they have to follow in order to get me healthy again.

"Nina? Are you listening to me?" Tessa snaps her fingers in front of my face with more amusement than ire.

"What? Yes, sorry." I duck my head, twin flames rising to both of my cheeks.

"I was just asking if you're doing okay," she repeats, stumbling briefly over her words. "I know the guys have taken an interest in you."

"They've been good friends," I agree with a soft smile.

"Friends?" Tessa releases an unladylike snort. "Honey, they do this shit all the time. They find a new plaything every time a woman comes to the prison. They use her and then discard her. I just don't want to see you get hurt. Believe it or not, I actually like you, Nina, and I don't like a lot of people." She leans even closer to me, her mouth millimeters from my ear. "They're not good men. You don't want their attention on you."

"They're my friends," I protest weakly.

Tessa connects our fingers and gives them a quick squeeze. "If they're truly your friends, they'll leave you alone. They have a lot of enemies, and you now have even more than them." Her voice is a hushed murmur, barely audible over the raucous inmates currently present in the cafeteria. "The other women are getting mad at you. They no longer have the attention they once had, you know? I'm afraid of what they'll do to you."

"Do to me?" My brain struggles to understand all the information she just pelted at me, but it's like a bucket that's already overflowing. Every new gallon of water just slides right over the edge.

"Be careful." Tessa gives my hand another squeeze before hurrying away. Not even a second later, Abel drops a plate of food in front of me.

"What did she want?" His voice is cautious, wary, and one glance through his eyes confirms that he's staring after Tessa. "Did she tell you I fucked her or something?" He tries to laugh, but there's a slightly manic edge to it. His gaze flickers back to me and settles there.

"What? No, she didn't say that." I shift uncomfortably at the thought of Abel "fucking" Tessa. I know the guys aren't exactly saints...

"Oh, she didn't?" Abel's voice is heady with relief.

"No, but you just did." I try to keep the accusation out of my voice, I really try, but it spews out before I can take it back. Internally grimacing, I slip out of Abel's head and stab at the chicken with my fork.

"Bambi," Abel begins placatingly. He grabs both my wrists and pulls my hands towards him. "Didn't I tell you that the past is the past? I don't do that shit anymore."

My heart begins to gallop like a stampede of wild horses.

"Don't do what?"

"You know...shit."

Giggling, I pull my hands out of his and resume eating. Bronson will have a fit if I don't eat everything on my plate. "That doesn't seem very healthy."

"I mean, it's...wait a minute. Are you teasing me?" His voice is suddenly closer, a hairsbreadth away, and I imagine he's leaning over the table. God, I wish I could see him. The golden hair flopping over his forehead. The tanned skin with a crescent white scar just under his left eye. The thick lashes. The high, chiseled cheekbones.

I have his face memorized, despite the fact that I've technically never seen it.

"Maybe I'm teasing you. Maybe not." I shrug, hiding my smirk with my hand. "But it would be quite painful not to poop. You should see the doctor. Brina, was it? You should see Brina about that problem."

"You little..." Abel jumps over the table and takes me in his arms, his hands roaming up and down my sides, tickling me. I laugh hysterically, attempting to swat him away, but Abel is relentless. When he finally stops, I'm breathless and panting and smiling like an idiot. I reach out and cup his cheek, his days' old scruff rubbing against my palm. He leans closer until his nose nuzzles mine. "What are you doing to me, Bambi?"

It's suddenly difficult to talk. To breathe.

"I don't know what you mean." There. That sounded coherent enough, right?

He leans even closer, hot breath fanning across my lips, but in the next second, he's ripped off me. I scream, throwing myself into his eyes to see Kai towering over the trickster demon. Scales cover his arms and cheeks, and red, reptilian eyes are currently narrowed.

"I can explain," Abel protests, lifting his hand to protect his face. Kai roars, smoke and a tiny bit of fire emerging. With a grace and stealth suited for a trickster demon, Abel sidesteps the next swipe of Kai's clawed hand. "I thought it was actually kind of funny."

Is this about what had just happened between me and Abel? Is Kai mad about that?

"You switched my BODY SOAP WITH GLUE!" Kai roars, stalking forward.

Abel chuckles once, turns towards me, and then breaks into laughter. I can't help but join in; his laughter is contagious, addicting, but the expression on Kai's face? The indignation, anger, and latent amusement? That's priceless.

Of course, it doesn't hurt that he's shirtless, with peeling white strips of glue on his muscular torso.

With a whoop, Abel takes off in a run down the hall, leaving Kai in his wake. I slip into a random prisoner's head when Abel's out of range. The entire cafeteria watches with bated breath as Kai's fangs and claws recede and his eyes return to normal. With a self-satisfied grin, he plops down into the seat Abel vacated. I slide out of the prisoner's mind and into Kai's.

"He's right. It was actually kind of funny," Kai says, stealing a piece of my chicken.

"Then, why did you go all 'dragon' on him?" I ask. When he tries to steal a second piece, I swat at his hand.

"So he would leave, and I could have you all to myself."

Smiling, I pick at the strawberries Abel put on my plate. A rare treat in the prison, reserved only for the inner circle. "Clever."

We sit in companionable silence for a couple more minutes until I say what has been burning a hole in my gut. No, not just a hole. A gaping chasm.

"We should tell the others," I blurt, dropping my fork and pressing my palms flat against the table.

Kai's gaze doesn't waver from my face. "No."

"No?"

"It's too dangerous. If the others knew..." He shakes his head ruefully. "No."

His words are the flames to my tinder, and my temper flares red hot. "It's my choice."

For a moment, Kai doesn't speak, stewing in silence. I expect him to yell, to scream, to demand that I listen to him, but he surprises me when he says, "You're right."

Every argument I had conjured up flees. "Huh?"

"If you want to tell them, I'll support you. You know that I'll do anything for you." He places one hand on top of mine. "But, Nina, you have to understand the dangers."

"Do you know what I am?" My words are a whisper, and I can't ignore the stab of betrayal. If he knew this entire time...

"No." His vision distorts as he shakes his head. "But that's the problem. Not one supernatural species can do what you can. The men... I trust them to an extent, I honestly do, but everyone has a price. A turning point."

I pull my clammy hand out of his own. Through his eyes, I see the blood drain from my face, leaving me even paler than normal. My silver, milky eyes stand out starkly. "And you think my unknown species will be the price. The turning point."

It's not a question.

Am I worth really that little? One minuscule detail will alter someone's entire opinion of me?

My heart seems to be growing in a steadily shrinking vise. What little air remains in my lungs leaves with my next swooping exhale. Pain grips me and refuses to let go.

Pain. Anger. Hurt.

My stomach is a tumultuous mixture of a dozen different emotions.

"I don't know," Kai settles on at last. "But I don't want to test it."

CHAPTER 23

DAMIEN

The man's a screamer.

The noise is melodic to my ears. Addicting. Better than any drug on the market.

At four foot nine, he's significantly smaller than the average man. Orange hair sticks out in all directions, matted down in the center with blood. Freckles dot his sinewy face and large nose. In normal circumstances, I would consider him ugly.

But when he screams?

He turns beautiful.

Not as beautiful as my Angel, of course, but nothing compares to her.

"Sean, Sean, Sean." I shake my head in feigned disapproval. "This will all be over the second you tell me what I want to know."

Sean had been a part of the guild with me. Plucked off the streets at sixteen years old, he has always been a condescending prick. I don't understand why Narian chose him. Maybe because he was small and could get into locations the average man could not.

Narian.

Just his name sends anger coursing through me, seeping into my bone marrow. The air around me lights up in a red sheen.

Fucking Narian.

I hate him with an intensity and passion that leaves me breathless. The fucker was the one who gave me a home, a purpose. Trained a ten-year-old boy how to be a lethal killer. He's also the same man who took that ten-year-old boy's innocence away.

And yet, he's the man I'm desperate to find.

"Come on, Sean. I know you still talk to him." I dig my blade into the werewolf's neck, and blood sputters out, staining my favorite pair of shoes.

"Go to hell, Damien," Sean pants before another scream cuts him off. I could use my magic on the simpering fool, but I much prefer getting my hands dirty. Well, bloody.

Twisting the second knife beneath his ribcage, I listen to his satisfying gurgling as more blood erupts from his mouth.

"You'll set up a meeting with Narian for me, won't you, Sean?" I pat his bloodied cheek. "I have some questions I need to ask him about a particular job."

"The Raphael Turner job?" Sean spits, face creasing with pain. "I heard you're shacking up with the bitch that killed him—"

Before he can finish whatever vulgar thing he's going to say, I reach a hand into his chest and grab his still beating heart. His face goes slack, wide, sightless eyes staring at something just above my shoulder.

I really hadn't meant to kill him.

"Oops," I murmur, dropping the organ onto the ground. He shouldn't have referred to Nina as a "bitch," then. Just hearing that degrading term causes snakes to come to life in my gut, slithering and hissing.

Using my knife, I cut the ropes that are holding Sean up, and he falls to the ground with an audible thump. While he may not be able to physically deliver my message for me, it'll still be heard. I just killed one of Narian's men. That's a call to war if I ever heard one.

And this time, I'll be ready.

Using magic, I eliminate the blood coating my body and run a hand through my slicked back hair. I shove both my knives into my sleeves before walking briskly down the hall towards the throne room.

While Blade had instructed me to reach out to my old connections in the guild, he has been working tirelessly to get answers out of the batshit crazy Rion, Lionel Green's old assistant.

What can I say about Lionel Green? Hmmm.

He's a self-righteous asshole who believes that all species should be segregated, humans should be slaves, and women should be demoted to the kitchen. He's a shifter, a powerful one, with four forms, a feat that is nearly unheard of. A wolf, a dog, a human, and a hyena.

What role did he play in Raphael's death? What does that have to do with Nina?

"Oh, hey, buddy!" Rion lifts his head from where it's lolling against his chest. Both his eyes are swollen shut, and blood coats his dark skin. His hands are raised above his head, held immobile by magical chains. He swings back and forth like a pendulum.

Blade stands in front of him with an indolent, almost tired, expression. Cain and Abel are leaning against the wall, whispering to each other.

That means Bronson is with my Angel.

"Has he talked?" I ask without preamble, stalking forward.

"I'm always talking. All the time. Talk. Talk. Talk. My

momma says I have an asshole for a mouth, that I'm always spewing out shit," Rion says, offering me a deranged laugh.

Crazy fucker.

"In answer to your question, no." Blade forks his fingers through his thick black hair, looking as if he wishes to be anywhere else. Or with anyone else. Particularly, a certain blind female.

"I told you." Rion spits some sweaty hair out of his mouth. "I hate Lionel. Yeah, I worked for him. Yeah, I was his little bitch boy for a couple years." His laughter increases, cutting off abruptly when a pained cough shakes his body. "But I don't know anything about his feud with Raphael. Did he hate the guy? Hell, yes. But murder him? No fucking idea. Look, I'm only putting up with this shit for my little cuddle buddy. I can easily free myself and kill you all."

"Please." I roll my eyes, removing one of my daggers from my sleeve. My hand stumbles across the swath of fabric still wrapped around my wrist—Nina's dress, from when she bandaged me. "You're lucky I don't kill you now."

"You won't," Rion protests with the utmost confidence. "Because you know my snuggle buddy will be sad without her Mr. Scruffles."

"I want to be Bambi's snuggle buddy," Abel whispers to Cain.

Ignoring them, I turn to face Blade. "We have to get going."

Blade lets out a ragged sigh, stepping back from Rion with a pained expression. The dragon shifter looks tired. Weary. In a span of seconds, he has aged years, maybe centuries. Lines crease his once flawless face.

"Nina still with Bronson?" Blade directs at the twins, and Cain nods once. "Good. She can't witness this."

"Ohhh...we're talking about my snuggle buddy, aren't we?" Rion rambles. "If you're going to see her, tell her I miss her boobs. But, like, not in a creepy way. In a cat way. They're fun to sit on. And tell her that I'm a nice, generous person, willing to share her with all of you assholes. Oh! And tell her about the turtle dove. Wait...don't tell her that. I repeat: do not tell her that."

A gag is placed in Rion's mouth before he can verbally run himself into a brick wall.

"Watch him," Blade instructs the twins, and Abel's eyes glint mischievously. It's a dangerous, scary look.

The guys like to act like I'm the most psychotic here, and though that may be true, the others aren't far behind me. I'm willing to bet my nut sack that the twins will engage in questionable torture techniques while we're away.

Without another word, Blade stomps down the hall, waiting only a second for me to catch up. We move quickly through the ever-changing passageways, only having to backtrack once when we make a wrong turn.

The tunnels are vast, but we are as familiar with them as we can be.

Finally, we stumble into an immense gray room surrounded by bleachers, all of which are currently occupied. I can't remember the last time someone cleaned this place, but it doesn't bother me. It actually adds something to the animalistic environment. Blood stains the cement floors and walls, and a musty smell barrages me, intermingling with the pungent stench of sweat and copper.

Two men stand in the center of the room, in the makeshift clearing the arena-style bleachers create.

Blade's face could've been carved from stone as he walks forward, stopping directly between them. The raucous cheering cuts off immediately when the prisoners set eyes on their king. For the longest time, I thought you could either be vicious and brutal or respected, never both. Blade has proven me wrong.

"A challenge has been issued!" Blade roars, and the crowd cheers, thirsty for blood. Animals. All of them. They live off the blood and death that occur within these very walls. "Timothy Rojas has challenged Michael Joel to a duel!" The crowd's noise ratchets up a notch, the energy infectious. I almost want to crack a smile at the bloodlust permeating the air.

We have these dumbass duels once every week in a brutal fight to the death. It's the way we maintain control of the prison and everyone inside it. Once a challenge has been issued, you can't refuse. You either fight...or die. And if you decide to be a little bitch and run away, then it's open hunting season.

Timothy raises his fists into the air, basking in the crowd's enthusiasm. Michael, on the other hand, looks as if he wants to shrink into his shell and disappear.

I give him a few minutes.

No words are spoken as Blade stares between the two men. A silent conversation is exchanged until the dragon shifter steps back, arms crossed over his chest. I stand just to the side of him, in his shadow.

Always his fucking shadow.

The fight begins.

There's no declaration. No announcement starting the fight. The second Blade steps back, the men charge at each other, throwing punches and kicks.

For such a scared man, Michael is a surprisingly good fighter. Fast. He easily sidesteps every punch thrown his way.

For the first time since the fights have begun, Blade doesn't look like he's enjoying himself. His eyes are shadowed, haunted, and his tattooed hands are clenched into fists.

"She doesn't have to know about this side of things," I murmur, easily able to read him.

"This will break her," he replies, and I can't help but agree. My Angel doesn't do well with violence.

The crowd begins to chant when Michael is knocked down to his knees. Blood leaks into his eyes, but he doesn't let up. Instead, it only makes him fight harder and faster, the need for vengeance and retaliation the driving force. The sight of his own blood makes his attacks feral and unhinged, each movement gradually becoming more and more chaotic. He delivers a punishing blow to his opponent's ribs, and the larger man falls to the ground, blood splattering everywhere.

Chest heaving, Michael crouches down, grabs Timothy's neck, and snaps it.

The cheers and roars are nearly deafening.

Blade steps forward, his frosty persona once more in place. Ignoring the blood still coating the other man's skin, he interlocks their fingers and holds their hands up in the air.

"We have a winner!"

I stare at the faces in the audience, salivating for blood. For death. For pain.

No, my Angel can definitely never learn about this.

CHAPTER 24

NINA

"I want to see Mr. Scruffles," I say abruptly, grabbing the dice off the table before Cain can roll them. Through Damien's eyes—who is standing sentry in the corner of the room—I see Cain quirk a blond brow.

"You know his name isn't actually Mr. Scruffles, right?" He leans across the table, opens my closed fist, and takes the dice.

We're having a "game night," as Abel calls it, in the twins' cell. The demons have procured a significant collection of various games and cards. Abel had insisted we play "Pretty Pretty Princess," calling it the best party game of the century. When Damien took a knife to Abel's throat, the trickster demon quickly retracted his claim, and we settled on some random board game that was missing more pieces than it had.

"Now, Bambi," Abel cuts in, and I turn my pleading gaze towards him, my lower lip trembling. He breaks off abruptly with a curse. "Fuck, I can't say no to that. She's doing the face, brother. The *face*. You can't say no to the face." To me, he adds, "I'll give you anything you want. Jewels? A crown? A majestic steed to ride...? And I don't mean a horse. It's yours."

"You might not be able to say no to her, but I can," Damien retorts, his vision shifting as he lunges forward with long, elegant strides. He tenderly caresses the side of my face before pulling his hand back as if I burned him. For a moment, he merely stares at me, both our hearts pounding in tandem. With a petulant shake of his head, he turns away. "Never mind. I can't."

"For fuck's sake..." Cain leans back in his chair and crosses his arms over his chest. "Princess, that's a fuck no."

"Is he..." I swallow around the lump in my throat. "Is he dead?"

Panic swirls in my stomach, a hurricane, and I absently rub at the spot. I haven't known Mr. Scruffles for long, but I have come to care for the cat...shifter...thing. He's my friend, and he saved my life more times than I care to admit. He saw me when I was at my most vulnerable, and he healed me. It might've been unintentional—he might've had malicious intentions—but he saw the cracked pieces within me, and he diligently repaired them. Comforted me. Allowed me to break down in a semi-safe environment.

"Shit, Trouble, what type of people do you think we are? Murderers?" Cain asks in exasperation, but I notice his lips twitch slightly. Abel definitely begins to smile before quickly masking his face.

"I want to see him," I insist, and I prepare myself for another denial. Instead, the cell gets abnormally quiet, and Damien's attention swivels towards the man now entering the room.

Kai looks tired—dark shadows outline each eye, and his face is paler than usual. Still, he smiles when he sees me. A brilliant smile that cleaves his face in two and makes butterflies dance and flutter in my stomach. My own lips curve up instinctively.

"Hi," I say shyly.

"Hi." He kneels down, placing his hands on both my knees. "Are you sure you want to see him?"

I don't even hesitate, nodding my head adamantly. "Yes."

"He's...he's not a nice man," Kai continues, seeming to choose his words carefully. He removes a hand from my knee to rub at the dusting of hair on his chin. "Remember how we talked about our friend group? Me, Damien, Abel, Cain, Bronson, and some of the others?"

"The prison whores?" I ask for clarification, and Abel begins to choke. I swear I see Kai's lips twitch.

"Yes, among others. The men and women in our group." I nod to show him I understand. "Well, your friend, Mr. Scruffles—" Another snort from Abel. "—He's a part of a rival friend group, okay? A group that doesn't quite get along with ours."

"For shit's sake, she's not a child!" Cain interrupts, and for the first time ever, I agree with him. I don't like the way Kai's speaking to me. It's not abrasive or cruel or anything, but it makes me feel like a stupid kid. It makes me feel like I'm back at the Compound, where the men and women considered me less than them, different. I already know that Kai is Blade, and he's the king of the Labyrinth. The gang leader. What else is there to know?

Kai opens his mouth to protest, but Cain forges ahead. "We're part of a gang, sweetheart. A prison gang. Blade's group and Rion's shifters. You see, there are probably one hundred shifters in this Labyrinth, and all of them bow to Rion. The rest of the supernaturals? They follow the ruling of your man, Kai, here. Right now, the shifters are being quiet, but we have no fucking idea how long that'll last. Rion isn't telling us shit."

My brain struggles to process his words. It feels as if I'm wading through tar: each step forward takes considerable effort and patience.

"And this Rion person..." I begin, my tongue snaking out to lick my top lip. "He's the leader of the rival gang? The one fighting with Kai's? And he's Mr. Scruffles?"

My head threatens to explode, but not because of the lack of information, but because I'm suddenly threatened with too *much* of it. Cain just lit the tinder, and we're all waiting for the inevitable explosion.

Why didn't they tell me this sooner?

My hurt and betrayal must be evident, for Damien takes a step closer and Kai tightens his hands on my knees.

"Rion is dangerous," Kai explains, his voice near pleading. Pleading for forgiveness? Acceptance? Something else entirely?

"He's my friend," I protest feebly. I suddenly feel just as tired as Kai looks.

"We also know that Rion was the assistant to Lionel Green before he was arrested," Abel breaks in, and for the first time, none of his usual mirth and cheer are audible. He sounds almost subdued and resigned, like a prisoner facing the executioner's block. Which, come to think of it, isn't a horrible analogy.

"And we believe Lionel might've been behind Raphael's murder," I deduce. "But why do you think Rion is involved? Hasn't he been at the prison for a while? I was only arrested and convicted recently."

Cain blows out a breath, as if my incessant questioning is annoying him. "He might not be involved directly, but that doesn't mean he's a good guy. He still has information that could be helpful to discovering the truth."

"Shouldn't I talk to him, then? See what he knows?" It may sound crazy, but I know in my heart that Mr. Scruffles—Rion—will never hurt me. If anyone is capable of getting information out of him, it's me.

The men exchange an eloquent glance, a glance I'm not intended to see, before Kai sighs in defeat.

"You have twenty minutes. And you're not getting within two feet of him."

~

KAI LEADS ME DOWN THE TWISTING, CURVING HALLWAY until we stand in front of the throne room door. Two unfamiliar men stand guard in front, hastily crafted knives held at the ready. I have to wonder how much damage something so little can do, but I keep my mouth shut.

"Bronson still inside?" Kai asks the one on the left. The man nods once, casting sly glances in my direction. "Send him out and then leave."

Without having to be told twice, the men skitter inside and return only a few moments later. They lower their heads submissively before slinking away. Bronson exits shortly after, face twisted in irritation.

"What?" he rasps, scowling. That scowl diminishes when he catches sight of me, replaced by something sweeter and softer. He reaches for me, and I willingly step into his arms. The scent of sweat, musk, and pine surround me, the smell uniquely his. "What are you doing here?" He pushes me back slightly to inspect my body, searching for injuries.

"Visiting Rion," Kai answers for me. Something in his tone gives me pause, and I slip out of Kai's head and dive into Bronson's. The giant man is staring intently at Kai over my shoulder, and I'm able to see Kai give a barely perceptible shake of his head. "I'll be going in with her."

Bronson immediately grunts and begins to argue, but Kai cuts him off with a wave of his hand. "You stand guard out here."

The air between the two men seems to crackle and spark

with electricity. They're two magnets with the same pull, repelling against one another. It's not like I expected anything different: both Kai and Bronson are alpha males in their own unique way, especially when it comes to me. I don't quite understand it, but I know that my safety and needs surpass everything else.

Finally, Bronson releases me with a decidedly pained whimper. He reminds me of a man whose puppy was just kicked. Wanting to comfort him—but not knowing how—I lean into his embrace and place my hands on both his cheeks. Memorizing his features through touch alone, I pull his lips up into a forced smile with the pads of my thumbs.

"Don't be so grumpy," I huff. He snorts, muttering something incoherent, before wrapping me in his arms one last time. "Good grief. I'm going to visit my cat, not a funeral."

"Not a cat," the wolf snarks.

Kai waits until Bronson releases me before interlocking our fingers and pulling me through the wide doors.

"Ten minutes, or I'm coming in," Bronson snaps just as the door swings shut on silent hinges. I immediately slide into Kai's mind to get a visual of Rion. Mr. Scruffles. I haven't seen him since that first time in the bathroom, what feels like months ago.

Instead, I find Kai's gaze intently on me.

I could be mistaken, but it almost seems intentional. Kai is the only one who knows what, exactly, my power can do. Is there a reason why he isn't looking at Mr. Scruffles? I feel the beginnings of irritation grip me with cold fingers.

"Buttercup!" an enigmatic voice squeaks from in front of me. I immediately turn a blind gaze in his general direction, but Kai remains focused on me. It's unnerving—his attention —to say the least.

"Rion?" I ask tentatively, trailing a step closer. Kai immediately tightens his hold on my hand, keeping me in place.

"Rion." The man snorts dismissively. "Only my mother, family, friends, and strangers call me that. Please, refer to me as Mr. Scruffles."

"Shifter scum," I hear Kai mumble beneath his breath.

"That's Mr. Shifter Scum to you," Rion retorts.

Tears burn my eyes as I consider the man, the stranger, in front of me. What's his story? How did he end up here? Why did he save me? Questions build, but I don't know how to put a voice to them.

I settle on the easiest one. "What have you been doing the last few days?"

"Oh, you know," he begins flippantly. "Just *hanging* out with my new buddies. Real sweethearts, those men."

I nod silently, suddenly unsure of what to say or what to ask. Thousands of questions clamor for attention, and I can't seem to settle on just one.

"Is it true that you're part of a...rival gang?" I timidly venture. To be honest, I couldn't care less about his affiliations inside the prison. I don't know enough about the social structure to care. All I know for certain is that I'm friends with Kai, Bronson, Damien, and Abel, and Mr. Scruffles saved my life. Oh, and Cain's a butt.

Rion sighs heavily, the forlorn noise causing acid to churn in my stomach like an active volcano. "It's true we don't get along. Usually. But we never had a common goal until now. They pissed on me first, Buttercup, and I just lifted my leg to pee back. Wait. Don't quote me on that. Actually, please do. Maybe I can become Instagram famous."

Okay, first: what does he mean by that?

And second: what's Instagram?

Shaking the cobwebs out of my head, I ask, "What do you mean *they pissed on you first?*"

"We really should get going," Kai urges, placing his hand

on the small of my back. His attentive, unwavering gaze causes heat to bloom across my body and ignite in my chest.

"I want to hear," I protest, stepping away from him.

"It's a long and complicated story, Buttercup," Rion states sadly. "But needless to say, there's bad blood between us that can't be solved overnight. They've hurt people I cared about, and I've hurt people they cared about. But I can promise you: you're the person I'll never hurt. Unless you ask for it...in bed. You're not into that kinky shit, right? I mean, we can probably get handcuffs pretty easily, but nipple clamps are a whole different—"

"We're leaving," Kai interrupts, ushering me towards the door. Rion's manic laughter continues to follow our retreat.

"And let me make one thing clear!" the cat shifter calls just as we reach the door. "I know nothing about Raphael Turner's death. And when I find the person who framed my Buttercup..." His voice lowers to a seductive purr, his cat personified. "I'll make them wish they had never been born."

CHAPTER 25

CAIN

I don't know what it is about this female that has captured the attention of all my brothers, even my asinine twin. They're positively enthralled by her, those dumb shits, even my asinine brother.

Sure, she's beautiful, but I've seen my fair share of beautiful women.

And she has a smile that can lighten up any day...

And she has this cute dimple on her cheek...

And she has this addictive little giggle...

And she seems to actually care...

Fuck me. No, fuck *her*.

Scowling, I cross my arms over my chest and watch her from a distance. She's sitting in the cafeteria beside Tessa, her fellow female inmate. The other girl is showing Nina a few dresses that no longer fit her.

"This will look great with your skin tone," Tessa says, holding up a little red number. I'm pretty sure Bronson and Kai would blow a nut if she ever wore that. For one, it's entirely too revealing, with a dipping neckline and slit up the side. For two, I'm pretty sure some random fuckboy originally bought it for Tessa. The last thing the shifters want is another guy buying clothes for their girl, even if it is indirectly.

I'll admit, spiders crawl up my spine at the prospect.

Nina touches the skirt, her hands trailing reverently across the silk. A beatific smile erupts on her stupidly pretty face.

I don't trust Nina. Not completely.

No, I don't believe she has malevolent intentions. The girl captures flies and sets them free. It's almost sickening how sweet she is. Vomit-inducing.

What I don't trust is her apparent "blindness." I'm not a complete asshole. I know she is, technically, blind, but I also know she can see things an average person cannot. I don't know exactly what that entails, but I do know it's not something she's sharing with the class. Why is she keeping it a secret?

When Tessa whispers something that makes Nina laugh, my chest tightens almost painfully. It shouldn't bother me as much as it does. It really, *really* fucking shouldn't.

I become aware of the female stepping up behind me only a second later. My body freezes as if it has been encased in ice.

"I haven't seen you and the others around," Haley purrs in what she probably thinks is a seductive voice. Haley was one of the girls the inner circle used to share, many months ago. I haven't ever touched the wench, but I know the others have.

"Jealousy isn't attractive on you," I say breezily.

"What is so special about her?" Haley continues, ignoring the warning in my tone. "Does she have a magical cunt or something?"

She reaches out and places her fingers on my bicep. It's an innocent touch, chaste in comparison to what it could be, but it seems to slam into me with the force of a wrecking ball. My vision blurs as fire erupts on my palms. Haley gasps, backing away, but I'm too far lost in my own mind to notice.

"Get up." A kick to the ribs accompanies the order. Abel is already up, knees pulled up to his chest and eyes staring despondently ahead.

"Both of us?" he whispers, and my heart breaks at the pensive expression on his face. The broken spirit. He was once joyful and lively, but that has long since been sucked out. He's nothing but a carcass of what he once was.

"Just the sex demon," Boris sneers. The collar around my throat gives a threatening tingle, warning me of what is to come if I refuse. Abel's eyes flash to mine, full of fear and pain and loathing. I can't tell if the loathing is directed at himself, me, or the monster who claimed us.

I'm led down the hall to a chorus of hoots and hollers. It's as undignified as anything can be. The fishnets I'm wearing leave very little to the imagination, and my chest is bare.

I know Boris—the sick fuck—has a second female club a few towns over. Exotique or something stupid like that. This one is exclusively for males.

Boris pushes me inside one of the plush red rooms that have starred in more than one of my nightmares. It's like Valentine's Day exploded in this room. Heart-shaped bed, velvet red carpeting, and red-painted walls. It's so disgustingly cliché that, in any other circumstance, it'd be almost comical.

Lionel Green sits on the bed, already naked. His hairy chest, hardened nipples, and half-erect cock are on display for all to see.

Boris gives my back a shove, and I stumble forward, vomit churning in my stomach. To Lionel, Boris says, "One hour."

The door closes with a deafening click.

"Get on all fours on the bed for me," Lionel purrs, cupping my cock. "Be a good doggy."

I'm shaking, shivering, but I know refusal will hurt not only me, but my brother.

I need to protect him.

I need to.

"CAIN, LOOK AT ME. LOOK. AT. ME." GENTLE HANDS REST on both of my cheeks, holding my head steady.

I'm trembling as if I've just been electrocuted numerous times in a row. Lead the size of a watermelon takes residence in my stomach, mingling with the ball of nerves already present.

"I can't," I sob. Weak. So weak. Pathetic. "I can't."

"You can," she whispers. "Just follow my voice. Come back to me."

God, I want to. I want to so fucking bad. She calls to me, her song melodic, and I want nothing more than to answer.

She takes deep, exaggerated breaths, and I work to match my breathing with hers. In and out. In and out. In and out.

I focus on her hands on my face, the only real thing in this world, and her sweet breath fanning across my lips. Slowly, the panic begins to recede like water being tossed into a strainer. I'm left with nothing but sharp, jagged pieces of glass.

That's all I am. Broken glass.

When I finally have myself under control enough to speak, I open my eyes.

Nina stands directly in front of me, a vision of ethereal beauty. Her black hair cascades around her delicate, heart-shaped face. And her eyes...

Her fucking eyes...

Those glassy orbs peer up at me, seeing me with a clarity no one else has ever possessed.

One flick of my eyes in both directions shows the cafeteria to be empty. I don't know how she was able to manage it, but somehow, she cleared everyone out. Thank fuck. I don't know if I would've survived if everyone had borne witness to my meltdown.

Seeing that I'm okay, Nina slowly begins to extract her hands from my face, but I capture them before they can leave. Leaning into her palm, I press a kiss against first one wrist and then another. My heart flutters like the damn wings of a bird.

At that moment, I'm entirely under her spell.

Everything around us freezes. All that exists is her. She's all I see, all I smell, all I hear.

Like a puppet on strings, I lean towards her, my lips hovering over hers. How will she taste? Will she moan my name?

"Cain!" I squeeze my eyelids shut, suddenly hating my brother's piss poor timing. "Cain!" Abel runs towards us, and Nina immediately steps back, cheeks flaming. My brother grips me in a bone-crushing hug. "Shit, man. I heard rumors that you completely demoned-out. What happened?"

I hug my brother back just as tightly, remaining silent. The memories are too raw, too brutal, pulling back my skin and revealing the blood and guts underneath.

"Thank you," Abel whispers hoarsely, but he isn't talking to me. He's staring at the slowly retreating girl over my shoulder. "Thank you for taking care of my brother."

I reluctantly step out of my twin's embrace to face her fully. For the first time in my life, there isn't a gaping chasm where my heart once was. That's not to say that I'm completely or even marginally healed—far from it—but it doesn't hurt as badly. It's a survivable pain, a pain that reminds me that I can emerge victorious.

"Thank you," I choke out, hoping she can hear the sincerity in my words.

She smiles softly.

And I think...

I think that's the moment I fall for her.

CHAPTER 26

NINA

It's two days after Cain's breakdown when Tessa arrives at my cell. Well, not my cell. Not technically. It's Kai's, but he has given me free rein to do whatever I want in it. Already, the stark gray walls have a splatter of coloring from the paint I found inside Abel's drawer. Kai has also taken it upon himself to get me more clothes. Bras, dresses, skirts, and beautiful blouses are neatly folded in the dresser, alongside his own clothes. A jewelry stand sits regally on the wooden surface, though why I would need jewelry in prison remains a mystery.

"Knock! Knock!" Tessa's chipper voice immediately brings a smile to my face.

"It's open."

I quickly slide into her head to see that she isn't alone. Two unfamiliar females stand beside her, one holding a small bag and the other a silver dress. Maybe not completely unfamiliar. I'm pretty sure I have seen them both before, but for the life of me, I can't figure out where.

"Are you alone?" I ask Tessa, despite already knowing the answer.

"No. No. Some of my girls are with me. Nina, this is Haley and Rebecca. Rebecca and Haley, this is Nina," Tessa introduces, and I notice Haley's lips thin into a solemn line. Rebecca, on the other hand, smiles cheerfully. She's an older, robust woman with brown hair, teal eyes, and a larger than normal body. Still, her smile is contagious, and her eyes glimmer with an inner mirth.

"I've heard a lot about you, and let me just say...you're even more gorgeous in person," Rebecca praises.

Fire enters my cheeks, and I duck my head. "Thanks."

"Bronson sent us to get you ready for tonight," Tessa proclaims, turning her head to stare at the hulking shadow wolf.

He's asleep in the cell opposite mine, chest rumbling with his snores. He looks tranquil, almost peaceful, with his thick lashes resting delicately against his strong cheekbones. His blond hair is tousled, and he's wearing only a thin white shirt that leaves very little to the imagination.

Earlier, I had been in the cell with him as he told me stories about his mother and siblings. He told me how he used to be a "little shit" and steal his sisters' diaries. As revenge, they stole his clothes after a shift, and he had been forced to walk the six-mile trek back to his house, naked. In the middle of his story, his eyelids had drooped, and his breathing had evened. Pressing a chaste kiss to his forehead, I pulled the blanket up to his shoulders and tiptoed into the cell opposite.

Kai has a collection of Braille books from the prison librarian. I'm not an expert at reading them yet, but I'm proficient. Kai had started teaching me back in the Compound, before he left me.

Setting down the book I'm currently reading—a riveting tale about a female vampire and her harem of lovers—I turn in the direction of the females.

Tessa saunters ahead first, immediately capturing me in a tight embrace. I tense instinctively before willing my body to relax and returning her hug.

"What's going on tonight?" I query, tilting my head to the side.

Haley drops the dress onto Kai's bed, and Rebecca moves to stand in front of me.

"Why, you have a date!" Tessa squeals, and when I throw her a warning look, she works to lower her volume. "Bronson asked us to come by and help get you ready."

"A date?" I parrot dumbly. I've never been on one before. Heck, I haven't even been asked to go on one, least of all by Bronson.

"We're here to make you look beautiful," Tessa continues.

"We're not doing it out of the goodness of our hearts," Haley snaps, flashing a bit of fang. "The guys are offering us... other things. Well, we're offering them, though it's not a difficult feat." She smooths a hand down her platinum blond locks before daintily sitting on the edge of Kai's bed. Her hand hovers above his pillow, and I have the irresistible urge to snap at her. To remove her scent from his belongings.

But the last thing I need is for these females to know the truth about my abilities.

Taking a deep breath, I focus on Tessa and Rebecca, ignoring Haley and her blatant lies. I know what she's trying to imply, but I also know the guys. They wouldn't touch her.

"Ignore her. She's just a jealous bitch," Tessa says with a wave of her hand.

"That's not what Damien said last night," Haley counters with a smug smirk.

I know her words are only that—words—but it feels as if I've been punched in the gut. I allow anger, rage, and hurt to seep into my bone marrow.

No. No. No. She's lying.

But the most important question: why do I care so much?

"Do you want to get killed, Haley?" Rebecca chides, unzipping the small bag and holding up a battered black pencil. It's unnaturally thick, the size of her thumb, and when she takes off the lid, I see a brilliant red color. "Let me put the lipstick on first, yeah?"

"No, the dress and hair first," Tessa protests. "Makeup after."

Haley grumbles and moves to stand behind me, her hands expertly pulling and twisting my hair.

"You don't have to do this...if...if you're not comfortable," I stutter out, placing a hand on her wrist to still her. Through Tessa's eyes, I watch Haley's face slacken with shock, but she quickly schools her expression.

With an impassive shrug, she resumes forking her fingers through my hair. "They're not paying me to just sit around," she huffs, and though she can't see it, I offer her a tentative, wobbly smile. Her hands pause once again. "And they're paying me in cash, by the way," she finishes at last, and my heart swells in my chest, almost to the point of bursting.

"Thank you," I whisper hoarsely, and she rolls her eyes.

"Whatever. Let me just make you look somewhat presentable."

The next hour consists of me being poked and prodded to within an inch of my life. At one point, Bronson wakes up and glances over at me before curling his lips into a predatory smile. He hooks a sheet in front of his cell door, effectively obscuring him from view.

"Stay still!" Haley scolds, whacking my shoulder good-naturedly. I feel like an errant child caught with my hand in the cookie jar. She pins back another section of hair with a dramatic flourish. "And...there! Perfect!"

Tessa helps me into the gorgeous dress, zipping it up and smoothing down the skirt. At least it's better than the outfits

Tessa bombarded me with only a few days ago. That had been a sea of colorful, tight-fitting, revealing clothes.

This one cascades down my body like silver starlight, the sequins catching in the artificial prison lighting. It's tight—tighter than anything I have ever worn—and accentuates my lithe but curvy frame. I'm not busty, like some of the other women, but I consider myself well-endowed (at least, that's what Tessa assured me when I began to fidget). A slit up the side showcases my pale, toned leg and thigh.

My makeup, thanks to Rebecca, is light and natural. I haven't actually worn makeup before, though I have heard some of the female guards at the Compound complain about theirs. The older woman puts something on both my eyelashes—mascara, she calls it—before lining my eyes with coal. The cherry red lipstick is applied to my lips, and blush dusts each cheek. I want to tell her that the blush isn't needed, that my cheeks color more often than the average person, but I let her have her fun. Rebecca is an artist with an empty canvas, and her face practically glows as she painstakingly applies each layer.

And my hair...

Even Haley can't hide her smirk of satisfaction. My wavy black hair now hangs in perfect ringlets down to the middle of my back. She braided it away from my face, and placed half the curls in an elaborate updo on the top of my head.

I feel wanton and beautiful. Powerful.

It takes considerable effort, but I manage to hide my reaction when Tessa finally turns to stare at me. She whistles beneath her breath. "Damn, you look hot."

"You look beautiful, honey," Rebecca agrees warmly. Haley, of course, just rolls her eyes and places her fisted hands on her hips.

"We shouldn't keep your date waiting..." Tessa titters, grabbing first Haley's hand and then Rebecca's to pull them out of the cell. Tessa pauses once to turn back to me. "I'm sorry about what I said before. In the cafeteria. Just...be careful, okay?"

Bemused by her warning, I nod once to show her I understand.

"Don't do anything I wouldn't do!" Rebecca calls as she's dragged around a corner.

Haley snorts. "You'll do just about anything, ho."

I giggle at their antics, stopping to brush my hands down the waist of my dress. This entire situation feels almost surreal. I'm about to go on my first date...while I'm in prison for a crime I didn't commit. It reminds me of one of the romance books I've just started reading.

Only, instead of dashing princes, my men are dangerous, psychotic criminals.

A sharp intake of breath alerts me to Bronson's dominating presence. I smile widely, spinning to show him the entire gown.

"What do you think?" I ask, suddenly shy.

"I think..." He takes a deep breath. "I think you're the most enchanting woman I have ever laid eyes on, and I might kill anyone who looks at you twice."

Ignoring his threat, I lean forward to place my hand on his bicep.

"Don't you usually have to ask the girl out on a date?" I jest with another smile. I feel...giddy. Girly, almost, which is entirely unlike me. I've never had material things and never wanted them. Until now. Standing in a musty prison cell, I have never felt more like a princess.

"I did," Bronson says. "Don't you remember?" I honestly don't, but before I can tell him that, he curses again. "Shit, Nina, you look like a goddess. *My* goddess."

My heart gains wings and soars at his admission.

"What do you look like?" I timidly ask, trailing a finger down his arm and to his hand.

"I'm...uh...wearing a suit, I guess, and I combed my hair." There's a distinct note of embarrassment to his voice that has my grin widening.

"What color is the suit?" I whisper, moving my hand across the lapels of his jacket and to the fabric underneath. His breath hitches, his heart tempo increasing beneath my hand.

"Is this some sort of foreplay?" he asks gruffly, and my confusion ratchets up a notch. I think through my recent collection of books, trying to remember if that word was mentioned at all. I can guess what it means well enough.

Having fun before a date, obviously. Teasing each other.

"What do you mean?" I settle on at last.

"Never mind, my goddess." He places my hand in the crook of his arm and leads me forward. "I have a lot planned for tonight."

CHAPTER 27

BRONSON

She's a fucking vision.

Radiant and perfect, someone plucked straight off the cover of a magazine.

And she's mine. Completely and utterly mine.

As I lead my goddess through the curving passageways of the Labyrinth, my heart pounds unsteadily. My entire essence is intricately entwined with hers. My wolf cries, demanding escape, but I silence him with a stern glare. The last thing I want to do is mark her and make her mine before she's ready.

Before *I'm* ready.

There are other men I have to consider, other men who consider her theirs just as much as I do.

Nina smiles up at me, and her attentive gaze causes heat to bloom across my body. My brain is scrambled like fucking eggs, and all I can think about is how badly I want to kiss her. Bite her. Claim her.

Sweeping those thoughts beneath the proverbial rug, I lead her to the room I set up earlier. It took convincing, but Damien eventually agreed to use his connections to get me the supplies I desired.

A single table sits in the center of the room, with a white tablecloth draped over the top. Unlit candles sit directly in the center, with two plates on either side. Roasted chicken, beans, and rolls are splayed out on silver platters. It's the best I was able to get on such short notice. My mate should be treated like the queen—the goddess—she is.

I hurry over to her chair and pull it out for her. Of course, she stares blankly over my head, unaware of my chivalrous gesture. Shit.

Retaking her hand with my own, being very careful not to startle her, I guide her towards the seat, then push her in. She smooths her hands down her silky dress, a gorgeous smile lighting up her face, and I'm momentarily struck dumb. I'm pretty sure I forget how to speak.

Recovering my wits, I grab a cloth napkin—read as: a clean shirt I ripped in half for this occasion—and daintily place it over her lap like the fucking gentleman I am.

"I really don't remember you asking me out on this date," she says, and my smile turns smug.

That's probably because I didn't.

Wolves take what they want, and me? All I want is her.

"Did I tell you yet that you're gorgeous?" I ask, scooping a hearty helping of beans and chicken onto her plate.

"Once or twice." She giggles, the sound both innocent and melodic, and I swear it sends heat straight to my cock. Fuck, what I wouldn't give to be inside of her...

But, no. That's not what she needs. She needs me to be her friend and protector, not a lover. Maybe, with time, we can get to that level, but I'll never force her.

"You're beautiful every day, but right now, you're enchanting. I swear I could stare at you for hours and still find something new to ogle over," I confess. Only when her plate is full do I fill up my own. It's been ingrained since I was young: my mate comes first. Always.

She blushes adorably, heat climbing up her neck and to both of her already rosy cheeks. She may find her constant blushing embarrassing, but I find it beautiful.

I watch her take her first bite of chicken, eyes closing in bliss, before digging into my own. We're silent for a moment, each reveling in the delicious assortment of food Damien procured for us, before she speaks.

"Are you going to tell me more stories of Momma?" she asks eagerly, setting her fork onto her plate. She must sense my glower of disapproval because she immediately grabs the fork and begins eating with gusto. My goddess is way too skinny.

I don't even admit to myself how giddy I get when she refers to my momma as her own. Soon, my mom will be. As my mate, my wife, my partner, my family will be hers.

"Actually..." I trail off to dab at my face with my napkin. Again, I'm a super classy motherfucker. "I was hoping we could talk about you."

The color drains from her face, and this time, I don't stop her when she drops her silverware. "Me?" She looks as if she has seen a ghost, as if the memories of her past are circulating in her head, haunting her. My heart aches—physically fucking breaks—at the pain in her expressive white eyes. What did my mate endure before I found her?

"We don't have to talk," I say roughly, unable to handle her agony. It makes me want to hurt someone, anyone. It makes me want to escape this fucked-up prison, find the Compound, and kill everyone inside of it. I might not even use a weapon. No, they deserve to die by my bare hands.

"No," she says, shaking her head once. "No, it's fine. You deserve the truth. What do you want to know?"

Now that I have the opportunity, I suddenly find myself speechless. I don't want to know anything, least of all what they did to her. My hold on sanity is tenuous, at best, and I'm afraid her words will send me spiraling over the edge. Already, my beast is prowling just beneath the surface, preparing to strike. He hates what has been done to his mate nearly as much as I do.

"I don't even know what to ask," I admit on a shaky, rumbling breath. Rubbing a hand through my short-cropped hair, I ask the first thing that comes to mind. "Were you ever happy?"

"Oh, yes!" she says without missing a beat. "That's where I met Kai." The way she talks about him...

I can only hope she'll talk about me like that one day.

"You really love him, huh?" For some undefinable reason, that realization doesn't pain me as much as I thought it would. I always knew my girl had a greater capacity to love than most people. Even after all she'd been through, she came into the prison with an imperious set to her chin and a sparkle in her eyes. She's a real and vibrant light, igniting the walls around my heart in flames and setting me free.

"He's my best friend," she says wistfully, lowering her head. "But he doesn't like me...in that way," she adds, almost as an afterthought. "Like, he never asked me on a date like you did."

I just barely hold in my snort. The girl is utterly oblivious. Blade—Kai—is head-over-heels in love with her. Anyone with eyes (ignore the pun) can see that. There can be a thousand people in the room, and his eyes will only ever be on her. I can understand his obsession with her, mainly because I feel it myself. I may be forced to reside in the shadows, but she reminds me that there is light.

Blade really needs to get his head out of his ass and confess his feelings for her. But tonight is my night, and I'm determined to show her what it's like to be loved and cared for by a shadow wolf.

"Tell me a happy memory. Anything," I press, leaning across the table to grab her fork and hold it up to her plush lips. She opens automatically, a rosy hue to her cheeks.

"My twelfth birthday," she blurts, and I raise my eyebrow at her. Blushing, she stammers, "Kai always tried to do something special on my birthday. At least, the day we decided was my birthday. I don't know the real date. Anyway, when I turned twelve, Kai convinced one of the guards to let us take over the kitchen. I don't know what Kai gave him for him to agree, but we were led to the kitchen only a few minutes later. Kai made me a big chocolate cake with delicious strawberry frosting. It was one of the first cakes I'd ever eaten. Actually, I'm pretty sure it was the first cake I ever had. The *only* cake I ever had. Kai was somehow able to find candles and a lighter, so I would have something to blow out. It's one of my happiest memories." She trails off, her lips curving up dreamily.

For the first time ever, I'm immensely grateful that Kai had been in that shithole with her. He had given her that memory and, consequently, that smile now gracing her perfect face. I'll be forever indebted.

"When's your birthday?" I ask, brushing my thumb across her knuckles. Goose bumps rise on her delicate skin, filling me with a masculine pride.

"February twenty-fourth," she whispers.

"I can promise you that you'll only have the best of the best from here on out. Cakes, candles, presents...whatever you want. Goddess, you'll never feel pain or fear again. I'll protect you for the rest of my life, with everything I have within me."

There's a long, potent pause as my vow settles between us. She blinks at me, startled by my declaration, before her eyes fill with tears.

Shit!

Jumping from my seat, I move to kneel before her. I'd promised myself I would never kneel to anyone, but for her, I'll get down on all fours. Anything to worship at her temple.

"Don't cry. Please don't cry," I plead, brushing a finger beneath first one eye and then the next.

"Why me?" she sobs.

I continue to collect one tear after another as I consider what to tell her without scaring her away. I settle for the truth. "I'm not a perfect man. Hell, I'm not even a good one." She opens her mouth to protest, but I talk over her. I need to get these words out before I decide not to. She deserves to know the truth about me—the good and the bad. "You want to know what I did to get here? I killed a man. A man who worked for the council. Unbeknownst to my family, he began seeing my little sister, Ali. She fancied herself in love with him, but he only saw her as something he could fuck on the side." My hands clench into fists as my anger courses through me. Even now, years later, the memories continue to bombard me. "Ali eventually told me about him, and I tried to warn her away. I swear I did."

This time, it's Nina who's catching the tears as they fall from my eyes. Her soft hands rest on both my cheeks, holding me hostage.

"She wanted him to leave his wife, but he refused. Ali then threatened to tell his wife the truth about their affair... and he killed her. Raped and killed my baby sister." I'm crying harder now, my entire being unraveling with each word. In a demented, self-deprecating way, I wonder if I could've done more for her. What if I had fought harder? What if I had told my momma?

What if?
What if?
What if?

"And then what happened?" Nina's crying as well, silent tears that glimmer in her eyes like a milky pool.

"And then I killed him," I say on a breath. "I murdered him for what he did to my sister. I'm a monster. A fucking monster."

Leave me.

Don't leave me.

Run away.

Don't leave me.

Run. Run. Run.

Nina cranes her neck and presses her soft lips against mine. I'm so startled that I freeze, heart dancing, before wrapping my arms around her and pulling her to me. Almost hesitantly, asking a question without words, I press my tongue against the seam of her lips. She replies by opening her mouth, accepting all I'm willing to give her.

And I'm willing to give her everything.

Her tongue wrestles playfully with my own, and I have to wonder if this is the first time she has ever been kissed. Ever been touched, at least willingly.

Don't think about that.

All thoughts flee as I allow myself to live in the moment, live in her. Her taste, her scent, the feel of her body pressed against my own.

"Bron," she whimpers, and I groan at the nickname.

"I want to take care of you, goddess. Let me take care of you." I curve my hand around her delicate neck before trailing it lower, pushing down the straps of her silver gown. Her chest heaves with each breath she takes, her desire evident. "I'm not going any further until you say it. What do you want, my queen?" I press a tantalizingly soft kiss to her collarbone.

"I want... I want you to make me feel good," she breathes, and I swear I almost blow my load right then and there. I feel like a fucking virgin boy seeing a tit for the first time.

"Anything for you, goddess," I murmur, pushing her dress farther down until the dark skin of her areola is revealed. White hot pleasure cascades through me, coursing straight to my cock, and I begin to grind myself forward. I kiss each new swath of skin exposed until her dress settles just beneath her breasts, her pink nipples already pointed. "Fuck, you're perfect. Absolutely perfect." Moving cautiously, unwilling to startle her, I kiss the skin around first her right nipple and then her left, never touching her where she so desperately needs me to.

"Bron," she cries, arching her back. Her hips begin to move in tandem, seeking friction. "Please."

My goddess shall never beg for anything. Obediently, I take one of her pert nipples into my mouth while squeezing the other one. My other hand travels down her stomach before curving around her ankle and hoisting it up. Her gorgeous dress slides up her thighs.

"You're perfect," I whisper, trailing my hand up her smooth skin until I reach her inner thigh. "God, I never thought I would meet you. I didn't think I deserved a mate. But you...you're everything. Absolutely fucking everything. Let me worship you."

She mewls something inarticulate, hands tangling in my hair to keep me in place. I want to bury my cock in her, but I know she's not ready for that. Not yet.

The tip of my finger grazes her soaked panties, and both of us moan. She's so ready for me, so wet.

My perfect, beautiful goddess.

I don't bother teasing her. Instead, I shove her panties to the side and stick one finger into her slick hole. She tenses, muscles as taut as a rubber band, and I instantly freeze.

"Do you want me to stop?" I ask, immediately removing

my hand. Her own leaves my head to wrap around my wrist, holding me in place.

"No," she whimpers. "I know it's you, and I know you'll never hurt me. It's just..." I wait for her thoughts to formulate, acid churning in my stomach like a whirlpool.

"At the Compound, did someone hurt you?" I whisper, and I don't mean the torture I already know about. She's silent for a moment, body shaking, before she gives a barely perceptible nod of her head.

Anger threatens to turn my vision red. A tsunami of rage crashes over me.

"Bron, please. Come back to me. Please. Make me feel good." She guides my finger back to her slit. "Make me forget."

I press my lips back to hers, kissing her with a primal, almost animalistic, need. Her body responds in kind as her tongue tangles with my own.

My thumb brushes over her clit as my fingers begin to scissor in her slick channel, and she gasps into my mouth.

"Come for me, goddess," I whisper against her lips as I press down on the sensitive numb. Tears spill from her eyes as she moans, riding out her pleasure on my still moving fingers. Her white eyes hold mine, trusting me to catch her as she falls.

"Bron," she sighs, pressing a kiss to my sweaty neck. "Let me take care of you."

"No, my love. This was about you." I pull her off the chair and into my lap. Her breasts are still bared to me, tiny marks from my teeth marring the porcelain skin. "You're my queen, my goddess, my life. I'll always take care of you."

She rests her head against my shoulder with a contented sigh.

For the longest time, I believed I had died and gone to

hell. My sister was dead, my mother was depressed, and I was in prison.

But now, with my beautiful mate in my arms, I think I have died and gone to heaven. Currents of happiness spiral through my mind as I kiss the crown of her head.

No one is going to take her away from me. I'll kill anyone who even tries.

CHAPTER 28

NINA

Bronson feels warm. Safe.

With his arms around me, all thoughts fade away until all I can focus on is him. His familiar, comforting scent surrounds me, consumes me. I have the irresistible urge to press my face into his neck and breathe him in.

My body still tingles through the aftershocks of pleasure. It had come out of nowhere, crashing over me like a tidal wave. I felt myself reach the peak of the cliff, but I knew that Bronson would be there to catch me as I fell.

I thought I was too tainted to enjoy such pleasures. I have heard other women ranting and raving about their sexual experiences, but I never even dared to hope. To be intimate with someone you care for, someone you genuinely want in your life, is an indescribable feeling. My heart feels weightless, as if it has suddenly sprouted wings and taken flight in my chest.

My emotions confuse me, unnerve me. Rattle me, in a way, until I'm unrecognizable. Give me the dark any darn day. I know those demons, this taint on my soul. It's the light that petrifies me. It brings me to my knees until I'm a simpering fool. No, allow me to live in the dark, an oblivion I understand, instead of forcing me into the sun.

"You're quiet," Bronson whispers against my head. His large hand is stroking my freshly curled hair as his lips pepper kisses to my scalp. "You don't regret—"

"No," I answer immediately. My heart hammers in my chest, but it's a good pound. An elated one. Emotions surge through me, and I struggle to grasp just one in particular. "No, not at all. It felt...amazing."

More than amazing, actually, but I swear if my cheeks get any hotter, I'll have to go to the hospital. There's a pain between my thighs, but it's a good one—completely different from the first time I was touched there.

"That's all I want for you." Bronson kisses my forehead.

We sit in silence for a minute, but it's not awkward. His presence, his arms around me, and his rhythmic breathing are all comforting.

"Are you sore?" he asks at last.

"A little," I admit, rubbing my thighs together in an attempt to alleviate the ache. "But it's not too bad."

"Goddess," he begins in his grumbly voice, and fireworks shoot through my body—as they always do—at the nickname. I'm many things, but a goddess is most definitely not one of them. "You know I'm a shadow wolf."

When he doesn't say anything immediately, I nod my head slowly, hesitantly. "Yeah?"

"Wolves can be either solitary creatures, or they can move in packs, you understand?" He seems almost uneasy, unsure. I place my hand over his hand still resting on my breast. My touch seems to ground him, and he takes a steadying breath. "My wolf has...for lack of a better word... claimed you as his mate." My breath leaves me in a swooping burst, but he continues before I can cut in. "But he has also claimed a bunch of the assholes here as part of his pack, understand?"

No, not at all.

Bronson's wolf has claimed me as his...mate? What does that mean? Did Bronson claim me as well? Did he even have a choice in the matter? Oh god. Is that why he...pleasured me? Because of his wolf?

Left unattended, my thoughts are running rampant, and Bronson easily picks up on my unease. He places a hand beneath my chin and tilts my face up. Soft, luscious lips press against my own. One would think that they would be hard and chapped from years in this prison, but they're surprisingly smooth.

"I'm your mate?" I whisper, and my heart thunders in both elation and trepidation. The juxtaposed emotions give me a blinding headache.

"Not yet," he replies. Crippling disappointment surges through me, but I mask it quickly. "If I were to bite you..." He trails off. "What I'm saying is: what we did solidified the bond for me. We may not be officially mated, but I want you. I always have, and I always will. But my wolf will not be angry if you decide to also pursue relationships with other members of our pack. *Only* our pack. Do you understand?" Kai's face immediately flashes to mind, followed closely by Abel's and Damien's. Even Cain's comes to the forefront before I push it back.

"Okay," I whisper.

I don't know what else to say. This—all of this—is decidedly not normal. I need time to process all the information he's given me. Bronson has murdered a man, for one, and though the death was deserved, I can't ignore the tiny voice in my head screaming profanities at me for trusting him. I know that not everything is black and white, light and dark, but it would be so much easier if you could separate everything and everyone into individual boxes. Unfortunately, that's not how the world works. You can't judge a man based on one past accident any more than you can judge someone for saving your life in the future. There's a delicate balance between good and evil, right and wrong, and I'm currently toeing that blurred line.

"We should get back to the others," Bronson says, moving me off his lap and kneeling before me. His hands tenderly rearrange my dress around my breasts before he helps me to my feet. He treats me as if I'm fragile. I've never had anyone besides Kai treat me like that before. Though the sensation is unusual, it's one I could get used to.

Bronson leaves the table and food behind, taking my hand in his own. I marvel at how big his palm feels—it swallows mine up whole. Still, there's no denying the innate sense of rightness as we walk down the hall.

His hand belongs in mine.

"Shit," Bronson curses suddenly, tugging me to a stop.

"What?" I drop into his head to get a sense of our surroundings. We're somewhere in the middle of the Labyrinth. In every direction, I see stone walls, rusty lead pipes, and shards of rock.

"I think I took a wrong turn." He sounds hesitant, unsure, as he leads me back in the direction we came from. Water rushes above us from one of the pipes. Urine, blood, and dust barrage me the longer we walk. After taking a few more turns, we end up in the exact same place we were originally.

"We're lost," I point out unhelpfully, and Bronson grunts.

"We're not lost."

"Yes, we are." Tugging on our combined hands, I use them to point at one of the rocks protruding from the wall. "Look at that rock. We passed it two times already."

Every muscle in Bronson's body goes rigid. At first, I'm

confused, wondering if he senses something I don't. As my wits gradually return to me, I realize my mistake instantly.

"Nina," Bronson asks slowly, carefully. He turns his head until I fill up his entire vision. "How can you see the rock?"

I open my mouth, close it, and then open it again. A thousand excuses pop into my head, but I know I can't lie to him. Not after he has been so honest with me.

I open my mouth to confess everything—Kai's wishes be damned—when Bronson suddenly grabs my shoulder and pushes me behind him. I stumble, pressing a palm against the wall to steady myself, as claws extend from the tips of Bronson's fingers.

From this angle, I'm unable to see myself, but I do see the figures approaching us on silent feet.

Five men and one female, all with an elegant, predatory grace. The men are tall and muscular, the ridges of their muscles visible through the thin shirts they wear. The woman doesn't even reach the men's shoulders, and her body is slim and almost delicate. Her elfin face peers first at Bronson and then at me.

"Shifters." Bronson's voice is unrecognizable. Throaty, almost guttural, as if he's speaking around a mouthful of abnormally sharp teeth.

"I'm surprised Blade let you off your leash," the woman says with a lilting laugh. Bronson growls threateningly but doesn't rise to her taunt. "Anyway, we're not here for a fight. You have someone we want. Give us back our leader, and we'll let you live." This is all said with a nonchalant shrug of her shoulders, as if she couldn't give a crap either way.

"Mr. Scruffles?" I break in, and Bronson immediately pushes me farther behind him, shielding me completely with his large, muscular body.

"Who the fuck is Mr. Scruffles?" the woman questions, glancing at her companions. "Have you guys heard of him?"

Turning back towards me, her voice turns mocking. "Little girl, run as fast and far as you can. We don't play well with Blade's bitches. I think he needs to be taught a lesson."

"Run!" Bronson roars.

A flash of light illuminates Bronson's vision a moment before he shifts. The transition is so effortless that, if I were to blink, I would've missed it. One second, a man is standing in front of me, and the next, he's lower to the ground as his wolf breaks free. Without delay, the wolf rears back on his hind legs and pounces.

I remain against the wall, stricken, as I watch his teeth cut through skin and bone. The vision provides me a vivid image of every gruesome detail—the sharp incisors breaking through skin and tendons, the gushing of blood, the open mouth as the man screams for mercy.

A white light shines directly in my eyes—Bronson's eyes—as one of the men pulls out a flashlight.

Distantly, I remember Bronson telling me that his wolf can only come out in the shadows.

With the spotlight on him, Bronson falls to the ground, his vision changing once more as he returns to his human form.

"Nina," he growls, crawling to his hands and knees. His gaze is intent on the man holding him hostage in the flash-light's thin beam. "Run."

And I run.

I pull out of Bronson's head as I run through the twisting cement halls. I pull my dress up, so I don't step on the train, and race around the corner, only to run face-first into a wall.

Wincing at the pain, I press one hand to my forehead and the other to the cold, wet wall. Using it for guidance, I continue to venture forward.

Come on, Nina. Come on.

My ankles throb as I stumble over loose rocks, but still I charge forward. For Bronson.

God, is he okay? Please, please, tell me he's okay.

I left him.

I. Left. Him.

Tears flood my eyes, but I don't allow them to deter me. I need to keep moving; I need to find help. With a purpose in mind, I tentatively venture farther down the Labyrinth's halls.

"Going somewhere?" a cold voice murmurs in my ear. I spin on my heel, throwing a punch at the intruder's throat. Before my fist can make contact, the girl grabs my wrist and gives it a twist. A cracking sound reverberates throughout the hall, and I scream. "Blade is going to pay for taking our leader," she hisses, spit flying into my face. "I hope you have a good stomach for torture, little girl."

I only have a second to pray that Bronson made it out alive before a fist connects with my face.

Darkness claims me.

CHAPTER 29

KAI

Lionel Green is an unassuming, ugly man.

I stare at the picture of him with narrowed eyes, unable to decipher whether he is capable of committing such an atrocious act against Raphael Turner.

Large and pudgy, with red cheeks and greasy hair, there's nothing about Lionel that makes me think he's powerful enough to kill a centuries-old vampire. Sure, he's a shifter, but is an animal really capable of beating a vampire in a fight?

Sighing, I hand the picture back to Maverick.

"Any other news?" I query, leaning back in my chair. The cafeteria is empty at this time of day. No surprise. The second I arrived to hold court, the others scattered like I'd seared their asses with my dragon fire.

"Damien has received a shipment of food and clothes from above," Maverick recites. I nod seriously. I knew Damien had planned to get more supplies for our gang, particularly Nina, from some of his contacts.

"Any shifter attacks?" My hands clenched into fists as I think of the vile, vicious gang. They've been silent, almost unnaturally so, which is especially strange, since we have their leader tied up in our throne room.

"Silent," he says. "But there have been three deaths since yesterday."

"What happened?" I ask, only half listening. Deaths aren't uncommon in the Labyrinth. We lost both men and women every day. It's sad, I suppose, but a necessity. There are checks and balances in every aspect of life. The strong thrive, and the weak succumb to their inevitable fate.

Maverick tells me about the most recent brawl between a werewolf, vampire, and succubus. Both the werewolf and vampire were killed.

Halfway through the story, my mind begins to wander. I can't help but wonder how Bronson's date with Nina is going.

Should I be jealous? Upset? I admit, my emotions are turbulent. A part of me is thrilled that Nina is able to enjoy life after months of captivity, but another part of me is immensely jealous.

Soon, I'll be the one taking her out on ravishing dates. I don't even care that other guys are as well, as long as I'm one of them.

Yeah. I'm pussy-whipped for this girl. My thoughts revolve around her like the earth circles the sun.

"Anything else, sir?" Maverick's words wrench me out of my thoughts. After I wave him away, he nods once before retreating, his metaphorical tail between his legs.

I heave myself off the table I've been perching on, grab an apple from the magical buffet line, then head in the direction of the throne room.

Damien is currently with our resident shifter. Probably has his innards separated from his body by now.

Snort.

I have just turned at a fork in the tunnels when a pungent,

coppery scent assaults me. My vision narrows, nostrils flaring, as I whip my head in the direction of the prominent smell.

Air escapes my lungs in a swooping whoosh as terror fills me.

Bronson places a bloody hand against the wall, stumbling forward. My eyes take only a second to catalog his injuries—bruises and scratches marring his face, torn sleeves, and a twisted ankle—before I'm lunging forward, gripping his shoulders. He hisses out air before facing me directly, eyes wide and wild with panic. Crazed. Feral.

Hints of umber appear in his irises as his wolf shines through.

"Where is she?" I ask slowly. Panic pulsates through my veins, accompanied by a fury unlike anything I have ever felt before.

"They took her," he growls out, saliva dripping from his sharp canines.

"Who? Who fucking took her?"

I'll rip whoever it is limb from limb until they're nothing but a torso and head. Then I'll use my dragon fire to burn off their noses and eyes. I'll leave their mouths, if only to hear their screams of agony.

Bronson's one-word answer causes shards of glass to swirl around in my stomach. "Shifters."

～

"HAVE ANY NINES?"

"This game is stupid."

"Any tens."

"Kai, seriously?" Nina asks, dropping her cards onto the musty cell floor. She stares up at me with blind, milky eyes. "You just like playing this game because you always win. It's not fair. I can't see what the heck I have!"

I chuckle, dropping my own cards onto the floor. She's not wrong. I do love playing this game, but for an entirely different reason. She always gets so flustered and angry, red splotches erupting on both of her cheeks, that I can't help but smile.

Playing Go Fish with a blind girl? I highly recommend it.

Only cold metal bars separate us. I sit cross-legged on one side, while she sits on the other. As always, she's dressed in a flowing white gown, with her black hair loose and wild. Staring at her, I feel something...different. It's no longer just concern and protectiveness that courses through me. For the first time, my body is noticing all her delicate, soft curves and heartbreakingly perfect features.

I yearn to memorize her lips with my own. Trace the contours of her face. Test the weight of each of her heavy breasts. She has always been pretty, but over time, she has become gorgeous.

I'm not the only one who has noticed.

I see how the other men look at her. The guards. Their vile thoughts are depicted in every action they make. Etched into their leering smiles.

Acid churns low in my stomach at the prospect of any of them touching her.

"Kai!" She flicks a card at me, and I blink, coming back to the present. "You're staring at me, and it's weird."

"I'm always staring at you," I admit with an easy-going smile. She giggles, taking my words as a joke, but it's closer to the truth than she knows. When she's gone, my heart cries out for her. I feel physical pain when I think about what she has endured. What she will continue to endure. I want nothing more than to break her out of this hellhole and give her the life of luxury she deserves. A life of fucking roses and chocolates and expensive jewelry.

For now, I'll just have to work on keeping her alive.

Pounding footsteps alert me to the guard a moment before Nina's cell is opened. I jump to my feet, rage burning a fire through my veins, and place my hands on the bars.

Man steps into Nina's cell. Broad-shouldered and dressed in a suit *of black armor, Man is a scary motherfucker. He always wears a dark visor that obscures his features from view. Only Nina has seen him, and she describes him as monstrous. Evil.*

He grips Nina's thin arm, propelling her to her feet, and my girl releases a helpless whimper. Anger like no other burns low in my gut like lava.

"Let her go!" I growl, voice barely recognizable.

Man laughs coldly, ignoring me, and proceeds to lead Nina down the hall to the torture room.

No!

Something breaks inside me—snaps in half—and the next thing I know, claws have ejected from my fingers. Brilliant red scales line the insides of my arms.

My mom always told me stories about my heritage—dragons— but I had never been able to shift before. I was beginning to believe that her stories were fabricated.

I suck in air and then release it with a deafening roar. Fire bursts from my mouth and sets the bars aflame. The metal begins to bend and contort under my assault, smoke filling the air. Both my lungs and throat burn, but I don't let up.

Nina.

I need to get to Nina.

"Hey! Watch it, kid!" a strident voice screams. The door to my cell is wrenched open, and I find myself on my back, a cattle prod electrocuting my stomach. Pain consumes me as a second, then third one joins the first.

Nina.

"He's getting stronger," I dimly hear someone say.

"We can't contain him," someone else agrees.

The very next day, I'm shipped to Nightmare Penitentiary.

~

STOMACH MUSCLES CLENCHING, I STORM INTO THE THRONE room. The door clatters loudly as it closes, the sound almost an ominous warning.

Rion lifts his bloody head, a coy grin playing on his chapped lips. Damien stands just off to the side, absently spinning a blade between his fingers without a care in the fucking world.

Both men freeze at whatever expression they see on my face.

Bronson, behind me, has shifted fully into his wolf. It'll help both alleviate the ache of losing Nina and heal his extensive injuries. In any other circumstance, I'd check on my longtime friend, but I have more important things to focus on.

"Where is she?" I hiss, slamming my fists into Rion's shoulders. There's an audible crack, and there's no doubt they're dislocated, but Rion doesn't even blink.

"What the bloody hell are you talking about?" he asks with genuine curiosity.

"Nina!" I press my thumb into an open wound on his chest.

"Nina?" Damien asks slowly, carefully. His eyes are wide with panic before he quickly schools his features. A muscle in his jaw twitches. The man looks as if he can take on a dozen different men and women...and win. The scary motherfucker grabs a second dagger from inside his sleeve and holds it at the ready. I'm worried he'll kill Rion before I can get information out of him.

"Your shifters took her!" I roar.

My grip on my dragon is fragile, feeble, almost. Trying to stop him is like trying to push the waves back into the ocean. Smoke flares from my nostrils, and I briefly close my eyes, attempting to rein in my beast. I can't help Nina if I'm too fucking big to maneuver the hallways.

"My shifters," Rion repeats, and my eyes snap open. For the first time since I've known him, there's no manic insanity in his forbidding gaze. He twists on the cuffs restraining him, and they snap easily. He falls gracefully to his feet, long chains dragging behind him. Unperturbed, he grabs first one manacle and then the other and snaps them in half.

Shit. The man wasn't kidding. He really could've broken free whenever he fucking wanted to.

"I'll find her," Rion announces darkly, already stalking past me. I move to follow, but Rion whirls on me before I can take more than a step. "They see you, and they'll kill her. No question. If you want to get her out of this alive, you need to fucking trust me."

"I don't trust you."

"You need to," he snaps. "Shifters or not, whoever took her will pay for what they did. And if they hurt her..." He trails off with a dark, raspy laugh. In that moment, I don't see the crazy prisoner we've kept suspended from our ceiling. I see the ruthless, vicious gang member who has created a following that rivals my own.

"I'll go with him," Damien says briskly. His voice leaves no room for argument...not that anyone would argue with him. The man's eyes are devoid of any feeling, any warmth. The eyes of a psychopath.

Rion nods once, already turning on his heel.

I release a guttural roar, my final grip on sanity breaking. As my skin sizzles and expands, I eagerly give in to the shift. My dragon has to crouch to not hit his head on the ceiling.

Bronson's wolf whimpers, attempting to follow Damien and Rion, but because of his disfigured leg, he's unable to.

Nina...

If anyone has hurt her, they'll get to experience the complete and unobstructed wrath of my dragon.

And if Rion betrays me?

Torture doesn't even begin to encapsulate what he will endure.

CHAPTER 30

NINA

I wrap my arms around my knees and sink farther against the wall. A musty, coppery smell perfumes the air, though I can't decipher if it's from the lead pipes on the ceiling or the bloodstain on the ground.

The woman—whose name I discover is Braelyn—had led me through a series of passageways and halls until we ended up in a large room. Dozens of shifters sat ramrod straight when she entered. Somehow, that tiny slip of a female was able to innately command respect from anyone and everyone who stared directly at her. It's the type of power I yearn to have myself. When the shifters turned towards me, their expressions became leery and distrustful. More than one had growled at me.

I was paraded through the throng of unruly men and women until I got to a cage in the corner. Through Braelyn's eyes, I saw the cage wasn't large enough for me to stand in. I doubted I could even sit upright. Rust was beginning to form on the bars, and a puddle of what I hoped wasn't urine dripped over the sides.

Not another cage...

"Please," I had begged desperately, dragging my feet. But my pleas had fallen on deaf ears as I was pushed unceremoniously into the minuscule cell.

Now, I push my consciousness into the nearest shifter's mind, who is sitting indolently on a cafeteria table. At least, that's what I'm assuming the room is used for. Besides the cage in the corner, the rest of the room is filled with long wooden tables easily able to hold a dozen, the kind I'd expect in a cafeteria. Men and women laugh, have sex, and throw punches. For the most part, I'm left alone.

I attempt to make myself as small as possible, placing my head between my knees. Fear thunders through me, and my breathing is labored. Cage after cage after cage. Is that all I'm good for? Being a prisoner? I inconspicuously brush a stray tear away. The last thing I need is to give in to the panic threatening to consume and swallow me whole.

Deep breath.

In and out.

In and out.

In and out.

"What do you plan to do with Blade's whore?" a masculine voice inquires. The rowdy cheers and laughter diminish like a flame being blown out until the room is utterly still and silent. All eyes focus on Braelyn.

She's sitting on one of the tables, her arm around a petite female. Her cold smile is a contrast to her elfin features and tiny stature. This woman is obviously not a stranger to killing. If the flames that enter her eyes are any indication, she revels in it.

"We could kill her," she suggests almost lazily, planting a kiss on her lover's head. Untangling herself from the other woman, Braelyn stands and crosses the room.

I cower, pressing my body flush against the bars.

Deep breaths.

In and out.

In and out.

In and out.

"She's so fucking skittish and weak, it would be like killing a puppy," a man protests.

Braelyn clicks her tongue, kneeling until she's level with me. Her tiny hands slip through the bars and capture both my cheeks, holding me steady. I blink rapidly, attempting to dislodge the tears building.

I can barely hear over the pounding of my heart. Terror clamps down on the organ in an impenetrable iron vise.

Cage after cage after cage.

Always a prisoner.

Always. A. Prisoner.

"Or..." Braelyn touches the skin beneath my right eye. "We could cut out her pretty eyes and send them as a present to Blade." She releases me suddenly, turning back towards the others with a deranged smile on her normally beautiful face.

In the next second, the door to the cage swings open on squeaky hinges. I press myself as far as I can against the corner, but it's not enough. It'll never be enough.

An unfamiliar man reaches for me. Instinctively, I kick my foot out, catching him in the kneecap. My momentary spurt of satisfaction dissipates when he grabs my ankle and drags me out of the cell. My beautiful silver dress pulls up, bunching around my thighs, and tears of mortification burn my eyes.

"Let's teach Blade's bitch a lesson, shall we?" Braelyn says, standing over me with her hands on her hips.

I begin to sob.

I've learned to compartmentalize my pain. Group it into tiny boxes and bury said boxes at the bottom of the ocean.

Experiencing pain doesn't make you weak. It makes you human. How you handle yourself after the fact is what makes or breaks you as a person. Do you give in to your instincts and cry? Do you scream and fight? Do you empty yourself, so you'll feel nothing at all?

There's a delicate balance between being brave and being stupid. Do you dare to fight when you know the outcome will only be worse for you? Is it strength to accept your fate...or is that weakness?

I've learned to embrace my pain. It makes me feel human. It reminds me that I can still feel, still endure.

As Man stands over me, a malicious smile on his lips, I give in to the sensations battering for attention in my head. Blood wells on my leg from his scalpel, eliciting a hiss from my lips, one I quickly smother.

My hands are secured on either side of my body. A thick rope digs into my waist, restraining me.

"Are you going to scream for me, Little Monster?" he asks, red eyes glimmering in the sunlight streaming through the windows. At first, I thought the red eyes were fake, but now, I'm beginning to believe that they're very, very real.

He's a monster, through and through.

"Stop," I say weakly. Tiredly. I poke my tongue out to lick my unbearably dry lips.

"I'm afraid I can't." He tsks. "You're mine, Little Monster. Mine. I created you. Made you. You. Are. Mine."

"I'm nobody's," I manage to stutter out before unconsciousness consumes me.

CHAPTER 31

RION

I am a storm.

I'm the wind rustling the boughs of trees, the lightning striking a deserted plain, and the thunder cackling up above. I'm the rain pelting your face, blurring your vision, and I'm the mud prohibiting forward momentum.

I am wrath. I am rage. I am vengeance personified.

Pace brisk, I hurry down the familiar halls of the Labyrinth. Gray stone walls turn smoother and wetter the farther we venture. Metal and lead pipes line the ceiling, sprouting in all directions. Somewhere in the distance, I can hear a man laughing. A woman's sated moan. Screams.

Damien follows silently behind me, an unwavering shadow. Not my shadow, but Nina's.

"Stay behind me at all times," I instruct curtly. The last thing I need is Blade's lapdog in shifter territory, but I know arguing with the mage would be futile. Damien will not be deterred. "Don't engage. Don't talk. Just shut the hell up."

With a nonchalance I know he doesn't feel, Damien says, "You know, shifter, that I will kill you if anything has happened to her."

My hands clench at the thought before I force myself to relax, my tight body loosening incrementally.

"Don't worry. If she's hurt, I'll help you."

We're silent as we maneuver the maze-like basement. Shifter territory is opposite Blade's. There's an invisible line that no one dares to breach—a red rock that protrudes at an unnatural angle from the stone wall. Crossing said line is a declaration of war.

But it's a line I'll cross a million times if it means being with my fated mate.

I still remember the first time I saw her, despondently leaning against the wall. Her beautiful, heart-shaped face was downcast, but her milky eyes held a fierce determination. For a moment, I merely watched her. I balanced my human body precariously on one of the pipes, peering down at the beautiful female. Something in my chest tightened the longer I looked at her. A knot, almost, with the remainder of the rope connected to her. The longer I stared, the more persistent the tug became before I couldn't resist the urge to crawl towards her.

If my own people have hurt her...

I don't know what I'll do.

They better fucking hope they can run fast enough.

Whistling beneath my breath, I shove my hands into my pockets and hesitate at a fork in the wall.

"Left or right?" I ask Damien, and the scary man scoffs.

"You don't fucking know?" he roars.

I hold my hands up placatingly. "Calm your titties, magic boy. No one knows where to go in the Labyrinth," I say, staring down one direction and then the other. Both seem to go on forever—an endless black abyss you could get lost in.

Is Nina down one of them, scared to death? Is she hurt?

My thoughts begin to swirl like a damn whirlpool, and I know they will only be settled by her magnetic presence.

"Let's go," Damien growls, shoving past me and walking down the right tunnel. I follow behind, my claws digging into the stone and leaving behind a trail.

After a few more right turns, we enter a cavernous room that serves as our cafeteria. Or, at least, one of them. We have three on our side of the prison, and Blade has two. This is the smaller one I took Nina to so many days ago.

Long, wooden tables are evenly distributed in the center of the room, all of them occupied. There's a hole in the right wall, leading to a makeshift kitchen. While the cafeteria itself is powered by magic, capable of creating food whenever anyone enters its walls hungry, most of my shifters prefer to make their own. Only a year ago, we tore a hole in the wall and bribed the guards to provide us with stoves, microwaves, and other stainless-steel appliances.

Rowdy shifters talk amongst themselves. Some are in human form, fighting and fucking, while others are animals. I spot a monkey hanging from the pipes and an alligator resting in the corner.

A single cage is against the wall at the front of the room, the door hanging open on its hinges. It was my idea to have it in plain view of everyone. A way to shame and demean the person in question. Normally, we reserve it for out-of-control shifters or murderous assholes.

If they shoved Nina into that fucking cage, I'll kill them all.

The shifters go deathly silent as I stalk forward, bending down to stare into the cage. Tapping into my enhanced senses, I inhale deeply. Piss, blood, and mold permeate the air. Underneath it all, subdued, is the familiar floral scent of my precious mate.

Fucking hell. Murder spree it is, I suppose.

Growls reverberate behind me, low and threatening. No doubt, Damien has entered the room as well. I glance over my shoulder as the tall, slender man moves forward with a grace and elegance that belies his predatory nature. He doesn't seem at all perturbed that he has basically entered the lion's den. Those cold, dead eyes of his survey each and every face with unwavering intensity. More than one shifter blanches, lowering their head.

Maybe Blade did something right keeping Damien on hand. I can see how appealing it can be to have my very own psychopath at my beck and call.

At that moment, he's not the prey, but the apex predator.

"The prisoner who was here..." I nod towards the empty cage. "Where is she?" My voice is low and quiet, but it carries in the room as if I've been screaming. The dominance I exude is capable of bringing grown-ass men to their knees. Shifters, like all animals, follow a certain hierarchy. Power is key. You're a predator or you're prey. There is no fucking in between.

I have always, and will always, be the predator. The tiger pursuing the tasty selection of morsels spread out before him. The hunter. The monster.

Her monster.

One of the men, an avian shifter, points towards the far hallway leading to the cells.

Without another word, I storm in that direction, not bothering to check if Damien is following me. For all I know, he was feeling cute and decided to get stabby.

Square cells are evenly spaced three feet apart. Some are nicer than others, bedecked in clean sheets, carpeting, and have a separate room for toilets and showers. Others are nothing but gray boxes with a sleeping mat, one scratchy blanket, and a chamber pot.

As I said before, there's a hierarchy.

We pass a couple fucking, and both immediately cover themselves when we stalk by, eyes wide with fear. A bear shifter rears back on his hind legs when we invade his space, pauses, then ducks his head in submission.

At the end of the hall, we veer to the right and to a familiar block of cells. My inner circle.

Jerome, Klaus, Manny, and Braelyn. Four of the most ruthless, vicious shifters I have ever laid eyes on. They had arrived in the Labyrinth with chips on their shoulders, and I had worked tirelessly to fuel their anger and rage. I provided the tinder in order to create a brilliant, all-consuming fire.

And while they're loyal, they're also fierce haters of Blade and his gang. If they've gotten to Nina...

Cursing, I pick up my pace, shoving lone shifters out of the way. Damien, sensing my unease, moves to stand beside me, a dagger in each hand. I don't bother to tell him to hang back; the man needs blood just as much as I do.

The door swings open on silent hinges, and the sight in front of me makes my blood run cold. The ice squeezes my heart, crushing it.

My mate—my motherfucking mate—is tied to a table in the center of the room. Her black curls are matted with dirt and sweat, cascading off the side. Her eyes are closed, head lolled to the side. A form-fitting silver dress is ripped, revealing her creamy white thigh. Dirt discolors her beautiful face.

Standing around her are members of my inner circle. Braelyn is smiling slightly, a knife held loosely in her hand. Jerome and Klaus rest against the door, the latter appearing uneasy. Manny is tying the last rope around her ankle.

"You have three seconds to move before I kill you," Damien says in a deathly calm voice. Braelyn's head whips up, and she flashes me a smug smile. That smile falters when she catches sight of first my—and then Damien's—expression.

"Rion. You're back," she breathes. Manny drops Nina's

ankle, slowly backing up. Smart man, going under the assumption that he values his good-for-nothing life.

And...

Just kidding.

Damien's knife embeds itself cleanly in Manny's eye. The shifter's mouth opens in shock, blood gurgling, before he falls to the ground, dead.

"Anyone else?" the mage asks, holding up his second knife. Jerome and Klaus turn on their heels and run out the door.

They can run... It'll make the hunt all the more exciting later on.

Braelyn hisses, feline eyes hurling daggers at me.

"Rion!" Her voice is high-pitched in accusation and anger. "How could you?" Normally, I would have agreed with her. What leader shows up at their home with the enemy? But alas, I'm going to have to murder her, which is a shame. She was a damn good vice president.

"Step away from my mate," I whisper darkly.

Braelyn's eyes widen almost imperceptibly, flickering between me and Nina and then back to me. Slowly, she backs away, hands raised, as if fending off a dangerous predator.

A funny and accurate analogy, if I do say so myself.

"Mate?" she asks, notable terror in her voice. Good. She should be afraid. Friend or not, she was going to hurt my mate. Hell, she might've hurt her already.

"Why else do you think I've been gone for so long?" I purr, stepping forward.

"I thought—"

"Lies. You have no thoughts. I imagine it's kind of lonely in that little head of yours." I rap my knuckles against her forehead, and she winces, despite the fact I hardly applied pressure. Braelyn really has been an asset to the team. It's such a shame I have to kill her. "You don't ever question my decisions, Brae." I tilt her chin up to meet her eyes directly. "I told you I would be gone for the foreseeable future. I told you the reasons were personal. You had one job to do and one job only: look after this place and my people." I tighten my grip on her—not to the point of pain, but enough to get my point across.

"We came across an opportunity," she stutters out. "Our sources told us that this girl is Blade's lover—"

"Shifters have been known to share their mate," I cut in, giving her a pointed stare. Her eyes widen at my revelation, but smartly, she doesn't respond. "From now on, we will work on making peace with Blade's people. Blah, blah, blah. I'm boring myself with this talk."

"Can we kill her?" Damien cuts in savagely.

I glance over my shoulder as the mage steps back into the room, dripping with blood. I didn't even hear him leave. Interesting. He really lives up to his reputation: an esteemed serial killer and assassin. I'll give him a solid five-star Yelp review.

"Did you just kill my last two inner circle members?" I ask, morbidly curious but not at all upset. I'm actually a little peeved I didn't get to kill them myself. Sigh. Another day.

Damien shrugs once before moving towards Nina's side. He lifts a hand, as if to stroke her hair before immediately lowering it. Instead, his eyes caress her body with a warmth that melts his frosty exposition. Awww. The little psychopath actually has a heart. I'm touched.

"Now, how should we kill you?" I muse, turning my attention back to Braelyn. She trembles, her fear contaminating the small, barren room. Fear always has a distinct scent—a heady combination of sweat and piss.

"Don't," a frail voice calls, and I spin towards Nina, my mate. Her blind eyes are open and staring at a spot on my shoulder. She opens her mouth, snaps it closed, and then opens it once more. "Don't... Don't kill her."

CHAPTER 32

NINA

There's a stillness to the air, like the calm before an impending storm. I feel it sweep over my legs and arms, an almost palpable entity, before settling on my chest. There's no pressure, no weight. It just sits there like an uncomfortable pest I'm unable to remove. I would almost describe it as a feeling. What that feeling is, I can't say.

Time is momentarily suspended as I float in this strange, in-between place. Darkness consumes my vision, but it's not frightening. Sometimes, I embrace the dark because the light is too much for me to handle.

Slowly, I regain feeling in my body. My wrists and ankles burn fiercely, but the pain is dull in comparison to what I have felt before. My mind feels groggy, sluggish, like it's full of cotton balls.

I extend my senses outwards, aware of hands removing the ropes from my ankles.

What....?

Who...?

The last thing I remember is being dragged out of the

cage by an unfamiliar male while Braelyn watched in morbid amusement. And then...nothing.

I push my awareness into the nearest person's head to see him staring down at me. My face is sweaty and pale, dark bags beneath both my eyes. The makeup Rebecca applied is now smeared, giving me a distinct raccoon quality. My black hair is tangled, and the gorgeous silver dress is ripped down the sides.

As his hands diligently work to untie me, I realize that my savior is Damien. He's the only man I know who wears a pressed black suit with white cufflinks.

I want to thank him for coming for me, for saving me, but the words get lost in my throat. Damien's a lot of things—most of them terrifying—and I'm not sure how he'll take my gratitude.

Mr. Scruffles's accented voice penetrates the fog in my brain.

I whip my head in his general direction, unable to see him with Damien's gaze firmly on me.

"Now, how should we kill you?" His dark tone sends prickles of unease up and down my spine. I've heard his voice high-pitched from laughter, I've heard him teasing, but I've never heard him so mad before. If Damien is ice, Rion is fire.

Finally, Damien lifts his head to stare in the cat shifter's direction.

Rion has his hands on either side of Braelyn's face, holding her steady. The female shifter is trembling, eyes cloudy with terror. I don't like that. Not one bit.

Yes, the woman was going to torture me, maybe kill me, but I'm not about to condone Rion's decision to kill her.

"Don't..." I say weakly. His head swivels in my direction, and relief dances in his eyes. That relief seems to soften his harsh, masculine features. "Don't... Don't kill her."

"Buttercup," Rion breathes, stepping closer to me. I flinch away immediately. I'm familiar with the cat, but the man is a stranger, one I have only spoken a few words to.

A flicker of pain crosses Rion's handsome, exotic features before he hides it behind his signature, manic grin. With his attention no longer on her, Braelyn steps backwards until her body is against the stone wall.

"Rion," I whisper, unable to attribute my cat to this hulking beast of a man. With his sleeves pushed up, I can see the tattoos covering his muscular biceps. His dark hair is slightly greasy, and his face is a canvas of bruises and slashes.

What the heck happened to him?

"Are you hurt? How do you feel?" Rion steps even closer until he's hovering over the table. He lifts a hand, as if he means to brush at my mangled hair, before dropping it. Indecision flares to life in his bright eyes.

"I'm okay."

Damien's gaze lowers, so it's once more on me. It's the strangest sensation to know you're the sole focus of two powerful, larger-than-life men. I know they're seeing everything—the fear I can't quite hide in my eyes, the scrapes on my arms from when I was dragged out of the cage, the blood still coating my scalp. Damien, especially, seems to see more than the average person. I'm stripped bare when his penetrating gaze is on me.

"Since you're okay, I'm just going to kill this bitch, and then we'll leave, m'kay?" Rion says with a jovial laugh. "I want you to be looked over by a doctor—"

"We have someone," Damien cuts in scathingly. His gaze lowers to my collarbone as his rough thumb traces a pattern only he can see.

"Oh. Of course. What's yours is mine, mi amigo. Why am I even speaking Spanish? Or is that French? You know what?

Never mind," Rion rambles, some of his trademark cheer returning.

"We hate the fucking shifters." Damien scoffs, bending down to scoop me up. I brace myself for the impending flashback, for the memories to bombard me, but when they don't, I breathe out a sigh of relief. I don't know if that means I'm healing or that Damien makes me feel safe. Both options terrify and exhilarate me.

"Well, suck a duck, Mage Bitch. We need to start working together now. We have a common goal, and I don't know about you, but I'm not giving my Buttercup up for anything or anyone. Get it? Got it? Good. Besides, we totally had a bonding moment earlier. A bromance. I think we should have a ship name. Dion? Ramien?" Rion continues to babble incessantly as Damien's eyes leave mine to face the enigmatic shifter.

Rion is once again hovering above Braelyn, claws extended. He's humming softly as he prepares to make the fatal blow.

"Rion!" I scream, and once more, the shifter pauses. "Please. Don't. Hurt. Her." I emphasize each word separately as my heart thunders in my chest. "Please. I can't take any more violence."

He whirls towards me with lethal intensity in his gaze. His abrupt change in mood reminds me of a flip being switched on and then off. There's something tenuous about the hold he has on himself. Something fragile.

"She was going to hurt you! She was going to take you from me!" he hisses, and despite his ire not being directed at me, I press myself farther against Damien's chest. Upon seeing my flinch, Rion physically works to calm himself. A deep breath. An unclenching of first one fist and then the other.

"If you kill her, I'll never forgive you," I whisper. I don't know if my words will hold any weight—we're virtual strangers, after all—but I know that they mean something to me. He was my first friend in this hellhole. My only friend. Yes, he lied to me, omitted important details, but he still protected me.

With a start, I realize I *want* to get to know him, both his beast and the man who tames it.

For a prolonged moment, he merely stares at me. Silence stretches between us before he sighs heavily, retracting his claws and stepping away from the trembling female.

"By the decree of my Buttercup, you are spared. Blah. Blah. Blah." Rion steps around the table towards me and Damien.

"Thank you," Braelyn stutters out. "I am forever in your debt. I am yours to do with as you please. Protect. Fight. Whatever you need."

"Just stay the hell out of my way," Rion says cheerfully, stopping in front of me to pet my cheek.

"Not you," Braelyn hisses. Her tear-filled gaze turns in my direction, awe, wonderment, and fear battling for dominance. "Hers. I am her loyal servant."

"Me?" I squeak, wiggling in Damien's arms. The mage glances at me before focusing intently on Braelyn, eyes narrowed in what I suspect is suspicion. Through his gaze, I watch Braelyn bow her head submissively.

"You need a protector—"

"She has a protector," Damien says through clenched teeth.

Braelyn continues, as if he hadn't spoken. "And a friend. I can be that for you."

My heart warms at her declaration. Besides Tessa, I don't have a lot of female friends. In a world as gruesome as this one, I need all the friends I can get.

"You can't trust her, Angel," Damien whispers softly.

"You can, actually," Rion cuts in, sighing deeply. "Shifters are able to pledge loyalty to one person. It's why we're often kept as bodyguards and assistants. If Braelyn pledges her fidelity to Nina, she'll never be able to hurt her, and she'll be bound to protect her at all costs."

"A bodyguard," Damien muses, his voice thawing marginally as he warms up to the idea.

"And since both Rion and I are important figures in the shifter community down here," Braelyn cuts in, "no one will be stupid enough to harm her. On *our* side, at least."

Damien ignores her jab, his arms tightening around me like steel bands.

"What do you think, Buttercup?" Rion peers down at me curiously. His hand brushes at my hair, pushing it behind my ear.

"Bring her with us," Damien breaks in before I can answer. "We'll talk to the others." He focuses on the small female. From this angle, I can't imagine her being a bodyguard, let alone a fighter. She's petite, and her features are child-like. Yet, there's a glint in her eyes that hints at an underlying coldness. This girl won't hesitate to do what needs to be done.

"But just a warning, my old friend," Rion says with a grin. Braelyn gulps once before steeling herself, meeting his gaze head on. "The others aren't very nice to shifters. They don't believe in friendship bracelets. So, if you're serious about this, be prepared for a lot of *hanging* around." He laughs at some joke I don't quite understand.

Braelyn nods her head once, a barely visible jerk of her chin.

"I'll go. And I'll protect her from all of you assholes." With that declaration, she stalks forward, tossing her hair over her shoulder.

Is it wrong that I'm beginning to like this girl? The same girl who intended to torture me?

Yes, it's most definitely wrong, but I can't find the will to care. Having her as a friend might just save not only my life, but the lives of my men as well.

CHAPTER 33

NINA

When we step back into the cafeteria, all eyes immediately turn in our direction. An array of emotions is visible on each of their faces. Fear, respect, and anger are the most prominent.

I notice, somewhat dizzily, that the man who dragged me out of the cage is leaning against the wall, his throat slit. I have no doubt which man was behind his demise.

Surprisingly, the thought that Damien killed this man on my behalf doesn't terrify me. Does that make me a horrible person? I was scared when Rion threatened to kill Braelyn, but seeing this man dead sends a wave of cool satisfaction through me. I don't even dare to begin analyzing my emotions.

Damien, whose head I'm still in, turns towards Rion and Braelyn. The two step forward in unison, proud sets to their chins and steely eyes.

"Nina is under our protection," Rion says in a cold voice. Braelyn nods in the affirmative.

"You're choosing Blade's whore over us?" a shifter exclaims, and Rion charges forward, preparing to strike.

But before he can, Braelyn has her claws pressed to the unruly shifter's neck. "You dare to question your king?" Without waiting for his response, she swipes her claws across his throat. His hands move to cover the slashes, blood welling, before he collapses. "Anyone else have something to say?"

When no one moves, Braelyn huffs, stalking toward the pretty girl I saw with her earlier. She grabs the girl's hand, whispers something in her ear, then pulls her to me.

"I'm Jenny," the new girl says in a soft, almost timid, voice. "I, too, pledge my allegiance to you. Thank you for saving my mate." Her emerald eyes turn in Braelyn's direction, as if she holds the moon and stars. Nothing but love emits from her gaze.

"Are you sure you want to do that?" Rion asks, moving to stand in between us. He settles a hand on my thigh, squeezing once. "With this type of bond, you'll be obligated to put Nina's life before your own and each other's."

Braelyn and Jenny exchange an eloquent look before turning back towards Rion in unison. "We're sure," Braelyn answers for both of them, and Jenny nods her head once in agreement.

I yearn to have that sort of connection with someone. A bond and trust that courses through my veins and seeps into my bone marrow. For someone to stare at me as if I'm their entire world.

I'm shaken out of my musings by Damien carrying me out of the cafeteria and into the Labyrinth.

"Are you sure you're okay, Angel?" he asks once we're far enough away from the others to not be overheard.

I consider his question seriously, taking a moment to catalog my injuries. Though the skin on both my wrists and ankles burn, there are no noticeable marks. There's a slight throbbing in my head, but nothing overwhelming. Mostly, I

merging me beneath the ocean line. I take one last breath
before I allow the water to carry me away.

I'M PULLED OUT OF MY SLUMBER BY A NOSE NUZZLING MY hand. A familiar whine greets me.

Bronson.

A moment later, human flesh replaces coarse fur as I'm ripped from Damien's arms.

"You're okay. You're okay. You're okay," Bronson murmurs repeatedly, burying his face in my hair. He rocks me gently, side to side. The original darkness creeping on me like a phantom dissipates the longer I'm in my protective wolf's arms.

"I'm okay, Bron. I'm okay."

He releases a breath, body shuddering, before his entire body goes rigid. I push myself into his head to see what has ensnared his attention.

Bronson's gaze is fixed firmly on Jenny and Braelyn, the latter of which meets his stare with a defiant one of her own.

"I'm going to kill you," Bronson roars, blowing the tiny hairs at the base of my neck. I fist my hands on his chest, both keeping him with me and grounded to the present, as well as stopping his pursuit of Braelyn.

"No," I say firmly, pressing a chaste kiss to his cheek. "Trust me."

"Isn't this adorable?" Rion asks cheerfully. He bounces from foot to foot. "All my people are getting along. I could write a sonnet right now."

"We're not your people, shifter scum," Bronson spits out, and I inwardly wince at the venom in his tone.

Ignoring the men, Braelyn steps forward and raises her chin. Her eyes spew fire as she focuses first on Rion and then on Bronson. Finally, her eyes rest on me. "My mate and I have sworn our loyalty to your mate, Nina. She saved my life, and I hope to return the favor."

I know Bronson thinks I'm his mate, but I can't ignore my feelings for the other men. Is it possible for someone to have more than one? What does it mean for all my relation-ships? Right now, I'm so relieved that he's alive and well that I can't resist tracing the contours of his bare, broad shoulders. Bronson wrenches his gaze away from Braelyn to pepper kisses on my neck. It's an oddly arousing sensation to see the pathway his lips take across my skin.

Pulling out of Bronson's head, I settle in Braelyn's. Her gaze encompasses the entire room we have found ourselves in. Rion is standing over Bronson's shoulder, a surprisingly tender expression on his handsome face as he considers me. Damien has his arms crossed, stone-faced, a frigid aura emanating from him.

"Bambi!" a voice screams from down the hall. A moment later, the twins appear in the doorway. Abel has a bright smile on his face, eyes glimmering, while Cain's expression is as stoic as usual. Though, I could've sworn I saw his body sag in relief when he caught sight of me.

Abel races forward and pulls me off Bronson's lap—ignoring his growl—and spins me in a circle. A laugh escapes, unbidden, at his antics. I can always count on cheerful Abel to pull me out of whatever mood I'm in. He's light personi-fied, the sunlight I so desperately need to not only survive but thrive.

"You need to learn how to fight," Damien cuts in suddenly. "By the time I'm done with you, you'll know a thou-sand different ways to incapacitate a man with your bare hands."

My body goes taut as I process his words. Me? Fighting? Before, I would've laughed at the absurdity of such a state-ment. Now, with both fear and adrenaline pulsing through me, I find myself nodding eagerly. I don't want to have to rely on others to save me. I have spent enough time as the damsel in distress.

Maybe I should be stronger. Maybe I should learn to

fight. That isn't to say I'm not going to need someone to save me every once in a while, but maybe, in the long run, I can learn to do the saving myself. It'll be a process—a long, drawn-out one—but a process I'm willing to endure.

And sometimes, your biggest strength is trusting others to shoulder half of the burden. You still feel the weight, the pressure, but it's not nearly as overwhelming.

"I want my angel to bathe in the blood of her enemies," Damien says stoutly.

Abel blinks at the mage. "I know what you're going for, man, but you needed to dial it down a notch. You're here." He moves his hand above his head. "And you need to be here." He lowers it to his chest. "Remember what we talked about: girls don't like crazy."

The glare Damien throws him is capable of cutting glass.

"Guys, we do have a problem," Cain cuts in, casting me an anxious glance. Braelyn immediately drops Jenny's hand and moves to stand beside me, knife at the ready. Cain's eyes flicker to her and narrow before settling once more on me.

"What kind of problem?" I ask, abusing my lower lip with my teeth.

"A fifteen-foot, scaly kind." Cain steps forward to grab my hand and pull me down the hall. I mentally squeal at his initiation of contact but manage to keep my face blank. I slip out of Braelyn's mind and comfortably settle in Cain's.

The sex demon leads me to the opulent throne room just as a deafening roar echoes from all around me.

"Are you fucking kidding me?" Braelyn interjects before I can enter. "You're going to make her enter a room with an out-of-control dragon?"

"He won't hurt her." Cain dismisses her concern with absolute certainty. "But she's the only one who can bring him back. Think you can talk some sense into him, Trouble?" He gives my hand a squeeze, and warmth migrates to the center of my chest.

"I'll try," I agree tentatively. None of the guys seem worried, and that bolsters my confidence.

Taking a deep breath, I push open the heavy doors and listen to them thud shut behind me.

I pull out of Cain's head—now on the other side of the closed door—and embrace the darkness. Welcome it like an old friend.

"Kai," I whisper as another roar sounds from directly in front of me. I take a timid step closer, followed by another one. My hands are outstretched in front of me as I rely on my other senses.

A moment later, my searching fingers connect with something cold and scaly. Warm air blows back my dark hair.

Kai.

No, his dragon.

"Kai?" I whisper. Another burst of air is the only reply I receive. "Malakai, you need to come back to us. To me. Can you do that? Please?" I stroke his scaly muzzle as warm air continues to waft across my face.

In the next second, his scales shift into skin as iron bands wrap around my torso. My hands shake slightly as I rub his now-human back.

Despite him being back in human form, his words are audibly beast-like when he speaks next. "*You. Are. Mine.*"

CHAPTER 34

NINA

"Kai," I whisper, unable to say anything else. He's all I can sense, all I can breathe. His tangy scent invades my lungs as I inhale sharply.

"Mine," he growls again in an unexpected spurt of possessiveness. His large hands capture my shoulders, holding me steady. "Say it. Say that you're mine."

I consider my answer very carefully. He reminds me of a ticking time bomb, one second from detonating. Though I can't see him, I can feel the tension in every line of his rigid body.

My disappearance shook him. Bled him. There's something distinctly primal in his actions now.

"I'm not just yours," I reply at last, and when his hands tighten, I fear I said the wrong thing. After a moment, he loosens his steel grip and presses his forehead to my own.

"Even a little piece of you is better than no piece at all," he whispers, breath fanning across my lips. "You can be mine...but you can also be theirs."

I'm left speechless by his words, my jaw dropping.

Surely, he can't mean what I think he means?

"Nina…" He cups my cheek tenderly, reverently. I know that, if I were to go into his head, I would see only myself. His eyes are a physical caress on my suddenly overheated skin. "Can I kiss you?"

I swear my brain forgets to function as my breath leaves me. This proud, beautiful man is asking for a kiss from me, as if it's the only thing he needs. The only thing he wants.

Kai. My first true friend—my best friend. My protector.

"Kiss me," I agree breathlessly.

Still, he hesitates, lips hovering over mine.

"If you need me to stop…" He trails off, continuing to knead both of my shoulders.

"I'll tell you," I say instantly. And I know he would, no matter how far along we were.

His lips are tentative against mine at first. Soft and careful, as if he's afraid the slightest pressure will break me. It's such a contrast to Bronson's heated, desperate kisses—though I can't compare.

I place my hands on his shoulders, trail them down to his biceps, and then raise them once more. I repeat this pattern three times as we exchange the most innocent, sweetest kisses imaginable.

At this moment, it's not just lust, though there's plenty of that too. It's a merging of souls reconnecting after years apart.

I reluctantly pull away, my lips tingling from his kiss. *His kiss.* How many times have I imagined this exact moment? It's even sweeter, better, than I had hoped.

"Nina…" He caresses the skin of my neck, each touch sending lightning through my veins. My body feels as if it's on fire, as if the heat his dragon emits is palpable.

"I need to shower," I reply, brushing my thumb over his plump lower lip. "I'm gross and sweaty and bloody."

"You're perfect," he declares immediately.

A swarm of butterflies escapes in my chest, fluttering their wings in tandem to my rapidly beating heart. Kai has always made me feel valuable and loved. In his arms, there's not a storm we can't face.

"I'm gross," I counter with a giggle. "There's a lot we need to talk about." Pressing my forehead against his, I lean closer, our lips a hairsbreadth away.

"We'll talk," he agrees at last. With a pained groan, he steps away from me. "But just remember, Nina. You're mine." His husky voice causes flames to burn throughout my body, filling the space with a cloistering heat.

But his possessiveness doesn't scare me. If anything, it only reinforces what I already know.

Maybe, just maybe, I've always been his.

KAI LEADS ME TO HIS PRIVATE BATHROOM, THROUGH A door in the throne room. After quickly relieving myself, I fumble into the shower and scrub myself raw. Kai provides me with a fluffy towel, a change of clothes, and a shampoo bottle.

When I finally force myself out from under the spray, I feel relatively human again. The last few hours are nothing but a horrible dream. A nightmare.

Dressing in the satin white nightgown Kai has provided me, I drape the towel over the sink and step back into the throne room.

It's silent when I enter, eerily so. I push myself into the nearest mind, marginally surprised that only one person is here with me. The tattooed sleeves crossed over his chest allow me to see that the man is Kai.

"Where are the others?" I query. Through his vision, I see myself step closer. My dark hair cascades down my back in wet curls, and my face is devoid of the makeup Rebecca had applied earlier.

"I sent them away," Kai announces quietly. His eyes track me—a lion hunting a gazelle—as I perch on his throne against the far wall of the room. "I told the twins to make rooming arrangements for...Braelyn and her mate." His voice lowers to a rough tenor as he speaks about my kidnapper.

"And Rion?"

Kai's head dips once as he nods. "We set him up in a room as well. As far away from you as fucking possible."

I want to scoff at his overprotectiveness but wisely remain silent. Rion will never hurt me, but Kai doesn't know that. Heck, even *I* don't know how I know that. It's the same sixth sense that made me comfort a little boy so many years ago in the Compound.

"We haven't really talked since you've been here," Kai says. He doesn't take a step towards me, but I feel his daunting presence almost physically.

"We talk all the time," I point out.

"Not about what's important." Finally, he moves forward until he's leaning over me. His eyes focus on my lips before moving up, staring in first one eye and then the other. "I never meant to leave you."

His voice is like a cold trail of water sliding down my back.

"At the Compound?" I whisper, anxiety clouding my face.

"I've known about the supernatural world since I was a young boy," he admits, dropping to the ground. This position puts his face at level with my breasts—he's intimidatingly tall, while I'm painfully short. "My family is descended from dragons. The last of our kind. I was kidnapped from my mother when she took me to the fucking supermarket." He releases a humorless laugh. "If that isn't a fucking cliché, I don't know what is. Kidnapped at the supermarket."

"Why didn't you tell me?" Tears burn my eyes, but I refuse to let them fall. Instead, they hang suspended on my eyelashes like raindrops. In a matter of seconds, he has ripped the security straight out from underneath me. I'd thought I wasn't alone during my years at the Compound. I'd thought that Kai was stumbling blindly through the dark with me.

Stupid, stupid me.

I'm the only one with lost vision.

"I thought... I wanted to protect you."

"By keeping me in the dark?" I snap back. "Because, Kai, as someone who has spent her entire life in the dark, it's not that fun." Rage swirls low in my stomach like a tsunami. It courses through my bloodstream. Interwoven with the rage is betrayal. Disappointment.

Crippling loneliness.

"I was a little boy, baby," Kai pleads, taking hold of my hands. I immediately pull away, his touch too much. "I was a stupid little boy who wanted to be your knight in shining armor. I wanted—no, I *needed*—to protect you. You're my mate. When I started showing signs of being more powerful than them, they took me away. Took me from you." His voice lowers to a whisper, but it echoes in the cavernous room.

"Why...why does everyone keep saying that? That I'm their mate? Bronson. Rion. You. What does it mean?" My fingernails dig into my palms. That one simple word causes goose bumps to bloom across my skin. My heart gains wings and flies around my rib cage.

Kai unclenches my fists, dropping his gaze to my hand. It's soft and delicate compared to his. Despite all I've endured, my hands have remained relatively clean. They're not as tainted as the rest of me.

"It means you're made for me, and I'm made for you. It means you're mine to protect and love and cherish. It means that I'll never leave you again, that I'll go to the ends of the earth for you. That not even bars can keep us apart. It means that I'm yours, despite you deserving ten times better than a monster like me."

His eyes lift to my face, my lips, and an insatiable hunger fills me. I pull out of his head, embracing my customary darkness, and smash my lips to his in a feverish kiss.

He freezes beneath my assault, hands stilling on my own, before he wraps them around my waist and pulls me to him. I lower myself onto his lap, kneeling on either side of his thighs, and brush my fingers through his hair. It's getting longer now, the strands cascading through my fingers like silk.

I... I want him.

That thought pierces me with its intensity. I want him in the same way I wanted Bronson only earlier today.

"Nina...my Nina," he murmurs against my lips. Dozens of fires blossom through my body, a bomb exploding, and I embrace the sensations they evoke within me.

"Yours," I agree, because at that moment, I am completely.

He lowers us both to the ground, me still on top of him, and slowly begins sliding down the straps of my nightgown.

"Is this okay?" He pauses with bated breath, awaiting my permission. When I nod, leaning down to kiss him again, he places a gentle hand on my chest. "I need to hear your words, Babygirl."

"Yes, Kai. Yes."

He pushes down my dress until my breasts are revealed. I didn't bother to wear a bra after my shower, and my nipples are currently beaded nubs.

"Do you know how often I imagined this?" he whispers, trailing kisses down my neck and to my aching breasts. I moan as he captures first one peak and then the other in his mouth.

"Kai..."

"Say my name again, Babygirl. Say it."

"Kai." I pull his lips back to mine, sliding my dress down the rest of the way. I shift my body awkwardly to kick it off my ankles. Through it all, Kai never breaks our heated kiss. "You. Can't. Leave. Me. Again." I punctuate each word with a kiss to his lips.

"Never," he agrees.

I lower my hands to his broad shoulders, memorizing the contours of his muscular chest. Shakily, I begin to unbutton his shirt, desperate to feel his heated skin against my own.

Kai doesn't rush me as I take my time removing his garment. He continues to leisurely caress my sides and breasts, never touching me where I need him to.

When I reach the final button, he slides the sleeves down his arms and takes my hands in his, bringing them to his chest.

"Touch me." His voice is half a whisper and half a plea.

I take my time mapping out every tight muscle and the grooves of scars. I don't need sight to know that he's beautiful.

"I made a lot of mistakes in my life," he whispers hoarsely as I bend my head to kiss his chest. "But loving you isn't one of them."

His words give me a pause. My lips pause their trajectory across his expansive planes.

"You love me?" I can scarcely breathe. Having someone love me, having *him* love me, is all I've ever wanted. I've spent my entire life as a prisoner to not only my surroundings, but my own mind as well. It was a loveless, lonely existence, bathed in darkness and shadows, with Kai's presence the only bright spot in my life. A part of me has loved him since that first day, when I recognized him in myself.

"More than anything."

Our lips meet once more as Kai fumbles with the button

on his pants. One moment, there's rough denim beneath my legs, and the next, it's prickly skin. I tense, my breath coming in quick bursts, as memories from the past drag me down like a pit of quicksand.

"What's the matter, Little Monster?" Man caresses my cheek before lowering his hand to my naked chest. "You don't want to play with me?"

"Nina! Nina!" Kai's desperate voice pulls me out of my flashback. I'm trembling, cocooned in his vise-like arms. "Shit, I'm sorry. I'm so fucking sorry."

I take a deep breath to steady myself, to ground myself in the present.

I'm not there. I'm here. With Kai. Who loves me.

I'm safe.

"I'm okay," I assure him. "I'm okay." I grasp his cheeks firmly between my hands. "I don't want to stop."

"You just had a fucking flashback." His voice is heavy with horror and pain. "I don't want our first time to be because you feel like you need to or some shit."

"I don't feel like I need to do anything." I brush my thumb across his lips. "I want to. With you. It's not just because I'm trying to trade that bad memory with a good one, though I admit that might be part of it. It's because I love you." He releases a shuddering breath at my confession, arms tightening. "I love you, and I want you."

"I haven't ever..." He trails off, and I imagine that, if I were to see him, he would be blushing. My own cheeks catch fire when I realize what he means.

"Not ever?"

With my hands still on his cheeks, I feel him shake his head adamantly. "No. I was a young boy when I was brought to the Compound, and after I left, I didn't want to. You're it for me, Babygirl. You're my queen." He lowers his forehead to my shoulder and takes a deep breath. When he exhales, his hot breath elicits a barrage of goose bumps. "I want you so damn much."

"You have me. Now and forever."

Because, with him, the darkness isn't too much for me to handle.

Kai's cock lines up with my sopping wet entrance.

"Are you sure?" he asks one last time.

"I've never been more sure about anything in my life," I reply earnestly. I don't know what this means for me and him, me and the others, but in this moment, my soul cries out to his. After years of separation, he has finally supplied me with the missing puzzle piece needed to make me whole. I could've died today, and that brush with death taught me that I can't take the people in my life for granted. I'm scared, yes, but I'm also hopeful. There's no telling what the future will hold and how we'll survive it. All I know for certain is that Kai makes my life a little bit brighter.

He enters me slowly, both of us groaning at the connection. He curses, muttering about how good I feel, before kissing my lips. His words keep me cemented to the here and now. Inch by inch, he sheathes himself fully inside of me, pausing his movements to allow me time to adjust.

Panic threatens to choke me, but I push it away. I'm with Kai, who will never hurt me.

Kai.

My best friend.

The man who loves me.

"Ride me," Kai whispers, kneading my breasts. "Take what you need."

I move my hips, familiarizing myself with him. I feel full, almost too full, as I ride his cock. One of his hands grips my hip while the other rubs at my clit.

"You feel so good, Babygirl. So fucking tight."

His praises make me move faster until I feel myself reaching the precipice, the impending explosion.

"Come for me," Kai whispers, claiming my lips in one last kiss. I explode around him, tears burning my eyes. It feels... glorious. Perfect.

I never knew sex could feel that good.

I collapse on Kai's chest, sweaty and sated, and play with the hairs on his chest. For a brief moment in time, everything makes sense.

CHAPTER 35

ABEL

Nina sort of looks like a constipated puppy when she fights. Her beautiful face is scrunched in concentration, arms raised, as those blind eyes survey everything and nothing.

Damien considers her with a tilt to his head. There's a permanent bend to his lips that gives him a cruel, haughty look.

"You can do it, Bambi!" I cheer supportively from the side. "Kick some mage ass!" She gives me a look. You all know the one I'm talking about—like she can't decide whether she wants to roll her eyes, knee me in the crown jewels, or laugh. I tend to have that effect on people, particularly women.

We're currently in the throne room while the rest of the inner circle moderates another fight. The guys insist on keeping Nina in the dark, but I know my Bambi. She's made of tougher stuff than you'd expect.

We arrived earlier that morning to find Kai and Nina in the room carved into the far wall of the throne room. Both were naked, Nina's head resting on Kai's chest as she slept soundly. Even the memory of her serene expression, heaving breasts, and toned stomach causes heat to rush straight to my cock. Misbehaving bastard (my cock, that is). The air in the throne room stank of sweat, sex, and cum—my three favorite things.

Bronson took one look at the sleeping couple and mumbled something inarticulate before storming out of the room. He's been in a mood ever since we found Nina. At first, I thought it was just the stress of losing someone his wolf obviously cares about. His mate, if I am to believe the rumors.

But now, I wonder if it's something else entirely. He eyed Nina with a mixture of anger, pain, and suspicion. When she tried to talk to him, he muttered an excuse and stalked away.

Something had transpired in those tunnels before Braelyn kidnapped my girl, but I can't put my finger on what.

"Fight like your life depends on it," Braelyn cuts in, pulling me out of my thoughts. The shifter is leaning against the wall with her mate, Jenny, eyes intent on Nina sparring with Damien. "It might at some point."

Damien scoffs, his face impassive. "No one will touch her. They'll have to get past me first."

"I seem to remember kidnapping her quite easily," Braelyn muses, tapping a nail to her chin. "And, funnily enough," she says, sarcasm clear in her tone, "I don't recall seeing you there."

Damien goes still, eyes chips of ice, but Nina's hand on his arm recaptures his complete attention. "Braelyn's right. I want to learn everything I can. Let's start from the beginning."

Her thick black hair is haphazardly tied in a ponytail, and sweat coats her skin in a silver sheen. Still, I don't think I've ever seen anyone more beautiful. There's a confidence to her gait that wasn't there before.

Damien critically examines her face, searching for any

deceit, before he nods once, stepping away. Only when his back is turned does Nina wince, shifting her weight to alleviate the obvious ache between her thighs. My eyes are automatically drawn there. What I wouldn't give to be Kai, that lucky bastard. To have her pussy squeeze my cock like a glove...

Okay, Abel, remain in the present. Please and thank you. Kay. Thanks. Byeeee.

With that mental pep talk, I lean against the wall and cross my arms over my chest. "You got this, girlfriend!" I do an enthusiastic fist punch. See? I can be supportive and shit. Hell, I was even willing to write her name in blood on my chest for her first fight, but Cain warned me that she would find it a "little odd." His words, not mine.

Her lips twitch, but she schools her features as Damien begins to instruct her on how to escape a backwards hold.

"We'll run through it a few times," he says curtly, "before moving on to other things."

They've been working for nearly an hour now, but Damien is miraculously sweat-free. In his impeccably tailored tuxedo, he looks as if he's on his way to prom instead of partaking in fight training. Granted, I don't think the psychopath serial killer would ever step foot in a school, but you get the analogy.

"If you don't mind me asking," Nina drawls, twirling a piece of black hair around her finger. "Why do you use knives when you're a mage? I mean, obviously, you're immensely powerful. I can practically feel you radiate it from here, yet you prefer other methods when in a fight. Why?"

Oh, god. Damien's going to start getting teary-eyed because Nina showed an interest in his deranged hobby of stabbing people.

"Because it's more fun," he deadpans at last, and Nina nods her head seriously. I'm pretty sure she doesn't understand the extent of his obsession with knives and sharp things. Oh, well. Ignorance is bliss and all that shit.

"Now, I'm going to wrap my arms around you from behind. We'll walk through, step by step, what you have to do." Without waiting for acknowledgement, Damien steps behind her and takes her in his arms. I notice that his nose brushes the top of her head, nostrils flaring as he takes in her scent. I also notice that his body is much, much closer to hers than necessary, her soft curves pressed against his hard ones.

Fuck.

My cock jumps in my pants at the enticing sight before me.

Even knowing that Kai slept with Nina doesn't lessen her appeal to me. I've never felt this way about a girl before. Usually, they're new and exciting for about a day until I get bored of them. With Nina, I yearn to memorize the shape of her body, listen to her addictive laugh, and confess all my secrets to her always-listening ears.

I could try looking for my balls, but I'm pretty sure they're inside her dainty palm, alongside Damien's knives.

I've suspected for a while that Nina is Kai's and Bronson's mate. The Rion thing? Didn't see that coming, but I can't complain. It's better to have him as an ally than an enemy, especially when it concerns her. Currently, the little shit is with Kai and the others, getting him acclimated to this area: particularly, the fighting ring. If he is to stay with us, he needs to know his place.

Namely, getting the shit beat out of him by our gang members. It's a rite of passage, one we all had to take.

I'm so distracted by my own thoughts that it takes me a moment to notice something is severely wrong with Nina. Her eyes are wide in her face as her breath saws in and out. Damien immediately releases her, his expression changing from focused to concerned, the only crack I've ever seen in his apathetic exterior.

"Angel?" he asks softly.

Nina drops to the ground, curling in on herself, holding her knees up to her chest and wrapping her arms around them. Desperate sobs shake her tiny body as she falls apart before our eyes, thread by thread.

"Fuck." I drop to my knees before her, being mindful not to get too close too fast. "You triggered her, asshole."

For the first time since I met him, he looks lost. He takes a step backwards until his back is pressed against the wall.

Ignoring him, for now, I crawl on my hands and knees until I'm in front of the diminutive female. My brother has the same type of panic attack on a monthly basis. It's less frequent now, thank fuck, but I'm equipped on how to handle it.

"Nina," I say softly, melodically, using her full name instead of her silly nickname. "Nina, sweetheart, come back to me. You're safe. You're not in the Compound. You're with me. With Damien. You remember Damien, right? The stabby mage? The murderous mage? The mage-with-stabby-tendencies?" As I talk, I continue to move closer and closer to her until my hands are capable of reaching her knees. Slowly, like a man approaching a feral animal, I place my hands on her skin where her dress has ridden up.

"What the hell did you do?" Cain explodes from behind me. I don't bother pulling my attention away from Nina. I can deal with my asshole brother later. "Abel!"

"Shut the fuck up," I say to him, my tone still soothing. To Nina, I plead, "Come back to me. You're safe, Bambi. I'm here."

"Flashback?" Cain is easily able to put the pieces together. I nod once. "What triggered it?"

"Someone grabbing her from behind," I fill in, casting a

glance in Damien's direction. He's still flush against the wall, face ashen.

"We have another problem," Cain says in a suddenly dark tone. I risk a glance at my brother to see livid eyes, sneering lips, and a clenched jaw.

I don't like this. Not one fucking bit.

"What?"

"Guards. We have a visitor." He clenches his hands into fists, eyes spewing fire. Tiny horns protrude from his head as his demon peeks a single eye out.

"*We* have a visitor?" I ask for clarification. In all the years I've been in the prison, I've never—not ever—had someone come visit me. My disbelief must've been evident on my face.

"I reached out to some of our old connections," he explains crisply. "About Raphael and Lionel." His eyes shut briefly at the name of our old tormenter, but when he reopens them, they're hewn from steel. Ever since Nina helped him with his flashback, he's been more determined than ever to help her. There's nothing he won't do to uncover the truth about what happened to Nina that night.

Even if it means facing his demons. *Our* demons.

"We need to meet the guards before they come here," I say, flicking my gaze back to Nina. She's rocking back and forth, tears trailing down her cheeks. "I don't want that damn mage using his powers on her."

"Obviously." Cain crosses his arms over his chest before glancing at Nina worriedly. "But we can't leave her."

I turned towards Damien, the only other person in the room who I trust. Braelyn is staring at Nina anxiously, but I don't know how Bambi would feel about a virtual stranger comforting her. But Damien? For some undefinable reason, she trusts him. Cares for him, even. If anyone can help her, it would be him.

"Damien," I call in an unrecognizable voice. None of my

jubilance remains; my entire being is focused on comforting this girl.

His head snaps up at being addressed directly, eyes shadowed and haunted, before he takes a step closer. I wait until he's directly beside me before grabbing the cuff of his sleeve and pulling him to the ground.

"Remain low to the ground," I instruct. "You don't want to scare her or startle her. Talk to her. Comfort her. Hell, even sing to her. Anything to get her out of her own mind." From somewhere down the hall, I hear a flurry of footsteps. I have no doubt the guards had traveled first to the throne room and then to the fighting arena before coming here. It wouldn't surprise me if Blade and the others are already on their way back, desperate to get to Nina. "Damien!" I shout, snapping my fingers in front of his face.

The cold man turns his stony eyes on me, dark hair grazing his forehead.

"Go," he says at last. "I'll handle the girl." He tries to sound dismissive, like he's discussing a stranger, but his eyes soften as they stare down at her.

Still, I hesitate, unwilling to leave Nina when she's in this state.

"Abel, come on," Cain hisses, pulling at my sleeve. With great reluctance, I stand—being very careful not to startle Nina further—before backing out of the room.

"Fuck, I'm worried about her," I murmur as we move briskly through the halls, towards the raised voices of numerous guards.

"Me too, brother," Cain whispers. "But she'll be fine. Damien is half in love with her already, and I guarantee you that the others are on their way, including the shifter scum."

"Shifter scum." I snort. "You just don't understand his brand of crazy."

"I don't understand *your* brand of crazy," he counters with an eye roll. Abruptly, the smile from his face fades as he turns to stare at me. "Who do you think is visiting us?" There's genuine terror in his voice, a wobble that wasn't there previously.

"Who did you reach out to?" My heart hammers in my throat, stealing the air from my lungs.

"Everyone."

Before I can reply, the white-haired mage appears from around the corner, arms extended. Behind him, a dozen armed guards dressed in tailored navy-blue uniforms lift their weapons.

Pain explodes behind my eyelids, leaving me incapable of speech. In that state between wakefulness and sleep, I reach for my brother's hand.

We fall to the ground with our hands intertwined.

CHAPTER 36

CAIN

"Cain." Abel shakes my shoulder. "Cain, we have to go."

I drowsily lift my head, turning towards my brother. His eyes are wide, frantic, and his hands are stained with blood. It slides in rivulets onto the floor, blending into the red carpeting.

"Where am I?" I ask, attempting to clear the fog from my head. The last thing I remember is getting pulled out of my cage by one of Boris's bastards. Dragged into the familiar heart bedroom, where I spent hours pleasuring Phillip Manning, an assistant to Councilman Draco. He had given me something to drink, something sour, and I had slipped into unconsciousness.

Had he drugged me?

Nausea swirls in my stomach like acid at the thought. Anything can happen when you're not aware of your surroundings.

"Cain! We need to go!" Abel grabs my arm and heaves it over his shoulder. My head lolls, giving me a view of my naked body. Blood cascades down my thighs from where Phillip obviously...

Well, I don't want to think about that.

My gaze lands on Phillip lying on the floor. Blood pools around his flaccid body from a slit across his throat. Dead. He's dead.

And there's blood on Abel's hands...

We move into the hallway, where absolute chaos reigns.

Prisoners are running down the halls, screaming, crying, and fighting. Guards attempt to corral them back into their cells, but if there's one thing I know about prisoners, it's that the second they scent freedom, they'll grasp it with both hands.

"What the fuck?" I slur, relying on my brother to carry half my weight. Each movement is slow and sluggish, like I'm wading through knee-deep murky water. As the fog in my brain recedes, I become aware of a deafening siren and bright red lights flashing intermittently.

"Uprising," Abel explains as we turn at a fork in the hallway. "But we need to run. If they discover who I killed..."

"They'll kill us," I fill in.

His eyes turn distant, hazy, as he no doubt thinks about the paranormal prison rumored to house the worst of the worst. And us...two pretty boys with a reputation for sex.

"We need to keep moving," Abel says at last. "Let's go."

∼

"OH, FUCK," I GRUMBLE, MY HEAD POUNDING. I MOVE TO place my palm against my forehead, only to discover my wrist is restrained.

Fucking great.

"Abe?" I inquire, cracking open my crusty eyelids. Bright, artificial lighting pierces my eyes, and I immediately snap them closed with a groan. Fucking light. Taking a deep breath, I peel open first one eye and then the other.

I'm in a fucking interrogation room.

There's a floor-to-ceiling one-way mirror against the far side of the room. No doubt, there are a dozen armed guards peering in from the other side, safe and cozy. A single table sits directly in front of me, with a plastic chair opposite it.

My hands are cuffed to the metal legs of the table, the manacles rubbing into my skin. A bottle of water taunts me from its perch on the table. Fucking assholes. My throat is always parched after their bitch mage uses his magic on me.

The door to the room clicks open, and a timid man scuttles forward. My heart drops to my stomach as a ball of lead and nerves forms around the organ—like thorns protecting a rose.

The man is unassuming. Small, with light brown hair, glasses, and a triangular mustache. I recognize him immediately as Henry Miller, one of the clients I serviced. My hands ball into fists as I stare at the sinewy man, but I force myself to relax. I won't get any information out of him if he's dead.

"Henry," I purr, flashing him a sultry smile. On the outside, I'm calm and collected—sex personified. On the inside, I'm a trembling mess of nerves and fear. Where is Abel? Why isn't he here with me?

Henry's body notably deflates with relief at my welcoming greeting. No doubt he thought I'd be pissed, seeing how he'd practically raped me for many years.

I daydream every day about turning his ugly ass into a lobster, roasting him over hot coals, and then eating him limb from limb. My imagination is quite vivid, thank you very much.

"I got your message," he says, perching himself on the seat opposite me. Already, I can sense his arousal and excitement. His pupils dilate, breaths coming in pants.

My palms are unbearably sweaty. I hate this man with a passion, and I especially hate that I have to flirt with him. That I have to tolerate his disgusting presence.

But then I think of Nina—her soulful white eyes, obsidian black hair, and lilting laugh that always serves to bring an instinctive smile to my own face. For her, I'll do anything. Be anything.

Even if it's a monster I don't recognize in the mirror.

"I have some questions for you, Henry," I say, infusing each word with a wave of lust. Already, he's nodding his head like a damn bobble head.

"Anything."

"I missed you, you know," I continue, voice husky. He gulps audibly. "I missed your cock in my mouth."

Vomit churns in my stomach, but I push away the queasiness. They're just words, and if my time as a slave taught me anything, it's that words can't hurt you. Still, the mere prospect of flirting with someone other than Nina has my stomach in a knot.

"Yes," he agrees readily. The poor man is smitten. Fucking rapist shit.

"So, tell me what I want to know." A slow smile blossoms on my luscious lips. I purposely lick my bottom lip, and his eyes track the movement. "Raphael Turner. Did you hear the news?" My voice raises in mock sincerity as I cock my head to the side.

His eyes lower to the table. As an assistant to Draco, he would've had to hear about it. "Yes, it's quite sad."

"Do you know what happened?" I ask innocently, batting my lashes at him. "How did he die?" I lean forward as far as the chains allow and lower my voice to a conspiratorial whisper, as if we're telling each other a secret, something just between the two of us.

His breath hitches at my proximity, and his eyes flicker to my lips before lifting.

"I heard..." He casts a glance in both directions before leaning across the table. This position puts his face near mine, and I instinctively back away. Fortunately, he doesn't seem to notice my slip. "I heard he was murdered by a little blind bitch."

A growl escapes me before I can stop it. If I didn't have

the magic-dampening cuffs around my wrists, I imagine my eyes would've been red and black as my demon came out to play. No one, fucking *no one*, calls Nina a bitch.

Except for me. But I was a little shit back in the day.

"I met her," I drawl with a lazy smile. "What makes the council think she did it? Because of the blood on her?"

"That's part of it, yes." Henry leans even closer, until I'm forced to smell his rancid breath. Fuck, I'm going to need to burn my nose off after this. "But it's also what they found on *him*."

Well, this is interesting. I haven't heard anything about the dead body itself.

"What did they find?" I try to keep my curiosity to a minimum. Men like Henry thrive on dangling information over your head like a tasty morsel you can't help but chomp down on. Only then do you discover it's attached to a double-edged sword.

When Henry doesn't immediately answer, I send a wave of lust towards him. He releases a guttural groan, his hand sneaking to his pants. My eyes flicker to the mirror, but I know that whoever's in there won't stop this sick man if he decides to take his infatuation a step further.

Even with the table obscuring my view, I know Henry is jacking himself off.

"Henry..." I trail off with another trademark smile. "Did you get distracted, darling?"

Sweat beads on his forehead as he begins to stroke himself faster and faster, his breathing gradually becoming more erratic. With a sigh, I release another wave of lust, and Henry comes with a groan.

If I have cum on my shoes, so help me...

"Why are we talking about this?" Henry questions at last, regaining his senses. He stands, flaccid dick still hanging out of his pants, and walks towards me.

Fuck, no.

"Because I'm curious," I say indolently. "Is that a problem? Are you jealous I'm asking about another man? You know you're the only man for me."

The only man for me to *kill*. I may have conveniently left that last part out.

"Apparently, they found a picture of Nina in Raphael's jacket," Henry divulges at last.

"Wait, what?" I don't even bother to hide my shock and disbelief. Raphael Turner, the oldest vampire in this area, had a picture of Nina on his person?

"And her blood was beneath his nails," Henry adds finally.

My thoughts are circulating rapidly, unable to settle for more than a second. What. The. Fuck?

Was Nina's blood actually on Raphael Turner's body, or was she framed after the murder was committed? And how did he get a picture of her? Was that another attempt to frame her? My thoughts continue to swirl like smoke, so much so that I don't notice Henry until he's directly behind me, his hands on my shoulders.

Darkness coats my vision, my thoughts. It's a fucking ghost that hovers just over my body, never touching but making its presence known.

No. No. No. No.

No!

"CAIN, HURRY UP, YOU HEAVY BASTARD," ABEL PANTS. HE props me against the wall as he rushes to open the door.

Sunlight blinds me. I can't remember the last time I felt its natural heat on my skin. I squeeze my eyelids shut, pressing my forehead against the wall. I have spent years underground with little to no sun exposure.

I haven't even realized how much I missed the light until now. Fuck, I need it. I'm tired of this darkness, this pain.

"Let's go, brother." Abel helps me stand, and together, we hurry outside. The frigid wind and subdued sun hints that it might be late fall or winter. Dark clouds speckle the sky, not quite obscuring the sun completely from view.

The moment we take a step forward, armed guards swarm us. I count at least thirty, if not more.

"Get on your knees!" someone demands, pointing a gun at my head. "Get on your fucking knees!"

I exchange an anxious glance with my brother, noting the strain on his face and the circles beneath both his eyes. He's tired of fighting, tired of this life we've been unwittingly thrust into. Maybe, just maybe, it's time we gave up.

Maintaining eye contact with the person I love most in the world, I drop to my knees, placing my hands on the back of my head. Abel copies my movements, mouth a grim line.

Wherever we're going has to be better than this.

Anything is better than fucking this.

I'M WRENCHED FROM MY FLASHBACK AS PAIN ERUPTS DOWN my spine. I roar, back arching, as I come back to the present.

A lone cuff dangles from my wrist, no longer connected to the table. Claws have broken through all ten of my fingers, and I know that my skin is black and crispy from my demon fire.

At my feet, a burning mess of flesh, is Henry.

Oh, fuck.

It's the last thought I have as the guards converge on me.

CHAPTER 37

NINA

Someone is singing.

An angel. An angel is singing to me, lulling me to sleep. The oddly seductive sound feathers down my arms, as soft as a butterfly's wing. I breathe in deeply, filling my lungs up with the scent of copper and citrus, before exhaling.

I don't recognize the song, but a sense of comfort seeps into my bones. It penetrates the darkness consuming my mind.

Focusing on the voice, only the voice, I open my mouth to sing back. Reply to his melodic song with one of my own.

He trips over his verse, pausing momentarily, before resuming with gusto. His beautiful, ethereal voice soothes all the jagged edges inside of me.

Despite not knowing the words, I join him and sing a song from my past. It was a song Kai used to sing to me in the Compound. He told me that his mom taught it to him.

Slowly, I come back to myself. Instead of drifting above my body like a malicious phantom, I become aware of every ache and pain inside of me.

My arms are wrapped around my knees, holding them to my chest. Cold tears slide down my cheeks and hang suspended on my lips. A distinctly salty flavor overwhelms me. There is another pair of hands on my knees, where my dress has ridden up, rubbing soothing patterns into my skin.

"There you go, Angel. Come back to me," Damien whispers. I never would've believed that he was the owner of such a soulful, beautiful voice. I always knew there was light in him —light tainted by his own inner darkness. He just needs help feeding the flame until it reaches an inferno. He needs someone who accepts his darkness and embraces his light.

"Damien?" I sob.

"I'm here. I'm right here."

With a cry, I lunge forward and wrap my arms around him. My face settles into the crook of his neck.

At first, his arms are hesitant around me, limp and unsure, but the longer I hold him, the more courage he gains. His body molds to mine until I can't distinguish where he ends and I begin.

"Thank you," I say into the hollow of his throat. His arms are steel bands around me, evoking a sense of irrevocable peace and security. The remnants of my flashback dissipate with each second in his embrace.

"I'll do whatever you need," he replies resolutely. I feel something feather soft on my scalp—his lips. "What happened?"

"I don't know," I admit, reluctantly lifting my head. My arms remain twined around his neck, my fingers playing with the short hairs at the nape. "I don't usually get flashbacks. I guess it was when you grabbed me from behind." I shudder delicately. "That was how Man used to grab me."

"Man." Damien's voice drops to a deadly whisper, ice saturating every word. "Is he from the Compound?"

"I think he was one of the guards," I admit, recalling the

brief second I had seen his reflection in the window. It will haunt me until the day I die. "He would come into my cell and call me 'Little Monster.' Sometimes, I wouldn't even hear him enter. I would be minding my own business when he grabbed me from behind." I rub at my arms, hoping to dispel the sudden surge of goose bumps pebbling on my skin. Fear pulses through me, tainting my body with the pungent, sour smell of it. "I don't want to be scared anymore. I don't want what he did in the past to dictate my future."

Damien cups my cheeks with a tenderness and warmth that belies his frigid disposition. It's hard to associate this Damien with the man others claim him to be.

"Fear is not a bad thing," he says after a moment. "Having feelings is not a bad thing. It just means that you're human. I once thought I would be happier if I didn't feel, if I didn't let my past consume me. I was like you, in a way, though I don't think it's wise to compare one tragedy to another." He pauses, breaths feathering in and out, before beginning again. "When I was a little boy, I was plucked off the streets and taken into an assassin's guild." His hands tighten almost imperceptibly on my face. "I did a lot of bad things when I worked for them, killed a lot of people. And you know what? I liked it. Maybe it's because I'm a sick, coldhearted bastard, or maybe it's because my sins and choices were already piling up on me, burying me in a coffin I created. It terrifies me, but that's the thing about fear—it's not rational and it doesn't listen to reason."

He doesn't speak for a moment, holding me in an embrace that is anything but cold. Warmth emanates from where he touches me, migrating to the center of my stomach. My heart begins to palpitate.

"I see you, Damien," I whisper. "The good and the bad. I see you."

"I really wish you didn't." He presses his forehead against

my own. "I've killed people for the fun of it. I've done horrible, horrible things. Things that would scare you away if you ever heard of them."

"I'm still here, aren't I?" I place my hands over his on my cheeks, holding him to me. Holding the broken pieces of this proud man. "You're not made of ice, Dam. I see the warmth in you. If you really didn't feel, didn't care, you wouldn't have sung to me until I crawled out of my flashback. You wouldn't have offered to train me to fight. You wouldn't have looked after me. You're warm."

"Only with you," he answers immediately. "Only ever with you."

Footsteps echo from down the hall, and Damien moves away from me, as if he's on fire. I want to be sad that he's reverting to his ice-cold persona, but I know that, with me, at least, he has a different facet. And maybe a tiny part of me wants that warmth to only belong to me. Wants to be the only witness to the snow melting and the brilliant flowers taking its place.

"Move out of the way, Braelyn," Bronson hisses. "Let me see my mate."

I push into Bronson's head to see Braelyn and Jenny guarding the door, their backs to me. I have no doubt they at least heard some of my conversation with Damien. Hopefully, for their sakes, they don't mention the fracture in his mask of apathy.

Braelyn and Jenny both move to the side, lowering their weapons as Bronson lunges for me. Briefly, I catch a glimpse of Damien leaning against the wall, a bored, disinterested expression marring his handsome face.

"Bron," I whisper, hugging him back just as tightly. I inhale his spicy, masculine scent as he rocks me from side to side, his body rumbling with his growl.

"The guards went looking for the twins. I got worried and

came as quick as I could. Are you okay? Are you hurt?" He puts his hands on my shoulders, holding me away, as his eyes roam my body. "Fuck. We need to complete this mating bond soon. I don't know how much more my wolf can take. How much *I* can take."

"Complete the mating bond?" I question. "What does that entail?"

"A bite, usually, from my wolf." The words are said almost dismissively as he continues to survey my body. "I'll be able to sense you anywhere in this world. Your emotions. Your pain."

I don't know how I feel about that. My entire life has been made up of pain. The last thing I want is for someone else, especially someone I care about, to experience it firsthand.

Something Bronson said shakes me out of my stupor.

"Wait a minute. What do you mean the guards were looking for the twins?"

"Apparently, they had a visitor. They've been reaching out to some contacts who might have information on Raphael Turner and Lionel Green." He gives my shoulders a squeeze. "Don't worry. They're safe. They'll be back and annoying us soon."

"Did someone mention me?" Rion's voice reverberates from behind Bronson. "Hey, Buttercup!" With a grace only Rion can pull off, he sidles up between me and Bronson. All of a sudden, Bronson's vision is filled with the back of Rion's head. "Did you miss me? Don't answer that. I'll probably cry if you say no. Well, maybe not cry. I'm pretty sure someone ate my tear ducts when I was a child. But I'll be sad for sure! I'll have to call home to my parents and grandparents and tell them that my mate didn't miss me. My grandpa will probably piss himself, laughing—the bastard always hated me—and my grandma will start pulling out our family tree to compare dicks. Yup. The crazy bat believes that you'll only get a mate if you have a big wanker. My Uncle Paul had seven mates because, apparently, he was sporting a python under there. But now that I'm thinking about it...it's kind of weird that my grandma knows all this, huh? Anyway, my mom and dad will probably put pliers under the nails on my toes—"

"And that's enough," Kai cuts in. He moves to stand behind me, resting his hands on the small of my back. "I don't want you to finish that sentence."

"Don't be an assburger just because you sauced the pickle first." Rion huffs. Sauced the pickle? What does he mean by... ohhhhhh. My cheeks go up in flames. "She's my mate too. Oh! Look at this knife! It's shiny. Isn't it shiny, Buttercup? Ah, shit. I forget that you can't see. Well, unless you're using your magical powers, but I'm not certain about that. It's just a theory I have..."

He trails off as the silence becomes suffocating. I suddenly can't breathe. It's physically impossible. My lungs are incapable of taking in air as my thoughts stutter to an abrupt halt. All I can hear is the harried thumping of my heart.

"Oh, shit." Rion runs a hand through his tangled hair. "I totally didn't mean to say that out loud."

"Your magical powers?" Bronson asks in a dark, growly voice. He puts his hands around Rion's waist, picks him up, and deposits him a foot away. "Is that how you were able to see in the halls after our date?" His voice is thick with hurt. He grounds his teeth together, works his jaw, and flexes his hands.

"I would like to know as well," Damien drawls lazily from his spot in the corner. He tries to sound casual, but his eyes sharpen on me, and he begins fiddling with one of his knives.

"You're right," I say, ignoring Kai's muttered warning. "I should tell you all the truth. I care about each and every one of you." I take a deep breath, my pulse skittering. I notice, somewhat distantly, that Damien stepped forward the moment I confessed I cared about him. It's the first time I have admitted my feelings out loud, and the words claw at my heart, demanding me to say *even more*. "But should we wait until the twins come back?"

Bronson once more pulls me into his arms. "My wolf demands we know now. In his mind, we can't protect you until we know the entire story," he says gruffly.

Guilt eats at me, gnawing at the chasm-sized hole in my stomach.

"Rion's right. I do have strange powers that no one has ever seen before. I don't know what kind of supernatural I am...or if I even am one. At first, I only had accelerated healing. The people at the Compound loved testing out how fast I could heal myself and how close to death I could get."

Bronson growls low in his throat, his arms constricting around me in an attempt to shield me from the world. Unfortunately, he can't protect me from the ghosts of my past who have come back to haunt me.

"I vote we kill them," Damien says coolly.

"Seconded!" Rion pipes in.

"Give me their heads," adds Bronson in a guttural voice.

Ignoring them, I continue. "Soon, I realized that I could do something else as well." I begin to rub Bronson's thick, muscular back, hoping to soothe his tension. His body relaxes in my embrace as he takes a deep breath of my scent. "I could go into people's minds and see through their eyes. I thought that, if I told them, if they knew what I could do, they wouldn't hurt me as much..."

My brain is sluggish, the events from my time there coming to the forefront reluctantly, as if being dragged through tar. The pain. The fear. The hurt.

"I've never heard of that before," Damien says at last.

"Can you only see through their eyes, or can you use their other senses?"

Immediately, my mind flickers to Cain in his cell, his hand wrapped around his cock. My face's temperature ratchets up a thousand degrees at the memory, heat blossoming and unfurling in my stomach.

"I fell asleep once and was able to see through Cain's eyes. I heard what he heard and saw what he saw," I admit at last.

"And by the blush on your cheeks, I'm pretty sure our demon friend wasn't just playing a game of checkers, am I right?" Rion jests.

"Maybe, with training, you can use more than just the person's eyes," Damien muses. "Maybe you'll be able to feel what they feel, smell what they smell, hear what they hear. Hell, you might even be able to hear their thoughts."

"Hear their thoughts?" I squeak. The mere prospect is daunting and, quite frankly, terrifying.

"And you've never heard of a supernatural species who can do that?" Kai queries. Through Bronson's eyes, I watch all of the men shake their heads.

"Well, gang, it looks like we have another mystery on our hands!" Rion says, lips curling into a salacious smile.

Bronson places his lips against the shell of my ear. "Thank you. For trusting me with this."

"Thank you for forgiving me," I reply, ignoring the goose bumps on my skin from his intoxicating presence. "I should've told you sooner."

"There's nothing to forgive," he grumbles. "You were scared. Fear makes you do irrational, crazy things."

"Guys!" Braelyn's voice penetrates the safety cocoon I have found myself in. "We have another problem."

"What is it, Brae?" Rion snaps, whipping his head in her direction.

"Jenny just heard that the guards are back in the Labyrinth. Apparently, Nina has a visitor this time."

"Over my fucking dead bo—" Before Bronson can finish his threat, he keels over, groaning in pain. His lashes flutter once as darkness consumes his vision. I wrench myself out of his head as more groans, grunts, and screams resonate in the room. I know, without having to look, that my guys are all unconscious as the white-haired mage steps into the room.

"Nina, you have a visitor," he says in a silky voice. In the next moment, pain radiates behind my eyebrows as my body collapses to the ground.

I lose myself to the darkness.

CHAPTER 38

NINA

This time, I'm not shocked when I wake up cuffed to a metal table in the center of an interrogation room.

I push myself into the nearest eyes, unsurprised to see Alyssa's face in the reflection of the mirror. Like last time, she's a picture of elegance and grace. She walks over to the table with a casual gait, her shimmery gown cascading around her like fire. A slow smile blossoms over her luscious lips before they lower into a frown. Sitting across from me, her vision shifts so I can no longer see her reflection in the mirror.

Instead, I see the room for the first time. There's a dark stain on the floor—almost as if the cement had been burnt—and the air smells heavily of bleach. I practically gag on the pungent scent perfuming the air. The table itself looks brand new, not a mark insight.

"It's good to see you again, Nina," Alyssa says softly. She sounds tired, forlorn, and her eyes drift down to her hands in her lap.

"I wish the circumstances were better," I reply with a self-deprecating laugh. Instead, the circumstances consist of me imprisoned for the murder of her close friend.

"I've been talking to some of my colleagues," she begins, getting directly to the point. "Did you know that Lionel Green's assistant was arrested many years ago for murder and theft?"

"Rion?" I question before I can stop myself.

Her eyes snap back to my face in surprise. "You met him."

I take a deep breath to control my suddenly erratic heartbeat. "I've been asking around," I settle for at last. I don't know Alyssa, and I don't trust her; I have no idea how she would react if she discovered Rion was my friend.

She bobs her head once, resuming her inspection of her long, slender fingers. The nails have recently been clipped and polished, the ruby red matching her dress.

"I'm sure Rion told you that Lionel was enemies with Raphael," she states after a moment.

"Did you discover something?" My heart still pounds in my chest, and I struggle to keep the jittery shivers down.

"As we suspected, Lionel has an alibi for the night Raphael was murdered. He was seen at one of the clubs he owns until early the next morning, in a town a few hours away from where Raphael was found." She sighs, slumping forward.

"So, Lionel wasn't involved in Raphael's death?" I deduce hesitantly. The one lead we had...shattered. Disappointment swirls in my gut like a thousand shards of glass.

"I didn't say that." She sits up, suddenly eager. "It just means that he found someone to do his dirty work for him. Have you had a chance to talk to the mage Damien?"

I nod warily. "Yes. I don't think he's heard back from his contacts yet."

"I have it on good authority that Raphael was killed by the guild your...friend...worked for." Her voice twists with disgust at the word *friend*.

"I'll talk to him," I assure her.

Alyssa drops her gaze to her hands currently fisted on the silky fabric of her dress. At my words, she relaxes them incrementally—one finger at a time—until they're flat against her thighs.

"You probably wonder why I care so much," she says softly, distantly. Her gaze focuses on a spot above my shoulder, lost in a memory I can't even begin to understand. Instead of answering, I remain silent, giving her the opportunity to share with me if she wishes. There's pain inside of her. An undeniable pain that calls to me. I recognize it because I experience it myself. It's the pain that hints she's been shattered, broken, and is struggling to reconnect the pieces.

It's a pain that speaks of loss and hurt.

"I loved him," she says at last, voice wobbling. "For hundreds of years. He was my everything."

Hundreds of...?

"Yes." She chuckles at my flabbergasted expression, the jubilant noise momentarily breaking her out of her melancholy. "I'm three hundred and sixty-seven years old, as of January."

"Wow," I breathe, unable to hide my shock in a quick enough manner. She doesn't look older than thirty. Shaking my head, I manage to add, "You sound young."

"I feel young." She chuckles good-naturedly before sobering. "I met Raphael when he had first been turned into a vampire. He was charismatic, idealistic, and the light of my life. He saw something in me that many others didn't. We've been together ever since." Her voice is low and distant, stuck in a memory invisible to my own eyes. "We weren't a traditional male and female couple. We both had our fair share of lovers on the side, but we always came back to each other."

"I don't know how you could deal with that," I blurt out before I can stop myself. There is no way to scoop the words out of the air and put them back into my mouth. "I would get jealous."

"It doesn't work for everyone," she agrees, not at all offended by my intrusive statement. "I know that I would prefer for him to be loyal only to me, but all relationships are different. Some are conventional and others aren't. Some require delicate maneuvering and others allow you to forge ahead."

I think of Kai and Bronson. Damien. The twins. Rion. I don't know how I would feel about them with another female. Does it make me selfish? Wanting them all when they can't have anyone except me? Do they even care for me like that? Do I care for them in *that* way? A romantic way? I already suspect that our relationship is...odd. One moment, I'm on a date with Bronson, and the next, I'm in bed with Kai. And the very next, I'm cuddling with Damien and being called *Bambi* by Abel.

One thing is painfully clear: I care for them all.

Alyssa sighs once more, glancing to the side and staring at her reflection. Anxiety clouds her beautiful face. "I want—no, I *need*—to uncover the truth about what happened to Raphael. I don't have proof yet, but I know Lionel is behind it." Her voice is frigid, colder than even Damien's, and causes ice to skate down my spine. "I want him to pay for killing my lover."

"I understand," I whisper, fidgeting in the cold plastic chair. If anything happened to my friends, I would go insane. I care for them all immensely, in a way I have only ever cared for Kai before. My stomach knots uncomfortably.

"I'll come visit you again," Alyssa says at last, rising gracefully to her feet. She brushes at a strand of hair grazing her eyes. "And Nina? Thank you. Between the two of us, we'll uncover the truth."

Her eyes focus on me before she turns on her heel and

leaves the room. I stay in her head as she turns at a fork in the hall, waving at one of the guards present. It's only then that I notice the bloody heap lying unconscious on the ground. Blond hair, matted with blood. Bruises marring his face. Eyelashes feathered shut.

My heart leaps to my throat as panic fills me.

Abel? Or Cain?

I try to search for any definitive characteristics, but Alyssa turns before I can get a good look. I'm wrenched out of her mind as she steps out of range.

Tears cascade down my cheek, wetting my lips.

When the guard arrives to take me back to the Labyrinth, I don't bother to struggle. My mind is consumed with worry for the twins. If one is lying unconscious in the hallway, where is the other? Did he already get led back home?

And when did I start thinking of the prison as home?

Stomach somersaulting, I allow the guard to stick a needle into my skin.

I'M NOT IN MY OWN MIND.

I know that immediately. It takes me a moment to pinpoint whose mind I've slid into.

His eyes are focused on his hands, naturally tanned and freckled. When he finally lifts his gaze, I see that he's in an interrogation room similar to the one I just left.

"Hello!" he calls, banging his cuffed wrists against the table. "Cain?"

Abel. This must be Abel.

That means the unconscious man is my dark twin, Cain.

"Motherfucker," Abel curses as he inspects the barren room. He begins to kick his feet, humming beneath his breath.

After a long, potent pause, the door to the room is thrown open. A large man with a potbelly, receding hairline, and sweaty lower lip enters the room.

Abel freezes, staring at the man. His heart rate skyrockets the longer he gazes at him.

"Lionel," he breathes, his voice heavy with fear.

Fear. It's an emotion I've never heard from my sunshine twin before.

The man, who I'm assuming to be none other than Lionel Green, enters the room with an imperious set to his chin. Instantly, I hate him. I don't even know why. It could be because he's framing me for murder, but there's something more to it, something entirely instinctual. I have the irresistible urge to punch him in his pudgy, smirking face.

"Abel, my boy!" Lionel says enthusiastically. Abel tenses under the older man's scrutiny, his knuckles turning white from how tightly they're clenched.

"Where's my brother?" Abel whispers softly. "Where's Cain?"

"I didn't ask for Cain." Lionel waves his hand dismissively. "I wanted to see you. I hear you've been asking about me."

He steps around the table and presses a kiss to Abel's hair. That gesture is...strange. Off. What the heck is going on?

Abel, if it's even possible, goes even more rigid, back ramrod straight.

"I've missed you," Lionel continues, either oblivious or choosing to ignore Abel's reaction. When the trickster demon doesn't immediately answer, Lionel steps away and sits in the chair opposite him. "I take it you missed me as well. My sources say you've been asking questions about my whereabouts."

"I...I...I..." He's speechless. Abel, the flirty, teasing demon I have grown to care for, is unable to utter a coherent word.

Who is this man to him?

"You should be thanking me, you know," Lionel continues, leaning back in his chair and placing his clasped hands on his protruding gut. "A little while ago, your brother ran into some issues."

That declaration finally penetrates whatever funk Abel has found himself in. He leans across the table desperately. "What happened? Is he okay? Is he hurt?"

Lionel chuckles with a derisive wave of his hand. "He's fine. Got into a fight with his visitor, apparently. Guards wanted to put him down, but I convinced them to give him another chance. You've always been my favorite, Abel, but I can't forget about the good times I had with your brother." A shark-like smile spreads across his face. "Don't look so sad, my love. There's no need to be jealous."

My love? Is Lionel Abel's lover?

The thought causes acid to churn in my stomach like lava.

If they're lovers, then why does Abel appear so skittish? Why do his hands shake and knee bob?

"I wanted to, um, ask you about Raphael Turner," Abel stutters out, lowering his gaze to his clenched fists.

Lionel's laugh is capable of slicing glass. "Why? Were you fucking that man too?" Abel doesn't answer, continuing to study his hands intently. "Did that Alyssa bitch put you up to this?" Lionel demands at last. "She seems to think I murdered that bastard." He scoffs and rolls his eyes.

"Did you?" Abel queries softly.

"Of course not! I may have hated that asshole, but I'm not fucking stupid. Killing him would be a declaration of war. Besides, didn't his murderer already get arrested?" There's a pause during which Abel flicks his eyes upwards. "Now that I think about it, that bitch has been placed here, hasn't she?" When Able remains silent, Lionel continues with a curl to his lips. "She's the reason you're questioning me, isn't she? My dear Abel, are you in love with her?"

Abel doesn't respond, meeting Lionel's frigid gaze without blinking.

"You know, I'm curious to meet the girl capable of killing Raphael Turner. Perhaps I should inquire about a meeting—"

"Don't you fucking touch her!" Abel explodes, his tenuous hold on his temper splintering.

Lionel smiles, as if he got exactly what he wanted out of Abel. His smile reminds me of a lion staring at a gazelle. There's something predatory about it, all sharp teeth.

"I have to leave," Lionel says abruptly, pushing back from the table and getting to his feet. "You and your brother will be taken back to your cell." He pauses in front of Abel, expression unreadable. When he speaks next, his voice is dark and threatening. "Your heart may belong to that whore, but your body belongs to me." Lionel ducks down and claims Abel's lips in a harsh, aggressive kiss. When he finally pulls away, Abel's trembling from head to toe.

Fire lights in my belly at Lionel's display, but I push down the rage before it can manifest.

"You be a good boy, Abel. And remember, you're mine."

CHAPTER 39

"Your bodyguard won't stop looking at you," Tessa whispers conspiratorially from where she sits across the table.

The cafeteria is loud and raucous this morning. News of Rion's arrival has spread like wildfire. Everyone is curious about the elusive gang king. But rivaling the curiosity is fear and anger; the shifters have hurt a lot of people, and the demand for blood permeates the room.

"Damien?" I inquire, despite already knowing the stone-faced mage is lurking in the corner of the room. I can feel his eyes like a physical brand burning my flesh. None of the guys liked the idea of me visiting the cafeteria without them present, despite Braelyn's insistence that she'll look after me. It's no surprise that Damien followed me. I'm pretty sure Bronson and Kai are guarding the hallway as well.

Their overprotectiveness causes liquid pleasure to cascade through my veins. While some may find it suffocating, I find it comforting. They each have embedded themselves in my soul, my genetic makeup, and I know they'll protect me from any future harm.

"God, he won't stop looking at us," Haley hisses.

"Not us," Jenny contests quietly. "Nina."

"The girl with the golden vagina," jests Haley, but I sense no malice in her words.

There's a whacking noise, and Haley releases a pained groan. "You stop that disgusting talk," Rebecca chastises. "We may be prisoners, but we're still civil. Behave like a proper lady."

Haley mumbles something inarticulate as the rest of us laugh.

"The entire cafeteria is looking at *us*," Braelyn laments, voice dark. I know she's gesturing to herself and Jenny.

Kai's gang doesn't seem to know how to deal with the shifters' sudden arrival. Kai has assured his people that they mean us no harm, but one man's affirmation doesn't negate the centuries of prejudice and discourse. For as long as anyone can recall, shifters have been the enemy. No one can expect the social standings to change overnight.

Even Kai doesn't trust the shifters completely, hence Damien's presence.

"It's because of your stunning good looks," Jenny teases. If there's one thing I've learned about the two shifter females who have pledged their loyalty to me, it's that Braelyn is brass to the point she comes across as rude, while Jenny is shy and quiet. The two of them are as different as night and day, yet they complement each other perfectly.

"Thanks, babe," Braelyn drawls, and I imagine she's rolling her eyes. Still, she sounds slightly flustered by her mate's words.

"I still can't believe Rion is here," Haley breaks in around a mouthful of food.

"I don't understand why," Tessa adds, and there's a distinct hitch to her voice that I can't quite place.

At Rion's insistence, we've been keeping the revelation of our bond a secret.

"The world can't know you're my weakness," he had said earnestly.

All they know is that Rion is negotiating peace with Kai and that Braelyn and Jenny have become friends with me.

"It's because of a girl." Rebecca huffs. "It's always because of a girl."

Haley chuckles, and Tessa's breath hitches once again. Something about her reaction makes me uneasy. My blood simmers in my veins as a nest of snakes slithers and hisses in my stomach.

Racking my brain to change the subject, I ask, "What have you guys been up to lately?"

Tactful, no. Helpful, yes.

Immediately, the ladies regale me with stories about their weeks in the prison since we last caught up.

Haley is in the midst of telling us a story about her Incubi lover when I feel hands on my shoulders.

Startled, I drop into Rebecca's head.

Rion stands behind me, looking as gorgeous as ever. Dark hair frames a proud and arresting face. Chiseled cheekbones, a strong jawline, and jubilant eyes complete the ensemble. There's a beauty to him—a barbaric, untamed type of beauty—that reels me in like a fish on a hook. With his sleeves pushed up, I'm able to see the numerous tattoos coloring his tawny skin.

"Ladies," Rion says with a wink. Haley giggles, ducking her head, and Tessa's eyes go wide, pupils dilating. A wistful expression crosses her pretty face as she stares up at the shifter.

Braelyn and Jenny are the only two who don't seem mesmerized by his beauty. If anything, they look annoyed at his intrusion.

Braelyn quirks a brow. "Don't trust me?"

Rion's grin grows as he intertwines our fingers.

"Excuse me, ladies, but can I borrow Nina? I have something I need to talk to her about." Without waiting for their response, he tugs me out of the seat, eyes dancing with mischief. My confusion grows as he begins to drag me out of the congested cafeteria. I thought we decided to keep our relationship—if you can even call it that—a secret.

But Rion does what Rion wants. I don't know why I expected anything different from the enticing, eccentric man.

Just before I pull out of Rebecca's head, I catch a glimpse of Tessa's face contorted with unbridled rage. Hurt flashes in her eyes as she stares after us. I pull myself out of Rebecca's head, stomach churning uncomfortably.

What did I do wrong? Is it because Rion showed interest in me? Is it because I left them?

As my mind races, so does my heart—anger, hurt, and frustration vying for attention.

Rion pulls me out of my thoughts with his next words.

"I want to take you on a date," he says abruptly, pulling me to a stop in the hallway.

"What?"

"A date," he repeats. He places his lips to my ear, and warmth radiates through my body, accompanied by a kaleidoscope of emotion. "I want to take you on a date."

A date. With Rion.

The thought both exhilarates and terrifies me. I imagine a date with Rion would be just as crazy as him. He's an enigma, someone I can't quite understand but yearn to know more about. One moment, he's silly and teasing, and the next, he's a stone-cold killer. I still remember his voice when he threatened Braelyn.

Who exactly is Rion?

"Earth to Buttercup." Rion snaps his fingers in front of

my face. "Do I need to get a space shuttle? Learn to moon-walk? I tried moonwalking once, but I tripped over a plant and broke my wrist. And ass. Did you know you can break an ass? I didn't. Apparently, it's a real fucking thing. And when I say 'fucking' thing, I mean it literally. It can happen when someone fucks you in the asshole real hard." He pauses, breathing unevenly, before continuing. I wonder if he can even help himself. "I'm not propositioning you for anal. Don't worry about that. I am, however, asking you on a date. A real date. Not a fake date. I was going to take you to one of those classes where you can get drunk and paint pictures, but the last time I tried crafting, I glued my hand to my face. Ten out of ten, would not recommend."

"Rion," I cut in, gripping his face between both my hands. Though I can't see him, I picture his tawny skin framed by thick black hair. God, I wish I could see him. Actually see him and not just rely on others' perceptions. You never know whose vision of the world is skewed. "You want to take me on a date?"

"Either that or sleep," he confesses. "It's the cat in me. Actually, if you have yarn, I can play with that. Shit. No. Abort. Abort. Abort. Playing with yarn on a date is not what the lady wants, is it? Don't answer that! I can use my mate-mind-reading capabilities to tell you the answer would be no. Just kidding. I don't have any mate-mind-reading capabili-ties." His body shakes beneath my hands as he practically bounces with excitement.

I think he's wrong about being an extension of his animal. Rion is a puppy personified.

His enthusiasm is infectious and brings a smile to my lips. If I could, I would bottle up Rion's essence and inhale it deeply. There are very few people who can make me smile like he can.

"Wolf Man already had his turn," Rion continues, and I

can almost picture his luscious lips pushing out in a pout. "It's time for Cat Man to show you a purr-fect evening. Wait. Don't quote me. That sounded ten times better in my head."

"Yes," I cut in before he can continue rambling. He's a verbal freight train barreling straight towards a brick wall. But, for some reason, I find it endearing. "I would love to go on a date with you."

"Thank fuck, or this would've been super awkward. Come on! I already have it set up." He recaptures my hand and leads me down the musty-smelling halls. A moment later, he pushes open a door and guides me through.

I slide into his head to realize we're in the throne room. A single easel sits in the center of the room, a barrage of paint on a table beside it. In front of Kai's throne, Abel rests on a sofa cushion, naked, with a blanket covering his groin.

"Um...?" My cheeks blaze as I take in his expansive, golden chest, blond hair, and muscular thighs. An easygoing smile dons his face.

I haven't talked to Abel and Cain about what I saw in Abel's mind. His encounter with Lionel feels personal. They've been more reserved since they returned, lost in thought more often than not. I know that I wouldn't want someone sifting through my mind without permission. I did tell the twins, however, about my abilities, both of which they took as well as I expected. Needless to say, not that well.

I can't forget the flicker of pain that crossed both their faces at my confession. The betrayal. The hurt. Despite their grim smiles, I know I'd hurt them immensely by omitting the truth.

It's been a week, and Cain has yet to talk to me.

"I lied earlier!" Rion's vision shakes as he jumps up and down. "We're totally painting and drinking wine."

"Errr..."

"You'll paint Abel first while I focus on him for you, and then I'll paint you. It'll be super fun!"

"I've been sitting like this for two fucking hours," Abel gripes. "Do you know how awkward it is to have my brother walk through the door and see me in all my glory? I think I traumatized the poor bastard, despite the fact we have identical fucking bodies—even our cocks."

Cocks.

My cheeks turn even redder as all my blood flows there.

"Don't worry." Rion presses his lips to my temple. "We won't do anything you're not comfortable with. If you want to do something else, we can. If you want Abel to leave, he will. You're in charge, Buttercup. Always."

My stomach twists as I stare at Abel through Rion's eyes. He really is a work of art. Though he isn't as muscular as Bronson or even Kai, defined muscles make up his arms and stomach. There's a spattering of golden hair trailing beneath the blanket.

And the blanket...

As my breath hitches, my mind utterly enraptured, the blanket begins to tent with Abel's arousal.

"Fuck, Bambi. You can't look at me like that. I don't want to blow a load with Rion's eyes on me. I'm into a lot of kinky shit, but that's next level."

Rion snorts, guiding me towards the easel. I honestly don't understand how they expect me to paint Abel with no vision.

"You should be honored," Rion huffs at Abel. "My eyes have been known to give multiple people orgasms. They don't call it an eye-fuck for nothing."

Placing his hands on my shoulders, Rion positions me how he wants me. This angle allows him to see the top of my head, the easel, the paint, and Abel still languidly propped up on the floor.

"I'll probably paint you looking like a cactus or something by mistake," I admit with a blush, grabbing the paintbrush from the table and dipping it into the yellow paint.

"You don't have to be good, Bambi. I'll love and cherish it, even if it sucks ass," Abel calls. He moves to get himself into a more comfortable position, his hand resting on his hip as the blanket slides down even lower, revealing dark pubic hair.

Heat throbs through me, settling in my lower region. I press my thighs together tightly, hoping the pain will abate.

"While you paint, I'm going to ask you some questions," Rion says, gaze momentarily flicking down towards me before he corrects himself. "I want to get to know my beautiful, perfect mate."

"I'm not perfect," I protest meekly, using the yellow to paint Abel's hair. It doesn't quite encapsulate the hues of gold scattered throughout, darkening the strands, but it's the best I can do with the limited supplies I have. "How did you even get the paint?"

"Damien knows a guy," Rion replies dismissively. "Now, we'll start easy. Have you ever painted before?"

"No," I answer instantly, dipping my brush in a cup of water. Using Rion's vision for guidance, I blend some white and brown paint together. "Never. I don't think I've really doodled before, either."

I think Rion is going to ask me to elaborate, but graciously, he changes the subject. "*Grey's Anatomy* or *The Vampire Diaries*?"

"Huh?" I pause mid-stroke to quirk a brow at him.

"You never watched *Grey's*?" he asks in horror.

"Team McDreamy," Abel calls.

"We'll have to change that straight away," Rion agrees. "Do you remember the cell I first brought you to? I have a television there that I might be able to connect to Netflix. You know, because I'm awesome and all that."

"And so incredibly modest." I giggle, focusing on the painting once more. Unfortunately, Abel's body resembles more of a blob than any human anatomy I've ever seen before. "Do you have two cells? The one we visited on the shifter side of the prison is in a different location than the other one."

Cheeks crimson, I begin working on Abel's nether region with a dollop of red paint. I draw the "blanket" over his thighs and just below his belly button.

"I have two cells," Rion admits. "One is with the other shifters, and the other—the one I took you to—is in an entirely separate hallway, not a part of either gang. It's a place I can be myself without worrying about the pressures—and why does Abel look like he's taking a mean shit?" Rion's vision cants to the side as he tilts his head, focusing on my painting.

"It does not!" I protest immediately, though now that he's mentioned it, I can see the resemblance.

And this is even before I started working on Abel's facial features.

"Don't worry, Bambi," Abel says easily, playing with the golden hairs on his chest. "I'll take a shit every day of my life if it means being with you." He winks at me, face glowing with mirth.

"I'm sure that was supposed to be romantic, but it came across as a little weird," Rion muses. "Now, I can't stop picturing you kneeling over Nina and shitting in her—"

"Stop!" I squeal, placing my hands over my ears. I barely resist singing "la, la, la" until they stop talking.

"So, you don't have a poop fetish, Buttercup?" Rion queries with amusement.

"No! Stop it! Ew!" I whack him with the brush, paint splattering. Still, I can stop the giggles from shaking my body.

Out of all the guys, Abel and Rion are the most light-hearted. It's very, very rare that I see cracks in their jubilant masks. They embody a warmth and light that seep into my very soul, setting me aflame.

"My turn!" Rion cheers suddenly, grabbing my shoulders and spinning me around. I place my hands on his waist to steady myself, and his muscles contract under my touch. His attentive gaze causes heat to bloom across my body, unfurling like a flower in spring.

"Your turn...?" My question is answered when Rion grabs the paintbrush out of my hands and trails it down my cheek. My jaw slackens, eyes widening, at the cold liquid.

"Rion!" I squeak, pulling out of his head and dancing away.

"I'm right behind you, Bambi. I'm not going to hurt you," Abel says softly—a warning. A moment later, his strong arms wrap around my chest, holding me steady. For the first time, this position doesn't trigger a flashback. I know that it's Abel who has me, and I know he'll never intentionally hurt me.

I laugh, the sound utterly carefree and joyous, as Rion's footsteps get closer and closer. His hot breath wafts across my lips.

"I told you I was going to paint you," he purrs, brushing paint down my other cheek and to my neck.

"You'll ruin my clothes," I protest, breathless from laughter. Abel's teeth clamp down on my earlobe, and my laughter quickly dissipates. My breathing, however, remains ragged.

"Then, perhaps we'll have to take them off of you," Abel whispers seductively. My heart ricochets around my rib cage.

"I've never felt this way before," Rion adds, taking another step closer. At this point, there is only a sliver of space between my lips and his. "You hold me in such a way that I don't feel broken."

I'm panting now, consumed by an insatiable need I have

only ever felt with first Bronson and then Kai. Rion steps back, and I suddenly miss his warmth.

Abel presses languid kisses down my neck and to my shoulder, pushing down the strap of my gown. "Do you want me to stop?" he whispers against my skin.

"No." My answer takes even me by surprise as he slips the other strap off my shoulder.

My dress pools around my feet, leaving me in only a lace bra and tiny panties. Heart hammering, I push myself into Rion's mind once more.

The sight before me is erotic and sends my lust skyrocketing.

The gauzy material of my bra does very little to conceal my cleavage. My beaded nipples are noticeable through the fabric. Lower, I see that my panties are visibly soaked through.

Abel stands directly behind me, kissing my neck and shoulders. He's still naked, but this time, he doesn't have a blanket obscuring his cock from view. He holds his body a bit away from mine—no doubt, not wanting to scare me—but through Rion's eyes, I can see the long, erect length of his cock.

I pull myself out of my shifter's eyes once more, content to experience this moment in my customary darkness. I don't understand a lot of things, but the dark? I understand it intimately. I embrace it like you would an old friend.

Without sight, I can focus on my other senses. Abel's lips feathering kisses across my skin. His hands on the waistband of my underwear. The smoothness of his face as he nuzzles my neck.

"Rion," I whisper, wanting him. Needing him.

Abel's hand travels to the clasp of my bra, expertly undoing it and pushing it off my shoulders. "Isn't she beautiful?" he asks, kneading my heavy globes. His thumbs and fingers twist my nipples, eliciting a hiss of pleasure from my lips.

"I need to paint her," Rion replies in a soft voice.

As Abel pushes down my underwear, his cock brushing my wet entrance, Rion moves closer to me once more. The brush, which I know to still be slick with red paint, travels down the valley of my heaving breasts. The combined stimulations are nearly overwhelming—Abel's hands on my thighs and the whiskers of the brush against my chest.

Rion paints a circle around one nipple and then the other before lowering.

"Rion," I groan, placing my hands on his shoulders.

"You're so beautiful," he breathes. "A work of art. My muse."

When the brush reaches the inside of my thighs, I can't stop the desperate mewl that leaves my parted lips. I want him to touch me, but at the same time...

"I don't want paint in my vagina," I whisper, resting my head on Abel's shoulder. My words bring a spurt of laughter out of first Abel and then Rion.

"Don't worry, my love." Rion's voice sounds from farther below, as if he has dropped to his knees. "I'll put something else in there instead." The next moment, his tongue licks my slit, tasting me. I jolt into Abel, gasping and reaching out to grab the top of Rion's head to hold him to me. He pulls back with a groan. "Fuck, you taste good."

He brings his lips back to my mound as his fingers press at the bundle of nerves. Abel turns my face towards his, kissing me fiercely as his hands drop to my breasts. Kneading the skin, he moans against my lips, muttering indecipherable praises.

"I want to feel you," I say breathily. Despite my encounters with Bronson and Kai, I haven't ever felt a cock in my hand. I've never felt the need to pleasure a man like that before this moment.

"Yes," Abel agrees, guiding my hand to his cock. The hardness belies how soft it actually feels beneath my palms, the skin and muscles contradicting one another. It's smooth velvet over steel. I run my fingers over the tip, my hand coming away wet and sticky.

As Rion continues to pleasure me from below, my body lighting up in pleasure, I work on memorizing the feel and shape of Abel's cock. I want him to feel the lust and desire that I'm feeling. I want him to unravel completely with me, one string at a time. When I reach his balls, Abel releases a hiss of air, his cock jumping in my other hand.

"Sorry!" I say instantly, pulling my hand away. "I didn't mean to hurt you."

"Fucking hell, woman, don't stop," Abel breathes, pulling my hands back to his throbbing member. I begin to stroke him base to tip, reveling in every sharp intake of breath and grunt he makes. "Faster. Fuck, faster."

Rion pulls his lips away from me abruptly, and I cry out at the loss of contact. Before I can protest, Rion pulls me into a desperate, feverish kiss. I taste myself on his lips, and my arousal ratchets up ten notches at the erotic flavor.

"I want to be inside of you," he pleads.

"God, yes," I cry, reaching for him with my free hand. He stealthily steps away, and I hear the sound of clothes being ripped off. A moment later, he stands in front of me once more, his cock inches from my dripping channel.

"Are you sure?" Rion asks, hands cupping my breasts, despite the paint he placed on them.

"Yes," I moan, stroking Abel faster. The trickster demon's breath hitches as he turns my face to kiss my lips once more. His kiss is possessive and needy, claiming me as thoroughly as

I claim him. Our tongues tangle together in a story of passion and lust.

Rion enters me slowly, lifting one of my legs to hold me steady, and allows me to adjust to his girth. He's thicker than Kai, his cock filling me so completely, I can barely breathe.

"Are you okay?" he asks, freezing.

"Move," I beg, wrenching my lips away from Abel's. He starts moving inside of me with slow, measured thrusts. I cup his cheek with the hand not pleasuring Abel. "Rion..."

"God, you're beautiful. Isn't she beautiful, Abe?"

"Fuck, yes," Abel pants as my hand moves faster and faster. He claims my lips once more, as if they have always been his, as if they belong to him. As if *I* belong to him.

Rion's strokes become harder and faster as his fingers find my clit. I am halfway delirious with pleasure and lust.

Abel pulls his mouth away from mine to flutter kisses along my neck and shoulders. His breathing is just as uneven as mine.

My body pulsates with desire, my inner walls clenching around Rion's hardened length. Rough grunts leave him, and my own moans mingle with his growls.

I sink my nails into the skin of his broad shoulders as my pleasure rises and rises, reaching an inescapable clifftop. Any second now, I'm going to fall straight over the edge.

"God, you're perfect," Rion whispers as my walls clamp down on his cock. His teeth sink into my neck hard enough to draw blood as I finally stumble headfirst over the edge. He follows me as my core tightens and clenches around him, milking him for all he's worth. Abel is quick to follow, exploding in my hand with a roar. "Mate," Rion asserts in a dark, possessive voice against my neck. "My mate." I'm too lost in my own pleasure to really hear and understand his words.

"Ours," Abel counters, sucking on my skin where Rion bit me.

"Yours," I agree as we collapse to the ground. "Always yours."

CHAPTER 40

DAMIEN

Travis Hudson was one of the best assassins in the guild.

Was, being the important term.

Lean and limber, Travis has a face that seems to be hewn from stone. His small body belies how dangerous he actually is. The curl to his lips makes him appear lethal, and his eyes are glowing with years of amassed wisdom.

Without a word, I hand him the bag of drugs.

While money may work in the real world to assert your dominance, here, we rely on a different currency. Drugs, booze, sex, and favors.

And since I don't give out favors, and I sure as fuck don't have sex anymore, drugs and booze it is.

Travis critically eyes the contents in the bag before nodding once, confirming I've done what I said I'd do. I should be offended, but in this world, everyone's a crook.

We're all a little mad here.

"I'm surprised the great Damien, Narian's favorite little protégée, got caught," he muses, leaning against the pillar with his arms crossed over his chest. He brushes at the white locks framing his face.

"And I'm *not* surprised that you got caught," I retort in the cold voice I reserve for my enemies, friends, and acquaintances. Frankly, everyone who isn't Nina. Travis stiffens at the proverbial ice I hurl at him. Weak. Fucking weak. How he was able to rise in the ranks as an assassin is beyond my comprehension.

Despite working for the same guild, the same man, I haven't seen Travis since I entered the prison. He's a shifter, a powerful one, and was immediately taken under Rion's wing. With relations between shifters and the other supernaturals no longer as tenuous as they once were, I reached out to my contact.

"I heard you were caught trying to assassinate Raphael Turner," Travis states.

"And I heard you were balls deep in the corpse of Councilman Draco's intern," I reply, face blank.

Travis throws back his head in laughter, slapping his knee. "Fuck, I missed your sense of humor, Red," he says, referring to the nickname the other men at the guild called me.

My hands always ended up stained that color after a job.

"Did you get me what I wanted to know?" I ask, cutting to the chase. I've never been into this "small talk" shit.

"Yup." Travis pops the P, lips circling. The easygoing smile on his face only serves to grate on my nerves.

"Tell me...before I kill you," I deadpan, removing my favorite gilded knife from my jacket sleeve. I've considered giving this dagger to Nina as a gift—a little token of me that she'll always have on her—but Abel talked me out of it.

"You're hilarious. Good one, man." He places a hand on my shoulder, and I eye the limb with narrow, penetrating eyes. Realizing his mistake, he quickly removes it and shoves it into his pocket. Smart man, going under the assumption he would like to keep it.

"Speak," I demand.

"You're right. The guild was asked again to take out Raphael Turner. Apparently, the client called Narian himself. There's no way of knowing if it was a man or woman, due to voice distortion."

"Did Narian take the job?" I ask curtly, already sifting through the numerous possibilities running rampant in my head. I'm still struggling to piece together how Nina fits into all this. Why her? Was she merely in the wrong place at the wrong time?

"Fuck, no." Travis snorts. "Narian isn't stupid enough to send his men after Raphael again. You were his best assassin, and you got caught." He shrugs his shoulders.

"Is the same person who hired me the first time the one who contacted Narian the second time?" I inquire. I feel desperate, gnawing at the first real lead we have. My head spins with the onslaught of information.

"No clue." Another nonchalant shrug. "Like I said, the voice was distorted, and we never met the client in person."

But whoever that person is obviously has a shit ton of money. Narian's services are not cheap.

"So, you're positive Narian didn't take the job?" I query.

"Positive." Travis bobs his head decisively. "He laughed before hanging up on them."

That sounds like Narian, twisted bastard.

"Anything else relevant?" I need to get to Blade and the others and discuss all that I've learned. More than that, I want to see Nina again.

"Yeah." Travis scrubs at his smooth jawline. "Narian mentioned something about a compound. I think the client mentioned it too. Do you know what he's referring to?"

My breath leaves me, and my lungs struggle to replenish their air supply.

Not just any compound, but *the* Compound.

Could it be the same one? The one my Angel escaped from?

It's too much of a coincidence for me to think otherwise.

Was Raphael Turner's murderer involved with the group who hurt Nina?

Red splotches erupt in my vision, and my hands curl into fists. I have the sudden, irresistible urge to enact vengeance on all those who wronged my Angel.

Including the assassin before me.

He may have helped me, but he's still a threat. His loyalties are as fickle and precarious as a shard of glass. At the drop of a hat, he could be the one slicing a knife across her throat.

I can't let that happen.

Before he can blink, I lunge forward and cut a clean line from ear to ear. Those glacial eyes of his glance up at me in shock and horror. Gradually, that horror turns into understanding. At the end of the day, we're all murderers. I have no doubt he considered doing the exact same thing to me.

I don't relish in this particular killing. It's not fun or orgasmic. It's a job, one that I need to do in order to protect Angel.

Wiping the knife on Travis's shirt, I slide it back up my sleeve and enter the corridor. Someone, at some point, will find his body.

I won't be around when that time comes.

∾

AFTER REVEALING MY FINDINGS TO THE TWINS, RION, AND Blade, I move to the cellblock where Bronson is with Nina.

They're sitting on his bed, her head beneath his chin, as he talks to her about his mom and sisters. Apparently, the oldest sister is a skilled hacker who once hacked the government's system to remove a parking ticket from her record.

"I wish I could meet them." Nina sighs, leaning farther against the hulking shadow wolf. Bronson kisses her head, a serene expression on his face. He looks at utter peace with her in his arms. For a brief moment, jealousy burns a hole in my chest.

"You will, my queen. One day. You're not going to be stuck here forever." His words scratch at the hole, rendering me breathless.

The thought of Nina leaving...

Is it selfish that I don't want her to ever leave? That I can't compute a future without her? I'm so used to her light that the darkness seems like a distant memory. The prospect of her leaving...

How long will it take her to forget about me?

Everyone eventually does. I'm a shadow, a ghost, hovering just on the outskirts but never participating. With Nina, with my Angel, I feel whole. Warmth suffuses me, wrapping me in its heated embrace.

Clearing my throat, I step forward, interrupting their interlude. Bronson's eyes flash umber, but he doesn't stop me from entering his cell. I keep my voice and face inscrutable—vacant, almost—as I stare at him.

"Blade has requested to see you," I say haughtily. Lie.

Bronson hesitates, staring from me to Angel, but she gives his bicep a reassuring squeeze.

"Go," she urges. "I'll stay with Damien." When he refuses to budge, she giggles, getting to her feet and pushing at his shoulder. "Go!" He turns, snaking an arm around her waist, and devours her lips with his own.

The little green monster makes an appearance again at

how easily he claims her. Like he has every right to. Like he's hers and she's his. Like they belong together.

A flush spreads up her cheeks, softening her dewy features, before she steps away from him and links her arm with mine. With anyone else, I would have them flat on their back with a knife to their throat.

But this isn't anyone else. This is Nina, and she's the only one allowed to touch me at will. I actually encourage it.

"Bye, Bron!" she calls, wiggling her fingers. He kisses her forehead, his eyes swarming with a dozen different emotions she'll never be able to see without the help of her powers.

"Bye, goddess."

He gives me a look that threatens pain if any harm comes to her. I nod back to show him I understand and comply. No one will be stupid enough to hurt my Angel when I'm beside her.

"Where are we going, Bitch Mage?" she asks, skipping beside me.

I stumble to a stop at the horrendous nickname. "What?"

This lady never ceases to surprise me.

"Rion told me that *Bitch Mage* is your nickname," she explains with another twinkling laugh. I could listen to that sound every second of every day and never tire of it. Warmth infuses my entire body.

"He did, did he?" I question lazily, already picturing a million different ways to murder the shifter.

But alas, he's her mate, so I suppose I'll let him off with a warning. One.

"Do you not like being called Bitch Mage?" she asks innocently. When I remain silent, staring stonily ahead, her lower lip wobbles. "I'm sorry, Damien. I didn't mean to hurt your feelings."

Oh, shit.

As tears flood Nina's milky eyes, panic overtakes me. I

desperately grab at her shoulders, my mind scrambling to come up with a solution to stop her tears. Chocolate, wine, and books. The perfect combination for any emotional female.

Shit. Shit. Shit.

A beatific smile overtakes her face, and she throws her head back in laughter.

"Were you...?" I trail off, dropping my hands to capture one of hers. "Were you teasing me?"

"Yup! And you fell for it!" She laughs, the sound so joyous and carefree that my own laugh escapes, unbidden. Her gorgeous eyes widen as she turns towards me. "Damien, did you just laugh?"

"You're evil." I drop her hand to wrap my arms around her thin waist. Over the weeks, she has gained a sufficient amount of weight back. She's nowhere near her ideal weight, but she's better than the skin and bones she'd arrived as.

As she tilts her face up, I have the irresistible desire to kiss her.

I've never kissed a girl before.

Sure, I've fucked them, but I always considered kissing an intimate act between two lovers, one that involves feelings and emotions. It was the one thing Narian never did to me. I thought I was broken, even more so than everyone suspected.

What type of man hasn't kissed a female?

Her luscious lips are curved up in a radiant smile, and I wonder how soft they'll feel against my own.

I step away, my body crying out as her warmth leaves me. She would never want to kiss a man like me.

I'm a monster.

Some people are monsters through circumstance only, but there are others who enjoy what they do. I fall firmly in the latter category. There's nothing more satisfying than my knife entering flesh and watching as the life drains from my enemies' eyes. Nothing more satisfying, that is, except for the temptress in front of me.

"Let's go to my room." I pull her down the corridor, my cold mask firmly back in place. If the mask was to ever break, I'm afraid the entire world would understand exactly how much she means to me.

We pass a group of Incubi who stare at Nina appreciatively. One glare from me has them cowering in the corner. Women and men alike eye us as we move down the hall of cells, curiosity, disbelief, lust, and anger in their gazes.

I mentally tally the number of people I have to kill. Hopefully, Blade can forgive me.

My room is at the very end of the hall, the only one without bars as a doorway. It used to be a guard's station back before we scared them all off.

It's my personal sanctuary, the one place I can go to escape the dissonant chaos of this world. Never before have I allowed someone to enter it, not even Blade.

Holding my breath, I push the metal door open.

I know she's in my mind when a soft gasp escapes her. Surprisingly, it doesn't feel invasive—I actually don't notice she's there.

I love that she can use me, use my eyes, to experience the world. It's an empowering feeling, and it makes me feel even closer to her.

Despite wanting to turn towards her, I keep my gaze fixed on the room, allowing her to look her fill.

A single bed rests against the wall, adorned in pristine white sheets, not a speck of color in sight. While the rest of the prison floor is variations of cement and stone, I have rich brown carpeting. Two dressers flank either side of my bed, and my acoustic guitar rests against the wall. It's one of my prized possessions. It took me weeks of favors to procure. A door against the far wall of the room is open to reveal a spacious and surprisingly modern bathroom.

"You live here?" Nina breathes in amazement. I don't bother to confess the reasoning for my arrangements—that I beheaded the guard who once occupied it.

"Yes. It's not much, but I made it my home." Finally turning towards her, I see that her eyes are dilated and her lips are parted. I yearn to rub my thumb across the plush lower lip, but I restrain myself. "It can be your home, too, if you'd like." My voice is cold, expressionless, but even I can't hide the hint of longing just beneath the surface.

To have her in my personal space...

It reminds me of the only thing I've ever wanted in this world—someone to trust, to love. Her. Forever.

"I'm actually kind of jealous," she admits after a moment. She gesticulates wildly. "I don't even get a cell to myself."

I smirk, placing a hand on the small of her back to propel her towards my bed. She sprawls across the mattress, her thick obsidian hair cascading around her. Any other girl would be wary about being in a room alone with me, or they would be scheming to get me in their beds, but not Nina.

Fuck, she's too good for this world. For me.

"I didn't know you play the violin," she states after a moment of comfortable silence.

I stare at the girl oddly. "Violin?"

She gestures in the general direction of my guitar.

"Angel, did you mean to say a guitar?" I ask with a twitch to my lips.

She sits up abruptly, cheeks crimson, before lowering herself back onto the bed with a groan. As always, she's wearing a short dress that reveals her ample curves and shapely legs. As she stretches, arms raising, the hem rides up past her thighs.

If anyone else were to see this, I would probably kill him or her on the spot.

My cock twitches in my pants, desperate to escape its confines and bury itself, balls deep, inside of her. Would she sheath my cock like a glove? Would she be warm? I imagine so, especially since she was made for me.

I have no doubt about that.

"I can play for you, if you like." The offer escapes my lips before I can reconsider. As soon as it's out there, I can't take it back.

Her white eyes gleam as a slow, beguiling smile pulls up her thick lips. It's hard to believe that something as simple as this could cause such genuine amusement. But, then again, Nina has never been a normal girl.

"Yes! Please!"

Chuckling at her enthusiastic response, I grab the guitar off a hook on the wall and adjust the strap. Quickly, I strum each string to make sure it's still in tune.

The last person I'd played for was my mother when we lived on the streets, before Narian took me in. Her pimp had given the instrument to her as a gift, and she had given it to me. I remember awkwardly plucking at the strings as a god-awful screech emitted from the instrument. It took dozens of trips to the library and over fifty hours of YouTube videos before I taught myself how to play.

Nina sits up completely, eyes trained on me, and I lose myself in her hypnotic stare. Those blind, sightless eyes see me with an unnerving intensity. I'm stripped bare before this gorgeous female, all my sins on display. However, I don't feel as if I'm being judged.

She sees me, the good and the bad, and accepts every facet.

Continuing to stare at her, I begin to play. It's an easy

piece, something I could even teach her, but one that holds a special meaning.

It's the first song I ever wrote.

Weeks ago, after she fed me in the throne room. This tiny slip of a girl had gone up to a grown man capable of evoking fear in the strongest of prisoners and fed him. They saw my ice; she saw my warmth.

Tears well in her eyes, and a soft smile breaks open her face. She looks so fucking beautiful. Angelic. With the light from my lamp haloing her head, I can almost believe she was sent straight from heaven to redeem me. Save me.

When I finish, those tears have dried, but the smile remains.

"Damien..." She trails off, slack-jawed. "That was beautiful."

"That was for you," I admit.

She moves to her feet, smoothing down her white dress and then wringing her hands in front of her waist. Indecision flashes across her face before it turns into resolve. With sure strides, she steps forward until she's directly in front of me.

"I want to try something," she whispers. I can scarcely breathe, scarcely think.

Before, my heart was racing. Now, it stops momentarily before stuttering to life again. It thunders in my ears.

Her smell wraps around me, like oranges and ginger. I wonder whose body wash she used this time.

Before I can focus on that further, she leans forward and presses her lips to mine. I freeze beneath her tender assault, body going rigid, before I force myself to relax.

My first kiss.

I timidly move my lips over hers, familiarizing myself with what she likes and dislikes. She tastes even better than I imagined. Her hands rest on my shoulders, pulling me closer, and I let her.

She's my anchor, keeping me tethered to the here and now.

Her fingers deftly undo the first few buttons of my shirt as our tongues swirl in a languid tango.

I want her.

I need her.

A knock on the door interrupts our moment.

I snarl, lips pulling back from my teeth, as Nina separates from me. My body immediately misses her soft curves pressed against my hard ones.

Fucking shit.

Who knew a kiss could feel so amazing?

And that kiss would've definitely led to other avenues if the cumstain hadn't interrupted us.

Removing my dagger, I stalk towards the door, preparing to slaughter whoever dared to knock.

I'm surprised to see Blade standing at the door. His face is taut with strain, dark shadows beneath his eyes. His haggard appearance isn't all that uncommon, but when his eyes flicker around me, towards Nina, I feel my own unease escalate.

"Nina," he breathes in relief.

"What happened?" I ask, donning my ice mask again.

Blade's eyes flicker to me once before settling on Nina, as if he can't look away. "Someone challenged Nina to a duel. She has to fight in the arena."

CHAPTER 41

NINA

"What do you mean?" I ask, stumbling forward. My face still burns from Damien's heated, passionate kiss. He may claim to be cold, but when he touched me like that, he was an inferno.

I slide into Kai's head while wrapping my hands around Damien's arm.

Engaged in a silent standoff, neither of the guys answers me. Damien's cold blue eyes are locked on Kai's dark ones. The air around them seems to crackle with electrical currents, a storm brewing.

"Cancel it." Damien's voice could turn water into ice. It chills me to the very core.

"I can't," Kai replies through gritted teeth. "She publicly made a declaration in front of at least one hundred of our men. If I refuse, we'll have an uprising on our hands. This system works because supernaturals can take out their aggression in the ring. It weeds out the weak and makes the strong feel powerful. You know the rules: refuse to fight, and it's open fucking season."

Damien's jaw is clenched so tightly, I'm afraid it'll break. His marble-like face could be carved from stone.

"We'll protect her," he hisses at last. He wraps a protective, possessive arm around my waist, tugging me closer to him.

My mind struggles to understand this conversation.

Ring?

Fight?

Me?

Random words filter in one ear and out the other. Try as I might, I can't catch enough to form a complete, coherent sentence.

"We'll lose our entire fucking gang, our army." Kai suddenly sounds tired. Older, almost, as if he's aged centuries in minutes. I pull myself out of Kai's eyes and into Damien's, warily eyeing my volatile dragon shifter.

Kai agitatedly runs his fingers through his hair, making it appear even more disheveled. When he drops his hand, I realize it's shaking.

"Then we leave the gang. Join the fucking shifters. I don't care. She's not getting in that damn ring," Damien argues. His gaze dips to the knife now in his hand. I didn't even realize he grabbed it.

"We can't!" Kai roars, the feeble hold on his rage exploding. To my horror, glistening red scales sprout on his arms and cheeks. Reptilian eyes, narrowed into slits, focus on Damien with unnerving intensity. At that moment, he looks positively lethal. Deadly. This is the man who has risen up the ranks of a gang to become their leader.

Kai isn't just my best friend and lover. He's a dangerous, murderous predator currently out for the kill.

"We can't," Kai repeats through clenched teeth. He takes a deep breath, chest rising and falling, before spinning on his heel and pacing the small expanse of hallway. "Rion is already having trouble keeping control of his shifters, due to this fucking alliance. They don't want us, and we sure as fuck don't want them. If we join, Rion can't guarantee our safety. *Her* safety. I'm not fucking risking her life."

"Then we kill the bitch who challenged Nina," Damien settles on at last, and I blanch at the word "kill." I'm not completely oblivious to Damien's recreational activities, but hearing it said so bluntly causes a shiver of unease to skate down my back.

"Can someone please tell me what's going on?" I break in at last. Detangling myself from Damien, I move to stand between the two fuming alphas. "Kai. Damien."

I feel Damien's hands on my waist, but through his vision, I'm only able to see Kai's piercing eyes. An inner conflict plays out in their depths before he releases a heavy sigh, nodding once.

"You're right. You deserve to know." His shoulders slump, as if a heavy weight is resting on them. I ache to comfort him, but I don't know how that will be received. "We have a system down here in the Labyrinth, at least on our side. Fights."

"Fights?" It sounds so simple, but I know that, with these men, nothing ever is.

"It's a way for the prisoners to take out their aggression. And it's a way for us to keep order," Kai explains, another sigh racking his body. "Someone can challenge another person to a duel, and that person has to fight. If they refuse or they try to run, we no longer offer them protection. They're cowards in our eyes, undeserving of our help." His words are matter-of-fact, but his eyes are anguished. "They're usually hunted down and killed in days."

"And someone challenged me to a fight?" I ask numbly, my mind unable to wrap around the sudden surge of information. Why would someone want to fight me? I mostly stayed to myself and the guys. I've never done anything to harm someone, at least not intentionally.

"There has to be something we can do," Damien argues in a cold, dark voice.

"The others are in the throne room. We'll talk there," Kai says briskly. Despite the urgency of the situation, he waits for me to place my hand in his. Unlike some of the others, Kai will never manhandle me. With him, everything is my choice.

As we walk, my mind wanders to Kai's confession.

They host...fights? And from what I understand, fighting is mandatory. To forfeit the fight is to forfeit your life.

Pain grips my heart in an iron claw and refuses to release. I've always known the guys weren't made of sunshine and rainbows, but I never suspected them capable of being this cruel. Would they really kick someone out of their gang because he or she refused to fight?

I have no doubt that with no alliance, you'll die pretty quickly in the Labyrinth. If not by your fellow inmates, then by the maze itself. I've only just begun to see what the Labyrinth has to offer. What else lurks behind every door, in every corner?

I don't even realize I've slipped out of Kai's head until we reach the throne room. Angry voices reach me, penetrating the fog in my mind.

"You're not fighting," Bronson announces immediately, his voice a growl, when I enter.

"You *would* find yourself in the ring already, Trouble," Cain quips. Despite his sarcastic tone, I can sense a hint of worry. If even Cain is nervous...

"Who challenged me?" I ask, allowing Kai to guide me to the throne. I don't bother protesting as I sit daintily on the edge, the other men gathering around me.

There's a long, potent pause before Rion answers, voice thick with self-loathing. "Tessa."

"Tessa?" I gasp, sure I heard him wrong. I consider Tessa a friend, one of my closest. What could I have possibly done...?

My mind snaps back to the day in the cafeteria when Rion came to get me. The rage in her eyes before it transformed into hurt. The frigid aura emitting from her. The unusual bend to her lips that gave her a cold, haughty look.

Oh, Tessa, what did you do? My heart drops like a stone into my stomach.

"Rion," Abel growls, my sunshine twin lost to his darkness.

When Rion doesn't answer, Braelyn cuts in with a resigned sigh. I didn't even realize she was in the room with us. "Tessa was one of the girls Rion used to have sex with," she says without preamble, ripping off the metaphorical bandage.

"You couldn't have been a little more fucking tactful?" Rion snaps. His voice suddenly comes from directly in front of me. His rough hands, the same hands that brought me to orgasm only a few days ago, touch my shoulders. Only, this time, I can't control the sudden flinch at his proximity. Pain and jealousy spear me at the thought of him with Tessa. "Buttercup—"

"Don't call me that." I shrug out from underneath him, stepping closer to the nearest guy. Abel, if the hard, lean body is any indication.

"I'm not a saint, and I never claimed to be one. Before you, I admit, I was with a lot of fucking women and men. I liked sex. A lot. It was just a way to pass time."

"Is that all I am to you?" I whisper as hurt cascades through me. The arms around me tighten, and I rest my head on the twin's shoulder. "A way to pass time?"

"No!" Rion shouts adamantly. "Fuck. No!" Working to moderate his volume, he adds, "The time with you...it was everything. Nina, since I met you, I haven't been with anyone else, and I don't want to be with anyone else. You're it for me, even if I have to share you with these idiots." He releases a sharp, humorless laugh.

"None of us are saints," adds Bronson quietly. "We all have pasts we'd rather not talk about."

I take a deep breath, knowing that's true. What happened in the past has to stay in the past. I can't allow the sins and transgressions of long ago to bury this relationship. Heaven only knows the ones I committed. I lashed out at Rion because I was jealous and hurt, but I know my reaction was irrational. He never intended to hurt me, and whatever relationship he had with Tessa was before he met me. He hadn't even looked at her in the cafeteria, his eyes on me like no one in the world could compare.

"I'm sorry," I whisper, tears filling my eyes. "I just got..."

"Jealous?" Rion supplies. At my nod, he pulls me into his arms, uncaring that Abel still has me in his. "I would rip the balls off any man you slept with before us. You're jealous because you're my mate. Hell, it could even be because you have feelings for an asshole like me. Either way, jealousy is completely natural."

"I don't know why we don't feel it towards each other," Kai muses, and Bronson grunts in agreement. "Maybe because this is fate: all of us together."

All of us together.

I like the sound of that.

Regathering my previously lost wits, I ask, "So, what happened with Tessa?"

"She liked the appeal of an off-limits shifter." Braelyn speaks up. "She would sneak over to our side of the prison."

"Only a few times!" Rion says immediately. "And it didn't mean anything to me. We would hook up, she would leave, and I would be with someone else an hour later. It was before I met you, of course. Now I'm a one-woman type of man. My heart is yours. My soul is yours. My fists are yours. My dick is yours. My pubic hairs are—"

"We get it," Kai cuts in. "Continue."

"Tessa fell in love with him," Jenny adds, speaking up for the first time. I imagine she's standing beside her girlfriend against the wall. "Or, more specifically, his power."

"It's not uncommon for betas and omegas to fall in love with alphas," Braelyn elaborates. "Those weak on the power hierarchy gravitate to those stronger. They want to be protected, and they contort those feelings into something resembling love."

"She probably thought Rion united our gangs for her," Damien breaks in vehemently. I suspect he's glaring at the tattooed shifter. "Fucking hell, Rion. Did you have to fuck everything that moved?"

"You're one to talk," Rion retorts. "I hear stories about your cock. It's as cold as the rest of you, capable of freezing a girl's vagina right off."

"Enough!" Kai roars, and the room immediately falls silent, no one willing to face the wrath of a feral dragon. "Nina will have to fight."

Protests immediately begin, but Kai cuts them off with another earth-shattering roar.

"I said enough!" he shouts. He takes a deep, calming breath. "The fight isn't until next week. That gives us time to train and prepare Nina. Fortunately, Tessa isn't allowed to use her powers. Unfortunately, if anyone suspects that Nina has any sort of unconventional sight, her secret will be out."

"Does that mean...?" I trail off, voice wobbling.

Kai's voice is grim when he speaks next. "You'll have to learn to fight blind. If anyone were to discover the truth about your abilities, I have no idea what they'd do. It'll be a witch hunt. People fear what they don't understand, and you, my love, are the biggest enigma here."

I'm barely holding on to my sanity. My breath rushes in and out as my heart picks up speed. Panic creeps around the edges of my mind, threatening to consume me completely.

"Damien, you'll need to teach Nina how to fight without her powers. Every fucking day. No breaks for either of you, understood?" I imagine Damien nods because Kai moves on. "Cain, you're going to be at the edge of the ring during the fight, ready to heal. If anything goes wrong, you jump in there, okay? I don't care what people say or think. I'm not losing her."

Cain? A healer? I never would've suspected.

He's more aloof than even Damien at times, and his bedside manner is atrocious.

"Yes," the man behind me agrees.

It's only then that I realize I'm not being held by Abel, but by Cain.

The man who cried when Haley touched him is now holding me tenderly against his chest.

My heart thunders in my ears as warm tingles radiate throughout my body.

"And Nina?" Kai addresses me last. When I turn in his direction, he says, "You fight until you can't fucking fight anymore, you hear me? You give it all you've got. Because if you don't, and something happens to you, I might just burn down this entire fucking world."

CHAPTER 42

NINA

There's a tension contaminating the room the day of the fight, polluting the air and filling my lungs with its toxicity.

Kai once read me a book about a man being led to the gallows. I imagine he felt similar to how I feel now. Worry and fear move through me like a winter's breeze. My hands are sweaty, and my heart beats rapidly against my rib cage. In the copious light, I see the blade seconds before it drops, dismembering the first of many heads. I know my time is quickly approaching, but I'm unable to move away. One step at a time, I walk towards my impending demise. Never stopping. Never looking back.

All I can do is keep my eye on the blade.

Braelyn has outfitted me in a stretchy pair of leggings and a skin-tight tank top. I've never worn anything like this before, and the fabric clings to my skin. My dark hair has been brushed into a tight braid cascading down my back, the flyaway hairs held back by a headband. I can't leave Tessa anything to grab during the fight, especially my hair.

I bounce on the balls of my feet, the darkness closing in

around me at all angles. Even though I can't see, I know Kai is pacing, Bronson's scowling, Damien is stone-faced, Rion's biting his nails, and the twins are huddled together. The anxiety in the air is particularly pungent, leaving behind an acidic, sour smell.

When a hand clamps down on my shoulder, I offer a feeble smile.

"Don't worry about me. I'll be fine." Even to my own ears, I know that's a lie. Braelyn and Damien have both worked with me, but there is only so much they can do with the limited time we've had. I'm confident that I won't die, but that's about it.

"Sure." Cain snorts derisively, squeezing my shoulder. "You'll probably only get your ass slightly kicked instead of completely kicked. Hell, maybe you'll still have an ass once this is all said and done."

I glare at him, but he only laughs.

"I'm not going to—errr—get my ass kicked." I wrap my arms around myself to fight off the sudden chill.

"You are, Trouble," Cain contests. "But don't you worry your pretty little head. I'll be here to fix you up afterwards."

"Is that supposed to be comforting?" I inquire. "Because it's really, really not."

"No. That's more of my brother's specialty. I'm just being honest with you. Do you know what Tessa was arrested and convicted for?" Cain asks, and I shake my head mutely. It has always felt too personal to bring up in conversation, so I have never asked. "Murder. She caught her boyfriend fucking another girl—his fated mate—so, she cut off his balls until he bled out. Then she went to the girl's home and murdered her too."

My breath whooshes out of me at his statement. What Tessa had done...

The lives she took...

In her mind, I did the same thing with Rion. She won't hesitate to kill me in order to prove a point. Ice-cold fingers squeeze my heart, effectively stopping my blood flow.

In a way, she's more dangerous than anyone else here. Her rage is driven purely by passion, which makes her volatile and unpredictable. When emotions are the driving force, a person is exponentially more dangerous.

"Is she here?" I ask, dreading the answer.

Maybe she decided not to go through with this. Maybe she realized that it's ridiculous and petty to fight over a guy— though I can't blame her for being head over heels for Rion. The man is capable of evoking strong feelings from anyone who spends time with him. Heaven only knows the number he did on me.

Unbidden, I slide into Cain's mind. Though his eyes are intent on me, over my shoulder, I spot Tessa's sleek brown hair. It's pulled into a tight bun on the top of her head. The bra and shorts combination leaves little to the imagination. Haley is standing in front of her, hands on her hips, but I'm unable to see the expression on her face.

To my shock, Rion steps up to the pair of females, a somber expression on his handsome face.

Jealousy churns low in my stomach, tasting like vomit. Why is he with her, the girl who wants to hurt me, possibly kill me? Why isn't he here with me?

As my emotions twist in my stomach like a ball of yarn, something unusual happens. Normally, I can sense the minds around me like flickering balls of light. I'm easily able to guide my consciousness inside the one of my choice.

This time, I'm slammed into Tessa's head with the ferocity of a freight train. Through her eyes, I see Haley's lips purse, like she's trying to keep from swallowing something sour. Rion looks livid, an unusual expression on his normally cheerful face.

I'm dimly aware of Cain saying my name, shaking my shoulder, but I'm too focused on Rion to hear what he says.

My awareness of Cain wanes as I focus intently on Tessa's mind. What she sees. What she feels. What she smells. What she hears. Slowly, Haley's words filter to me, as if through a tunnel.

"...fucking stupid. I keep telling you," the girl says, anger evident in her jewel-like eyes. "What did she ever do to you?"

"End this, Tessa," Rion demands. His tone is pure vitriol, and I'm shocked to hear it coming from my fun-loving shifter. "Call off the fight."

"Why the fuck should I?" Tessa retorts, turning towards the scowling shifter. She moves to place a manicured hand on his crossed arm, but he steps back before she can make contact. "I thought you loved me. I thought you came here for me. I was willing to be her friend when she wrapped her vagina around Damien's cock first and then Abel's. I even tried to help the bitch. But she took it a step too far. Why did she need to go after you too? Why couldn't she just be happy with what she had?" Tessa's voice breaks, her vision distorting with tears. The part of me that recognizes pain in others wants to comfort her. The larger part of me is too angry to care.

"Tessa." Rion's voice is considerably more gentle. "I was never yours to begin with. I thought you knew that. I don't— *didn't*—do relationships or anything serious. Especially here. But Nina's different."

"Why?" Tessa cries. "What does she have that I don't?" Her grief quickly morphs into rage.

Rion takes a fortifying breath. "She's my mate." That declaration causes my heart to stutter once, stop, before restarting with a vengeance.

Haley inhales sharply before blowing out a breath. "Damn. I always suspected something was up with her." She gently touches Tessa's shoulder, garnering the fuming female's attention. "Please reconsider, Tess. Nina didn't know about your relationship with Rion. Hell, I didn't even know about it, and I'm your best friend. Don't blame her for Rion being a fuck-boy."

"Rude," Rion mutters petulantly, but he doesn't argue with her.

Tessa's gaze flickers from Rion to Haley and then to me, standing on the other side of the stone arena. Only the top of my head is visible around Cain's broad back. Bronson stands behind me, speaking urgently into my ear, but I can't decipher any of his words.

"You'll be making a lot of enemies if you go through with this," Haley warns. "Even if, for some reason, Nina escapes unscathed, those guys of hers will still go after you. Hell, even Rion, the man you're fighting for, won't hesitate to kill you."

Tessa swings her gaze in the shifter's direction, and he shrugs sheepishly, once again not denying Haley's claim.

Before I can hear Tessa's reply, I'm wrenched out of her head and returned to my customary darkness. Steel bands wrap around my waist from in front. Behind me, someone's scratchy beard rubs against my cheek.

"What the fuck, Trouble?" Cain demands.

"Are you okay?" Bronson asks nervously. "Do we need a doctor? Cain, get a doctor. Or can you look over her? Fuck, I don't think you have your medical degree. Get an actual licensed doctor."

"I'm fine," I say quickly, hoping to alleviate the tension. Cain, who is still standing in front of me, takes a step backwards. Bronson uses that to his advantage, twisting me in his arms so he can nuzzle my neck. Licks of fire creep up my spine at the contact.

"Where did you go?" Bronson murmurs. "You just zoned out."

"Jesus Christ, Trouble," snaps Cain. "I thought you were seizing or some shit."

"No." I shake my head adamantly, untangling my arms from around Bronson to grip Cain's hand. After giving it a reassuring squeeze, I release it. While he has been more touchy-feely lately, I don't dare push my limits. Lowering my voice to a whisper, I add, "I went into Tessa's head."

"And?" Cain asks with a snort. "You always go into people's fucking heads."

"And..." I throw him a scathing look over my shoulder. "I was able to hear her conversation with Haley and Rion."

Bronson goes rigid in front of me, his arms iron vises. "And that's different?"

"Very different," I admit with a nod. "I'm usually only able to see through the person's eyes, except for the two times with Cain and Abel, when I was able to hear through their ears as well."

I realize my mistake a second too late. At that moment, my careless words wrap around Cain like rope, seep into his skin, and change something fundamental inside him. My heart simultaneously shrivels up like a raisin.

"Wait a fucking minute." The disdain in Cain's voice drips like acid eroding rock. "What do you mean 'except for the two times with Cain and Abel'? You've been using my ears? How often? When? What did you hear?"

"I was going to tell you," I begin urgently, spinning around, but my pleading words fall to the cement ground and get trampled on by his rage.

"You only say that because you got caught. You're drowning in a sea of your own lies, and sooner or later, you're not going to have enough air to breathe." I know, without needing vision, that his eyes are hurling daggers into my forehead. "I knew I shouldn't have trusted you."

"Cain..." Bronson's growly voice is both a warning and a

threat. His muscles are taut around me as a growl rumbles through him. "Shut the fuck up."

"I'm done," Cain snaps, ignoring Bronson completely. His ire is directed solely at me.

"Cain, wait!" I plead, desperately grabbing at his arm.

"Don't fucking touch me," he snaps, a hitch to his voice that wasn't there previously. I hear the stomp of his footsteps fading away, each deafening step an ominous omen. I wonder if he'll ever come back or if I broke his trust for good.

"He's so mad at me," I whisper, turning towards Bronson once more to bury my face in his neck. I inhale his spicy, masculine scent. It's like Cain ripped my heart out of my chest, threw it on the ground, and now I'm staring at the shattered pieces, unsure how to put them back together again.

"He's hurt," Bronson rumbles. "He doesn't trust easily, and he feels as if he's been betrayed. I think he's hurt more than anything that you didn't trust him."

"But I did—"

He cuts off my protests with a kiss. "I also think he's scared. He doesn't like being vulnerable, and he's terrified of what you heard while you were in his brain."

Tears slide down my cheeks, but I don't brush them away. Each trail reminds me of the pain I inflicted on someone I care about.

"He hates me," I whisper, the mere prospect shooting bullets into my heart. Claws desperately scratch at the organ until I'm unsure where the pain ends and I begin.

"It's not hate he feels, and that's why he's so scared." Bronson presses another painfully tender kiss to my forehead before releasing me. Abruptly, he changes the subject from Cain to the upcoming duel. "Remember, fight like your life depends on it. I don't care what you have to do, my queen, but you're coming out of this mess alive. I won't stand anything else."

He guides me to the center of the room, where I know Kai is standing. The dragon shifter is coiled with tension. It emanates from him in tangible waves.

"Remember what Damien told you," Kai whispers in my ear. The next second, I'm pushed forward.

The crowd is cheering and screaming, their excitement ratcheting up when I step into the ring. Blood rushes to my head, rendering me immobile.

There's no announcement, no official declaration.

But when Tessa punches my cheek, I know the fight has begun.

CHAPTER 43

NINA

My cheek stings fiercely.

Instinctively, I bring my hands up to guard my head. There's the telltale sound of her footsteps retreating a few steps. No doubt, she's gearing up for another attack.

"Tessa, please," I beg, blood forming in my mouth. She may be petite, but her hand seems to be carved from stone. "We don't have to fight."

"Why don't we?" Her voice comes from directly in front of me, and I duck just in time to avoid her next assault. "You stole Rion from me, you bitch. I thought we were friends."

"We are!" I plead. This time, I hear a whoosh of air, but I'm unable to move out of the way in time. Her fist lands in my stomach, pain exploding like fireworks. "This is ridiculous. I never meant to hurt you."

"But you did." The grief and rage are evident in her voice. For the first time since the fight began, genuine worry tumbles through me, like an intoxicated gymnast. I'm afraid Tessa might actually kill me.

I take an emboldening breath, bracing myself. "And I'm sorry I hurt you. Honestly. I never meant to."

"Then give me Rion," she hisses, catching her elbow in my shoulder.

"He's not something I can just give away," I protest immediately. "He's a person with a mind of his own. If he wants to be with you, that's his choice. I won't stop him or stand in his way."

That seems to be the wrong thing to say. She charges forward, a ferocious snarl escaping. She sounds positively feral and unhinged.

"Fight back, bitch!" she screams, slashing at my cheek with her nails.

Something solidifies in my stomach—a sort of resolve. My mind conjures up memories of Cain's betrayal-laced voice. The pain in Tessa's eyes when Rion retrieved me from the cafeteria a few days earlier.

And then Man, the last time I was with him. In a desperate bid to escape, I had clawed at his face the same way Tessa clawed at mine.

Am I as bad as Man? Is that why she's fighting me? Do I deserve this?

I have hurt so many people. I don't want to become the monster I once hid from.

"No," I say at last, my voice reverberating throughout the room. The screams and jeers of the crowd become dimmer until they're merely background noise. I focus entirely on Tessa's heavy, erratic breathing.

"No?" She pauses mid-assault, the warmth from her hand burning my throat.

"No, I'm not fighting you." My steel voice rings out clearly. The raucous cheers turn into murmurs of confusion.

"Nina, what are you doing?" Kai roars from the edge of the arena. I ignore him. I ignore everything.

"I'm not fighting you, Tessa. Not over this," I repeat softly. A second later, her fist connects with my opposite cheek. Pain blossoms as I collapse onto my hands and knees. I feel like a wilted flower that has been trampled on until it's merely a husk of what it once was.

She takes the opportunity to step on my back, bringing me completely to the ground. Tears cascade down my face, but I refuse to openly sob in front of her and the crowd. The pain is unbearable, agonizing, but I keep my reactions to a minimum. I have dealt with it before, and I'll deal with it now.

If I were to follow Damien's training, I would sweep my leg out and knock Tessa off balance. Instead, I keep my face pressed to the icy cement. I have no doubt nasty bruises are now marring my pale face. Fear makes my brain go blank, makes me retreat to the place I used to go as a child. Unlike before, I can't just hide under a blanket and hope the monsters don't get me. This is the real world with real monsters, and they don't only come out at night.

"Fight back!" Tessa screams, grabbing a fistful of my hair, lifting my head up, and then shoving my face back into the ground. A resounding crack echoes around me, and I know my nose is broken.

She waits until I amble back to my feet before attacking me again with renewed vengeance. Each kick, punch, and scratch causes lightning to radiate through my veins.

"I'm. Not. Fighting. You," I hiss. The crowd has gone eerily silent, as if they're waiting for something. But what they're waiting for, I haven't got a clue. "Take your anger out on me. Give me your pain. I'll survive it all because you know what? I have lived my entire life in hell. This is child's play."

I don't want to talk about the next few minutes. I don't want to discuss the agony that crawled up my spine as her foot stomped on it. The pain in my fingers as they were snapped back. The crunch of my nose as she punched me while I huddled in a fetal position on the ground. Kai's enraged snarl. Bronson's melancholic howl.

I know pain. Heck, I'm even an expert on it. This is nothing compared to what I'd previously endured.

Unlike the previous times, however, I know I'm going to survive it. For the first time in my life, I have people looking out for me, people who are just as full of shattered glass as I am. They're painstakingly mending the holes in my body and soul; I'm not whole, but I'm no longer the carcass I once was.

"Enough!" I'm vaguely aware of Kai screaming. "I said, enough, dammit! The fight's over. It's fucking over."

Pain. Pain everywhere. It's all I'm aware of.

So. Much. Pain.

My eyes are shut, head lolling to the side, as strong arms wrap around me.

"Where the fuck is Cain?" I hear Kai shout.

I open my mouth to confess the truth—that my transgressions have finally caught up to me, killing me—but I'm unable to move. My eyes are swollen shut, and the pain in my ribs threatens to consume me completely.

This is how I'm going to die.

But no. I'm not going to die. Not yet. Not when I still have so many things to live for. First and foremost, I'm a survivor. I always have been. This is just another obstacle I have to hurdle over.

"Stay with me, baby. Stay with me."

Screams and shouts pierce my brain from all directions, and I dimly hear someone crying.

It's the last thing I hear before I succumb to my injuries.

CHAPTER 44

CAIN

I hurt people I care about. It's my thing, always has been. My heart is shielded by barbed wire and prickly thorns. Anyone who dares to get close will get stabbed.

I can still picture Nina's tear-stained face as she stared up at me. The pleading in her voice. The sudden paleness in her cheeks, as if all her blood had been drained. I wanted nothing more than to take her in my arms, promise her that we'll be okay, and hold her until she was able to fight the demons plaguing her gorgeous mind.

Instead, like the asshole I am, I left her. Fucking left her. One look into her milky eyes, and I was putty for her to mold and shape. Whoever she wants me to be, I'll be. It's terrifying to think about the hold she has on me.

Fucking shit.

And now, because of me, she's no doubt distracted in her fight against that bitch, Tessa. If anything happens to her...

I throw my fist against the wall in the throne room, the cement denting with my enhanced strength. Blood seeps from my cracked knuckles, but I embrace the pain. Welcome it, even. Snarling, I prepare to punch the wall again when a warm body wraps around me from behind in a tight hug.

"Let me go, Abel," I hiss, my voice nearly unrecognizable as my demon makes an impromptu appearance.

"Nope!" My brother pops the P. "It's cuddle time!"

"For fuck's sake..."

It takes some maneuvering, but I finally manage to untangle myself from my brother's arms. Abel pouts petulantly before some of his signature cheer returns.

"What has your panties in a twist, brother?" Despite the amusement in his tone, I can hear the genuine worry and curiosity just beneath the surface. My brother is more than just the flirty, joking man others perceive him as. He has a side to him that most of the world has never seen.

I mask my pain by being an asshole. He masks his by laughing. Sometimes, those with the largest, brightest smiles are the ones who are hurting the most.

"Nina," I answer at last, forking my fingers through my blond hair. I slowly slide down the wall, pulling my knees up to my chest and wrapping my arms around them.

God, when will her face not haunt me? Those damn, soulful eyes...

I had promised myself I'll never hurt her, and what did I do the next fucking day? Hurt her. She had lied to me, sure, but that was no excuse for my explosive reaction. She had flinched back, as if my words were the slash of a physical whip.

Fucking hell.

"What happened?" Abel asks cautiously, moving to sit beside me. His eyes flicker towards the door before focusing back on me. I know he wishes he could be with Nina right now, supporting her at her first fight. Instead, he's stuck dealing with his selfish, asshole brother who, once again, put his foot in his mouth. My guilt blows through me like a

December breeze, when the snow is a white blanket on the ground and the sun barely peeks over the canopy of clouds.

"Nina's power changed today," I explain subduedly, glancing at my hands. White scars still line my wrists and palms from numerous years of captivity. There are very few things that can scar a demon, but cuffs laced in holy water are one of them. It was Boris's preferred method back at the sex club.

"What do you mean?" Abel inquires curiously. No doubt, he's wondering how Nina's shift in abilities caused such a volatile reaction from me, to the point where I ran from the room like a little bitch baby.

"She was able to see through Tessa's eyes and hear through her ears." My fingers tap a staccato against my pants leg as my mind wanders. "She let it slip that she had done it twice before...through us."

Abel is silent for a second, but unlike me, he doesn't get angry or even upset. Instead, his expression turns thoughtful and almost curious.

"So, she was able to go inside our heads and use our ears and eyes?" he surmises. At my nod, he goes silent again. Processing. Unlike me, Abel thinks things through before he reacts. People usually think he's the impulsive twin, but that couldn't be further from the truth. He methodically weighs every option in that analytical brain of his, the pros and the cons, before arriving at a conclusion.

"Are you mad that she kept this a secret, or are you scared about what she saw?" Abel, as always, is able to read me better than I can read myself. In a matter of seconds, he puts a name to the tumultuous thoughts rattling around in my brain.

Sighing, I scrub a hand down my face. "Both? Neither? I don't know."

We were both hurt at first that she had kept her abilities a secret, but we understand now why she had to. She hadn't known whether we were friends or foes. I certainly hadn't given her any indication that she could trust me. Once the hurt waned, I understood why she hadn't wanted to tell us. I would do the same if I was in her situation.

But this?

What could she have seen that would make her so hesitant to share? My mind sifts through memories of the last few weeks.

I haven't been with any other girl, so surely, that wasn't it. Did she see me murder that man in the visitor's room? Or, before that, had she seen me flirt with him? Does she feel like I betrayed her?

My thoughts continue to run rampant, unintended, in my head. I know that my abrupt departure will only add tinder to the already blistering flame.

Did I ruin the best thing that has ever happened to me?

"She'll forgive you, you know," Abel pipes up. "Knowing her, she's kicking herself for keeping it a secret in the first place. I know you hate lies and half-truths, but you have to remember where she came from. She was tortured her entire life. The only person she ever trusted left her. She's delicate, Cain, and she needs us now more than ever."

"I know," I growl, trying to push down another wave of self-loathing. "I fucking know that, okay? It doesn't change the fact that it hurts that she lied to me."

"She didn't lie to you," Abel points out. "She just omitted the truth." He hits my shoulder with his own. "But I see how happy she makes you, how happy she makes me. I know demons don't have fated mates or whatever, but I genuinely think she was made for us. Both of us. Yeah, we have to share her attention with the others, but I'd rather do that than not have her in my life at all." Abel trails off, voice turning contemplative.

I risk a glance towards him to see his eyes wistful and smile serene. For the first time ever, he looks at peace. The ghosts once inhabiting his body have been exorcized.

"Do you love her?" I whisper, suddenly desperate to hear his answer. My own feelings for the female are confusing, at best. I don't know love, but I do know that I can't imagine life without her in it. This daunting, dark world doesn't seem as terrifying with her by my side.

Once again, Abel doesn't immediately answer. He takes his time to think over my question and formulate an articulate response.

"Yes," he replies after a moment, eyes widening at his own epiphany. "I think I do." He pauses, scratching at his smooth-shaven chin. "I'm not even going to ask you if you love her. I know you do, but you'll never admit it. Emotions terrify you. You shut them behind a locked door in your brain, where you keep all the other unpleasant and painful things. But emotions and feelings shouldn't be scary. Love shouldn't be scary. It breaks my heart that your past is affecting you to this day."

My heart thunders in my ears as I consider Abel's words. He spoke them with such certainty that it almost felt as if he was speaking about himself.

"When did you get so wise, asshole?" I quip, not daring to express my true feelings. Maybe Abel's right. Maybe the thorns around my heart actually conceal a rose desperate to bloom. All it needs is sunlight and nourishment, which Nina supplies in spades. It's like I've been sleeping this entire time and only just now learned how to open my eyes. She's awakened me and given me courage to face my demons.

Just as I'm about to rise to my feet and go to her, raised voices erupt from the hallway. A moment later, the door to the throne room is thrown open.

Kai enters first, face haggard and drawn. Damien, directly

behind him, is impossible to read. He emanates a frigid aura that warns prey and predators alike to stay as far away from him as possible. I notice a cat scurrying between their legs, releasing a pitiful cry.

And then, I see her.

She's lying in Bronson's arms, her head resting on his shoulder. At first, I'm unable to get a good look at her, due to her face being twisted away. As she shifts, moaning in pain, I catch my first glimpse.

Her eyes are swollen shut, the skin around them already beginning to turn black and blue. Gashes disfigure the side of her face, the jagged marks seeming to come from fingernails or claws. One of her fingers is twisted at an unnatural angle, and blood pours from her cracked lips.

For a moment, I'm stunned, unable to do anything but gaze at her. How did this happen? None of us had expected her to win the fight, but we sure as fuck didn't expect this type of damage. It's like she didn't even try.

Abel bursts into action a moment before I do, racing to her side. His eyes are crazed, his carefree persona nowhere in sight.

"What the hell happened?" he demands. When he takes a step closer, Bronson growls, baring his sharp canines. There's no doubt in my mind that his wolf is fully in charge. Seeing his mate hurt tipped him over that steep edge. Already, I feel the flimsy hold I have on my own emotions exploding like a dam with too much pressure applied. I can barely think straight through the sudden rush of panic.

"Cain. Cain. *Cain!*" Damien's voice pierces the clouds fogging up my mind. I stare into his cold, icy eyes and then to the dagger pressed to my throat. "Fix her." There's not a shred of warmth or sanity in his gaze. His actions are purely instinctual, not a coherent thought swirling in that calculating mind of his. Numbly, I wonder what Nina's death will do to him.

I'm not sure any of us could recover from it.

Forcing myself into action, I race forward until I'm directly beside Bronson. The wolf continues to growl at me, amber eyes bright in his face, but I hold his stare steadily. Calm. I can be calm. I don my apathetic mask with practiced efficiency.

"She'll die if I can't help her," I warn. "Set her down."

"Bronson! Fucking do it!" Kai screams. Anxiety clouds his normally harsh face.

Bronson struggles for a moment to control his wolf's instinctual reaction. Slowly, he places her on the ground, refusing to budge from her side. I can deal with that.

As Bronson pointed out earlier, I never went to medical school. However, I was a licensed nurse with ambitions to gain my medical degree before I was kidnapped by Boris's men. My training has come in handy to save not only my and my brother's lives, but other inmates' as well. In both prisons.

The last thing we need is to involve Brina, the psychotic prison doctor who makes Damien look sane. She's a fae who thrives on pain and suffering—I still have nightmares from the one time she worked on me, back when I was forced to fight in the ring to prove my worth.

"I'll be okay," Nina murmurs now, voice garbled and pained. She tries to crack a smile, but her lips are unable to move more than a millimeter. The swelling on her face has intensified in the short time it took the others to bring her to me.

"I'm so sorry," I whisper hoarsely, starting my inspection at her ribs. I pray that none of them have punctured an important organ.

"It's my fault," she whispers, so softly I have to strain to hear her. "I refused to fight. Does that make me weak? Does that make me stupid?" Her lashes flutter against her red cheekbones.

"It makes you brave," I reply, voice choked with emotion. Emotion...for her. I regret our stupid fight earlier with my entire being. If I could take my words back, I would in a heartbeat. "You have a kind, gentle soul, and that makes you different than the others here but not any less strong." Her eyelids flutter, unconsciousness beginning to pull her under once more.

"Cain?" Her voice is a hushed, barely audible, murmur.

"Yeah, Trouble?" I try to keep my tone light and teasing, but it wobbles slightly. Shit.

Hold yourself together, Cain!

"I'm sorry."

Even when she's on death's door, she's still thinking about those around her. Apologizing to me, the asshole who left her. If anyone should be saying sorry, it's me.

"I know, honey," I soothe, gently using my talons to claw open her shirt. I hiss at the collection of bruises and protruding ribs on her once pale and unblemished stomach.

Come on, Nina. Fight. Fight harder than you've ever fought before.

She may have chosen not to fight in the ring, but I'll be damned if she makes that same mistake now. Because, if she dies, I'll relinquish my horns, gain a fucking halo, and fly up to heaven to be with her.

CHAPTER 45

KAI

It's been two weeks.

Two weeks since I watched the love of my life get beaten to a pulp by a jealous bitch.

Two weeks since I saw the life drain from her eyes a moment before they shut indefinitely.

Two weeks since I heard her lilting laugh and saw her breathtaking smile.

Two weeks since her body has slowly, gradually begun to heal itself. With anyone else, anyone human, she wouldn't have been able to survive. Her injuries were intense, and one of her lungs had been punctured. However, Nina isn't human.

Two fucking long weeks.

Tessa's dead.

Ironically enough, it wasn't any of my men who killed her. None of them—except for maybe Damien—would hurt a female, though I was sure tempted that day. Instead, we usually rely on other devices to subdue the threat. Banishment, for one.

Fortunately, we didn't have to worry about any of that. The second the fight ended, Braelyn strolled up to Tessa and snapped her neck. It didn't do anything to help shifter relations, but it made me feel better.

"They should've bonded over the fact that they liked the same dick—and I mean that in both ways. Rion is a massive dick," she said with a twist to her lips. "You know, this world would be a better fucking place if girlfriends and exes became best friends forever. Matching friendship bracelets and late-night wine talks just to bitch about the guy. Oh, you liked that ride? Me too! Now, let's get drunk."

I'm grateful that Braelyn eliminated the threat, but I'm terrified of Nina's reaction.

If she ever wakes up, that is.

Already, rumors are circulating in the prison about the new queen. The humble queen. The generous queen.

Queen.

Queen.

Queen.

It's all I hear during those brief hours a day I'm forced to lead people. Her stand during the ring accomplished more than she expected. The people have found someone they can rally around, someone gracious and kind, with a fleet of the most dangerous supernaturals at her beck and call. They know that, by controlling her, they can control us.

Queen.

Fucking queen.

"You need to rest," Braelyn says from where she stands sentry against the wall. There's noticeable concern and wariness on her face whenever she glances at Nina's prone, unconscious form.

"I'll rest when she wakes the fuck up," I growl, squeezing Nina's cold hand. Some of the bruises have faded already, while others have turned yellow and light green. The scars have all but disappeared, leaving behind smooth, unblemished porcelain skin. Cain has been working around the clock to ensure she'll wake up. The poor kid blames himself for leaving before the fight began. But I know that his appearance there wouldn't have made any difference.

Nina's a gentle soul, a kind one. It doesn't make her any weaker, but it makes her strengths different. This strength, however, managed to gain her a kingdom.

A soft cough has my head whipping towards the corner of the room. Damien stands in the shadows, suit wrinkled and face covered in heavy black scruff. The man looks like shit, and coming from me, that's saying something. He hasn't moved from the corner since Nina was injured. Sometimes he's sitting, sometimes he's standing, but he's always watching. Jenny has been bringing him food from the cafeteria. Without her, I guarantee you that the stubborn bastard wouldn't eat. He's too lost in his own thoughts, his own despair.

Is it healthy? Not at all. Do I dare say something? Fuck no, especially when I'm not behaving any better. I leave the room only when necessary to deal with matters of the prison, but I always come back to her. She's a magnet. No matter where I go, she'll always pull me back in.

Bronson has remained in his wolf form since that fateful day. Currently, his furry head is resting on the edge of the bed, eyes closed in sleep.

Abel has become a pseudo-nurse, helping his brother gather supplies and administering the necessary drugs.

Only Rion remains suspiciously absent. He claims that he has to deal with the shifters, but I know the truth: he feels guilty, even more so than Cain. It was Tessa's obsession with him that caused Nina's injuries. Though I know Nina doesn't blame him, he carries the burden like steel weights on his shoulders.

Sometimes, I see his cat lurking in the rafters of my prison cell where we brought her once she was stable.

I turn her hand over and grab the nail polish I had Rebecca procure for me. Both Rebecca and Haley have been by numerous times to check on Nina and see her progress. They both feel immensely guilty for not seeing Tessa's instability until it was too late. I worried Haley, especially, would want to seek revenge, and though the girl grieves Tessa, she doesn't seem too distraught. If anything, she appears more worried about Nina than her dead friend. But that's life here in the Labyrinth. People come and go every day. People *die* every day.

"You have to wake up soon, baby," I say softly, painting her pinkie a pearlescent pink. I trimmed the nails down a little bit earlier today. "I need to see those beautiful eyes. I need to hear your voice."

Damien audibly gulps, but he doesn't say anything. He never says anything, content to hide in the shadows until his light returns.

"We all miss you," I continue, moving to her ring finger. I pause, tracing the length, and imagine my ring adorning it. She would make a beautiful bride.

My wife.

My fucking wife.

My heart swells at the prospect.

Shaking my head, I move to the middle finger and begin to paint that one.

"Rion and Cain blame themselves. They both love you, you know. It should bother me. I mean, technically, I had you first. I had you all to myself, and ironically enough, those years at the Compound didn't feel like hell. Maybe because you were with me." After finishing her pointer finger, I move to her thumb, applying long, languid strokes. "But it doesn't bother me. Sharing you, that is. At least, with these men. Okay, maybe sharing you with Rion pisses me the fuck off, but I know he cares for you. Even Damien is mourning you in the only way the asshole knows how." I drop her hand gently back onto the table and grab her other one. "You're going to be okay, my beloved. We're not going to let anything happen to you."

After finishing her other hand, I press a tender kiss to her clammy forehead. Soon, those white eyes of her will stare up at me adoringly. Soon, I'll hear that sweet laugh again. Soon. Soon. Soon.

"It's been two weeks," Cain murmurs, scrubbing a hand down his face. A light, scratchy beard has appeared on his jawline, and his cheeks look thinner. Nina will beat our asses if she discovers how little we're taking care of ourselves. Beat our asses...with love and hugs.

"You don't think we fucking know that?" Abel asks, irritated, from where he's sitting on the ground, playing solitaire. He hasn't so much as smiled in the two weeks that have passed. His lips are pressed into a tight, somber line.

"I'm not talking about Nina," Cain snaps. "We've been so preoccupied with the fight and then Nina's health that we haven't had a chance to discuss what we all discovered." He meets each of our gazes, including Rion's in the rafters. At some point, he shifted back to his human form, lying on his stomach with his chin on his hands.

"Lionel Green is obviously lying," Damien speaks up for the first time in...who knows how long. Those glacial eyes focus on Cain. "He claims he didn't kill Raphael, but how do we know it's the truth?"

"We don't," I agree, reaching into my back pocket to grab the two printed pictures I had my men procure for me.

The first one shows Raphael Turner. His dark hair is slicked back from his handsome, smiling face. He's a strange combination of beautiful and terrifying. His blood-red eyes and sharp fangs give him a lethal look, despite the jubilant grin.

The second picture is the asshole Lionel Green. Fat, ugly, and insignificant in every way. He only won the council vote through fear. No one dared to run against him. I hate him with a burning intensity, especially after I learned the truth about his relationship with the twins.

They confessed the truth to us a few days ago, while we held vigil around Nina's bed. They told us that they were once slaves to the atrocious Boris, and Lionel was a frequent customer. Abel described his encounter with the slimy man, and I know that if I were to ever see him, I would kill him on the spot. True, undiluted fear appeared on Abel's face as he recounted the story. When he described the forced kiss, even Damien's impassive mask cracked as raw rage flashed in his eyes.

"Do you think the client got another assassin's guild to kill Raphael?" Abel asks Damien.

"No." Damien shakes his head adamantly. "There aren't any assassins who would take on such a high-profile case, especially after the last failed attempts." He taps a finger to his chin contemplatively. "Of course, I can't be certain, but from what I hear, the kill was too sloppy to be done by a trained individual."

"Unless that's what they wanted you to think," Cain points out, and we all fall silent again.

Reluctantly, I leave Nina's side and tape the pictures to the stone wall. Raphael Turner and Lionel Green. We know their connection, obviously—political rivals.

But we also know that they've been serving on the council for many, many years. What changed? Why would Lionel snap now and hire someone to kill Raphael? Damien's right. The kill was sloppy. Was it the work of an expert or an amateur? And what does Nina have to do with any of this? Damien claims that the client discussed the Compound during the phone conversation with the assassins' leader.

My mind continues to spin and spin like a carousel I'm unable to get off. Around and around and around...

"Cain?" a sleepy voice murmurs. "Kai? Abel? Damien? Bron? Rion?"

We all whip our heads in the direction of the bed. White eyes in a gaunt, pale face stare back at me. Or through me, is a more accurate description. As she blinks at me, I find myself igniting and burning on a pyre. Heat rushes through me, white hot.

"Baby?" I whisper, scarcely able to believe it. I feel as if I'm holding something precious in my hands, but any sudden movement will cause it to shatter.

Nina's face, if it's even possible, pales further. She trembles, tears filling her eyes.

"What's the matter?" Abel demands, jumping to his feet.

Damien steps towards her with his dagger raised, searching for an invisible threat.

Her shaky finger, still wet from the nail polish, points towards the pictures I just taped on the wall.

"Why...?" She trails off, swallowing. "Why do you have a picture of Man in your cell?"

CHAPTER 46

NINA

Man was a regular around the Compound for as long as I can remember. I'm not exactly sure when I first saw him; time moved differently in the Compound—slow and sluggish, like molasses.

I distinctly remember, though, when I met the *real* Man. I was eight years old when he revealed his true face, the face of a monster.

He never bothered to hide his identity from me, never bothered to conceal his grotesque face. Why should he? I was a blind, dumb child who still cried for a mother I'd never met. He took one look at me and dismissed me the way everyone did.

I remember that day vividly. The images were tattooed on my mind, etched into the skin behind my closed eyelids.

It's the first time I looked evil in the face. Even to me, a person who indirectly saw horrors every day of her life, he appeared monstrous, though I was under no misconception the others perceived him as that. I heard the ladies whisper about him when they thought I wasn't listening. Handsome.

Powerful. Rich. Three words that meant nothing to a prisoner like me.

What they saw was a charming man—dark, slicked-back hair, revealing a proud and arresting face. High cheekbones, a strong jawline, and wrinkles around his eyes that betrayed his true, ancient age.

But what I saw in private, when we were alone, was the evil lying in wait just underneath his skin. Eyes red as fire and fangs that contorted his mouth when he smiled, showing the remnants of blood on his teeth.

When I first saw his reflection in the window of the torture room, I'd accepted the inevitable conclusion that I'd been kidnapped by a monster. An honest-to-god monster. He looked like something that could crawl out from underneath your bed.

He only got scarier over time, colder and meaner as the days dragged on. And as the years passed, his beatings became more frequent and took me longer to heal from.

Man was a monster, through and through.

I still remember his cold, grating voice; it'd slithered down my spine like a snake. "You're mine, Little Monster. I made you."

What he made was a trembling, terrified girl with an ingrained need to escape and make a name for herself. To become something more than his plaything and prisoner.

Seeing his face on Kai's wall...

I am suddenly that scared child again, shivering beneath my scratchy blanket as I attempt to ward off the monster.

As I stare through my dragon's eyes at the photograph, a ball of lead forms in my stomach. Even after all these years, his abuse still haunts me.

Kai stalks forward and points to the picture of Lionel. "Him?" he asks, disbelief evident in his tone.

"No, him." I point to the other man, the dark-haired, red-eyed one.

"Raphael?" Abel questions in disbelief.

Raphael Turner.

The man whose death I was arrested for.

The man who tortured and beat me to a pulp, leaving behind nothing but bruised, mottled skin.

The man whose face haunted my every waking moment.

Man.

"Fuck," Kai murmurs, stumbling away from the pictures. He, too, experienced Man's abuse firsthand, though, unlike me, he never saw his face.

Nausea causes my stomach muscles to tighten.

No. No. No. No.

"Trouble, you need to calm down," Cain whispers, brushing at a strand of my black hair. "Your body is still healing, and you shouldn't get so worked up."

Healing?

Distant memories return in flashes of light. Tessa's furious eyes. The ring. My refusal to fight. And pain. So much pain.

"How long have I been out?" I whisper, pulling out of Kai's mind and sliding into Cain's. The sex demon is staring at me intently, his gaze sliding over the yellowing bruises on my face and then down to my wrapped ribs. The longest I was ever incapacitated back at the Compound was a couple of weeks, and that was after being an inch from death. Only my unknown supernatural blood saved me then. Apparently, it also saved me now.

At some point, the guys must've washed me. The blood and grime have been cleaned off, and I'm dressed in a comfortable white nightgown. Even my hair has been brushed and braided. My nails have a fresh coat of pink paint on them as well.

"Two weeks," Cain answers, voice choked.

Two weeks.

Two weeks, I have been unconscious and unresponsive, my body struggling to heal itself and repair the damage inflicted. Tessa *really* did a number on me.

Phantom pain cascades down my arms and legs, but it's not overwhelming. It's a dull ache, a pressure almost, like when you fall asleep on your arm, causing the limb to go numb. The worst pain centers around my stomach, where I have no doubt broken one or two ribs.

"And how's Tessa?" I query. Does she regret hurting me? Is she sorry?

Silence descends in the cell, nearly suffocating me.

"Tessa?" I repeat somewhat desperately. But before they can even speak, I know the answer. They may be kind and gentle with me, but in their cores, they're hardened, possessive men.

"I killed her," Braelyn admits at last, leaving me stunned and slacked-jawed. "I pledged my loyalty to you. I promised that no harm would come to you when you're under my care. She caused me to break that promise."

My head reels with this new information as pain grips my heart, squeezing until all the blood in my body rushes straight there. A part of me hated Tessa for what she did to me, what she wanted to do. I'm under no misguided notion that she would have spared me if Kai hadn't stopped the fight. Another part of me grieves for her, grieves my friend.

"Don't cry, Bambi. Please. You know I hate tears. They make me ragey, and you really don't want to see me like that," Abel pleads, moving to stand beside his brother.

"This is too much," I whimper. "Raphael. Man. Tessa. It's just too much." I continue to mutter incoherent words and phrases. I don't know if they understand me—heaven only knows, I don't understand myself—but the more I talk, the calmer I become. I no longer feel like I'm stuck in the vicious winds of a hurricane. Instead, I'm resting in the eye of the storm. I have no idea how long the peace will last, but I revel in it while I can.

Calmness cascades through me like a summer's breeze, blowing the doubt and anger away.

Okay, Nina. Calm down. You're no help to anyone if you allow your emotions to consume you.

"So, what do we do now?" I ask weakly. I push myself onto my elbows to move into a sitting position. Bronson's whine has me pausing, turning in the direction of the noise gradually coming closer to me. A moment later, his wet nose rubs against my hand.

"I'm okay, Bron," I whisper, petting his coarse fur. "I'm okay."

The wolf steps away, and very human hands caress my cheeks. Gently, as to not disturb my numerous injuries, he parts my lips with his thumb.

"You're okay. You're okay." He seems to be reminding himself as well as me. Still keeping his hands on me, he drags me into a sitting position on the table, allowing me to use his muscular, bare chest as a backrest.

Bronson. My shadow wolf. The man who has always—and will always—look after me. I feel so safe and treasured in his arms.

"So, Raphael Turner worked in the Compound," Damien mumbles harshly. He's silent for a moment, contemplative, before he says, "That explains why they found your blood beneath his fingernails and his blood on you. Didn't you tell me you guys fought during the escape?"

I swallow down a lump the size of an acorn. "He scratched me," I admit. "During the escape, he scratched me, and I attacked him."

There's a long, potent pause as we all consider the implications.

"But you didn't kill him?" Cain asks for clarification.

I gape. "Of course not!" Though the prospect of killing him had occurred to me numerous times during my stints down in the torture room. It was always a fleeting thought, there and gone in only seconds, but it was a thought all the same. I had contemplated the fragility of life and how easy it was to destroy.

I don't know if I was referring to Man's life or my own.

"I've done months of research on Raphael fucking Turner and never stumbled across anything like this," Damien snaps. I have a feeling, however, that his ire isn't directed at us but at himself. He likely blames himself for not seeing this connection sooner.

"He was obviously good at covering his tracks," Abel muses. He grabs my hand and absently plays with my fingers. Heat travels through me from that small connection, blossoming in my core.

"He probably hid the Compound under the guise of one of his charities," Cain adds. "Fuck, he probably even had fundraisers to raise money for his sick fetish."

"But why did he have the Compound to begin with? Why did he participate? What was the purpose?" Kai fires off. When Cain swivels his gaze towards him, I see the dragon shifter pacing in agitation. He pulls at the strands of his dark hair, making them appear even more disheveled.

"Because he's a sick fuck," Bronson rumbles, sniffing my neck. Goose bumps skitter across my body at the contact. "Who knows why sick people do sick things."

"I doubt the other council members know about this," Damien theorizes. "It's too fucked-up, even for them."

"So, we know that Raphael Turner wasn't the saint everyone suspected him to be," Abel says. "We know that he actually ran an illegal Compound, where he tortured and abused young supernaturals. We know that he was murdered after Nina escaped. But why? None of this makes sense. Why did they kidnap Nina and Kai in the first place? Why them?" He releases a heavy sigh, brushing my hand across his lips in a tender kiss. In a quieter voice, meant for my ears alone, he whispers, "I'm sorry all of this happened to you."

"I just don't understand." I feel the beginning of tears in my eyes. "Why me? Why does all this stuff have to happen to me?"

It's a question that haunted me when I sat in the dingy, seven-by-seven cell. It's a question that reverberated through my mind when I was strapped to the table in the torture room. I questioned it again in the ring with Tessa, a friend turned enemy.

Why me?

"I don't know, my queen," Bronson replies in my ear. He nibbles on my earlobe once before he releases me. "But I swear to you, we'll figure it out. Cross my heart and hope to die."

And that's exactly what I'm afraid of.

CHAPTER 47

NINA

My body has been bent and broken, twisted and reshaped, discarded and used, numerous times throughout my life. Yet, I have somehow managed to emerge relatively unscathed.

Sure, there are pieces of me that I can't get back, pieces left behind in the Compound and then at the court hearing with the judge. I'm less whole than I once was, but I'm still breathing. My lungs are still capable of taking in air. My heart can still beat, though the rhythm is unsteady. My hands no longer shake when I contemplate all I have endured and all I will continue to endure.

The week since waking up after Tessa's attack has proven to me how resilient I actually am. You can knock me down, stomp on me, but I'll always get back up with a determined glint in my eyes.

My body has slowly and surely mended itself back together again. My bruises have all but completely diminished, and my ribs no longer ache. And though I should feel one hundred percent, a part of me died in that ring with

Tessa. It's a minuscule piece, one I doubt anyone will miss, but it's still a part of me I'll never get back.

During the course of my healing, none of the guys dared to discuss Raphael Turner or the Compound with me. They believe they need to tread lightly around those subjects, as if the mere mention of my tormentor will send me spiraling over the edge.

Don't they realize I'm made of tougher stuff than that? Don't they see the armor I have erected around myself? It's made of steel and cement, a fortress not even my dragon can break.

Silently fuming, I curl my fingers around the ball Cain had gotten me. It's supposed to help with my physical therapy—something about regaining function in my broken fingers. For a human, this method would probably work. For me, it's just an annoyance. I didn't even realize my fingers were broken until Cain mentioned it.

Bronson is sitting opposite me, gaze steady on me. That isn't necessarily surprising. The man is always staring at me. Surveying me. Cataloging my injuries. This time, however, he seems agitated. His knee bounces up and down as his eyes flicker from my face to the bars of the cell. After the fourth rotation, I finally drop the ball and stumble to my feet. Immediately, he's across the room in an attempt to steady me.

"What's going on?" I ask softly, cupping his whiskered cheeks. The scruff bites into my palms, but the pain surprisingly sends heat to my core. I can still recall the feel of his light beard against the inside of my thighs...

"You almost died." His voice is rough, broken. It's not something I'm used to hearing from my confident wolf.

I caress his cheeks softly, allowing him to collect his thoughts. I know my injuries and near death have pained all of them, Bronson especially. He's always been overprotective

and overbearing, full of passion and emotion. My comatose
state had sent him careening over that edge.

"You almost died," he repeats in that same choked voice.
He kisses first one palm and then the other before capturing
my hands in his own. "It got me thinking..." He trails off,
uncharacteristically bashful.

"It got you thinking about what?" I ask, heart racing. My
stomach is suddenly in tight knots.

Does he regret meeting me? Caring about me?

I don't know why my mind automatically runs to the
worst-case scenario. Maybe it's because of the Compound and
everything it represents. Maybe it's my own insecurities.
Maybe it's because I don't know if I deserve love, especially
the irrevocable love he gives me.

Bronson takes a steeling breath, dropping his gaze to
where our hands connect. His thumb idly draws circles
around one of my knuckles.

"I want you to be my mate," he rushes to say. My body
freezes, going as taut as a guitar string, before I force myself
to relax. "Officially, I mean. I want to complete the bond."

Mate.

He wants to be my mate.

My heart gains wings and soars around my rib cage like an
enthusiastic butterfly. Blood rushes to my ears as the sheer
intensity of my emotions cascade over me.

Mate.

Mate.

Mate.

Bronson, mistaking my silence for rejection, hurries to
elaborate, his gruff, raspy voice eliciting full-body shivers
through me. "I know you already mated with Rion, but
shifters can have more than one mate." *Wait, I completed the
mating bond with Rion?* "I knew from the first moment I saw

you that you were my fated mate, the only girl I'll ever love. I understand if you want to—"

I cut him off by standing on my tiptoes and kissing him on the mouth. It's a soft kiss, chaste by some standards, but delicious tingles run up and down my body, from the tips of my fingers to my bare feet.

"Bronson, I would love to be your mate," I whisper with a shaky smile. "I don't know what that will mean..."

"It means that I'll always find you. That your pain will be my pain. Your hopes will be my hopes. Your love will be my love. Nothing can break a mating bond, except for death."

"Don't say that," I whisper as another wave of emotion swallows me whole. "Not even death will keep me from you."

He pulls me towards him and ravishes my lips again. This time, there's nothing soft about the kiss. It's possessive and angry. A fight of teeth and tongues. A fight against the monsters who want to keep us apart.

He lays claim to me with this kiss, devouring not only my body, but my heart and soul as well. When he finally pulls away, I greedily arch my neck, giving him access to the skin there.

"Do it," I whisper as his teeth graze my neck. I don't know if it's intentional, but his lips are directly above the spot where Rion bit me a few weeks ago. "Make me yours."

Because I already am.

His teeth clamp down, but it's not painful. Like with Rion, liquid lust travels through my veins, setting me aflame. I gasp, arching my back, as my soul merges with his. Everything I am belongs to him. Everything he is belongs to me. We're one and the same, two halves of the same heart. From this day forth, we'll beat as one.

"Nina," he breathes against my skin, voice heady with emotion. "My queen."

"Bron." I run my fingers through his blond hair, enjoying the way his breath hitches with each tug.

With his lips still against my skin, he whispers the words that change everything. The words I have only heard to my face once before, from Kai. Words that send delightful shivers through my body. "I love you."

It might be wrong or unconventional to love more than one person. I might be looked down upon, but in that moment, I need him to know the extent of my feelings. He owns my heart, but so do five other men. I didn't know it was possible. I didn't know a heart was capable of containing so much love. It's to the point where I fear the organ will burst.

"I love you too."

His lips are on mine once more, devouring me like I'm the air he breathes. Lust permeates the air like a perfume, dousing the both of us in its sweet scent.

My shirt and bra are soon discarded as Bronson squeezes my breasts. When he twists my nipples, evoking a sharp sting of pain, I moan louder. I never suspected I would like something like that, something rough.

I reach down his body and rub his cock through his pants. Through feel alone, I know he'll be bigger than Kai and Rion. Bronson himself is massive—a real giant of a man, with muscle upon muscle. It's only fitting that his cock would be just as big.

"Take your shirt off," I whisper, fingering the edge of the fabric. In the next moment, he yanks it over his head, the soft material brushing against my face with the motion. I run my hands over his defined, sculpted muscles before raising them to his face. I would never describe his features as beautiful—they're too masculine for that—but he's ruggedly sexy. He looks like he'd be at home in a cabin located deep within the forest.

I move my hands to his head as he takes one of my

nipples into his mouth, sucking gently before biting down sharply.

I moan again, tangling my fingers in his tousled blond hair.

"Is this all right?" he whispers, nuzzling my breasts. "Am I being too rough?"

"This is perfect. You're perfect."

"God, I could look at your body all day, my queen. It's perfect."

I shoot him a soft look that I hope relays the extent of my love for him, for this massive man with a heart of gold. I pull his mouth back to mine, attacking it with my own. It's rougher than anything I have ever experienced before, but it doesn't negate the pleasure pooling low in my belly.

The first time we were intimate, during our date, he was painstakingly gentle. This time, there's a primal edge to his actions that weren't there before. He wants it rough, and apparently, so do I. It's as if the last few months were leading to this moment, this lust-filled explosion. We were always fated to collide. It's no wonder we both combust when we finally join.

"We don't need a condom," he murmurs against my lips. "I'm clean, for one, and shifters can only impregnate their mates when the female is in heat. We can sense it."

"I don't think that will be a problem," I admit, twin flames in both my cheeks. "I think... I think the Compound did something to me. I've never even had a period."

Bronson pulls away, studying me intently. I flush under his scrutiny, feeling vaguely like an ant under a microscope.

Finally, he pulls me towards him and plants kisses down my neck. "We'll figure it out. I promise."

We pull at the remainder of each other's clothes, his thumbs hooking into the waistband of my panties as he pulls them down. I gracefully step out of them, my hands on his broad shoulders.

"Tell me you love me again," he pleads.

I smile up at him. "I love you, Bronson. More than words can say."

He gently guides me to the bed, pushing my legs apart to reveal my sopping entrance.

"You're already so wet for me, my goddess. My love. My world." He kisses my left thigh and then my right. I want his lips there, I always do, but right now, I want something else inside of me. I want the fullness I experienced with both Kai and Rion. I want him to complete me in a way only he can.

My protector.

My lover.

My wolf.

I guide his lips back to mine as he lines up the head of his cock with my entrance.

He sheathes himself inside me slowly, inch by excruciating inch, and waits, giving me a moment to adjust. Pressing his forehead to my own, he whispers, "I love the way you feel around me."

"I love the way you feel inside of me," I reply, blushing.

He chuckles, holding himself steady over top of me. Not for the first time, I wish I could see his face. The lust and love in his eyes. The curve to his lips. The flush to his cheeks. Is he in as much bliss as I am?

"Your dirty talk still needs some work, my goddess." He presses a gentle kiss to my sweaty neck.

"Are you really talking about my dirty talk—or lack thereof—when you're inside of me?" I hiss.

He chuckles again, body shaking, and I groan as his cock jumps in my tight channel. "You can practice on me anytime," he says, and I know he'll be smirking devilishly. He sounds more like Abel and Rion than himself in this moment, but maybe this is a side of him I haven't seen before. A playful one.

I really, really like it.

"Okay...hymen remover," I stumble, and he roars with laughter.

"Hymen remover?"

"What?! Is that not sexy? It's the first sexual term I could think of," I insist as he laughs even harder.

Then the laughter subsides as we finally—finally—begin to move together.

Our bodies find a rhythm as he pounds into me, first slow and languid and then fast and punishing. I hold on to him, digging my nails into his back, as he continues to use my body like he owns it.

Maybe a part of him does.

"I'm close," I warn. So, so close.

And then, I explode.

Colors pass in front of my eyes, a kaleidoscope, and for a second, I can't breathe. I lose sense of who I am, where I am, and what I'm doing here. All that exists is Bronson and his warm, sweaty body above me.

He holds on to me as he jerks his hips once, then twice, releasing his seed inside of me. He calls out my name as he comes.

Aftershocks of pleasure course through me, leaving me shaking. But it's not just the pleasure causing such a reaction from me. It's him. It's me. It's us.

He's a protector, a fixer, someone who will go to the ends of the earth for the person he loves.

If I let him, I know Bronson will fix everything that is broken inside of me.

∽

"You didn't tell me we completed the mating bond. After sex, when you bit me, you didn't tell me that made us officially mates."

I find Rion in the rafters above Kai's cell. Technically, Bronson found him. I just provided moral support.

With a kiss to my forehead, Bronson leaves me with the eccentric cat shifter.

When Rion doesn't answer, I cross my arms over my chest, fighting off the intense chill that passes through me. "Is that why you've been ignoring me?" I question softly.

Finally, I get a reaction out of him. There's a "thump" as he drops to the ground, and then his arms are around me.

"Fuck, no. It's just... I just..." He stumbles over his words. "I feel guilty!" he explodes at last, and his dogmatic declaration has me blinking at him stupidly. "I feel so fucking guilty. First, for mating with you without your permission, and then because of the whole thing with Tessa. I'm supposed to protect you, and what do I do? Get you beat up. I'm a cat, Nina. When I feel guilty, I hide in corners to lick my fur in relative peace. Though I really wish I could lick you... Gah! See? I'm a pervert. And technically, I did tell you. A few times. Don't you remember my post-sex claiming? Probably not, actually. You were a little out of it. I don't know why you haven't punched me in the face yet. You know what? Do it. Punch me in the face. It'll make me feel better."

I cut off his incessant ramblings by placing my hand over his mouth.

"It'll make you feel better...to have me punch you in the face?" I repeat slowly, carefully, wishing I could gauge his reaction. Why are men so difficult to understand? I swear there are one hundred underlying meanings behind what he just said to me. Surely, he doesn't mean for me to punch him literally.

Rion removes my hand from his mouth, intertwining our fingers together.

"I hate myself for what Tessa did to you. What my dick inadvertently did to you because I fucked that crazy bitch. Fuck, I shouldn't be talking about other women with my mate. My mate—who's you, by the way, if I still haven't made that clear—who I'm crazy in love with. But I just can't stop talking, you know? My mom always told me I'll talk myself straight into a volcano. Or maybe she said she'll push me into one. I don't remember. Either way, I'm sorry. I'm so fucking sorry. I should've asked you if you wanted to cement the mating bond instead of losing myself in the moment. And then the fight... Nina, I felt your pain. I felt each punch like I was experiencing it myself. Did you know I started crying? I never cry. Except for when I'm watching *Titanic*. But besides that, I never cry! Ever! And then there was you, looking so beautiful, even covered in blood and bruises. You held yourself regally, like a fucking queen, and I knew that you were it for me. I loved you then, and I love you now, but I don't know if I love myself anymore. I know, I know, it's hard to believe because I have a pretty kick-ass body and my personality is amazing. I really, really want you to punch me in the face. I don't think I can forgive myself otherwise. I deserve that and more. God, I fucking hate myself for what I did to you." Through his entire spiel, I'm not sure he has even taken a breath.

I don't want him to hate himself.

So...

I punch him in the face.

Damien has taught me how to throw a punch, how to accurately hit my target without sight, how to rely on sound and air currents. I believe I have pretty good form. There's a crack as my fist connects with Rion's cheek, and a startled yelp escapes the shifter.

"Holy shit!" Rion curses. I drop my hand and shake out my fingers. There's a dull pain, but it's nothing I can't handle, especially comparatively. "You actually punched me in the face." He sounds awed.

Heat blossoms in my cheeks, and I duck my head sheepishly. "You told me to," I murmur shyly.

Crap, did I do it wrong? Did he want me to punch him in the stomach?

Why did he even want me to punch him in the first place? Is it a guy thing?

Rion throws back his head in hearty laughter before pulling me into his arms. "Fuck, sweetheart, if I didn't love you before, I definitely love you now." A field of flowers bloom in my chest at his words, leaving me lightheaded. "But you want to know who else you should punch some sense into?"

I have to punch someone else?

"Who?"

"A certain little sex demon who's still wallowing in guilt and self-loathing." Rion pinches my butt cheeks, making me squeal and blush hotter. He leans forward to nip my bottom lip. "Let's go. Before I tie you up and spread you on Kai's bed, like my own personal feast."

He really, really isn't giving me incentive to leave.

I wouldn't mind being Rion's dinner...

CHAPTER 48

NINA

We find Cain sulking in one of the hallways in the Labyrinth.

Through Rion's eyes, I see the golden-haired twin sitting against the wall, eyes shut and lips curved into a despondent frown. He doesn't seem to notice our presence until we're directly above him. One eye lazily opens until he sees who it is. Scowling, he climbs to his feet and levels his penetrating glare at Rion.

"Why the fuck did you bring her here?" he demands, and the venom in his tone makes me flinch. His face softens slightly as he glances towards me before his emotions once again shutter closed. "Leave."

"Nope," Rion says with a giddy laugh. "You two need to talk and sort out your shit. And please, don't take that literally. The last thing I need is your shit in color-coordinated boxes." Rion gently places my hand on Cain's. The sex twin eyes the limb distastefully, lips pursed like he ate something sour, but he doesn't remove it. "I'm leaving. I need to find my bro toy."

"Bro toy?" I query, cocking a brow.

"Damien. We totally have a bromance. You know, the one where I sort of want to suck his dick," he teases, laughing at the delighted flush that rises to my cheeks.

"I will cut you and eat your guts if you come even close to my dick," a dark voice warns from behind us. We all turn, startled to see Damien lurking in the shadows. He doesn't even bother to glance up from his knife.

Was he following...?

You know what? I'm not even surprised anymore.

"And then I'll take my knife and cut off your sweaty balls," Damien continues nonchalantly.

Rion leans forward to whisper to me, "Awww. He likes my balls. Isn't it cute?"

Damien, in answer, lifts his knife.

Once more, Rion says, "Knife play is his kink, FYI. He likes it on his nipples."

I'm pretty sure the only reason Rion lives is because I step in between them.

"Can you guys wait over there?" I implore, sliding gracefully out of Rion's head. I place a hand on his chest, the muscles contracting beneath his thin shirt, before he presses his lips to my forehead.

"Of course. Anything for you. But please don't let the psychopath murder me." The last sentence is said in a hushed murmur.

Damien scoffs. "Just what type of man do you think I am?" he questions, amused.

"Umm...a stabby one?" Rion fills in. Damien snorts again in response.

As their footsteps retreat, I turn toward Cain. I know Rion and Damien are only a few feet away, pretending to give us privacy, but I still feel incredibly nervous. I never know how Cain will react to something. He's volatile and moody, a combination that's perfect for shredding my heart.

It's like I'm giving him a fragile, invaluable gift, awaiting his reaction. He holds it in his hands, throws it on the ground, and now, I'm staring at the shattered pieces, unsure how I'm supposed to put them back together.

I can admit to myself how utterly besotted I am by this demon, but I know he doesn't feel the same way.

He uses his anger as a shield, a weapon, a way to eradicate the hurt. And I know he's been hurt. He wears it on his sleeve, an indecipherable symbol I yearn to learn more about. I want to know everything.

"Cain..." I reach for him, but he steps away the moment my fingers graze his shoulder. That hurts, more than I'll ever show him.

"What are you doing here, Nina?"

Nina. Not Trouble.

Instead of the anger I expected, he sounds tired and sad. His tone of voice matches the face I saw through Rion's eyes only a minute earlier.

"I wanted to see you," I admit with a shrug.

"No." He scoffs at once. "You don't want to see me."

"Yes, I do."

"No, you don't."

Anger burns through me, briefly overshadowing the hurt. "Yes. I. Do." I stand toe-to-toe with him, eyes spewing fire. My blood simmers in my veins. Why does Cain frustrate me the way he does? Why am I still drawn to him like a moth to a flame?

Cain is so mercurial. Sometimes, I want to shake him, and other times, I want to kiss him senseless.

"Why?" he asks flippantly, and his tone only serves to piss me off further. "Because I saved you? I didn't do anything. I only fixed what I broke."

"What the heck are you talking about?" I explode,

shoving a finger into his chest. He captures it in both his hands, holding it still.

"I'm talking about how you should be furious with me. Pissed. I left you. At the fight, I left you. I ran like a little bitch boy with my tail between my legs." He takes a shuddering breath that stirs the hairs around my face. "Because of me, you nearly died. How can you stand to look me in the face? Aren't you furious at me?"

What the...?

His words leave me gaping. Stunned. Never once did that cross my mind. Even now, I struggle to understand why he thinks he is to blame. It was my own decision to not fight back, and though it did nothing to save Tessa, I don't regret my decision. I'd never forgive myself if I had hurt Tessa. She was angry and violent, yes, but she was also hurting. I could sense her pain, like it was an extension of my own.

"Are you blaming yourself for what happened?" I ask in disbelief. Rion's right. Maybe I should punch some sense into him. But I doubt it'll make a crack in his thick, stubborn skull.

"Of course I fucking am!" he roars. "If I would've been in the ring, I would've been able to treat you right away. Instead, the guys had to stumble around, looking for my dumb, selfish ass. I'm such a fuckup—"

"Stop it," I snap, cutting him off. "Don't talk about yourself like that." When he makes a sound of protest, I talk over him. "Do you want to hear me say I'm a dumb bitch for not fighting Tessa? Is that what you want to hear? I'm a dumb, stupid bitch."

Cain growls, the sound more animal than human. More animal than demon.

"Don't you dare," he hisses. "Don't you fucking dare."

"Then, stop it," I retort angrily. I step even closer, my feet on top of his, and rise up on my tiptoes. "What happened is not your fault. I lied to you. I hurt you. You had every right to leave—"

"But I didn't," he interrupts vehemently. "I didn't have a right to leave. Not over that. I was hurt, yes, but I did what I always do. I run, Nina. It's my thing. I run and pray to God that my emotions won't catch up with me." He grabs a strand of my thick hair and wraps it around his finger. "You're right," he admits at last. "You did hurt me. A lot. But I think what scared me most of all was what you heard when you were in our heads. Why did you keep it a secret?"

I take a deep breath, stomach heaving. "When I was in Abel's mind...I saw him with Lionel Green. They seemed to know each other intimately. But then, I saw Lionel kiss Abel, and I saw Abel's face through your eyes afterwards, when you came back here. I saw terror in his eyes, Cain. And I..." I scrub a hand down my face. "I recognized it, okay? I recognized the fear because it's what I saw on my own face every day at the Compound."

"Ask me," Cain says briskly. His breath wafts over my lips. "Ask me what you want to know."

"Did Lionel do something to Abel?" I finally ask, trembling. I don't know if I'll survive the answer. Not my sweet, fun twin...

"Abel and I..." Cain seems to be searching for words, struggling to form an articulate sentence. "We were like you, in a way. Prisoners before we technically arrived at prison. When we were in our teens, we were kidnapped by this man named Boris and brought to a club. A sex club."

Tears fill my eyes, trailing down my cheeks, but I don't avert my gaze. I hope he sees something other than pity and sympathy in my eyes.

I understand his pain. I empathize with him.

I also know that his past doesn't define his future. His demons aren't chains weighing him to the ground. I want him to see how incredibly strong I think he is, how much he inspires me, how I'll be with him every step of the way as he recites his story.

"As you can probably guess, Abel and I were the star clients. There were some days I prayed for death, and there were other days I wanted to fight. I never understood why, though. Why fight? What was the point? And now, I know it was for you. To come here. To meet you. To be with you."

He captures one of my tears with the pad of his thumb, wiping it away.

"I'm so sorry you had to go through that," I whisper, envisioning two scared demons in a cage similar to mine, fighting their own monsters. I know how long and tedious that battle can be. I know how seductive giving up, giving in, sounds. I know...because I experienced it myself. "I'm so grateful you continued fighting. Maybe it's selfish of me, but I'm happy I met you, Cain. So freaking happy."

His lips are inches from my own, breath warm, when he asks, "What did you see in my mind?"

The color drains from my cheeks. "What?" I ask meekly.

"What did you see in my mind, Trouble?"

Instinctively, my gaze drops to his crotch, despite not being able to see it.

I can hear the smile in his voice when he says, "Oh. You saw *that*."

Is it possible to die from embarrassment?

"Did you like it?" Cain lowers his voice to a soft, seductive purr.

"Like it?" I squeak, stumbling back a step. His arms immediately hook around my waist to hold me steady.

"My cock, Trouble. Did you like it? Did you like hearing me say your name as I came?"

My breath hitches, heart thundering, as I place my hands

on his chest. "You're not a prisoner anymore, Cain," I whisper, fisting my hands in the fabric of his shirt.

"Then what am I?"

"You're mine."

He doesn't ask. He just takes—my lips, my soul, my heart. All of them have always belonged to him, anyway.

He kisses me feverishly. Brutally. And I know bruises will sprout on my waist from his hold.

"I'm not letting you go, Trouble," he gasps, wrenching his lips from mine. "So, stop me now if you don't want that."

"I want you. All of you. All of your darkness and pain. Your ghosts and demons. Give them to me, Cain. Give me all of it."

Cain and I are like fire and gasoline. When we come together, we explode.

When his lips move back to mine, I'm drowning in him. Drowning in his taste, his scent, his touch. I can't get enough of him. One kiss just isn't enough; I'm insatiable.

It only takes us seconds to remove all our clothes. My body still hurts from Bronson, but in a good way. I have a moment of panic that someone will walk down this hall and see us, but then I remember that Rion and Damien are only a few feet away, guarding us. The thought that they're here, probably watching, should fill me with a sense of self-consciousness, but it doesn't. Instead, my lust only increases.

I *want* them to watch. To want me.

Without preamble, Cain enters me, lifting my legs so they wrap around his waist. It's hard and fast and brutal. Pain briefly erupts down below, but it's quickly replaced by an agonizing need. I need more of him, all of him. Everything this broken demon is willing to give me. I'll take it greedily.

His hips roll against mine, filling me even more completely. I know his eyes are on mine without me having to slip into his head. It's intimate, almost too intimate. Despite being already naked, I feel as if he's staring into my very soul, stripping me bare. Seeing the ugly but loving me in spite of it.

"You ruined me, Trouble. Ruined me." Cain's voice is muffled where his lips are now pressed to my neck.

"It's only fair," I reply back as his hands knead my bare ass. He pushes me backwards until my back is flush against the wall. "You already ruined me."

I brush the tips of my fingers across his taut stack of abs.

"You can't leave me, okay? Not after this." He begins to move faster and faster, our breaths intermingling. It's different than the others but no less intense. Lightning shoots through my bloodstream.

"Never," I whisper back.

And when we come together, the entire world burns.

CHAPTER 49

BRONSON

I bounce my knee, nervous energy coursing through me.

This will be the first time I have seen my momma and sisters in...who knows how long.

When the guards arrived at my cell, I was ready. I didn't even flinch as the mage asshole sent a wave of power at me, knocking me unconscious.

I glance around the barren visitation room with the stark white walls, metal table, and two plastic chairs. It's as unwelcoming as the rest of the prison. A tool designed to warn people away.

When the door to the room opens, a brilliant smile is already spreading across my face.

"Oh, my baby boy!" Momma calls, rushing to me and peppering my face in kisses.

"Momma, stop it," I growl half-heartedly, cheeks flaming at being doted on like a little boy. If Nina could see me now...

"Let me get a look at you, boy!" She whacks my shoulder, pulling away to give me a critical once-over. Her shrewd eyes narrow. "Are they feeding you right? Don't make me march to that warden and give him a piece of my mind. I'll beat him with my purse. Don't even test me."

I smile softly at the ferocious woman. I have no doubt she would.

Standing at barely five feet, Gemma Ferguson is a sight to behold. Her blonde hair, peppered with silver, hangs in a loose braid over her shoulder. Today, she wears a purple flannel shirt and ripped blue jeans. Despite her small stature, she looks plenty capable of charging into a battle, head-on. Her pouty lips and long lashes make her look younger than her actual age, emanating an innocence that contradicts the badass I know her to be.

"Are you going to ignore your favorite sister?" Marbella snarks, already sitting indolently on the plastic chair opposite the table.

"You dyed your hair," I observe, staring intently at my sister's indigo locks.

"I did." She nods her head once, a familiar smirk playing on her lips.

"And," my younger sister, Lola, pipes up, "she has a boyfriend."

"Lola, shut up!" Marbella hisses immediately.

Boyfriend? Bella has...a boyfriend? I'm suddenly grateful I'm restrained by cuffs. If I weren't, I might run out of this prison, track this boy down, and castrate him.

"Don't start growling, boy!" Momma whacks me again on the shoulder. For a little old lady, she packs a mean punch. "She's sixteen. Heaven only knows what you were getting up to at that age."

That only makes me madder. I know sixteen-year-old boys because I *was* one. All we think about are sex and drugs, not necessarily in that order. I'll be the first to admit I slept around and experimented with weed during my high school years.

"Who is he?" I growl, voice nearly unrecognizable.

"For fuck's sake, Bron!" Bella flicks a wadded-up gum wrapper at my head.

"Don't use that language, missy," Momma scolds, diverting her attention off of me. "Or else I'll go over there with my purse and beat you silly."

Bella pouts her lips out petulantly while Lola cackles. Those two always got on each other's nerves. Ali was the unofficial peacemaker.

At the thought of Ali, I instantly sober. Momma must read the change in my expression because she gives me a side hug.

"I miss her too. More than anything," she whispers, her voice choked with emotion and pain.

I lost my sister, but my mom lost her daughter. I can't imagine what she must be going through. I don't have children yet, but already, I can see dozens of little babies with Nina's glorious black hair. I don't want to know what I would do if anything happened to them, these babies that don't even exist yet.

"This place is crazy," Lola interrupts. I love my younger sister, I do, but sometimes, she's oblivious to the emotions of others. She's not purposefully trying to be malicious or rude; she just gets trapped in her own mind. "It's like a soap opera."

"Soap opera?" I scoff. Nightmare Penitentiary is a lot of things, but a soap opera isn't one of them.

"I heard some of the guards talking. Did you know that one of the guards, some dude named Rook, fucked and mated with an inmate? I heard the girl, the cockatrice, had a pretty badass shank business." Lola's face seems to glow as she talks, eyes bright with excitement. She feeds off drama like vampires do blood. "While we were walking through the halls, we came across this siren named Selena. She was really pretty. Have you met her? You should mate with her.

Unless..." She flashes me a Cheshire cat grin. "Unless you already have a mate."

"Don't be ridiculous." Momma scoffs. I note that some of the pain, the anguish, dimmed in her bright eyes the more Lola talked. I don't think she'll ever be whole, but she's slowly working on mending herself together again. For Lola and Bella. For me. "If my boy had a mate, he would've told me by now."

She glares at me disapprovingly, and I duck my head sheepishly. In a matter of minutes, my momma has made me feel like an errant boy getting caught eating something he wasn't supposed to. That glare turns into shock as she whacks me a-fucking-gain with the back of her hand.

"You have a mate and didn't tell your momma?" she cries in a stilted voice that conveys her annoyance and irritation. "I gave birth to you, boy. You don't keep things like this from me!" She begins to sniffle, wiping at her eyes. Oh, dear God. Not the tears... "When should I start hearing wedding balls? Grandbabies? I want babies, dammit."

The thought of babies saddens me as I recall what Nina confessed earlier. All my dreams of beautiful, black-haired babies dissipate like words written in condensation. I'll have to bring this up to Cain at a later time, ask him to look into it. Babies or not, I'll love Nina, regardless.

Besides, it's not a smart idea to bring babies into this prison.

"Momma." I blush, lifting my gaze towards her face once more. "It's still really new..."

"But you met her?" Lola asks eagerly, placing her arms on the table and leaning forward.

I smile when I think of Nina Doe. My mate. My world.

"I did. She's perfect." If my voice sounds like that of a lovesick idiot, can you blame me? "She has a way of making you feel like you're the only person in the world. She's so incredibly strong—I can't even begin to describe her inner strength. And she's sweet. You'll love her."

Momma's lips are curled into a soft smile. That smile seems to radiate through her expressive eyes. "You love her, don't you?" Though it's phased as a question, there is a knowing glint in her eyes.

"What...? How...?" Yup. I'm blushing. Like a simpering schoolboy.

Fucking hell.

"Do you remember your last girlfriend?" Momma questions, shooing Bella out of the only spare seat and perching delicately on the edge.

"Why does that matter?"

"When I asked you about her, you immediately began describing how she looks." Momma's smile widens. "Yet, with your mate, you didn't once mention her appearance."

"Because Nina's more than that," I snap before I can stop myself. "She's beautiful, of course, but she's also kind and funny and strong—" I break off at my momma's smirk. "Ah. I see."

"When can I meet her?" Lola asks, jumping from foot to foot. "Can we meet her now?"

"Calm down, spitfire," I say, rolling my eyes. If my hands weren't cuffed to table, I would've ruffled her bleached-blonde hair. "I promise I'll introduce you to her."

Lola and Momma exchange a mischievous look that promises trouble for that future encounter. I have no doubt that Momma thinks this girl isn't good enough for me. I'm sure all mothers think that about their kids. However, she'll come to realize that *I'm* not good enough for *her*. Momma will take one look into those white, compassionate eyes and be a goner. I'm pretty sure she'll disown me and then adopt Nina as her own child.

"Well, we can't stay for long." Momma reluctantly gets to her feet. "Lola has art class this afternoon."

"And Bella has a date," Lola says in a singsong voice.

Bella glares at our younger sister, eyes hurling daggers, before huffing and crossing her arms over her chest. "Before we leave, can I talk to Bronson alone for a moment?" she asks, turning towards me. She brushes at a lock of her indigo hair, pushing it behind her ear.

"Of course, sweetheart." Momma turns towards me and kisses my forehead. "Please, allow us to visit more. I know you didn't want us to see you like this, but I can't lose another child." Tears fill her eyes, and each one is a punch to my gut. I hate when women cry, especially my mother. Tears should be fucking banned.

"Okay, Momma." I rest my head against her chest like I used to do when I was a young boy. Her floral perfume surrounds me, evoking memories of late-night cookie baking sessions and horror movie marathons. "Love you."

"Love you too, boy. And don't forget to introduce me to that mate of yours." In a softer voice, she adds, "Your face glows when you talk about her. Any girl who's capable of earning your love is someone I need to meet. Hopefully, she's good enough for my son." If she was a peacock shifter, I imagine she'd be ruffling her feathers, attempting to assert her dominance.

"You'll love her," I assure her. "Promise."

"Is she pretty? What does she look like?" Lola continues to babble question after question as Momma leads her out of the room. "Bye, Bron! Love you, asshole!" The "asshole" comment gets her a whack on the head from Momma.

A moment later, the door closes with a resounding clank.

Bella sits once more in the chair Momma previously occupied. She adopts a languid pose, legs kicked back and arms crossed.

"Did you get it?" I ask my sister.

She eyes me warily, eyes keen, before nodding once. "I did."

She doesn't move.

My irritation growing, I ask, "Can I have it?"

"Of course." Once more, she doesn't even twitch.

I sigh. "Okay, fine. I bite. What do you want?"

Finally—*finally*—I get a reaction. She sits straight up in the uncomfortable plastic chair and smiles brilliantly. Hook, line, and fucking sinker.

"I want your room," she demands. "And I want you to call me 'the supreme sister goddess' for a whole month."

My lips press into a grim line. "Is that all?"

"Hmmm." She taps a finger to her chin before breaking into laughter, the noise deceptively light, and flashing me a malevolent grin. "When you leave here, I want you to buy me pancakes every day for three months. Every day. I'm not playing on this."

"Fine," I say through gritted teeth. "Now, give me."

She gracefully slides a file out from underneath her sweat-shirt. I have no idea how she was able to smuggle it into the prison, and I don't care. All I care about is the information it contains.

My sister's a hacker. A skilled one. Since a young age, she's been able to break into the school's computer, change her grades, and mark her attendance as perfect. Over time, her skills have developed significantly, and she even befriended some men and women from the dark web. Of course, I had argued profusely and threatened bodily harm on those creeps, but there's not much I can do now that I'm in prison.

I never suspected her skills would come in handy.

Narrowing my eyes at the folder, I huff with irritation. "I can't fucking read it with the cuffs on."

With a sigh, she stalks around the table and flips it open to the first page.

"I couldn't find anything on the Compound. Whoever ran it was good, very good. Probably better than me. Or they didn't keep records online. There's not a single trace of it on the web." She sounds affronted by that idea before she shakes her head and nods towards the paper. "I did, however, find Nina's hospital records from when she first left this mysterious Compound. The records were sealed, but the hospital had an extra, secret file on their computer. But this... Bron, this is big."

I hit the brakes on my thoughts so fast that there are skate marks on the asphalt and the smell of burning rubber.

"This...this can't be right," I whisper, stunned by what I'm reading.

Bella's face is uncharacteristically grim as she considers me.

"Your mate is in even more danger than you thought, if this is true," she says solemnly.

Horror swamps me, consumes me, as I stare at the words before me. I see them, but I'm not able to read or comprehend them. Icy numbness courses through my veins.

I think...

I think my sister may be right.

CHAPTER 50

NINA

I can feel Damien's eyes on me.

It seems as if he's always watching me. No matter where I am in a room, no matter who I'm speaking to, his eyes caress my skin like a cold winter breeze.

After my encounter with Cain, the sex demon guided me to the private showers and tenderly washed the cum and sweat off my body. Each touch felt erotic, like he was leaving a piece of himself behind in the process.

"I need to go talk to Abe," he'd said, kissing my forehead. "But I'll be back. And then, we can do round two. And three. And four. And five."

"Go!" I'd said, laughing. With another passionate kiss, Cain left, leaving me alone with Damien.

After I'd changed into my favorite white dress, Damien led me back into his secluded room at the end of the hall. Now, we sit.

"I don't bite, you know," I tease, patting his bed. "You can sit beside me."

Damien grunts something noncommittally but doesn't move any closer.

"Or is the big, dangerous mage scared?" I continue, giggling. I can practically envision his flabbergasted expression at my jests.

He huffs, finally sitting beside me on the surprisingly fluffy and comfortable bed. I'm almost jealous of it.

"I'm not scared," he snarks.

"Are you scared of a teeny tiny little girl?" My voice is saccharine sweet, one I reserve for small animals.

He grunts in amusement, placing his arm behind my back. I immediately lean against it—better than any backrest I've ever used.

"Hey, why are you being so quiet?" I tentatively venture, climbing to my knees and turning towards him. I reach and touch his face, hesitantly running my thumb across his downward curved lips. My own lips lower instinctively. "What's wrong?"

His hands settle on my lower back. "Just thinking, Angel."

"About?" I press, placing one finger on either side of his lips and attempting to press them upwards. He grabs my wrists gently and brings them to his lap.

"You love Cain."

It's not a question, but something in his tone makes me think he wants to hear a confirmation. Deciding for honesty, I nod.

"I love a lot of people." My cheeks burn at the confession, but I refuse to duck my head. Not with him. He always sees me, even when I try to hide.

"I'm sure you were told about all the horrendous things I did before I arrived here." Damien's voice lowers with disgust and self-loathing. I hate that—I hate that he sees his broken edges as something he should be ashamed of. I've always known he wasn't made of sunshine. Surprisingly enough, it's his darkness that intrigues me.

"What happened?" I turn his hand over—rough and calloused from years of work—and brush my thumb over the center of his palm. I feel his body shiver delicately beneath me. "At the guild, I mean. What happened?"

He takes a deep, fortifying breath, as if bracing himself against an incoming storm. I know he'll be building walls and impenetrable fences around his heart, designed to keep me out. He thinks that his words will scare me away, anger me, terrify me. He doesn't seem to realize that his monster is nothing compared to the monsters back at the Compound. He doesn't seem to realize that I love him, demons and all.

"I never knew my dad. He was probably some asshole mage who knocked up my mother, then ran like a bitch when he discovered she was pregnant." His voice holds a world of loathing and contempt for his absentee parent. I want to comfort him, but I have no idea how. "My mother turned to drugs. After only a few years of her addiction, she owed a shit ton of money to a pimp named Fangs. Fucking stupid name, if you ask me." He pauses, bringing my hand to his lips to kiss the sensitive, tingling skin there.

"And then what happened?" I whisper breathlessly.

"She died. Overdosed. And I was found and taken in by Narian." A spurt of anger accompanies that name, and I wonder who this Narian is to him and what he's done. "Narian is the leader of the guild. He trained me, conformed me into the heartless man you see before you. I don't believe I was a psychopath before I met him, but now?" He laughs humorlessly. "I love the kill. The hunt. The fight. It excites me more than anything else in this fucking world."

"What was Narian like?" I query, interested in the man who raised a young, innocent Damien. A little boy who had witnessed more than he should've. Who'd fought battles best served for someone older and wiser.

Damien releases another self-deprecating laugh. "Narian was a fucking pervert with a penchant for scared little boys."

At first, I feel horror. That horror abates quickly to be transformed into anger—a blistering hot rage that makes me see red stars. The intensity of my emotions takes me off guard. I've felt like this only once before, when I discovered what Lionel Green did to the twins. I don't remember ever being this mad at the Compound. Heck, I wasn't even this furious when Raphael Turner was revealed to be Man.

"Hey." Damien rubs his hands up and down my arms soothingly. "Where did you go just then?"

"I hate him," I whisper venomously. "I hate a man I've never even met because he hurt you. Does that make me messed up?"

"No, Angel." He lifts his hands to cup my neck, gently applying pressure. "It means that you care." He sounds breathless, disbelief evident in his voice. "Do you, Nina? Care about me?" There's a vulnerability in that question. I have to wonder if anyone has ever cared about Damien before. He has always been on the outskirts looking in, never participating. The inmates here fear him, and those who don't fear him, hate him. Those walls he erects around himself aren't a choice, but a necessity. A way to protect his fragile heart.

All he has ever wanted was to be loved. I don't know how I know that, only that I do.

"I care about you, Damien." I brush my hand through his slicked-back hair. "I think I even love you."

His breath hitches, and the next thing I know, I'm on my back with his lips on mine. There's nothing cold or calculating about this kiss—it's pure fire. Flames burst behind my closed eyelids like a firework explosion.

"Are you already wet for me, Angel?" Damien whispers, trailing kisses to my ear. "Is your pussy slick and ready for my cock?"

I whimper at his dirty words. Out of all my men, I didn't expect Damien to be into this kind of thing. Heck, I didn't even know *I* was into this kind of thing. When Haley had discussed it during dinner a few weeks earlier, I had blushed and giggled awkwardly.

Now, I can see and understand the appeal. Each word Damien says sends heat straight to my throbbing core.

Damien yanks me to him, our tongues dancing. It's a war for control, for dominance, but I don't hesitate to give it over. I'm at his complete mercy. Whatever he wants from me is his. I'll give him everything.

He stops kissing me, only to take off his shirt and throw it somewhere in the room. I have no idea where, and frankly, I don't care. I trail my hands across his chest, pinching both nipples, and then down his taut abs. He flexes, muscles clenching, but allows me to repeat the rotation twice.

"I need to see you," he declares, removing my hands from his chest. He pulls my dress over my head, leaving me in my matching bra and panties. I don't know which of the guys gave them to me, but I'm suddenly grateful. I do know that they look good on me, accentuating my curves and the muscles I'm beginning to form. "Fuck, you're even more beautiful than I imagined."

"And how often is that, Bitch Mage?" I tease.

In retaliation, he pinches my nipple through the fabric of my bra, and I hiss, moaning for more.

"Do you want me to punish you?" he asks coldly, deftly unclasping my bra and sliding it off my shoulders. He holds my breasts in both hands, pushing them together. His lips move from one nipple to the other, nipping and sucking until I swear I'm going to explode.

"Damien," I beg, my panties soaked through.

"You'll be patient," he snaps, biting down on my nipple. "And you'll take what I give you."

"Give me everything," I beg.

Abruptly, he releases my breasts and places a hand in the center of my chest. Applying a bit of pressure, he guides me onto my back.

"Today, I'll give you everything," he agrees. There's a rustle of fabric as he methodically removes his remaining clothing. A moment later, he returns to me, breath warm on my thighs. "Fuck, you're gorgeous."

Without waiting for my response, he slides my undies off and places my legs on his broad shoulders. He begins to plant tantalizingly soft kisses to the inside of my thighs.

"What are you...?"

"Shhh, Angel. I want to remember this moment. Today, I'm going to taste you. I'm going to make you writhe against my tongue as you come. But be patient with me. I haven't done this before."

"You haven't—"

My question is cut off by his tongue on my clit. I throw my head back and close my eyes as sensations rush through me. The stubble on Damien's cheek against my swollen pussy lips. His hands on my thighs, holding me steady. His own moans of pleasure as he devours me like a decadent treat. Each lick, kiss, and bite send me closer to careening over the edge.

He may have claimed he's never done this before, but his mouth is magic.

I explode in an intense stream of whimpers and praises. Tears form in my eyes at the sheer power of it. The orgasm rocks through me like a tidal wave.

"You taste delicious," Damien deadpans, and I almost laugh at his nonchalant voice. Almost. I'm too lost in the post-orgasmic bliss to care.

"Damien." I pull his face towards mine and kiss his chin, cheeks, and finally, his lips. I taste myself on him, and it only serves to heighten my arousal. These men are making me a sex fiend, and I find that I don't even care. "I want you."

"Are you sure?" he asks, the head of his cock poking at my aching entrance. His tongue parts my lips, breathing life back into me.

"I'm positive."

He doesn't need to be told twice. With a grunt, he enters me. He's not gentle or delicate like the others. No, not my mage. His fingernails dig into my hips as sheathes himself completely in my wet heat. I cradle him against my body, wrapping my legs around his waist.

"I need you to move," I beg, wincing at the pain. The fullness.

He rocks inside me slowly, circling his hips, but I don't want gentle. I want him the way he entered me: possessive and claiming, surrendering his soul to me completely.

"Harder, faster," I plead, pushing my hips up to meet each thrust. My words release something in Damien, a beast he had kept in a cage.

He pounds into me ruthlessly and viciously, his balls slapping against my skin with each punishing thrust. He captures my lips in a fierce, claiming kiss. There's no denying that I'm his, completely and unconditionally.

I arch my back as pleasure dances in front of my eyes. "I'm so close," I whimper, panting. "So close."

"Wait," he growls, continuing to move relentlessly over me.

"Damien!"

"I said wait!" His tongue invades my mouth, sweeping across my teeth, before he trails kisses down my neck. He begins to suck on my skin, no doubt leaving marks. "Come for me, Angel. Come around my cock."

I fall into bliss. Complete, ethereal bliss. Screaming

Damien's name, I hold on to his shoulders and wait for the aftershocks of pleasure to leave me.

After a few quick thrusts, Damien comes inside of me as well, his cum sliding down my thighs.

He collapses on top of me, and I hold him to me, unwilling to part. He chuckles darkly against my neck before planting a single kiss to the skin there. We lay there together in silence, savoring the moment, until Damien teasingly bites down on my earlobe.

"We should go find the others," he says lightly. I don't think I've ever heard Damien sound more carefree than right now. The power of sex, I suppose.

I hug him tighter. "I'm comfy, and you're warm. Like a human blanket."

He chuckles again, slowly untangling his limbs from mine, despite my protests. My body feels empty when he's gone, like a piece of me has been ripped away.

"Let's get you cleaned up and dressed," Damien says.

I don't move from my sprawled position on his bed. I'm not even sure I'm capable of it. My limbs feel like Jell-O.

I don't know what Damien uses to clean me up, but soon, I'm dressed once more in my white gown. His hands linger on me even after I'm dressed. Now that we've started, we can't seem to stop touching each other. His hand in mine, his pulse beneath my lips, his arm around my waist. I know that the second we leave the security of his room, the touching will end, but I'm desperate to soak up his affection while I can.

"Hey, Damien?" I whisper, suddenly shy. I shouldn't be after what we just did, what our bodies just did, but I still feel a blush rising to my cheeks. "I love—"

Pain flares behind my eyes, and I gasp, dropping to the ground. Damien releases a pained roar before he becomes silent. Too silent.

A familiar voice penetrates the incandescent pain radiating through my body.

"You really are strong," the prison mage muses. "Most people can't stay conscious for more than a second or two." He sighs suddenly, as if my inability to fall unconscious is a personal slight against him. "But, anyway, time to get up. You have a visitor."

CHAPTER 51

ABEL

I never thought I would fall in love.

It's not like I didn't want to—I did—but I just didn't believe that love was for me. Who could possibly care about someone as twisted and fucked up as me?

Yeah, I know how to smile—and I have a pretty damn good one, if I do say so myself—but that doesn't mean I'm happy. That smile obscures a darkness and pain lurking beneath the surface. I'm a perfectly wrapped gift of barbed wire and explosives. One wrong move and *boom*. We're both dead.

But then fucking Nina came into my life like a burst of sunlight. Her presence was impossible to ignore, impossible to resist. After living in darkness for so long, I craved the light.

Somehow, the beautiful girl was able to crawl not only under my skin, but my brother's as well. She saw the demons in both of us, but instead of fighting them, she wrapped them in a comforting, warm embrace.

"How was it?" I ask now, lazily taking a drag of a cigarette.

I pass it to Cain, and bliss contorts his features as he breathes in deeply.

We're sitting in the throne room, a cold draft blowing in from the propped opened doors. Nina is currently with Damien, and Bronson is still with his family. I have no idea where Kai and Rion are—probably stabbing people, those deranged shits.

"Fucking amazing," he declares, a dopey fucking smile on his face. "She was everything I imagined and more."

"I'm kind of jealous, you know," I admit, taking the cigarette back from him. "I always thought I would be the first twin to make love to Bambi. Not your ugly ass."

"Make love." Cain snorts, but once again, a dreamy, wistful smile erupts on his face. "We've turned into lovesick fools."

"So, you do?" When he turns towards me, I crush the butt of the cigarette out on the cement. "Love her, I mean."

I thought that realization would hurt me, gut me, but I only feel at peace. All I have ever wanted was for my brother to find love and be loved in return. If it just so happens to be with the same girl as me? No problem. Nina is more than capable of loving both of us equally, unconditionally. Her love has no bounds.

"That's actually what I came to talk to you about," he admits, scrubbing a hand across the top of his disheveled blond hair. I eye him curiously, waiting for him to gather his thoughts. "I love her, but I know you do too. And I suspect she loves both of us—as well as the others—equally." He takes a deep breath, eyes closing, before he drops his head back against the wall with a *thunk*. "What the fuck are we doing, Abel? Are we okay with this? Sharing her?"

I remain silent as I think through his words. It's what I always do, despite people's preconceived notions concerning me.

"Can you imagine life without her?" I ask Cain at last.

There's no judgment in my tone, just curiosity. His eyes snap open, the green so similar to my own peering back at me like jade gemstones.

"What?" His voice is raspy, hoarse, and he has to clear his throat before he can speak again. "What do you mean?"

"I mean"—I tap my fingers against my leg—"that I can't imagine a life without her in it. I love her, and I accept all the parts of her, even the parts that love other men. But that's my decision and mine alone. I don't expect you to as well. So, I want you to ask yourself: can you imagine life without her? Would you rather have a piece of her, a piece of her heart, or nothing at all?"

Cain gapes at me wordlessly before his mouth snaps closed. He turns his attention towards his hands in his lap.

I dread his answer. Can I still be with Nina, knowing my brother loves her and can't have her? Would that make me selfish? I know the answer to that thought even before it formulates completely.

Yes.

I can't give Nina up.

All I know for certain is that a part of me will die if my brother chooses to leave her.

Cain releases a heavy breath, lifting his eyes once more. He pierces me with a look amassed with so much wisdom and longing, I feel the ache physically in my chest.

"Yes. I love her. I don't care that she loves you and the other assholes as well. I want to be with her and only her, for as long as she'll have me."

The tension in the room lessens infinitesimally at his declaration. It's like we're both finally able to breathe again.

"How about we steal her from Damien and prove our devotion to her?" I suggest with a waggle of my eyebrows. It's not often that Cain and I share girls. Hell, the last time it happened was back at the sex club. But now, I can't think about anything else but enjoying our girl together. Seeing her flushed cheeks, demure smile, and cloudy eyes. Hearing her whimpers and moans of pleasure...

My cock jumps in my pants, instantly hardening. Fuck, just the thought of Bambi has me hard as rock.

"I call back!" Cain says instantly, and I curse.

"Dammit! Rock, paper, scissors for it," I plead, placing my fist on my hand and holding them both out.

"Nope. I called it first." Cain tilts his chin up stubbornly, a wicked glint in his mossy eyes.

"You suck."

"Yeah, her clit—"

Whatever foul-mouthed thing Cain was going to say is interrupted by Bronson's appearance in the entrance of the throne room. His eyes are wild, feral, flickering from one face to another but never sticking. A dusting of goose bumps erupts on my flesh.

"Everything okay, Wolf-man?" I ask just as Cain demands, "Where's Nina?"

Ignoring us both, he turns towards the empty throne situated in the center of the room. His brows furrow. "Where's Kai? I need to speak to him immediately."

"You're acting kind of weird, Bron Bron." I hesitantly take a step closer to him. You have to be careful when approaching an out-of-control wolf; you never know when they might bite.

"Seriously, what's going on?" Cain jumps to his feet and crosses his arms over his chest. Unlike me, he has no problem confronting the growly shadow wolf.

"Nina with Damien?" Bronson rumbles.

My brother and I exchange a long, eloquent look. A twin look. You know the type.

"Is this about Nina?" Cain asks slowly, warily.

Bronson growls sharply but grabs a folder out from under his shirt.

Exchanging another look with my brother, I grab the proffered folder and begin to flip through it. A lot of medical gibberish and terminology glares back at me. I do recognize Nina's name on the top of the form: Nina Doe, the name the court gave her when she revealed she didn't have a last name.

"I don't know what I'm looking at," I admit, feeling like an idiot. School and I never really went together. However, Cain had been training to be a doctor before Boris and his thugs took us. He had been able to skip three grades, graduating high school at only fifteen. He completed nursing school when he was seventeen, the same year Boris...

I sweep those thoughts beneath the metaphorical rug.

Not today, Satan. Not today.

I hand the papers to my brother and watch as his eyes change and harden the longer he stares at them. Horror douses his serene expression like a bucket of frigid water. His hands tremble slightly.

"Are you sure?" he whispers to Bronson.

The shadow wolf nods once. "My sister was able to hack the hospital records."

"Somebody better tell me what the fuck is going on before I get ragey. You really don't want to see me like that," I say somewhat petulantly. I hate being left in the dark, especially about the people I love.

"It's Nina's testing from the hospital, after she escaped the Compound," Cain states shakily.

"Someone tried to have these sealed," Bronson adds. "I have no doubt that everyone involved with her case had a mysterious, life-threatening accident shortly after she was discharged."

My head swarms like a nest of bees have been released, the incessant buzzing causing a headache to form behind my eyes. What the hell are they going on about?

Noticing my rising anger, Cain hurries to elaborate. "The

paperwork shows tests from the hospital. Including blood tests." He takes another deep breath. "They found angel blood in her body."

"Angel blood?" I ask, not understanding the issue. Shouldn't they be thrilled? "So, she's an angel?"

Damien will get a kick out of this.

Now that I think of it, I can totally see Nina with a halo and white, fluffy wings. Her mannerisms are certainly angelic.

I wonder if it hurt...when she fell from heaven.

Yeah, I have a whole arsenal of cheesy angel jokes at my disposal.

I can't help but smile softly. For her entire life, Nina hasn't known who or what she is. Now, she finally has answers. There are other angels in the prison, people we can reach out to and ask to train her—

Cain's and Bronson's somber expressions cut my thoughts off mid-rant.

"What?" I volley my gaze from one to the other.

"They found something else as well, something they didn't understand," Cain begins. "Demon blood."

"Demon blood," I repeat slowly, carefully. "So, she's a hybrid?"

Hybrids were uncommon in our world, but not unheard of. It still doesn't explain their reactions.

"A mage tested her blood. A special test, one that most people wouldn't normally think to do," Bronson takes over. The burly shifter sounds more scared than I've ever heard before. That immediately puts me on edge. If Tall, Large, and Scary is anxious, then I should probably prepare to shit my pants. "Apparently, the demon blood has been added. It's not natural."

"Not natural..." There's a strange roaring in my ears, drowning out their words. All I can see is Nina's heart-shaped face, shy smile, and fluttery lashes.

Not natural.

Not natural.

Not natural.

"Someone added the demon blood to her over time...sort of like a transfusion. The mage also found alternations to her DNA," Cain recites expressionlessly.

Vomit churns in my stomach. "Are you saying what I think you're saying?"

I'm gonna be sick.

"Someone fucked with Nina's genetic makeup," Bronson growls, eyes flashing amber. "They modified her blood to make her into a hybrid." Another growl reverberates through his body as he struggles to hold on to his wolf's leash. "The Compound isn't just a prison, but a lab. A fucking lab."

I barely make it to the trash can before I vomit up my breakfast.

CHAPTER 52

NINA

I 'm not surprised when Alyssa steps into the visitor's room. By this point, I have her footsteps memorized—the audible clack of heels against the white tiled floor.

I slip into her head just as she sits opposite me, gaze fixed on her manicured nails tapping against the table.

"One of my men contacted me the other day," Alyssa begins softly. Despite her words being directed at me, her eyes are glued to a water stain on the wall. It's the only blemish I have noticed in this nondescript room. Everything else is painted in stark white, with freshly scrubbed floors and wiped-down tables. I imagine the warden wants to give a certain impression to family members—that this prison is a respectable, clean place.

"What did he say?" I ask as Alyssa's gaze travels to the one-way mirror. There's a determined set to her jaw, and her eyes are clouded with pain.

"He doesn't think Lionel did it," she says quietly, demurely. "He doesn't think Lionel killed Raphael."

Raphael. Man.

Even just his name evokes full-body shivers. Does Alyssa

know about his past activities at the Compound, or is she just the poor, unfortunate soul who fell in love with an evil man?

Maybe she was blind to his demons. I know I can be when it comes to the men I love.

"I'm at a loss for words," she whispers brokenly. "I don't know what to believe anymore. If Lionel didn't kill Raphael, then who did? You? I doubt that." I catch the inquisitive look on her face in the reflection before she turns to me completely. "I still don't believe you killed Raphael, but now, I don't know who did."

"And you trust this source?" I query. What had she been told that changed her entire perspective of Lionel Green?

Alyssa's vision shifts as she nods once, a decisive head bob. "I do. He has been undercover for years now and is a close confidant of Lionel. I haven't been able to contact him since this whole thing went down, but he recently got in touch with me." She blows out a breath, stirring the curl that had fallen in front of her face. "Lionel is just as terrified as the rest of us. He believes someone is targeting council members. He's only left his house once since this whole thing began. Tell me, Nina, is that the behavior of a murderer? Or a scared little boy?"

I feel as if this is a test. My answer will determine how we proceed next. The tension and anxiety saturating the room is nearly stifling.

"I don't know," I answer. "I honestly don't know." I bite down on my lower lip as my stomach tightens into knots. I wish desperately that Alyssa would look away from me, towards her reflection. There's no way of knowing if I passed or failed her makeshift test.

"I'm going to get to the bottom of this," Alyssa says resolutely. "Raphael was my whole world. I loved him. One touch from him was goddamn nuclear. We destroyed each other in a way only loved ones could."

There's a potent pain to her words. I try to imagine a love like she's talking about, a love capable of destroying the parties involved, but I can't seem to visualize it. Love is supposed to be sweet and bright, breaking apart the monotony of darkness, one crack of lightning at a time. It's supposed to be gracious and calm. That's not to say you won't get hurt—you will—but the joy will overshadow the pain.

"I'm sorry this happened to you." Alyssa clears her throat, pulling herself out of her memories. She gracefully rises to her feet. "We'll keep searching. I want the truth. More than you can possibly know." My heart cracks like an aged stone being dropped. Her pain seems to radiate throughout the room, seeping into my skin.

"I'm sorry too," I whisper as she exits the room.

I don't immediately pull out of her head, watching as she walks down the twining halls of the prison. A few of the guards wave to her, smiling, and she returns their waves with her own pleasantries. Everyone here seems to genuinely like Alyssa, her presence magnetic.

What attracted her to a man like Raphael? What face did he wear when he was with her? I saw the monster, the demon, the nightmare. She saw a charming man who spun lies like a spider spins webs.

She's in love with a monster, but then again, so am I. With a few of them.

Alyssa finally exits the prison and takes a deep breath. Elation flows through me when I realize this is the longest—and farthest distance—I have been in someone's head. I wonder how long I can hold the connection...

She moves to a chain-link fence with gargoyles perched on the turrets. A rough-looking guard waves to her.

"How are you doing, Alyssa?" he questions.

Hearing.

I'm hearing through her ears.

I'm giddy with excitement, knee bobbing up and down.

What else can I do? Can I feel her clothes against my skin? Smell the fresh air?

God, I miss fresh air.

The sky is a brilliant blue canvas overhead with a golden sun directly in the center. It appears as if the prison is located in a barren wasteland. Nothing but red dirt spreads in all directions as far as the eye can see.

After speaking briefly with the guard, Alyssa moves to a black car idling just at the entrance. The driver rushes around to open the door for her, head bowed submissively. It's only when he lifts his head that I freeze, blood pulsing through my body. I feel lightheaded, and I swear my heart cracks open, weeping blood.

I recognize that man.

He has white-blond hair, curled around his ears, and a wicked, vertical scar marring his left eye and right cheek. His lips are pursed, as if he's eaten something disgusting and is trying not to swallow.

He's from the Compound.

I don't know his name—everyone called him M—but he's definitely one of the men who tortured me on the daily. One of the men who strapped me down, put a scalpel to my throat, and watched me bleed. One of the men who tormented a vulnerable little girl just because he could. He wasn't as bad as Man, as Raphael, but he still haunts my nightmares. Him and the dozen other men and women who deemed me a toy to play with and break.

Panic threatens to sweep me under like a ten-foot tidal wave.

Why is Alyssa with him? How does she know him?

Alyssa stops suddenly, her reflection visible in the passenger side window. Her ruby red lips curl up into a smile, but there's nothing warm about it. It reminds me of a frosted-over sword.

"Nina," she purrs, her smile growing, "I know you're here."

I pull myself out of her mind so fast that I get whiplash. Bright colors disrupt the darkness I'm so accustomed to. My head spins and spins and spins with this onslaught of information.

How is this possible? How does she know about my abilities? How did she know I was in her head?

My panic increases until it's nearly overwhelming. I can't focus on anything else. My heart picks up speed, pounding in my eardrums.

There's only one thing that makes sense. The final piece of this distorted puzzle.

Alyssa worked for the Compound. *Works* for the Compound.

Just as that thought forms, something sharp pricks my neck. I gasp at the initial stab of pain, stomach somersaulting, as my consciousness begins to wane.

Alyssa betrayed me.

That's the last thought I have before I lose myself to the darkness.

CHAPTER 53

NINA

My consciousness returns fleetingly. There and gone in seconds. It's like trying to grasp water in your cupped hand—no matter what you do, you can't maintain a hold on it.

After what feels like a century later, I sluggishly return to the land of the living.

The first thing I make note of is the stale air. Dust and dirt saturate the room, rendering even breathing a difficult feat.

I cough, pressing my face into the cold stone floor.

Where am I?

That one thought circulates in my brain, but I don't have an answer to it. The last thing I remember is meeting with Alyssa, and then...

My stomach tightens and twists until I swear I'm going to vomit.

Somehow, someway, she knew about my power. Not only that, she could sense my presence in her mind. The only logical explanation is that she was at the Compound with me.

I try to make sense of my surroundings, but without sight,

it's surprisingly difficult. There's a pungent, undefinable scent permeating the air, but I can't put my finger on where I've smelled it before.

Everything is cold. The ground, the air, my body. I half wonder if the room is hewn from ice.

Maybe the important question isn't where I am, but how I got here.

I rub at my neck where someone had pricked me. How did they get into the visitor's room without me knowing? I imagine I was so entranced by Alyssa and my enhanced abilities that I didn't hear the door opening and closing.

As the guys always say...

Fuck.

I'm painfully aware of a gnawing, gaping hole in my stomach. I whimper pathetically as it grumbles, demanding I feed it. Even my throat is unbearably dry, as if I haven't had water in weeks.

How long have I been unconscious?

As panic sets in, I take a slow inventory of my body. Fortunately, I appear to still be wearing the white dress I arrived in. The fabric clings to my thighs and stomach. Except for a slight sting in my neck and my weakened state, my body doesn't appear to have any significant damage. Maybe a bruise or two from when I was thrown into this... whatever the heck this is.

Okay, think, Nina. Think.

I push my awareness into the hall, searching for the nearest mind, but I can't sense anyone. That sends my panic ratcheting up a notch.

I have no idea where I am or what my new prison looks like. For all I know, there's a dead body a few millimeters away from me.

And God, I'm hungry. So unbelievably hungry.

"Hello? Is anyone there?" I cry weakly, moving to my

hands and feet and crawling forward. Something sharp digs into my left knee, and I fall onto my back, wincing.

Carefully, I cup my knee and feel around the edges until I grab whatever has embedded itself into my skin. Glass, if the shape and texture are any indication. The shard cuts my finger, eliciting a sharp hiss of pain. Slowly, I pull the minuscule fragment out of my knee and toss it to the side. Tears of indignation and pain trail down my cheeks. It doesn't seem to be bleeding too hard, but I still rip at the hem of my gown and wrap it around the wound.

Okay, now, figure out where you are, Nina.

Using my hands as guidance, I make a mental map of the cell.

Against the far wall is a single cot devoid of any blankets or pillows. The mattress itself is lumpy and reeks of urine. Nothing else is in the room with me, not even a toilet. There's a single door that leads into and out of the cell, but it's locked. Whoever took me has no intention of letting me go.

Alyssa.

Hours go by with no contact, no food, no water. I'm beginning to get claustrophobic, despite not being able to see the walls. Still, I feel them closing in around me on all sides like a steadily shrinking vise.

Panic and my own gnawing hunger bring me to my feet. I pound desperately, futilely, against the door. From the sound of it, the door is made of wood. I wonder if it's possible to break it down…

Even as I think that, a wave of dizziness courses through me. I'm too weak to stand on my feet, let alone break open an obviously thick door.

With a cry, I hobble away from the door and curl up on the bed. Am I going to die down here? Alone and forgotten?

I can't get over the irony of this entire situation. I escape the Compound only to be arrested and imprisoned. I escape the prison only to be brought to a new cell.

I'll never be free.

DAYS PASS. WEEKS, MAYBE. I LOSE TRACK OF TIME.

At the Compound, I at least had guards stopping by my cell. I'll take that torture any day over this solitude, this silence.

This hunger.

A few days ago, I found a leak in the ceiling of my cell. The water is rancid and dirty, but it does wonders to relieve my parched throat. It doesn't alleviate the hole in my stomach, though.

I haven't peed since I arrived here. Not once.

I know I'm dehydrated, but there's nothing I can do besides open my mouth and hope the leaking water enters it.

My muscles are beginning to ache from the lack of hydration. Soon, I won't be able to pull myself from the water leak to the bed and back again. I'll have to choose between water and comfort.

I'm so, so hungry.

At one point, I swear I hear a mouse squeaking in the distance. Is it a shifter coming to save me? A friend of Rion's?

When he presses his whiskered face against my cheek, I realize he's not a shifter but a plain old mouse.

A mouse I imagine eating.

I feel light, disembodied, like my soul isn't even in my body but hovering a foot above.

How long do they plan to keep me like this?

I think of Kai and Bronson. Cain and Abel. Rion and Damien. The sexy men who have claimed my heart and soul. I imagine they'll be worried sick about me by now.

If I die, who will be Damien's light? Who will help Cain and Abel conquer their demons? Who will listen to Rion's ramblings and be his shoulder to lean on? Who will love Bronson and allow him to love her in return? Who will take care of Kai while he worries about taking care of everyone else?

I think of them, only them, as the darkness once again pulls me under.

I'M IN THE LABYRINTH. I RECOGNIZE THE LEAD PIPES ON the ceiling, the stone walls, and the mold growing on every available surface.

I appear to be in someone's head. A male, if the height is any indication. When he raises his hands, balls of fire forming in each palm to illuminate the pathway, I realize the man is Kai.

"How much longer?" Rion demands, his honey, accented voice as cold as ice. Kai turns towards him, and I see my four other men as well. All five of them have somber expressions, eyes tight with worry, and there's an urgency to their gaits that wasn't there previously.

"Do you think I fucking know?" Kai growls.

"We've been through this hall already," Bronson cuts in. His eyes flash amber, seeming to emit a golden glow as his wolf makes an appearance. Sharp incisors cut into his bottom lip before he takes a deep, steadying breath. His teeth return to normal, and his eyes lose their luminescent glow.

"You need to calm the fuck down," Abel snaps at the shadow wolf. "You can't wolf out down here. You know you can't control your instincts, and the last thing I want to be is puppy chow."

Bronson whips his head in the demon's direction, a growl

emanating from his chest. He steps forward threateningly, looking every inch the dangerous predator I know him to be.

"Enough!" Cain shoulders his way in between them. His hair is unruly, as if he'd run his hand through it one too many times. His lips pull back from his teeth in a snarl. "We can't fucking fight." When he's sure he has both of their undivided attention, he turns back towards Kai. "Okay, so, Bronson's right. We have been down this tunnel before. We turned left at the upcoming fork, so, this time, let's go right."

The guys—excluding Damien—all nod their agreement. I notice my mage's eyes are as blind as my own. Seeing but not understanding. With dark hair framing a proud and arresting face, chiseled cheekbones, strong jawline, and icy eyes that never seem to freeze me, he's beautiful. Cold and beautiful. That beauty reels me in like a fish on a hook. This angel, however, is bathed in blood and menace. An avenging angel, then.

My avenging angel.

Kai turns back around, focusing on the flames dancing in his palms. When they reach the fork, they turn right.

Kai is so focused on his hands that he doesn't notice the scythe dangling precariously against the wall. Directly below it, on the floor, is a square slab of darker stone, slightly raised.

Stop! I scream mentally, and Kai surprises me when he stumbles to an abrupt halt.

"What the hell, Blade?" Rion snaps, spinning on his heel.

"I... I heard her," Kai whispers breathlessly. "Nina. I heard her."

"You feeling okay, buddy?" Abel asks placatingly. He steps forward to feel the dragon's forehead. "Fuck, I think he's hallucinating."

He can hear me?

Giddy elation travels through me.

Kai, can you hear me? I ask tentatively.

"Nina?" His voice is high with wonder and veneration.

Yes! Yes! If I had a body of my own, I would be crying right now.

"How is this possible?" Kai demands.

I don't know! I reply. *But be careful. I think there's a trap right in front of you.*

"What?" Kai looks first at the uneven square tile before lifting his gaze to the scythe. Without hesitation, he reaches into a pack I hadn't realized was slung over his shoulder and grabs an apple. Crouching down, he rolls the apple across the dark square. Immediately, the blade drops in a swooping arc before settling once more against the wall. I have no doubt it would've decapitated anyone in its line of fire.

"Pressure sensor," Kai says darkly. "Another one of the Labyrinth's traps."

"Fuck," Cain breathes from somewhere behind Kai.

Where are you? I ask desperately.

"We're fucking getting out of this place," Kai announces vehemently. "Rumor has it that there's a staircase that leads to the roof. From there, I can turn into a dragon and get us all out of here. Now, where the fuck are you? Bron and Rion can sense you nearby, but they can't get an exact location."

"You're talking to Nina." Damien's face appears in front of Kai's, eyes wild. "Are you there, Angel?" Before Kai can respond, Damien presses his lips to mine—Kai's—in a desperate, wild kiss.

And... I feel it.

I feel the softness and the scratch of his stubble. I feel his tongue poking the seam, demanding entrance. I feel it all, and tingles of desire blossom in my body.

All too soon, Kai shoves at Damien's shoulder, pushing the mage away. "What the fuck, man?" he snarls.

Damien doesn't answer, grabbing a knife from his sleeve

and leaning against the wall. I notice that warmth has bled into his once glacial eyes.

I felt that, I whisper to Kai.

"We're not using my body to give you orgasms," Kai says immediately. "Because I felt that too, and now I'm terrified my ass will be used for a bunch of horny penises."

Despite the direness of this situation, I laugh. I don't know if the noise translates in Kai's mind, but his own answering chuckle greets mine.

"Where the fuck is she?" Cain demands, bringing us back to the topic at hand.

I don't know. Insidious fear slithers down my spine like an icy snake. It seeps through my skin and squeezes my heart. *I think I'm in a cell. But no one has visited me in days. I'm so hungry and thirsty, Kai. I don't know how much longer I can last.*

"You're going to fucking hang in there, okay?" Kai's vehement voice pierces my depressive fog. "We're coming for you."

I don't want you to risk your life for mine, I protest weakly. But I know my words will fall on deaf ears. They will do anything and everything for me. Some people promise you the moon; others actually lasso it down for you.

I'm so weak, Kai, I try again, but his growl cuts off the remainder of my protests. It's no use arguing. I could sooner move a brick wall.

"Buttercup, hang in there, okay?" Rion cups Kai's cheeks to peer deeply into my—his—eyes. "We're coming for you. I know you're hungry, Buttercup, but you need to hold on a little longer. I can feel you, my love, and I'm coming."

"If you kiss me too, shifter scum, so help me..." Kai growls, and Rion reluctantly pulls his hands away.

"Bambi, do you remember who took you?" Abel questions, and the mood immediately turns suffocatingly tense.

Alyssa. She works for the Compound. I don't know in what capacity, though.

The guys pause suddenly, and through Kai's eyes, I see a hall of nails. I'd guess there's at least a thousand protruding from the walls, ceiling, and floor.

"How much do you want to bet we have to go in that direction?" Cain says dryly.

Without a word, Damien stalks forward, seemingly unaware or not caring that the nails dig into his skin on all sides. I let out a soft sob at the blood darkening his white dress shirt.

Please, don't do this. I don't want to lose you guys, I beg Kai.

His voice is terse when he answers. "And we can't lose you, either."

I make a move to reply when something hard snaps across my face, jerking me awake.

"Oh, good. You're awake," Alyssa says, saccharine sweet. "Now, we can talk."

CHAPTER 54

NINA

I open my mouth to demand that she let me go, but only a pitiful moan manages to escape. I'm terribly weak and dehydrated; each of my limbs feels like weights of lead.

"Are you hungry? Thirsty?" Alyssa giggles, the noise distinctly childlike. A moment later, a bottle is placed in my hand.

At first, I want to refuse her offering. I want to be strong enough to throw it in her face. Instead, I desperately fumble with the cap and down the bottle in less than a second. The water is warm, a little hotter than room temperature, but it feels like heaven in my dry mouth. Only when every last drop is gone do I put the bottle down.

"Damn, you really were thirsty," she muses, her voice coming closer. This time, she places a fluffy block in my hand. Bread, if the texture is any indication.

I know I need to eat slowly, but I'm positively famished. My stomach churns in protest as I shove the entire piece of moldy bread into my mouth.

"Why are you doing this to me?" I manage to stutter out. My voice is raspy and hoarse from lack of use.

"It's nothing personal," she says immediately, jubilantly almost. "I'm just tying up some loose ends."

"You work for the Compound," I whisper. It's not a question. There's no doubt in my mind that this councilwoman has played a part in my lifelong torture.

"No, silly girl." She laughs, the sound deceptively light-hearted, before petting my sweat-soaked, greasy hair. "I *run* the Compound."

Ice-cold terror skids down my spine as I process her words. She isn't just a pawn to the Compound; she *is* the Compound. There are thousands of questions clamoring for my attention, but I settle on the easiest one.

"Back at the prison, how did you know I was in your head?" For all I'm aware of, no one has ever sensed me lurking in their mind. The fact that Alyssa had...

She chuckles again, and I hear the springs on my bed creak as she sits. "I'm an angel. We're gifted in evading mind control. It's like an alarm system in our brain. Of course, not all angels are as old or as skilled as me. I'm sure that anyone else wouldn't have noticed your annoying presence where it doesn't belong." Her conversational tone transitions into rage. Even with no sight, I can feel her eyes spewing fire on my back. "Or it could be because you're my daughter." This last statement is said nonchalantly, as if she is merely discussing the weather, but it causes all my organs to stutter and stop. I'm not even sure I'm breathing.

"What?" I gasp. Surely, I heard her wrong. Surely, she didn't just confess to being my biological parent.

For years, I have lived with no identity. No true name. I thought that was all I would ever be: a nameless, faceless female. Surprisingly, that thought provided me with a great deal of comfort. I didn't want to know if I had family out there, crying for me. Missing me.

Laughing at me.

"I fucked a human male," Alyssa says dismissively, as if she didn't just drop a life-changing bomb on my lap and hit the detonate button.

"I'm part angel and part human?" My voice cracks. "I'm a hybrid?"

Alyssa releases another undignified snort. "No, silly girl. You're a tribrid." She moves to her feet once more before dropping another water bottle on my head. I wince at the initial stab of pain before eagerly devouring the water. I try to sip this one slower, my stomach already protesting how quickly I drank the first. "Raphael and I had a plan," she says, stroking my hair back. I wonder if she means for the touch to be motherly. Instead, it causes disgust to run rampant through my veins. "We wanted to create a world where supernatural creatures could love freely. Could procreate freely. We realized quickly that the best supernaturals embodied the characteristics of more than one species."

My plan to drink the water slowly backfires. In only a second, the bottle is empty. My stomach howls and gurgles in protest.

"We had the Compound open for years, since the twenties," Alyssa continues, and I realize blankly that she's telling me all this now because she has no intention of letting me go...or keeping me alive. "At first, we would just find compatible supernatural creatures and force them to mate."

Force them to mate. That sounds an awful lot like rape.

Disgust churns like acid in my lower stomach. I feel queasy, but I can't be certain if it's because of Alyssa's words or my gnawing hunger.

"As technology advanced, so did our techniques. We learned how to inject supernatural blood into our subjects. How to alter their DNA." She sighs dreamily.

"You experimented on them? On me?" I croak out, stumbling to my hands and knees. Even that movement pulls at muscles I didn't know existed.

"Of course." She doesn't sound at all apologetic. "There was an issue when we tried adding the demon DNA to you. I'll give you one hint. Well, two." She pokes at both of my eyes, and I let out a scream at the immediate, burning pain.

Alyssa isn't just evil. She's positively deranged. That makes her dangerous and unpredictable.

I fall onto my back, sobbing.

"Why now?" I cry. "Why are you doing this now?"

She sighs heavily, as if I'm an imbecile for asking such a ridiculous question. "I didn't want to kill you, Nina. It's why I put you in Nightmare Penitentiary. However, one of your boy toys received classified information the other day. Information that he shouldn't have." Her words send my mind in a tailspin, but before I can ask, she continues. "Enough about that." She blows out a breath. "I really don't want to kill you, Nina, just like I didn't want to kill Rafe. But sometimes, you have to do things for the greater good."

"You killed Raphael Turner?" I squeak as horror washes over me like a tsunami. "I thought you loved him!"

"I did. I mean, I do." The ire in Alyssa's voice makes goose bumps dust across my skin. "But he was getting too power hungry. He wanted to tell the council about our experiments. You see, over time, we have made over one thousand hybrids and tribrids. Hell, during the time you were in the Compound, we made at least fifty, if not more. An army's worth. Raphael wanted the world to know."

"So, you killed him?" I conclude, heart hammering in my chest. If she can do that to the person she loves, what will she do to me? Daughter or not, I'm under no illusion I'm getting out of this mess alive.

"It had to be done. Besides, he let you escape." Her tone

darkens considerably. "I needed to contain you somehow, but I knew returning you to the Compound would draw too much attention. You already had his blood under your nails, so it was the perfect idea. You go to prison—I get to keep an eye on you."

"What about Kai? Is he like me? A hybrid or whatever?"

Alyssa scoffs. "The dragon? No. He was meant for you, actually. What would be better than a quarter angel, quarter demon, quarter human, and quarter dragon baby? We intended for you to mate when the time was right." She cuts off abruptly when I begin laughing. Not just tiny peals of laughter, but full-on, grab-your-belly-and-rock-back-and-forth laughter. "What the hell is so funny?" she hisses.

"The flaw in your plan." I wipe at the tears that have escaped my eyes, attempting to regain some semblance of control. "I haven't had my period yet. You guys did something to me. I don't think I can get pregnant."

I expect her to get angry, get annoyed, heck, maybe even get somber. Instead, *she* begins to laugh. The jovial noise knots my insides.

"Stupid, stupid girl. You don't think that was intentional? I had a mage put a spell on your dumb ass, so you couldn't conceive until I was ready for you to."

The laughter dies in my throat as horror swamps me.

"Of course, my plan changed when Kai showed signs of being your fated mate," she says with a huff. "Dragons are normally dangerous, but when their mates are threatened, they become volatile. I knew I couldn't keep him around, so I ordered his imprisonment at Nightmare Penitentiary."

Poor Kai. Ripped away from his family to satisfy the twisted obsession of this power-hungry bitch.

"Are you going to kill me now?" I question tersely. I always suspected my death was inevitable. You don't live the life I did and expect to come out unscathed. I suppose I have accepted this chapter of my story—my death. I can only pray that my males will survive it too.

Alyssa releases a twinkling laugh. It reminds me eerily of the wind chimes I always heard in the Compound.

"Who said anything about killing you?" she asks, cupping my cheek. I try to twist away, but her hand only tightens, nails digging into my flesh. "You're my daughter, Nina, but you're also a powerful weapon. I have plans for you and plans for my future grandchildren."

Grandchildren?

The bread I just ate threatens to come back up.

With one more condescending pat to my cheek, Alyssa exits my cell.

CHAPTER 55

I don't see Alyssa for the next few days.

Fortunately, she deems that I'm worthy enough to have food and water. A guard delivers a single bottle of water and a block of bread through a slit in the door every day. It doesn't completely alleviate the hunger, but it helps pacify it.

Loneliness consumes me. At the Compound, I yearned for solitude. Now that I have it, I want nothing more than to rip all my hair out and scream at the top of my lungs.

I miss the guys fiercely. Bronson's overprotectiveness. Kai's leadership. Abel's jokes. Cain's snotty quips. Damien's cold stare. Rion's rambles. It's like I was given something infinitesimally precious and had to watch it shatter into thousands of pieces. Try as I might, I can't fix what I inadvertently broke.

I'm cold, dirty, and hungry. I want to cry, but I fight against it. Still, I can't stop the few tears that slip out. I'm surprised I even have water left in my body.

I attempt to clamp down on my emotions and think of a way out of this mess. If Alyssa has it her way, I'll be nothing more than a breeding mare, but I can't allow that to happen. I can't allow her to take that piece of me—it'll be the final nail in my coffin.

I feel like an animal. Actually, I feel like less than one. Animals, at least, are washed and fed. How long can I last like this? With the bare minimum of food and water?

Once again, tears threaten to choke me, but I stubbornly hold them in. Barbed wire coils around my heart, and venom pours into my blood.

You can survive this, Nina. You have survived worse.

With that pep talk, I allow my lashes to flutter shut.

THIS TIME, I'M NOT SHOCKED WHEN I ENTER ONE OF MY guys' minds. He's taller than the others, his head nearly brushing the tunnel's ceiling.

Bronson.

His eyes are intent on Rion as the shifter crawls forward. It appears as if he's on a black and gray checkerboard. He places his hands on the square directly to his right, and the tile breaks with a resounding crack. It caves in on itself, collapsing into a black abyss.

With a curse, Rion moves to the square on the left of him and repeats the process. Like before, the square cracks and breaks.

Bronson, I say. He jumps, startled, and whips his head around. Behind him, my other men are leaning against the wall, sweating and panting. Scratches and bruises mar their skin. Damien's white dress shirt is completely coated in blood, and he has a wicked scar on his cheek. Kai has nasty bruises on his neck, and he's favoring his right arm. Both the twins look as if they've been through the meat grinder, tiny cuts freckling their handsome faces.

"Nina?" Bronson asks, and all heads snap to attention.

I'm here, I soothe. *Where are you? What is Rion doing?*

"We're still in the fucking Labyrinth," Bron snarls. "It never fucking ends. And Rion is attempting to survive another puzzle."

Puzzle?

Bronson turns back to Rion just as the shifter crawls from one square to another. He breathes a sigh of relief when it doesn't immediately crumble.

"Tell my Buttercup that we're almost to her. And that she's the speckle to my shine. Actually, don't say that. It doesn't make sense. It's one of those things that sounded much cooler in my head." Rion cuts off abruptly as the square in front of him falls away and a spear pops up where it once was. "Fucking hell! That nearly took out my face. My sexy, beautiful face."

"Hurry the fuck up," Kai rumbles, stepping in front of Bronson and crossing his arms over his chest.

Tell him to be careful, I cry, fear skirting through me.

"He'll be fine," Bronson assures me. "Now, tell me what's happening."

Quickly, I tell him about Alyssa's visit and her claim about my tribrid status. Bronson doesn't sound surprised when I tell him I have angel, demon, and human blood in me.

"I had my sister do some digging," he explains somewhat guiltily. "Before I could tell you..." He trails off as a growl resonates through his chest. He stalks away from Rion and the others, pressing his forehead against the grimy stone. With a deep, fortifying breath, he whispers, "Please tell me you're okay, my love. I don't think I'll survive if anything happens to you. I can feel you, feel your pain, and it's killing me."

My heart swells with love and longing for this brave, beautiful man. His rough features belie a gentle soul and kind heart. He sheathes me in a cocoon of light, making me forget all about my monsters and demons. The darkness can't reach me when he's there to fight it off.

Bronson, I love you, I whisper reverently. *I love you so much that sometimes I can't breathe.*

He lets out a choked sob. "Hang in there, Babygirl. Hang in there for me. We're coming for you, okay? Just hang in there. I'm in love with you. I've been in love with you. But I feel like..." He gulps audibly, hands tightening on two rocks that protrude from the wall. "I feel like I'm failing. Failing at being your mate, your friend, and your protector. Failing at loving you the way you should be loved."

You have been anything but a failure, I protest adamantly. *You were the first person in the prison who showed me what it means to be loved. You cared for me when I didn't know how to care for myself.*

My resolve hardens, strengthens—a wall of steel and cement around my heart.

I'll come back to you, Bron. To all of you. I promise.

It's a promise I intend to keep, come hell or high water. Not even death will separate us.

Before Bronson can respond, I'm wrenched out of his head. It's like traveling through a whirlpool. My mind spins wildly until everything settles.

"Good. You're awake," Alyssa chirps, patting my cheek harder than necessary.

"Let me go," I groan. Almost instinctively, I slip inside her mind.

She's hovering over me with her hands on her hips. Pressing the toe of her heeled shoe to my stomach, she laughs.

"See? This is why you're an asset to me. Your powers are unlike anything we've ever seen before. Unlike anything we've ever created." I imagine her ruby red lips pulled into a smile. She oozes satisfaction. "You'll be a perfect little spy for me.

You've heard of that awful man Lionel Green? Of course, you have. I'm sure your twins told you all about him."

"Go to hell," I mumble weakly. The slap comes out of nowhere, stinging my cheek. A red splotch in the shape of a handprint darkens my skin.

"You're going to spy for me, Nina," she says in a dark voice. "You won't like the consequences if you refuse."

"What are you going to do? Kill me?" I laugh humorlessly. "Go ahead. I dare you, you spineless bitch."

Her hand snaps once more across my face, sending my head flying to the side. I lie on the ground, trembling, unsure of how to fight back. I know I need to—I promised Bronson —but I'm so painfully weak. My eyelids are as heavy as lead. I can feel blood trickling from my busted lip, but I don't lift a hand to brush it away.

She crouches down beside me until her face is only slightly higher than my own. "Don't talk back to your mother," she hisses.

"You're not my mother."

She sighs, as if my answer pained her. The next moment, she grabs my collar and hoists me to my feet, her other hand encircling my throat. Her strength surpasses that of even Bronson's. I dangle in the air, panic thrumming through my veins, as her hand tightens around my throat, cutting off my air supply.

"I can make those guys' lives a living hell. The shifter. The dragon. The mage. The twin demons. The wolf."

My panic turns into rage. No one—absolutely no one— threatens my men.

Before, I was scared and slightly irritated. Now, I'm furious. The anger coils around my heart like a piece of rope, tightening incrementally with each word she says.

"I'll have fun ripping the scales off your dragon. One piece at a time. I wonder if he'll cry? Hmmm. We never were able to break him in the Compound, you know. We tortured him like we did you, but he never cried. Not once. The only time he cried was when we made him watch you get your skin peeled off." She laughs at the stricken look on my face. "You didn't know that, did you? Ha! We realized pretty quickly that the way to destroy the dragon was to destroy you."

I begin to struggle in earnest, clawing at her fingers. Only one thought echoes through my mind: vengeance. For me, for Kai, for all the other experiments throughout time. How many people has she killed? And how many people are like me, confused and alone with powers they can't even begin to understand?

My rage continues to manifest deep in my stomach. It's unlike anything I have ever felt. It burns me. Each word she says is tinder to the roaring flame.

"I think I'll keep the twins," she continues with a lilting laugh. "I'm not sure if you know this, but I used to visit them at the club. They're good fucks, am I right?" She nudges me conspiratorially, and I see red. It coats my vision like shutters being drawn closed. "Of course, they don't remember that. I had a mage wipe their memory each time. Lionel recommended them to me." She loosens her hands, and I desperately take in air. My lungs are aching, my breaths raspy.

She drops me back to the floor, stepping away, as if I have a particularly pungent smell. At this point, I'm not sure that I don't. Through her eyes, I watch myself stumble to my feet, eyes livid and lips pulled back from my teeth.

"Don't get me started on that handsome wolf. Did you know it was his sister that found the information concerning your blood?" She tsks her tongue disapprovingly. "I suppose I'll have to kill her now. And her mom and sister. Poor Bronson will lose his entire family because of you."

It's that, more than anything, that sends me spiraling over the edge. Something inside of me clicks into place, something

I can't define or name. My rage continues to grow and grow until it threatens to explode. I'm an active volcano, and this murderous woman happens to be in my vicinity. Anger is a living entity inside of me. Fire spews through my veins, setting me aflame.

"You won't touch them," I say through clenched teeth. Through Alyssa's eyes, I see myself change. Dark horns, similar to the ones I saw on Cain's and Abel's heads, poke through my black hair. My eyes take on a crimson quality, the pupils rimmed in coal black. Sprouting from my back are two luminescent white wings. Each expands the length of the cell, the feathers white with a pearlescent shine.

I look beautiful and deadly.

Wrathful.

I am vengeance personified.

"You won't hurt them," I say in a low voice, and Alyssa actually stumbles away. "You won't hurt my mates."

"Nina, think about what you're about to do," she begins placatingly, but I've heard enough.

With a roar, I lunge for her, tackling her to the ground. I wish I could see her face at my attack.

Are her eyes wide with fear?

Is she trembling?

I can't focus on anything through the blinding, incandescent rage. I pummel her face with punches, enjoying her pained moans. They reach a part of my mind I can't access, a part that is buried beneath years of hurt and anger.

She wraps her legs around my waist and throws me off her. My back slams against the far wall, but I regain my balance quickly.

"Think about what you're doing!" she screams, spit hitting my cheeks.

"I am."

She comes for me, but I remain where I am, watching

through her eyes as she comes closer and closer. At the last second, I spring to action, throwing my fist out and catching her in the neck.

The hit rattles her, and she releases a guttural cough.

I spin her so her back faces my front. Wrapping my arms around her throat, I hiss in her ear, "You're done."

"You think killing me will stop the Compound?" she gurgles. "They'll always exist, and they'll always come for you. Their perfect specimen."

"Let them come," I say darkly. She scratches at my arm, but I squeeze tighter. She begins to go limp, body pliable, but just before she can hit the ground, I release her. "You're never going to hurt me again."

With a ferocious cry, I spin her around and shove my fist into her chest. I see my face through her vision—I look exactly like the monsters I once feared.

Strange choking sounds emit from Alyssa, and her vision steadily begins to dim before it turns black completely.

I remove my hand from her chest, still holding her heart in my hand.

"You won't hurt any of us again," I whisper brokenly.

Noise alerts me to the incoming assault a moment before the door to the cell is broken down.

"Freeze! Hands where I can see them!" a voice screams. I hear pounding footsteps against the cement, but all I can do is stare blindly in their general direction. "Get down on the ground! Get down on the fucking ground!"

Slowly, I come back to myself. I feel my wings retreat into my body with an audible snap. My horns lower until I can no longer feel them anymore.

Oh, God. What did I just do?

Panic gushing through me, I drop the heart and slowly fall to my knees. My body is shivering uncontrollably.

What did I do?

What did I do?

What did I do?

I bring my hands behind my head, only to have them brutally wrenched behind my back. I feel the familiar sting of handcuffs rubbing against my skin.

"Nina Doe, you're under arrest for the murder of Council-woman Alyssa Timmer," a familiar voice sneers in my ear. I recognize him as the detective who arrested me for Raphael Turner's death. William.

And this time, I'm actually guilty of the crime.

CHAPTER 56

NINA

"Doe!" The guard rattles his baton on the cell bars. "You have a visitor."

I sigh, throwing my legs over the side of the cot. The jail-issued orange jumpsuit scratches against my skin, dreadfully uncomfortable. Hopefully soon, I'll be able to wear my normal clothes again.

I slide myself into the guard's—Gregory's—mind. He's one of the nicer ones at the jail they're currently housing me in. He once told me that I remind him of his daughter.

On the other side of him, with a severe scowl on his face, is Jermey. Now, this is a guard I hate with a passion. He's evil personified and never fails to make me feel like the scum beneath his shoes.

It's been two months since I killed Alyssa. Two months of imprisonment for a murder I actually committed. Two months and one week since I last saw the guys.

When Alyssa kidnapped me from the visitation room, with the help of a nameless guard, she killed two of the warden's men in the process, including the guard she had greeted at the gate. The warden immediately contacted the paranormal police—led by William—who conducted a complicated tracking spell. Ironically enough, I never left the prison. Instead, Alyssa took me to a separate, uninhabited wing.

I half wonder if William actually arrived sooner, overhearing the entire conversation, but chose not to enter until Alyssa was dead. That way, he wouldn't have to worry about the politics involved with a councilwoman killing a fellow councilman. Either way, the detective is relentless.

Guilty until proven innocent.

And the entire world is now witness to my guilt.

Fortunately, I was able to contact the guys after Alyssa's death—and my consequential arrest—before they ventured farther into the Labyrinth. They had numerous injuries— broken bones and bloody gashes—but they were alive and back home before the warden realized they'd tried to escape. That was all that mattered.

Swallowing thickly, I wait until my bars slide open before stepping out.

"Come here," Jermey snaps with a come-hither motion. He pulls a pair of magic restricting cuffs and motions for me to turn around. Realizing I can't see him (to his knowledge), he grabs my shoulder and spins me. I try to ignore the surge of satisfaction that thrums through me when I can still see through Gregory's eyes. I don't know if it's my demon, angel, or human blood, but the cuffs that smother our powers never seem to work on me.

We step through the door at the end of the cellblock into a long, gray corridor. A door to my right buzzes electronically and swings open.

"Move, inmate." Jermey shoves my shoulder, and I grit my teeth to keep myself from saying something I'll regret. Gregory subtly steps in between us, indirectly protecting me from the cruel guard's wrath. I offer him a small, grateful smile, the tension in my muscles loosening until I feel like I can breathe again.

We reach a locked metal door that he unlocks with a keycard—surprisingly modern for a secure paranormal facility.

A plastic chair sits in front of plexiglass, and a phone is attached to the wall. Sitting in the chair opposite is a pretty girl with strange orange hair and a flicking tail. I'm positive I've never seen her before in my life.

Approaching with caution, I take the seat opposite her. As the guard exits back through the door, I pull out of his mind and surrender to the darkness.

Fumbling slightly, I grab the phone and press it to my ear. "Hello?"

"Nina?" She has a sweet voice. A trusting one. It doesn't completely eradicate the trepidation coursing through me, but it sure helps to ease it. "You don't know me, obvs, but my name is Sinclair Denali. A little birdy—as in, a member of my prison squad—told me you're trying to get into Nightmare Penitentiary. Been there, done that, checked off that bingo square." Her voice turns devious. "Basically, I was conveniently convicted, and I'm going to return the favor by helping you. Now, listen up. There's a lot I have to teach you, my young apprentice. Let's start with Pop Rocks…"

I'M SWEATY AS I SIT IN THE UNCOMFORTABLE WOODEN chair facing the judge's stand. My new friend, Sinclair, pulled some strings to procure me this particular judge.

Through my lawyer's eyes, I see a furry, bull-like creature with curving horns. A minotaur, if I remember Sinclair's warning correctly.

I shift anxiously as the prosecutor begins to read out my

list of offenses. Breaking out of prison (despite the fact Alyssa had technically broken me out against my will, and I never actually left Nightmare Penitentiary). Attacking a guard. Murder in the first degree.

His words claw at something raw and bleeding inside of me. All I can see is my face contorting as I rip out Alyssa's heart...

"What do you have to say for yourself?" Judge O'Vine demands, his voice thunderous. When my lawyer makes a move to stand, I gesture for him to stay down.

Clearing my throat, I get to my feet.

You can do this, Nina. You can do this.

"You look like pubic hairs," I stutter out, recalling the insults Sinclair gave me. This would be so much easier if I had notes.

Everyone pauses. My lawyer is no doubt sweating, flicking his eyes in all directions nervously, and even the prosecutor is staring at me slack-jawed.

"Um... Cash me outside, how about dat?" I wince as Judge O'Vine begins to growl, the sound more animal than human. "Your mom's so fat that...um...when she rolls over, she ends up in a country across the ocean." Pause. "Why can't the minotaur get laid? Because his hairy dick is stuck inside... um..." I sift through my memories for the ending to that joke. "Because, um, they're hairy?"

Judge O'Vine raps his gavel against his desk as the audience breaks into nervous laughter. "Order. Order. Nina Doe, have you ever had a psych evaluation?"

"Yeah, by your mom," I retort.

"This girl is obviously a menace to society," the prosecutor insists, and I see the judge nod once. Already, the minotaur is staring at me as if he wants to stomp me beneath his hooves. The animosity saturates the air.

I know, no matter what I say or do now, Judge O'Vine will

still find me guilty. There's an unforgiving glint to his eyes and a sneer to his lips.

"Ms. Doe, you have been accused of murder in the first degree of a council member. What do you plea?" he seethes.

"Guilty," I answer immediately. "Absolutely guilty. I shanked that bitch." And then, as an afterthought, I add, "Asshole cumstain. Go shove a bloody tampon up your nose."

His eyes flash with raw, unparalleled rage. Smoke emits from his pierced nostrils.

"I hereby sentence you to life in prison at Nightmare Penitentiary, effective immediately." He knocks the gavel once more, sealing my fate.

And my future.

I SETTLE INTO THE GUARD'S MIND, USING HIS EYES, AS THE door clangs shut behind us.

The warden's office is exactly as I remember it. Posh and elegant, with hundreds upon hundreds of strange, magical artifacts.

The guards escorting me turn towards the man in question, and the warden drops the cockatrice feather he's been playing with.

"Nina Doe. Long time no see," he says, opening one of his drawers and grabbing a box of cigarettes. He lights one, blowing smoke directly into my face. "You're lucky I'm giving you another chance after what you did to my men." He gives me an inquisitive stare, and I sense the underlying question behind his statement.

He doesn't believe I'm guilty of what I'm accused of. Ironic, considering I actually committed the crime. Well, part of the crime. I wasn't the one who attacked and killed his men.

I remain stubbornly silent, my face an impassive mask I have perfected over the last two months.

"This is your last chance, girly. Act out again, and I won't be so forgiving," the warden warns me, moving around his desk to lean against it. His long trench coat flutters around him as he languidly smokes his cigarette. He nods to the guards on either side of me. "Take her to the Labyrinth."

I try to hide my ecstatic smile, I honestly do, but I know it escapes unbidden when the warden's eyes narrow suspiciously. Still, he doesn't stop his men from injecting me in the neck.

Soon.

I'll see them soon.

~

I KNOW I'M IN ABEL'S MIND BEFORE MY CONSCIOUSNESS even settles. He's staring at himself in the mirror, humming beneath his breath as he brushes back his blond hair. Smiling at his reflection, he spins on his heel, using the brush as a microphone.

"And who's the sexiest man alive?" He points finger guns at himself. "You are."

He's wearing a form-fitting navy-blue suit that I have no doubt Damien got for him. It fits his athletic build like a glove, showcasing his muscular biceps and tapered waist. He's so beautiful that it physically pains me. Beauty like his, both inside and out, shouldn't exist.

He begins to sing louder—something about a lot of single ladies and putting rings on it—when Cain enters behind him, brows furrowed. In a dark-blue suit and black tie, Cain looks just as dashing as his twin.

"What the hell are you doing?" Cain asks, quirking a brow.

Abel spins towards him, grabs his shoulder, and begins to sing even louder in his face. "Fucking hell, Abe, get a breath mint."

"Ha. Ha. Ha. I have brushed my teeth ten times in the last four minutes. You want to know why?" He drops his head onto Cain's shoulder, despite the sex demon's grunt of annoyance. "Because our girl is coming home today!" He lets out a whoop, jumping up and down like a little boy. Cain can't hide his own wistful smile.

Butterflies grow inside of me.

"Talking to her mentally isn't the same as seeing her," Abel continues, gritting his teeth in the mirror to make sure there is nothing in them. "Though, we have great mental sex. It's like phone sex, but only mentally."

I giggle as I recall some of the conversations with my men during the last two months. While we couldn't be together physically, we got creative. It's strangely erotic to watch them masturbate. Heck, even Damien played along.

Abel pauses suddenly, head canting to the side, before his face goes slack in horror.

"Bambi!" he squeals like a little girl. "Are you in my head right now?" He throws his hands in front of his body, as if he's naked instead of fully dressed. "You can't see me yet! It's bad luck!"

Hi, Abe, I say fondly.

Abel spins to face the wall, but not before I catch the shit-eating grin on his face. "Are you here yet? Are you? Are you? Are you? Are you? Because I'm going to fuck you until you can't—"

"Ignore him," Cain speaks up. "I do. Daily. Are you here yet?"

The guards are bringing me down now, I answer.

Abel bounces from foot to foot before grabbing Cain's sleeve and pulling him out of their cell.

"Let's grab the others and go see our girl! Fuck, I missed you, Bambi. I swear my balls are permanently blue."

"Stop talking about your balls," Cain snaps.

Abel snorts. "Oh, please. Just yesterday, you were planning a candlelight date for Nina that will end with a big bang, if you know what I mean."

"Shut the fuck up, Abe," Cain retorts. "You were asking Braelyn for dating advice earlier today."

Braelyn, during the two months I've been gone, has been working on fixing relations between Rion's gang and Blade's gang. I've been able to talk to her a few times, and she told me she wants to implement a "foreign exchange program" between the two groups. Haley and Rebecca have already volunteered to travel to the shifters' side of the Labyrinth.

"Fuck off!" Abel hits Cain's shoulder, sending the sex demon stumbling back a step.

My vision—Abel's vision—begins to get blurry, my surroundings turning glassy.

I think I'm waking up, I say quickly.

"We'll be there," Abel assures me. "We'll always be there."

I WAKE UP TO SOMEONE BRUSHING AT MY TANGLED HAIR. I moan lightly, turning my face into the calloused hand.

"Open your eyes, Babygirl," Kai whispers in my ear. "I need to see your beautiful eyes. Fuck, I missed you."

A contented sigh leaves my lips as I finally regain consciousness.

I appear to be sitting on a fluffy bed, an equally soft blanket splayed out around me. There's a kink in my neck that's new, and my eyelids are unbelievably heavy.

With ease, I slide into Kai's mind to survey my surroundings.

We're in a part of the Labyrinth I haven't visited before. Gold trinkets and jewels are scattered around me, some mountainous in size. I spot everything from necklaces to tiaras to gold-capped teeth.

"Where am I?" I murmur dazedly, still struggling to regain my bearings. "Where is everyone?"

"I kidnapped you," Kai says in satisfaction. "And we're in my cave. Dragons like shiny stuff. It's a compulsion to steal and collect them. Though, you're the most beautiful treasure of all."

I blink my eyes open slowly, groggily, and place a hand to my forehead. It's surreal to think that, after all this time, I finally reunited with one of my mates. Alyssa and the Compound can't hurt me anymore. Tears trail down my face as I lift my arms to Kai.

"Babygirl," he whispers reverently, pulling me towards him. Wrapped in his arms, I feel sheltered from the world. Nothing can harm me now. "Fuck, I missed you so much."

"I missed you too," I whisper into his neck. His citrus scent surrounds me, encompasses me. I can't differentiate where I end and he begins. "I love you."

"I love you so, so much. God, being with you again... I thought you were dead. I was so fucking worried when Alyssa took you and then when you had to go to trial." He brushes his lips against my forehead, body trembling. "Why didn't you fight back?"

I pull away from him, cocking a brow.

"At the trial," he explains. "Why didn't you tell them the truth about Alyssa? That she kidnapped you? That she killed Raphael? Why did you allow yourself to be blamed?"

I cup his prickly cheeks tenderly. God, I missed him. I didn't even realize how much until this moment.

"Because I needed to come home," I reply at last. Not wanted to. *Needed* to. Being with these men is an innate compulsion inside of me, similar to my need to eat and breathe. "You're my home. You, Rion, Damien, Abel, Cain, and Bronson."

He brushes his lips to mine once, twice, three times, before resting his forehead against my own. His eyes close briefly, obscuring my view, before he reopens them.

"I'm so sorry you had to go through all of that. I'm sorry I wasn't strong enough to protect you." The despondency and self-loathing in his voice breaks my heart. It rubs at something already bleeding in my chest. I hate that he feels this way.

"It's not your fault," I say earnestly, punctuating each word with a kiss to his face. His cheeks, his jawline, and then finally, his lips. "Alyssa's dead. She won't hurt us anymore." I pause, gathering my thoughts. "The only thing I regret is that the Compound is still out there, still hurting people. We cut off one head, but how many more are still alive and well? Still experimenting on innocent kids?"

"That's not our problem," Kai insists, grabbing my shoulders. When I go to protest, he tightens his grip. "Nina, it's not. We did what we could, but we're not the heroes in this story. At least, I'm not. I'm the villain, and I refuse to lose you again to the fucking Compound."

"Alyssa said she was my mother," I choke out.

"We don't know that," Kai counters immediately, but I'm already shaking my head.

"What reason did she have to lie?" The muscles in my stomach clench. "I killed her. I ripped her heart out of her chest." The familiar tendrils of panic and hysteria grip me. "I'm afraid... I'm afraid something inside of me died when she did. I'm afraid that I lost a piece of myself that I can never get back."

"Oh, baby." Kai sighs, pulling me once more into his arms. I rest my head on his chest and fall apart, tear by tear. "If I could, I would trade places with you in a heartbeat. I can't stand to see you so...broken. I'll hold you forever if that's what you need."

"But you can't," I choke out. "You can't fix me, Kai. What if I'm too broken? What if killing Alyssa made me into a monster?"

His arms tighten almost imperceptibly around me. A reassurance and a promise.

"Then, you'll be my monster." His breath wafts across my lips, eliciting full-body shivers. "When I lost you, I felt like a piece of myself went missing as well. I didn't think I'd ever be whole again. Seeing you now, I realize I love you more than anything. More than the sun or moon, the stars or clouds. I'll be content to remain in this fucking hole for the rest of my life if it means you're with me." He pauses, brushing at my loose curls. "Nina, will you be my mate?" There's so much hesitancy and trepidation in his voice. All I can do is close the distance between us and press my lips to his, promising him without words that he'll always own a piece of my heart.

"Yes, Kai. A thousand times, yes."

When he speaks next, he sounds breathless, ecstatic, as if I offered him the world instead of just myself. Maybe, to him, that *is* the world.

"You're fucking perfect."

His hand shakes slightly as he brushes my hair away from my neck, baring my skin to him. I pull out of his head, choosing instead to focus on the intimacy of his touch. It's been months since he last held me in his arms, last kissed me, last nuzzled my neck. It sends tingles of pleasure racing through my body.

When his teeth close around my skin, drawing blood, I can't stop the moan of pleasure that escapes me. White-hot, liquid pleasure surges through my veins. It's a beautiful, empowering feeling. All the pain from my time at the Compound, all the guilt concerning Alyssa's death, all my conflicting emotions about my relationship with the guys fade away. It's me. It's Kai. It's us. Everywhere we touch, we dissolve into each other. An aura of completeness settles around me.

When he finally pulls away, I know I have been irrevocably changed.

"You were the first man I ever loved," I whisper, wiping my thumb across his plush bottom lip. He captures it in his hand, pressing tingling kisses across the flesh.

"I love you so damn much, Nina," Kai says. "You're everything to me." He intertwines our fingers, his touch electric, and leads me out of his cave.

I don't ask where we're going as we travel down the Labyrinth's winding hallways. When we finally stop, I ask the questions on the tip of my tongue.

"Where are we going? Where are the others?" I don't care that I sound whiny. The last few months have been a proverbial hell. I have all these powers I don't know how to control, and I haven't touched my guys in two agonizing months. Seventy-eight days, to be exact.

"Are you in my head?" Kai inquires. Unlike Alyssa, the guys can't sense when I mind hop, unless I announce my presence. Slowly but surely, I've been working on strengthening my powers. We're hoping, in time, I'll be able to control body movements as well. Maybe even read minds.

That thought terrifies and exhilarates me. As a girl who never had anything, having this power at the tips of my fingers is surreal. It's like I'm hearing a story about a different girl, a stronger girl, instead of one about me.

"I am now," I answer with a smile on my face.

We're directly in front of the throne room, though I'm not surprised. It's where we usually congregate all together.

Kai pushes open the door and leads me inside, his hand on the small of my back.

Candles, their flames dancing, line the perimeter of the room. Rose petals create an aperture towards the golden throne, raised on a dais at the heart of it.

My men converge on me before I even step fully inside.

They all look painfully handsome in their tuxedos and ties. Sexy, even. Bronson catches me first, eyes burning amber, and buries me in his arms. A contented hum rumbles through his body. He repeats my name over and over as he rocks us side to side.

"My turn, Dog Breath." When Bronson doesn't release me, Rion holds me from behind, inhaling my scent. "Fuck, I missed you, Buttercup. Do you know how awful it was to be separated from you? I felt like I was dying. And no, I'm not being dramatic."

Tears spring to my eyes as I kiss first my wolf and then my shifter. My mates.

"Cuddle party!" Abel practically jumps on me from the side, pulling me away from the two possessive men. Bronson growls threateningly but doesn't make a move to grab me back.

Cain appears beside his brother. "Hey, Trouble. I heard you got into a teeny tiny bit of trouble." His voice dances with amusement.

"Just a murder," I say noncommittally, and Abel throws his head back in laughter.

"Fuck, Bambi." He kisses the shell of my ear, lowering his voice to a breathy whisper. "Did you know that I'm the only one of us you haven't slept with yet?" His teeth graze my lobe, and I shiver in pleasure.

"We should change that," I agree breathlessly. The thought of Abel inside of me...

Heat cascades through my veins.

"I like the way you think." He laughs jubilantly. "It'll be your welcome-back present."

The twins step away, leaving me with one last reunion. Through Kai's eyes, I see Damien standing a little bit away. His eyes slowly travel across my body, assessing me for injuries, before they lift to my face. A softness crosses his handsome features, melting away the ice.

"Damien." I hold my arms out to him—an offering and a promise. He needs to know that he can always come to me, and I'll always be there to catch him.

With quick strides, he crosses the distance between us and sweeps me off my feet. I wrap my legs around his waist as he holds my butt.

He brushes his lips against mine, and that one kiss promises me the world.

"I love you," I say softly, knowing he needs to hear it.

"You're my everything," he declares, reluctantly dropping me back onto my feet. His hands stay on my waist, though, warmth migrating from that slight touch.

"What is all this?" I ask, gesturing towards the elaborate setup.

Abel begins to grin, bouncing on the balls of his feet. "Can I tell her? Can I? Can I?" He raises his hand in the air, like a schoolboy begging to be called upon by his teacher.

"We decided something when you were away," Kai cuts in. The guys begin to walk towards the throne, pulling me along after them. Up close, it's even more elegant than I initially suspected. I wonder how Kai managed to create it. It's a combination of golden and silver filigree melded together. A single red cushion is placed on the seat, and the high back is lined with similar red trim.

"What did you decide?" I ask quizzically as Damien leads me to the chair. My confusion grows when Rion helps me sit on the surprisingly comfortable cushion. "What...?"

As one, the men, minus Kai, drop to their knees before me. My dragon continues to stand beside me, being my eyes.

"I was terrified of the way you made me feel. From the first moment I met you, I knew you would change my life. I don't even know when I fell in love with you, only that I did," Cain says, a tender smile softening his features.

"I don't want to be a king if you're not my queen," Rion adds.

"You're my entire world. My queen," Abel says solemnly. "*Our* queen."

"Our world," Bronson grunts in agreement.

"We'll serve you," adds Damien.

Kai slowly moves from his spot beside me to kneel with the others.

My heart leaps to my throat at the display. These proud, beautiful men, kneeling before me.

"You don't have to do this," I whisper.

"Be our queen," pleads Abel. "Be our wife."

I begin to cry silently, my tears cascading down my cheeks and wetting my lips. I've been broken and beaten. Bruised and discarded. Imprisoned.

Yet, I'm still breathing. I'm still alive. I hurt and I love. I'm stronger than I've ever been, my skin made of steel, but my heart made of glass. Only these men are capable of holding my heart in their hands and protecting it from shattering.

"Yes," I say, sobbing. "Yes."

As they surround me, touching me and loving me, I feel that final, unnamable puzzle piece click into place.

I may have been blindly indicted, but I've never felt more free.

AFTERWORD

Wow! Writing Nina's journey took me on a crazy ride. I hope you enjoyed reading her story as much as I enjoyed writing it! Make sure to check out the final book Blindly Acquitted.

SUPERNATURAL PRISON SERIES

PARANORMAL
PRISON

Siren Condemned by C.R. Jane and Mila Young

Delinquent Demons by K. Webster

Conveniently Convicted by Raven Kennedy and Ivy Asher

Noir Reformatory by Lexi C. Foss and Jennifer Thorn

Blindly Indicted by Katie May

Stolen Song by Autumn Reed and Ripley Proserpina

Prison Princess by CoraLee June and Rebecca Royce

Succubus Chained by Heather Long

Wraith Captive by Lacey Carter Anderson

ACKNOWLEDGMENTS

As always, there's a whole team of people I would like to thank.

First, thank you to my parents and sister for supporting me unconditionally. I love you all so much!

I would also like to thank the other amazing, incredible authors who partook in this prison series with me. Rebecca, Ivy, Raven, CoraLee, C.R., Lacey, Mila, Autumn, Ripley, K, Heather, Jen, and Lexi.

Thank you to my incredible alphas—Kelly, Ash, and Ellen —for helping me make this book what it is today. I wouldn't have been able to write this without your help.

And thank you to all my author friends! You know who you are, and I'm so incredibly grateful for all your support.

ABOUT THE AUTHOR

Katie May is a reverse harem author with numerous books and series under her belt. She writes everything from contemporary to horror to fantasy. When not writing, she can be found curled up with a cup of coffee and a good book. Join her group Katie's Gang - a Katie May Reader's Group to stay updated on all her new releases as well as access exclusive content.

ALSO BY KATIE MAY

SERIES

Together We Fall (Apocalyptic Reverse Harem, COMPLETED)

1. The Darkness We Crave

2. The Light We Seek

3. The Storm We Face

4. The Monsters We Hunt

Beyond the Shadows (Horror Paranormal Reverse Harem, COMPLETED)

1. Gangs and Ghosts

2. Guns and Graveyards

3. Gallows and Ghouls

The Damning (Fantasy Paranormal Reverse Harem)

1. Greed

2. Envy

3. Gluttony (Coming Spring 2020)

Prodigium Academy (Horror Comedy Academy Reverse Harem)

1. Monsters

2. Roaring (Coming Spring 2020)

Tory's School for the Trouble (Bully Horror Academy Reverse Harem)

1. Between

2. Untitled (Coming Summer 2020)

CO-WRITES

Afterworld Academy with Loxley Savage (Academy Fantasy Reverse Harem)

1. Dearly Departed

2. Untitled (Coming May 2020)

Her Immortal Legacy with Elena Lawson (Time Travel Paranormal Reverse Harem)

1. Chasing Time

2. Finding Time (Coming April 31, 2020)

STAND-ALONES

Toxicity (Contemporary Reverse Harem)

Blindly Indicted (Prison Reverse Harem)

Not All Heroes Wear Capes (Just Dresses) (Short Comedic Reverse Harem)

ANTHOLOGIES

Merry Elfin Christmas (Featuring Addie and her harem from Together We Fall)

Made in the USA
Columbia, SC
29 December 2024